The Xenologist

Michael Joseph Dutton

First Edition
Copyright © Michael Joseph Dutton, 2025

The right of Michael Joseph Dutton to be identified as the author of this work has been asserted by him in accordance with the Copyright, Designs and Patents Act 1988.

All rights reserved. No part of this publication may be reproduced, stored in a retrieval system, or transmitted in any form or by any means—electronic, mechanical, photocopying, recording, or otherwise—without the prior permission of the copyright owner.

All images in this publication were created using a variety of commercially licensed tools and manually modified and enhanced by the author. The resulting works are original and are protected under applicable copyright laws.

This is a work of fiction. Names, characters, businesses, places, events, and incidents are either the products of the author's imagination or are used fictitiously. Any resemblance to actual persons, living or dead, or actual events is purely coincidental.

This book is set in UK English, following British spelling and grammatical conventions.

A catalogue record for this book is available from the British Library. *(Pending)*

Published by Rivenstone Media (an imprint of Brigante Aviation Ltd.)
Printed in the United States.

ISBN 978-1-0681605-0-9 (Paperback)

Typeface: Amazon Endure, designed by 2K/DENMARK in 2025.
Template ID: ST-414D415A-25-A01

For Ilona and Merlin.

The former with two legs,

for sharing the latter with four.

And the latter for the gift of time,

Without which, there would be no new world

For me to share with this world.

Contents

- PROLOGUE 9
- Chapter 1. 11
- Chapter 2. 15
- Chapter 3. 19
- Chapter 4. Part 1. 23
- Chapter 4. Part 2. 27
- Chapter 5. Part 1. 31
- Chapter 5. Part 2. 35
- Chapter 5. Part 3. 39
- Chapter 6. 41
- Chapter 7. Part 1. 45
- Chapter 7. Part 2. 49
- Chapter 8. 55
- Chapter 9. Part 1. 59
- Chapter 9. Part 2. 63
- Chapter 10. Part 1. 65
- Chapter 10. Part 2. 69
- Chapter 11. Part 1 75
- Chapter 11. Part 2 78
- Chapter 12. 85
- Chapter 13. Part 1. 89
- Chapter 13. Part 2. 95
- Chapter 14. 97
- Chapter 15. Part 1 103
- Chapter 15. Part 2 107
- Chapter 15. Part 3 111
- Chapter 16. Part 1 113
- Chapter 16. Part 2. 119
- Chapter 17. Part 1. 127
- Chapter17. Part 2. 131
- Chapter 17. Part 3. 135
- Chapter 18. Part 1 139
- Chapter 18. Part 2. 143
- Chapter 18. Part 3. 149

Chapter 18. Part 4... 151
Chapter 19. Part 1... 153
Chapter 19. Part 2... 155
Chapter 19. Part 3... 161
Chapter 19. Part 4... 163
Chapter 20. Part 1... 167
Chapter 20. Part 2... 171
Chapter 21. Part 1... 175
Chapter 21. Part 2... 179
Chapter 21. Part 3... 181
Chapter 22. Part 1... 183
Chapter 22. Part 2... 187
Chapter 23. Part 1... 191
Chapter 23. Part 2... 195
Chapter 24. Part 1... 199
Chapter 24. Part 2... 203
Chapter 25. Part 1... 207
Chapter 25. Part 2... 211
Chapter 26. Part 1... 215
Chapter 26. Part 2... 219
Chapter 27. Part 1... 221
Chapter 27. Part 2... 223
Chapter 28. Part 1... 227
Chapter 28. Part 2... 231
Chapter 28. Part 3... 233
Chapter 29. Part 1... 237
Chapter 29. Part 2... 239
Chapter 29. Part 3... 241
Chapter 30.. 245
Chapter 31. Part 1... 249
Chapter 31. Part 2... 251
Chapter 31. Part 3... 253
Chapter 31. Part 4... 255
Chapter 32. Part 1... 257
Chapter 32. Part 2... 259

Chapter 32. Part 3. 263

Chapter 32. Part 4. 265

Chapter 33. Part 1. 267

Chapter 33. Part 2. 269

Chapter 33. Part 3. 273

Chapter 34. Part 1. 277

Chapter 34. Part 2. 281

Chapter 35. 287

Chapter 36. 293

Chapter 37. Part 1. 297

Chapter 37. Part 2. 301

Chapter 38. Part 1. 303

Chapter 38 Part 2. 307

Chapter 38. Part 3. 311

Chapter 39. Part 1. 313

Chapter 39. Part 2. 317

Chapter 39. Part 3. 319

Chapter 40. Part 1. 323

Chapter 40 Part 2. 328

Chapter 41. Part 1. 330

Chapter 41. Part 2. 334

Chapter 42. 337

Chapter 43. Part 1. 339

Chapter 43. Part 2. 341

Chapter 44. 343

Chapter 45. Part 1. 345

Chapter 45. Part 2. 347

Chapter 46. Part 1. 351

Chapter 46. Part 2. 353

Chapter 46. Part 3. 357

Chapter 47. Part 1. 363

Chapter 47. Part 2. 367

Chapter 48. 371

Chapter 49. 373

Chapter 50. 377

Chapter 51. Part 1.	381
Chapter 51. Part 2.	383
Chapter 51. Part 3.	385
Chapter 52. Part 1.	389
Chapter 52. Part 2.	391
Chapter 52. Part 3.	393
EPILOGUE	395
VISUAL APPENDIX	397
GLOSSARY OF TERMS	401
ABOUT THE AUTHOR	405

PROLOGUE

Varinn's breath scraped through his throat, dry and shallow. The heat clung to his skin, suffocating. His arms ached under the weight of the body he carried, but he refused to slow down.

Far ahead, a ruined city rose from the desert, its futuristic spires like the vertebrae of some long-dead alien leviathan, white-clad, segmented towers stretching toward the sky. Its smooth curves and impossible angles reflected a level of engineering Varinn couldn't begin to understand. The surface structure was shattered in places, deep cracks running along the foundations and the upper platforms listing slightly; evidence of slow decay rather than sudden collapse.

Beneath the city's broken spires, the dunes rolled outward like a sea of ochre. In the distance, the heat shimmered, warping the horizon until the edge of the world blurred into pale nothingness.

Far beyond the dunes, nestled within the shadow of a massive escarpment, lay the underground city. It was newer, but more primitive. Hewn directly from the rock, its smooth walls and carved arches had the quiet elegance of ancient craftsmanship. The place lacked the technical sophistication of the ruined towers, but it endured against the lethal solar light. In that cool and dark sanctuary, Varinn's apartment was there, luxurious in a way he couldn't imagine feeling again if he failed out here in the dunes.

The Designer stirred in his arms. His tunic and outer protective cloak were light in colour and close-fitting. They were cut from a high-density weave that should have resisted the sun's intensity, but it wasn't enough. Red welts were already forming along the edge of his collar and sleeves.

Varinn's gaze fell to the Designer's chest. The familiar name patch, *D. Marinallis*, stood out as a stark white rectangle against his tunic.

Curious, Varinn opened the jacket. The Designer's pale skin was burning heavily, but directly beneath the patch, the skin was completely untouched, glowing in contrast to the angry red tissue surrounding it. "The meteorologists said the sun was getting lower in emissions now. This shouldn't be happening."

Tessara's shadow fell over him as she drew alongside. Her almost jet-black skin was already glistening with sweat beneath her radiation-blocking hood. Her gait was steady, controlled, but her narrowed eyes betrayed how much the heat was affecting her, too. "It's cutting through his clothes," Tessara said, her voice sharp with disbelief. "That's insane."

"Yeah." Varinn adjusted his grip on the Designer's body. "But the patch left a mark."

Tessara's gaze dropped to Varinn's arm, where the protective weave was starting to fray. A thin, sore-looking line was already forming beneath it. She glanced up, meeting his bronze eyes, satisfied at least that his UV-filtering contacts were enduring in the harsh radiation.

"Are you burning?"

"Starting to."

"I'll feel it for days." Tessara's mouth tightened. "Let's get inside a city before it gets worse."

Varinn forced his legs to keep moving, muscles screaming beneath the strain as the Designer's breath came thin and shallow against his shoulder.

"There's an access tunnel about four klicks out," Tessara said, scanning the dunes with the kind of tense focus that came from years of training. "There are several places to shelter on the way. We can make it."

The Device pulsed faintly at Varinn's side. He barely realised it was happening until the rhythmic pulse settled into the edge of his heartbeat.

A faint hum spread through his chest, a low vibration crawling up his arm, not painful exactly, but wrong. Like a sound vibrating on a frequency his body wasn't meant to feel.

Tessara's gaze sharpened. "Varinn."

Varinn's grip on the Designer tightened. The hum didn't stop. It was warmer now, almost inviting.

"Do you feel that?" Tessara's tone was cautious.

"It's... reacting." Varinn forced his expression flat.

Tessara's eyes narrowed. "It's not meant for us," Tessara said carefully.

Varinn's jaw tightened. The pulse from the Device steadied, matching the rhythm of his breath. "It's not hurting me."

"That's what worries me."

The Designer's hand twitched against Varinn's chest. It was a weak but deliberate gesture. His head lolled slightly. Varinn said quietly, "All we have to worry about is getting them safely home; otherwise, we may not have to worry about anything ever again"

Tessara's expression hardened. "Well, don't die carrying him there. Or this was all for nothing."

Varinn caught a nuance in what she said that he could not quite fathom but quickly dismissed the thought. He tightened his arm around the Designer's back as he adjusted his grip. The pulse from the Device hummed steadily against his side—a warm, steady rhythm that somehow aligned with the beat of his heart.

Tessara was watching him. "You feel it, don't you?" She said softly.

Varinn hesitated.

"It's protecting you," Tessara said. Her voice was quiet.

"Or it's using me."

Tessara stepped closer. Her hand brushed his arm as she steadied his grip on Marinallis.

"I hate that thing," Tessara said. Her voice was steady, almost calm. "We weren't supposed to use it."

"Maybe it's not up to us anymore."

Varinn's gaze lifted toward the broken skyline. He could feel the Device at his side, like it was breathing with him. He could feel the Designer's weight against his shoulder—the sharp, blistered heat of his burned skin.

Tessara's hand lingered on Varinn's wrist for half a breath. "We need to move," Tessara said quietly.

Varinn nodded. He adjusted his grip on the Designer, stepping forward into the wavering heat. Ahead, the ruined city loomed, distant and useless. Talemora's sun bore down on them, unforgiving and wrong. The Device pulsed steadily at his side.

Chapter 1.

The low hum of the shuttle's **gravitational sluice drive** faded as it settled onto the tarmac. A moment later, the hatch hissed open, and the blast of arid desert air struck Voss full in the face. Even through the polarised glass of his side-shielded sunglasses, the glare was blinding. The suit's cooling system ventilated his skin, filtering out the worst of the heat, but it was still an oppressive influence radiating up from the sand-blasted ground beneath his boots.

The landing site was a quarry, a colossal humanoid-made pit carved from the side of a rocky escarpment. The walls stretched upward in sheer slabs, heat shimmer blurring the edges where rock met sky.

Voss adjusted the dark lenses over his eyes as he stepped down the gangway. The ground beneath him was blasted rock polished by centuries of erosion and heat. As his feet touched the ground, *not Earth,* he paused and looked down, committing to memory his first moment on an alien planet.

He looked up. A sign to his right said, 'Welcome on behalf of the PCMA'. He thought, *Yes, use the acronym, because nothing says freedom like 'The Privatised Colony Military and Administration'.*

With a wry grin, he continued along the path. Behind him, the other workers and settlers moved in a similar, stunned silence. From the wide eyes and upturned faces, he guessed they were all as awestruck as he was. He walked onto a humble transport bus, much like he had seen many times on Earth.

Once enough passengers were onboard, it set off in eerie silence. They headed directly to where the quarry walls gave way to a massive hollow cut into the cliffside. The cut took the form of a cavernous opening five hundred feet high and nearly as wide.

Within that void, the city.

The transition from desert brightness to shadowed depth was immediate. Voss's gaze followed the sheer face of the cavern wall, where smooth, fluted columns stretched from floor to ceiling. Dark archways and long balconies overlooked the entrance like galleries of an ancient amphitheatre. Deeper within the cavern, blue crystal domes set into the roof filtered the lethal ultraviolet light, casting a softer glow across the stonework.

The underground city was vast and quiet, ancient in a way that settled in his bones. The architecture was unsettling, echoing Earth's Greco-Roman forms, but with a seamless blend of art and engineering that felt far beyond anything humanity had achieved in classical times.

A narrow causeway, suspended over a dizzying drop, extended from the metal gangway toward the city entrance. The metal gave way to stone as it crossed into the cavern's mouth, a transition from human design to Architect craftsmanship. The bright sandstone had a rough, pitted quality beneath the faint blue glow of the crystal domes.

A faint breeze rose from below, cool and dry, carrying the scent of dust and minerals. The sharp temperature difference between the desert heat and the cavern's coolness made his skin prickle.

A voice broke his thoughts. "You're the new Xenologist?"

Voss turned. A figure approached down the walkway—short black hair beneath a military cap, body armour over a dark tactical uniform.

Commander Greer's dark eyes swept over him with the efficiency of someone cataloguing weaknesses. "You'll want to watch your step," she said. "We advise new people to be wary of anything alien and glowing."

Voss followed her gaze toward the excavation site. Engineers clustered around an exposed wall, containment fields flickering faintly where glyph patterns glowed beneath the surface.

A blue flash arced from one of the panels. A technician stumbled backwards, clutching his hand. "Dammit!" someone shouted.

Greer's gaze didn't shift.

"How many injuries so far?" Voss asked.

"Six radiation burns, three electrical shocks, two concussions from structural collapse," Greer replied flatly. "And that's this week."

"That seems high."

Greer offered a faint, humourless smile. "Welcome to X-13294/B."

As they moved deeper inside, passing through narrow corridors lined with embedded glyphs, Voss paused beside a panel that felt strangely unwelcoming, almost angry. Curious, he reached out and touched the writing, immediately feeling inexplicably anxious. Greer stopped, watching him closely.

"Are you okay, Dr. Voss? Any sudden insights you'd like to share?"

"Not really," Voss said, masking his unease. "It's just the impact of seeing these things in person. They really are...alien."

Greer nodded. "Indeed. Some people react emotionally to the text, but everyone gets used to them eventually."

They entered a broad plaza beneath the tallest crystal dome, busy with scientists, engineers, and heavily armed guards who stood silently, watchful. Their dark tactical suits bore unfamiliar insignias, corporate rather than military.

"Private security?" Voss asked uneasily.

Greer's expression hardened. "They're here to keep the peace. Or that's the theory."

"They expect trouble?"

"They expect something," Greer said, continuing forward.

Voss's eyes lingered on the guards' posture—too stiff, too alert. They weren't just watching the engineers. They were watching the city.

As they passed a smaller chamber, Voss approached a slab etched with glyphs pulsing faintly beneath the stone surface. A low hum resonated subtly through his fingertips. Greer's gaze sharpened. "Feel that?"

"Yes."

"Most people don't."

"What are you suggesting?" Voss asked cautiously.

Greer's expression remained neutral. "Just an observation."

A figure shifted nearby, drawing Voss's attention. A woman stood at the base of a nearby column, short dyed-blonde hair framing serious features. Her dark grey utility suit was scuffed at the knees and sleeves.

"Dr. Voss?" Her voice was steady, carrying an Eastern European accent.

Voss approached her. "You must be Volkova."

She straightened, brushing dust from her sleeve. "Renata Volkova,

Xenoarchaeologist."

"Julian Voss," he replied warmly. "Xenologist. Like you, a completely new discipline."

She studied him quickly. "I was briefed that you were coming. Just arrived?"

"Yes. Just landed," he tugged slightly at his collar, indicating his discomfort with the temperature.

"You'll get used to the heat, but not the sunburn". "Best not to go outside, just stay in the shade."

Voss smiled slightly. "Not planning on going hiking."

Her eyes sharpened. "Not unless you want a sun-tan that lasts a year and an appointment with the oncologist."

Voss nodded. "Sounds like a good policy!"

"You should have just enough time to settle in. I think you will be impressed with your quarters," Renata said quietly, "And I will be seeing you there at dinner. We'll be able to discuss the current status of the ongoing archaeological projects during the meal."

"Good to meet you," Voss said sincerely.

A hint of a smile touched her lips. "You too, Julian Voss."

With a final nod, Greer turned and led the way, leaving Voss to follow, his mind already racing with the implications of private armies, glowing glyphs, and the promise of dinner with the enigmatic Director Raith.

Chapter 2.

The door to Voss's quarters hissed open with a soft sigh, revealing a surprisingly spacious and impressive room carved from the same smooth stone that marked the rest of the underground city.

He set his small travel bag beside the narrow bed and sat down heavily, feeling the faint uneasiness brought on by touching the angry glyphs. The sensation lingered, subtly disquieting, leaving him uncertain whether it was real or imagined.

He looked closer at the apartment. The walls were rough-hewn rock, with some walls rebuilt or made more functional with human prefabricated block tastefully blended into the apartment. In the corner was a whirlpool bath that looked like it had come straight from the industrial 3D printers that come with every exploration effort, but it blended in well. In front of it was a huge picture window overlooking the underground city.

As he walked over to admire the view, he saw that the shaded parts of the vast plazas below his apartment were lit by turquoise and blue glowing remnants of ancient technology embedded randomly within the rock walls, pillars, and ceilings.

In the cavern roofs, Voss marvelled at the blue crystal domes that allowed shafts of filtered, low-UV sunlight to enter. To Voss, the domes lived up to all the reports he had read. Their material was harder and more durable than anything modern humans could reproduce.

This single discovery, he thought, *justifies all our efforts to get here.* He took another moment to marvel at the miracle he was witnessing. *These domes have stood for over eighty thousand years, it's just impossible to imagine.*

As he paced the room thoughtfully, touching walls and looking at unfamiliar electronic artefacts, he pondered *What other treasures remained undiscovered, perhaps under my fingertips even now?*

He stared at an ancient screen, no longer working but left on the wall as a priceless ornament. *Or perhaps,* he thought wryly, *the treasures have already been discovered and we merely lack the understanding to grasp their true significance.*

A chime at the door startled him from his thoughts. He turned sharply as the door opened without awaiting his response.

Renata stood in the doorway, one hand raised apologetically. "Dr. Voss, I hope I'm not intruding."

"No, please," Voss said, gesturing for her to enter. "Make yourself comfortable."

Renata stepped inside, allowing the door to close behind her. Her gaze drifted briefly around the sparse quarters before settling on him. Without her outer suit, she appeared leaner, younger, but her eyes retained their guarded intensity.

"Dr. Voss," she began with cautious politeness, "I wanted to speak privately before you meet Raith. There are certain dynamics here you should understand."

"Such as?" Voss leaned forward slightly, intrigued by her tone.

Renata hesitated, choosing her words carefully. "Raith represents interests that don't always align with scientific inquiry. He believes this place is primarily a strategic asset, and only secondarily a research site."

Voss exhaled slowly. "The military-corporate mindset."

"Exactly," Renata confirmed. "He represents the consortium backing this expedition. He's cautious, controlling, and concerned less with discovery than with profit. You should be careful around him."

Voss frowned slightly. "You don't trust him?"

"Not entirely," she replied with caution, "and neither should you."

The quiet authority in her voice made the room feel colder, heavier. Voss considered her carefully, appreciating her candour.

"Why tell me this?" Voss asked. "Do I have a trusting face or something?"

Renata smiled faintly. "I know you through your work, Dr. Voss—"

"Julian, please," he interrupted.

"Julian, yes," she corrected herself. "I know your publications. When asked whom to bring in to bolster our efforts here, at least ten other people immediately suggested your name. Frankly, if we can't trust you, then honour in academia truly is dead."

"It may well be anyway," Voss replied. He immediately regretted the words as the conversation faltered. He thought wryly, *academic brilliance at the expense of social grace.*

Renata skilfully recovered. "Perhaps it is, but I choose to believe otherwise."

"Thank you," he finally said. "For what it's worth, I intend to honour your trust—and this conversation didn't happen."

Renata smiled softly as Voss said, "Have you heard about the planet's new name? It's in our official letters on the ship, so it won't be a secret for more than about 2 minutes".

Renata's face brightened up. Voss noted her ability to suddenly change demeanour as she asked, excitedly, "Ooh, what is it?"

Voss smiled in return and replied, "They're calling it Sikarra. Wentworth named it, finally".

Renata took a moment, her brows in a slight frown, then a moment of amused clarity: "No. He didn't!"

Voss said, "He's a big fan of twentieth-century science fiction novels." Shrugging and smiling wryly, "He insists he didn't realise this was a mostly desert World when he filed the name."

Renata laughed quietly. "He'll never live it down."

Voss continued, "Is there anything in return that I should know?"

Renata hesitated again, the smile fading, and she briefly glanced at the polished stone floor. "Only that there's more here than ruins and artefacts. I've observed Greer and Raith exchanging private communications. There's something significant they haven't disclosed."

Voss: "About the ruins?"

"About everything," Renata clarified sharply. "Why we're really here? what they're actually looking for?"

Voss absorbed this in silence before asking, "And what do you think they're after?"

Renata's eyes hardened slightly. "I'm not certain yet, but whatever it is, it's dangerous enough for them to bring private security teams and keep us on tight leashes."

Voss nodded slowly, recognising the undercurrent of tension he'd sensed from the beginning. "Thank you for the heads-up."

Renata stood, signalling an end to their brief exchange. "Just be cautious, Julian. This place holds secrets older than humanity itself. We may be uncovering

Pandora's box, Mark 2.0"

She moved toward the door, pausing briefly. "Rest up. You'll need your wits about you when you meet Raith."

"Renata," he said as she began to leave, prompting her to glance back at him. "Thanks for trusting me with this."

She nodded once, her expression neutral. The door closed quietly behind her, leaving Voss alone in the silence. An ache began at the back of his skull, a physical manifestation of the weight of unanswered questions.

Chapter 3.

The terminal in Voss's quarters glowed, cutting through the dimness with a soft blue hue. He tapped the screen, and the message unfolded in crisp text:

"Dr. Julian Voss, you are cordially invited to dine with Director Desmond Raith at 19:00. Follow the attached route. Five-minute walk."

A map blinked to life, tracing a path through the underground warrens. Voss synced it to his smartwatch, the qNav system on his qWatch, vibrated on his wrist as it locked onto the city's grid. Five minutes. Military precision from a corporate man, that alone told him something about Raith.

Voss glanced around his quarters. He wished he could take more time to explore. On impoverished, worn-out old Earth, it would have fetched a fortune. He would have months, perhaps years, to explore every nook of this place, he reminded himself. With a sigh, he stepped out, the door hissing shut behind him.

The corridor stretched ahead, its stone walls carved with fluted arches that caught the turquoise glow of crystal domes high above. Cool, dry air carried the scent of ancient dust and the echo of his footsteps. The path twisted past archways and balconies, carved with an intent not from a human mind.

An alarm shattered the quiet. Voss froze, his pulse quickening. Shouts erupted ahead: "It's Jonesy! He's back!" followed by a panicked, "He's burned, call the medics!"

The noise drew him toward a junction where bluish sunlight streamed through a jagged hole, a ruined, human-sized door opening to a ten-meter tunnel that breached the surface. Three men stood at its threshold, silhouetted against the harsh glare, reluctant to expose themselves. The figure staggered forward into their arms and Voss hung back, watching the shaken men launch into a practised drill. Knives came out, cutting the clothes from his body. One man, white as a sheet, turned away and retched.

In a moment of dissociation, Voss's attention wandered briefly to the CCTV camera hung above, its lens dark and unblinking. He frowned. Voss had read that nothing bigger than a rodent survived out there, and even those avoided the city as if it were cursed. He'd always wondered why.

A thought intruded. A trauma-memory. His first year at WTA's Xenolaboratory complex in Silesia. Hiking in the woods, he'd met an old woman gathering mushrooms. In his broken Polish, he'd asked how she knew which were edible. Her voice rasped over the fire, "If the animals don't touch it, something's wrong." He had laughed then, but now, staring into the ominous tunnel, the lesson resonated deeply.

Medics rounded the corner, boots pounding stone. Jonesy saw the medics and sagged, relief buckling his legs, slipping from his colleagues' grip to the stone floor near the exit-tunnel mouth. He was starting to scream louder now as the manhandling started to provoke his blistered, red skin. The medics sprayed foam across his arms and chest; it hissed upon contact, and Jonesy's cries mercifully began to dull into a low whimper.

Voss snapped out of it and stepped forward, but a medic waved him back. "It's okay, sir. We've got this. He'll live, but he's off-planet as soon as he's stable." Voss nodded, but Jonesy's screams stuck with him.

"Can I talk to him?" Voss asked.

The Xenologist

The medic shrugged. "Sure, but not now. He'll be sedated for days."

Jonesy's head lolled toward Voss, eyes glassy with pain. "I was helped," he rasped. "Something out there."

The medic snorted. "Scanners showed nothing but him past the perimeter. Pain makes you see things."

Voss nodded, but Jonesy's screams stuck with him. He'd experienced severe sunburn once himself, at sixteen, before a critical scholarship interview. He'd foolishly tried tanning to impress a girl who liked the beach-bum look. Pain and humiliation had cost him the scholarship, a sting that lingered years later. However, the level of Jonesy's suffering made that incident seem trivial in comparison. Determined, Voss decided he'd have to speak with Jonesy later.

The medics loaded Jonesy onto a stretcher. With military discipline, they ran, carrying the stretcher back the way they came. The shocked workers who helped Jonesy took a moment to breathe, slapping backs and taking deep breaths. Voss smiled and congratulated their composure.

One by one, the men dispersed, boots fading, until the corridor stood empty, eerie under the blue glare. Voss retreated instinctively to the shadows and started to walk on his way, somewhat mollified by the medic's reassuring words. A fiery baptism for Sikarra's mysteries.

The route ended at a metal door etched with geometric patterns, sliding open with a whisper. Warm amber light filled the chamber beyond. Renata stood near a long table, striking in a deep red evening dress that hugged her figure, her dyed-blonde hair catching the glow. Voss glanced at his functional grey jumpsuit, feeling underdressed yet again.

Across the room, Raith lounged in a metallic blazer, radiating wealth and power. He rose slightly, extending a hand.

"Dr. Voss," with easy confidence, "a pleasure to finally meet you. Your reputation precedes you. Please, sit."

Voss took a chair beside Renata, whose faint smile was unreadable. Raith poured an amber drink, leaning back confidently.

"I apologise for being late," Voss said. "There was an incident; someone got hurt."

Raith's brow lifted slightly. "Ah, yes, Mr. Jones. My qWatch alerted me. The poor man wandered into a sandstorm. We thought him lost. The surface is unforgiving, as you've seen."

Renata interjected softly, "I'm sorry you had to witness that. It's very distressing."

"He'll recover. Our facilities are top-tier," Raith said with a dismissive wave. Now, tell me, Dr. Voss, what's your initial impression of our newly named, Sikarra? A Xenologist's dream, surely?"

"It's singular," Voss replied cautiously. "The ruins suggest advanced civilisation, then decline and collapse. I'm here to understand why."

Raith chuckled. "Collapse or sacrifice. Ever consider they deliberately cleaned the slate?"

"Cleaned the slate?" Voss echoed.

Raith's eyes glinted. "A Marie Celeste planet. No bodies, no DNA, no Rosetta Stone, just half-working tech after thousands of years. Deliberate, no?"

Voss opened his mouth to reply, but Raith continued smoothly, "I'm sure it's in the glyphs, waiting to be deciphered. But that's your expertise, yours and Renata's." He turned to Renata. "Your thoughts, Dr. Volkova?"

Renata's fork paused mid-air. "It's a theory," she said coolly. "Surface tech predates these cities by millennia. Something catastrophic happened, UV flares, ozone collapse. They adapted underground, then vanished."

"Vanished," Raith echoed with a smirk, "or fled elsewhere, perhaps?"

Voss leaned forward. "You think there's evidence of evacuation?"

Renata shook her head. "No direct evidence, but the absence itself is suspicious."

Raith waved dismissively. "Speculation is fine, but I want results. This planet's a vault, and I intend to open it."

Raith's hand twitched on his glass, a flicker of strain beneath a forced smirk. Voss realised Raith had pushed his dominance of the conversation a touch too far. Not a mistake a man of his skills would normally make.

Is he under pressure? Voss wondered. Either way, he wasn't going to rescue him. He glanced at Renata, but her jaw was set, her gaze fixed on the table before her. Clearly, he concluded, she wasn't going to help either.

Before the silence got too awkward, Raith broke the tension and stood.

"Enjoy your evening. Excuse me, I must check on Mr. Jones. Tomorrow, we dig deeper. Literally. Mind your footing; mistakes here can be unforgiving."

The door closed behind him, leaving Renata and Voss alone. They exchanged cautious glances, each silently wondering whether their conversation was monitored.

Chapter 4. Part 1.

As the sun began its descent toward the horizon, Tessara and Varinn stood at the edge of the wreckage, their shadows stretching long across the ochre sand. The scuttled ship's hull was torn open, its once sleek form now a true fish out of water.

A long-forgotten sea had left its Leviathan behind to be consumed by the sand. Metal panels lay scattered across the dunes like discarded scales half-buried by the restless desert.

"We should wait for sunset," Tessara said, her gaze tracking the sun's position. "Temperature as well as the UV will drop. Safer."

Varinn nodded, already examining a large, curved panel of hull plating. "This will work. Help me clear it."

Together, they extracted the panel from the sand that had partially buried the wrecked craft, brushing away any dust that stubbornly clung to the smooth surface. With steady determination, they fashioned a crude but functional dray, using strips of high-density cable to secure handholds.

Exploring, Tessara ran her fingertips along the control panel of what was left of the bridge, pressing buttons that remained dark and unresponsive. "Nothing works. It's all properly sterilised."

"Would you expect any different?" Varinn asked quietly, not looking up from his work.

Tessara's eyes met his briefly, something unspoken passing between them. She turned away, scanning the horizon where distant rock formations rippled in the heat. "We'll need water before we attempt the crossing."

"The creek at the edge of the western ridge should still have some," Varinn replied, securing the last of the makeshift harness.

"There might be water dragons?" Tessara said, her tone casual despite the weight of her words.

Varinn paused, considering. "Sadly, there aren't many left now. Nearly all dead from UV."

Tessara said, "Sadly? Cute as they are, I like my legs as they are too. Attached to my body."

Varinn sniggered and adjusted his pack. "We'll stop quickly, fill the bottles, and make it to Vasantha before sun-up if we maintain pace."

The cooling breeze was funnelled by the wrecked superstructure, providing them some semblance of relief as they waited for dusk. The Designer lay unconscious between them, his breathing shallow but steady. Varinn applied a translucent salve to the man's burned skin, the angry red fading magically to pale pink as the medicine quickly took effect.

"He should be waking," Tessara observed, though neither of them seemed particularly concerned.

"His system is in shock. The salve will keep him stable," Varinn replied, wiping his hands clean.

Silence settled between them, comfortable yet heavy with unspoken thoughts. The dying light cast long shadows through the broken hull.

Looking at Tessara, still studying the old console and trying to puzzle out what had happened, he said, "I am sorry."

"What for?"

"For dragging you into this. You had one week of service in your contract left as a Pilot and have a potential genteel future as an Archaeologist. This kind of malarkey is for the 'in-for-life' types like me."

"You don't know, do you?" She replied. "Know what?" His face was genuinely innocent. "When was the last time you checked the gene-pool database?" she asked, her face a mixture of amusement and pity.

"A couple of years ago, I guess? Why?" Tessara laughed and rolled her eyes in mock despair. "Well, Mr. Secret Agent body-guard-superman, if you had checked recently, even in the last two months, you would have noticed the population drop is narrowing things drastically. Bottom line is, whether I like you or not, you are my last potential genetic match and you have only three choices left. One hates you, another is probably already gone and the last is looking right at you, so do you think I was honestly letting you out of my sight even for a moment?"

He looked at her, genuinely lost for words.

She leaned back on her arms and lowered her chin to her chest, her tone softer now. "I don't want to die childless. 2000 years of lineage could end with me."

With some amusement, he let the moment fester, allowing her time to reflect on her awkward moment. Then, to break the tension, he asked: "Why archaeology?" Varinn asked suddenly, his voice soft in the stillness, "Of all disciplines, why choose to study what's already gone?"

Tessara smiled faintly, her gaze distant. "I was seven. My mother took me to the excavation at Lunan Bay, where they'd discovered the foundations of a submerged ancient village. I watched the archaeologist divers as they brought up their precious treasures. I was completely fascinated as one man was carefully brushing away mud from a tiny object. I started to see the shape of a little carved ivory animal. A child's toy that had been preserved in the anaerobic slime for aeons."

She traced patterns in the sand beside her. "The lead archaeologist let me hold it. He said the last person to touch it was a child who lived before our calendar even began. I asked if they were humans." He said, "They were people. What kind, who knows? Nature keeps inventing the same solutions to the same problems." Then he added, "A child is a child. This one, whatever his or her name was, is lost to eternity except for this small, well-loved object.' In that moment, I felt connected to something vast and unending. I wanted that child to live again, if only in my mind and in the records we make."

She looked up at him. "That's why. Because nothing truly vanishes. It just waits to be rediscovered."

Varinn studied her face, his expression softening. "My simple science education would have me say that information is never truly lost. Your way is better."

"But you are not simple. You always questioned everything," she countered with a hint of warmth.

The sun vanished beyond the horizon, leaving a brief splash of crimson across the western sky before darkness began to claim the desert. Stars emerged overhead, brilliant and unfiltered by atmosphere, casting faint silver light across the dunes.

Varinn checked the Designer's vitals one final time before standing. "It's time." He tapped the device on his wrist, and a small holographic display flickered to life, projecting a three-dimensional topographical map with a pulsing blue marker. The glow illuminated his face from below, highlighting the determination in his eyes.

Tessara took her position at one side of the dray, fingers wrapping around the makeshift handles. Varinn mirrored her at the other side and together they lifted the Designer's unconscious form.

"Let's stay on the hard sand," Tessara advised. "Follow the old riverbed."

In one last careful gesture before they began to walk forward, Varinn put his hand to the Designer's carotid artery to check his pulse. Tessara glanced at him, "Are you sure you aren't overstating his usefulness? Are you letting your personal devotion cloud your judgment?"

Varinn's gaze hardened, fixed on the horizon. "If he doesn't make that ship with us, I can't overstate the loss to humanity."

They set off into the darkness, the only sound the soft crunch of their boots on ancient sand accompanied by the hiss of the trailing edge of the dray as they dragged it along the desert surface.

The glowing beacon on Varinn's wrist cast a faint blue aura ahead, guiding their path across the empty desert; two figures and their burden, moving steadily through a world that seemed to hate them. Beyond the wreckage, a silent drone hovered low, its sleek form skimming the dune's crest before dipping out of sight. Behind the rise, its unseen operator peered into a glowing orb, the projection swirling with the faint blue trail of their beacon, a predator's eye fixed on its prey.

Chapter 4. Part 2.

Morning light filtered through the crystal dome in the cavern above the plaza, visible from the picture window along the wall of Voss's quarters. It cast a faint turquoise glow, spilling across the pillars and pathways of the buried city. The air was cool, dry, carrying a mineral tang of ancient dust. The atmosphere had a calm that only comes with the solidity of stone, giving a primaeval sense of comfort, perhaps a genetically inherited memory stretching back to humanity's first cave dwellings.

Voss stood at the panoramic window, gazing over the subterranean magnificence: blue-lit arches and balconies carved into the rock, contrasting heavily with dark corners tastefully illuminated by soft, incandescent human lighting. A labyrinth alive with promise and secrets. Incongruously, a whirlpool bath sat carved into the centre of the main room. *A bizarre place to put it,* Voss thought. The human 3D-printed pumps purred faintly, an industrial anachronism amid the alien polish, absurdly luxurious in its presence.

A knock broke his reverie. Voss gestured to the housekeeping Artificial Sentience, and the door hissed open. Renata stepped inside, her dyed-blonde hair catching the soft light, a wry smile tugging at her lips.

"Two announcements," she said. "Nothing Sikarra-shattering, mind."

Voss grinned, leaning against the wall. "Intriguing enough." Renata placed a small box in Voss's hand labelled "extreme UV filtering contact lenses—no prescription".

"They are more convenient than the full-face visor. A cool bronze look, too. Did you sleep well?" Renata asked.

Voss replied with genuine surprise, "I'm good with contacts as it happens" smiling. "Sleep was better than good. Stupendous, even." He opened the box and walked to the nightstand to put the contacts in.

She glanced around, nodding appreciatively. "These rooms. Earth's richest will claim them soon. Enjoy the luxury while we're still useful to the developers."

"Yes, we'll eventually be farmed out to primitive lodgings with the riff-raff, I guess," Voss said dryly. "Can't wait."

Her hazel eyes sharpened, Tatar features striking in the soft glow—not gorgeous, but compelling. He caught himself staring, inwardly chastising: *Keep it professional, you mirror-owning fool.* He realised suddenly she was still speaking, and he dragged his focus back.

"—obsessed over space, these Architects. They likely knew they'd be underground forever. Surface was never coming back."

His mind flickered, recalling his mother's teasing reprimand: "I've never known anyone who could look so attentive while wandering so far away."

Ten-year-old Voss had replied, "It's all stored for review, Mom." She had given a long-suffering eye-roll toward the ceiling.

Voss quickly refocused, reviewing Renata's words: space obsession, a doomed surface.

"Duty, maybe," he interjected. "A slow wind-down, generations needed to dismantle an entire world."

Renata paused thoughtfully. "Obvious when you say it. But why sterilise it all? Unless they ascended—or got tired of breathing."

"Two announcements?" he prompted, eyebrows raised. "Spill."

"Oh yes. First, we're official," she said, a smirk flickering. "I vouched for you. You have two weeks stuck with me, then you're free to ditch. Passed muster, Dr. Voss."

"A trial run," he smirked back. "I'll survive."

"Second, the planet's name is out: Sikarra. Hilarity ensued, sand-worm jibes, but it's settled now. Professionals, mostly."

Renata paused, prompting the next question.

Voss obliged. "And?"

She leaned in, deadpan. "Oh, Wentworth wants to rename Petropolis... brace yourself..."

He just gave her a look, refusing the bait this time.

"Sikarra City!" Voss's laugh was sharp as he punched the air. "Genius."

"But don't worry, it's never going to happen". Renata said, her tone dry as the desert beyond, as she continued, prompted by Voss's puzzled look. "Local names have to be proposed by the head of Xenoarchaeology, then approved by Director Raith. Since Raith came up with the name 'Petropolis' after Petra on Earth, I think you can safely assume this idea dies before it flies."

"Well, thank God for that!" Changing subject, he added, "You're very chipper this morning?"

"Last night I was guarded. It's Raith's pompous shadow. But today's for digging. Xeno-morphometry day." She smiled happily.

His pulse quickened. "My thesis? Measuring alien forms through artefacts?"

"Yours was the only book," she replied, eyes glinting. "We're testing it in the field. There's a skimmer waiting to take us to a nearby overground city. The surface team found what looks like a HOTAS equivalent."

"Hand On Throttle And Stick?" Voss asked, already moving. "I hope we have plaster of Paris for casts. Let's go".

"For handprints or for our break?" she quipped, following. "You're the expert from here on."

They stepped into the corridor, the door hissing shut behind them. Voss noted her calm had descended quite suddenly, her earlier giddiness replaced by professional focus, her passion surfacing.

The skimmer bay was a short walk away, the craft's sleek frame humming gently as they boarded, settling into their seats behind the patiently professional flight crew. He glanced at her as they strapped in. "Why archaeology?"

She looked out the viewport, her voice soft. "A goat, a red dog collar, and the British Broadcasting Corporation. Long story. Not now." Her smile was faint, eyes briefly dimming.

The skimmer lifted off with a low growl from its engines, and the city fell away beneath them. Beyond the escarpment, the desert unfurled: flat rocks and small dunes glowing gold under the dawn, sand sculpted into frozen waves by a wind that moaned faintly through hidden cracks. Heat rose in a shimmer, blurring the horizon where cracked spires pierced the sky like broken teeth. Impossibly advanced ruins appeared ahead—each a small self-contained science-fiction city of unknown purpose. Gigantic alien blocks and towers stood isolated from each other by kilometres of wasteland, stark against the amber fade, their shadows stretching long and jagged across the tundra.

Voss leaned forward, the hum of the skimmer syncing with the pulse of unanswered questions in his skull.

Chapter 5. Part 1.

The desert night pressed down on them, no warmth in the starlight. Varinn's breath burned in his throat, and the weight of the dray cut into his shoulders with every step. The unconscious Designer lay still between them, his breathing shallow but persistent, face ghostly in the starlight. Their footsteps fell in a steady rhythm across the ancient riverbed, sand whispering beneath their boots.

"We need to pick up the pace," Tessara said, voice low as she studied the southern horizon. "Those clouds aren't natural."

Varinn glanced up, noting the thickening darkness where stars should have been. Not clouds, but something worse. He adjusted his grip on the dray's makeshift handle, his other hand instinctively touching the pack where the Module nestled. Even through the fabric, he could feel its presence, not warmth exactly, but a kind of awareness that set his teeth on edge.

"Vasantha's just beyond that ridge," he replied, nodding towards a jagged silhouette ahead. "We'll make it."

He blinked rapidly, reaching up to adjust his bronze-tinted contact lenses. "These UV filters are killing me," he muttered, rubbing at his eye. "Last pair I've got, and the sand isn't helping."

"Better irritated than blind," Tessara said. "I've seen what happens to runners who skimp on eye protection out here."

The Designer stirred, lips moving soundlessly before settling back into unconsciousness. Tessara watched him with narrowed eyes. "He knows more than he's telling. About that thing you're carrying."

"Maybe," Varinn said, his gaze fixed on the ridge ahead. "But right now, I'm more concerned with getting to Vasantha alive."

The silence stretched between them, broken only by the soft crunch of sand and the occasional scraping noise as the bottom of the dray dragged over a stone. Then, a buzz like a fly. Subtle at first, then the unmistakable sound of a drone's engine operating at a frequency designed to cause anxiety and a desire to get away.

Tessara froze, hand dropping to her belt. "Above us," she breathed. "It's not one of ours. Military?"

"No Markings," Varinn replied. He looked at his wrist navscan, "and no signal or transponder".

The drone appeared as if conjured from the night itself, sleek and predatory, hovering twenty metres up. Its sensors swept the ground in methodical patterns, the hum deepening as it paused, then began to descend.

"It's found us," Varinn said, easing the dray to the ground. "Or found something."

The Module pulsed in his pack, a surge of energy that seemed to answer the drone's call. Without thinking, Varinn reached inside, fingers closing around the device. It felt strange in his hand, awkward, with angles and surfaces that seemed to shift under his touch, but it responded to him all the same, humming against his palm.

"Varinn," Tessara's voice was a warning. "What are you doing?"

He stepped away from the dray, the Module held before him like an offering. The drone's hum intensified, synchronised with the device's pulse. Something passed between them, information, recognition, and Varinn felt knowledge unfurl in his mind that wasn't his own.

"I can feel it," he said, his voice filled with wonder. "It's doing something."

"Put it down," Tessara hissed, but the wind suddenly gusted, drowning her words in a spray of sand.

The Designer's eyes snapped open, his breath ragged. "The Veil," he gasped. "Careful, Varinn..." His pupils contracted sharply, then his body slackened as he slipped back into unconsciousness.

Varinn twisted the Module, following instructions that he somehow knew like a memory, almost a false memory, like a dream. Two lights in two colours he had never seen before, painted his surroundings in the manner of augmented reality, a hallucination that would have been as terrifying as the drone above, if it weren't for the fact that he knew it was only due to his connection with the device.

The colours were new, assaulting his senses. They were none of the eight primaries of his genetically engineered retina, not even the familiar, angry ultraviolet. This was something else entirely, a frequency his mind was never meant to perceive. He felt ready to mentally burst, then a strange relief came over him when he realised the two "colours" had "direction" and that extra information embedded into the colour was what he was seeing.

One colour was somehow at ninety degrees to the other. His mind was opened and he forgot the threat of the drone overhead. He was instantly aware he was visualising the electric and magnetic fields of the planet as they applied to the device. The device rewarded correct intention by creating an itch that was ecstatically scratched when he did the right thing. As he mentally turned the fields, in a way he could not describe, he 'flipped' or 'pulled down' the electrical field in a way he just "knew" was in the direction of the drone.

Physics became child's play. He saw the 'flipped colour' spread out, exploring every possible path to the drone but the direct one. This, he realised with a jolt of ecstatic understanding, is how the Universe truly works. A place beyond speed, beyond causality.

The pleasure in his brain was exquisite and indescribable. The drone shuddered, its hum becoming a shriek before cutting off abruptly. A blue arc shot from the drone's power pack as the energy flowed downhill into it. The Drone plummeted, striking a dune with a muffled thud and a shower of sand.

Just before Varinn was about to let go, he glimpsed something that made him look away, quickly. A hooded person or a tent, he couldn't tell. By force of will, he let go of everything to return to normality. Silence fell again, heavier than before.

This moment of mental afterglow, although less than a second in reality, seemed to last for an age.

The pleasure faded. He could no longer grasp it or truly remember it. His false "device-memory" told him that this was a "first time" and a "last time" he would never again feel that intensity. He must never chase it, for there lies madness. You can only ever have one first time.

Tessara stared at Varinn, her expression caught between fear and awe. "What did you just do?" she demanded.

Varinn looked down at the Module, its energy receding like a tide, taking with it the intuitive knowledge of this new exotic physics.

"I'm not sure," he admitted, trying to let her know that he was still himself. "It showed me how. Just now."

"Showed you?" Tessara stepped closer now, her hand hovering over the hilt of her knife. "That thing is communicating with you?"

"Not with words," Varinn returned the Module to his pack, his amber lenses catching the last faint glow from its surface. With feelings. Impulses, maybe some kind of implanted memories." After a moment, Varinn continued: "I don't understand it myself. It was..."

Tessara looked at him, her scientific curiosity overcoming the primal fear of the unknown in her eyes. "Fantastic," he breathed.

The wind picked up again, stronger this time, carrying the first stinging particles of a sandstorm. To the west, the horizon began vanishing behind a wall of approaching darkness.

Tessara shook off the tension, realising now was not the time to talk: "Storm's coming and so is whoever repurposed that drone and I bet he is as subtle as the decision to use that awful machine implies," Tessara said, eyes tracking the advancing front. "And I'll bet credits to water that wasn't the only drone. We need cover."

They painfully picked up the front end of the dray and pressed forward, muscles burning with renewed urgency. The outcropping ahead resolved into ruins, the sweeping curves of some ancient, yet advanced-looking structure, half-buried in sand but solid enough to break the wind.

As they reached shelter, the first blast of the storm hit, sand hissing against the plazstone of the building. Tessara dragged the Designer into the deepest recess while Varinn crouched at the entrance, watching the storm swallow their tracks.

"If there are more drones, they'll have to wait," Tessara said, settling beside him. "Nothing flies in this."

Varinn nodded, wiping dust from his eyes with a corner of his sleeve. Through his amber contact lenses, the sand took on an otherworldly glow, like embers in a dying fire.

"What did he mean?" Tessara asked, following his gaze to the Designer. "About the Veil?"

"I don't know," Varinn answered honestly. "But I think it was something very important and it's very possible that I could have got something badly wrong." After a pause, he added, "Because that cost him a lot of pain and effort to shout it out."

The storm howled around them, a living thing hungry for secrets. And in the darkness, the Module pulsed once, twice, and Varinn's pulse followed, synchronising to a rhythm he didn't understand

Chapter 5. Part 2.

The futuristic "ruins" were no ruins at all. They had endured the aeons in a way no Terran materials ever could.

Voss and Renata had been shepherded to a room that had been hastily shored up with plexiglass sealing the broken windows. The place had the look of a laboratory. Something that any scientist would recognise across species and cultures. A group of scientists stood by a cabinet on a lab bench. In the corner, a technician was attempting to diagnose a completely inert box that stood against a wall, which looked disturbingly like a sarcophagus.

Voss ran his hand along a weathered console that had at one time been exposed to the elements. "So we are calling this city 'Old Petropolis?"

Renata stood a few paces away, her posture relaxed, a faint smile playing on her lips as she watched him. "Yes." Then she came to where Voss was standing and touched the same ancient console. "It's incredible, isn't it?" she continued, her voice warm. "Unimaginable technology in manufacturing and design. Eighty thousand years old, and still not only standing, but with power traces still running through it. But if it was built so well, why did they abandon it to live underground?"

Voss replied, "The official narrative is that they wanted to shield from previously even stronger UV and other radiations, no?"

Renata answered, "Maybe. But they could surely build more shielding. Unless they started to lose their tech?"

Voss postulated, "War? A need to keep agriculture and habitation all in one place? Lower air-conditioning bills?"

Or, Voss thought, *was there a deeper reason to hide?*

Renata looked unconvinced. Voss, needing time to think on the matter, changed the subject. "I finally got the briefing documents delivered last night, but I haven't had a chance to do more than gloss over them. I was wondering why the secrecy. If the technology here is that advanced, no wonder it's been so secret."

Renata said, "There's a lot to catch up on. For instance, there are what we think are plutonium batteries here that still give a trickle of power to everything after all these millennia."

Voss nodded, glancing back at her. "The Sikarrans were so careful about sterilisation, it makes you wonder why they left batteries." Renata arched an eyebrow and tipped her head.

He continued, "These power traces could be spotted from orbit. A ground invader, if there was one, could gain advantage from those batteries. Maybe there was no ground or space invader? No threat other than the UV?"

Renata said, "Indeed, but if that was the case, why would they otherwise get rid of as many clues about themselves as they could? And why conduct such a planet-wide, thorough job on such a colossal scale?"

Voss nodded, thoughtful. Their easy camaraderie hung in the air, a rare moment of peace. Then, the sound of footsteps echoed through the chamber. Raith stepped into view, his sharp eyes scanning the ruins with calculated interest. The shift in Renata was immediate. Her smile vanished, her shoulders stiffened, and her gaze turned cold. She folded her arms, her silence heavy and deliberate.

Voss frowned, confusion flickering across his face. He opened his mouth to speak, but the tension in the air stopped him short.

Raith, oblivious or indifferent, strode toward the centre of the chamber where a team of scientists huddled around the newly uncovered HOTAS-like artefact. "What have we got?" he asked, his tone clipped.

One of the physicists, a wiry man with a perpetual frown, looked up. "It's unlike anything we've seen. Three-fingered handle, round base, definitely not human-made. We're calling it the Echo Key for now, and for a very good reason."

Raith said, "Now that is intriguing. Would you care to elaborate, Dr. Mainwaring?"

Dr. Mainwaring said, "I think a demonstration is the best thing here. Would our new Xenologist like to step forward? It does appear safe so far."

That was hardly reassuring, but insatiable curiosity usually won out with Voss and he stepped forward with some alacrity.

Beside him, a xenobiologist adjusted his gene sequencer, his fingers tapping impatiently. "I need more samples. If you're going to touch it, I want your DNA first."

Voss shrugged and turned to the xenobiologist, curiosity piqued. The Echo Key sat in a circular docking hole inside a cupboard that had been forced open by the team. Its surface was smooth and metallic, with three finger grooves instead of the human four, that seemed to shift under the light. As he passed by, it emitted a low hum, almost imperceptible, like a distant heartbeat.

The physicists exchanged glances. "Did you see that?" the wiry one muttered. "It reacted to him."

Raith's eyes narrowed, fixed on Voss. "Interesting."

The xenobiologist thrust a swab at Voss. "Cheek, please".

Voss complied, rubbing the swab inside his mouth and handing it back. The xenobiologist slotted it into the sequencer, his eyes darting between the screen and the artefact.

Then Dr. Mainwaring said, "Dr. Voss, please grab what looks like the handle and then tell us what you feel out loud".

Voss, only half-listening, felt an inexplicable pull toward the Echo Key. Before he could stop himself, he reached out and lifted it from the pedestal.

Renata glanced over: an oscilloscope being monitored by a physicist showed a faint ripple, a minor change that barely registered.

The hum intensified, not painful but resonating through his bones. A distant vibration in his chest. A flicker of warmth, of recognition.

Dr. Rebecca O'Donnell, a young physicist with dark hair, said, "How did you do that? It was stuck fast in the console!" But Voss barely registered her voice.

Dr. Mainwaring raised a hand. "Becky, let's hold off."

Voss turned the Key in his hands, feeling its shape fit his palm perfectly. Someone started speaking in the background, but he pressed on: "The echo-feedback doesn't feel wrong," then paused, catching their surprised looks. He could hear his own words echoing back to him before he fully spoke them, but stranger still, he was talking about the pre-echo before he knew there was one.

Before he could dwell on it, another thought surfaced: "It doesn't like me," Voss said, frowning at the Key. "Or maybe it's just unsure. I don't know why I feel that."

"That's not unusual," Dr. Mainwaring said. "Some people say it's indifferent. A few report outright hostility."

Renata's brow furrowed. "You're talking like it's sentient," she said cautiously. "Fair enough if it's got an AS, but how would it communicate without knowing our language?"

Raith stepped forward, taking the Key from Voss. He held it easily, studying it with a thoughtful look.

The oscilloscope showed another faint ripple, then steadied.

"Why is that happening?" Renata asked, nodding at the screen.

"It's a small fluctuation," the wiry physicist said. "We're picking up a slight anomaly in the Higgs field readings."

"It happens when the echoing kicks in, but it's tiny." The room went silent. The physicist looked bored, but Raith, Renata and Voss were focused intently on him. He carried on hesitantly, wondering if he was pushing the bounds of their attention, "Well, er, when something with rest mass, like Dr. Voss here, approaches the speed of light, its relativistic mass increases without bound. That's due to the Lorentz factor, γ, which blows up as you get close to 'c'. The speed of light…"

Filling in the brief silence, Voss said, "Right, so you'd need infinite energy to actually hit c. But the Key… it's doing something different?"

Dr. Mainwaring stepped in, rescuing the slightly awkward, wiry physicist. "Exactly. From what we're seeing, the Key seems to cap that mass increase. It's like it's modifying the Lorentz factor so γ doesn't go to infinity. Instead, it levels off, maybe at something like 10 times the rest mass. That means you could reach c with a finite amount of energy."

Renata said, "But how? The Lorentz factor is baked into the fabric of spacetime. You can't just change it."

Dr. Mainwaring answered, "That's where the Higgs field comes in. The Higgs gives particles their rest mass, but the Key might be tweaking how that mass interacts with spacetime as you accelerate. It's not reducing the rest mass itself—just limiting how much it amplifies with speed. Think of it as damping the usual relativistic effects."

Voss asked, "So, it's not making me lighter; it's stopping my mass from spiralling out of control as I speed up?"

"Precisely." Dr. Mainwaring looked pleased. "And for faster-than-light travel, it might be doing something even more exotic, like creating a tiny warp effect, bending spacetime just enough to let you slip past c without the infinite energy problem."

Raith smirked faintly, "Sounds too good to be true. What's the catch?"

Dr. Mainwaring replied, "The catch is, we're messing with fundamental forces. If we scale this up? Let's say, for a ship? The energy involved could change the energy state of the Higgs field.

Raith continued, "Change it how, exactly?".

The wiry physicist shrugged. "Think of the 'Mexican Hat' potential. If you push the field too hard, like with a lot more energy, it could go over a brow and then settle to a lower energy state. Might mess with particle masses."

"But that's a big if, of course," the wiry physicist interjected. "There likely isn't a lower energy state."

"But it could go into a negative energy state," Dr. Mainwaring added grimly. "And if that happens…"

Dr. Becky finished the sentence. "The gravitational attraction that binds matter would be too weak to hold even subatomic particles together, which would propagate out at the speed of light plus the universe's expansion rate. Obviously…" she left it hanging.

All the physicists nodded safely, but Raith's eyebrows lifted in faint amusement. "Obviously?"

Dr. Mainwaring rubbed his chin. "Yeah, it'd take a serious energy spike to make it an issue. We're just guessing at possibilities here."

"And" the sceptical physicist suddenly countered, "it could be localised. Self-correcting."

Raith's half-smile returned, though his eyes were cold. "Then we'd better not push it too far. Yet."

Voss, still standing near Raith, took the Echo Key back from Raith. This time it felt different, less uncertain, less guarded. As if it were willing to let him hold it.

You're fine. For now.

The thought wasn't a thought. It was a memory. A memory that wasn't his own.

Voss swallowed hard. He thought about saying something but then instinct, probably protective, prevented him from saying anything further.

Renata's eyes narrowed. A slight nod back from Voss meant that it was understood between them that more was to be said in private. Voss put the echo key back in place.

Raith moved to the Echo key. There were several astonished looks as the Key also allowed Raith to move it. With a satisfied look on his face, he placed it down again. His gaze lingered on Voss for a long moment. He smiled faintly. "Let's find out how far it bends before it breaks."

Chapter 5. Part 3.

It didn't know what it was and it didn't care. *It* had a master and a mission. *It* didn't know exactly where it was either, probably because it was quite spread out. Or at least it thought so.

All that mattered was the splendid, beautiful mission that let it do its favourite thing. A human might call it "dog-napping." *It* felt privileged that all it had to do was watch the lovely Universe function as it should. If something came along to disrupt that order, it disturbed its sleep, and that was unacceptable.

It was a lazy beast by design, not that it had much truck with introspection. It knew there was a Maker. It didn't know much about the Maker, except that once in an aeon, a soothing thought might drift through the fields. This was reassurance that Maker was still there, still watching.

Nothing and no one but Maker must ever disturb that field, or there would be no Universe within which to sleep. That would be bad.

Unfortunately, these inconveniences did crop up. Some 200,000 standard planet revolutions ago (it called them Spins), annoying spikes of energy appeared in the more sensitive of the fields in this region of space. As a result, *It* was assigned this solar system to monitor. The mission was simple: keep the fields of existence in certain states. Light and magnetism could be fizzy, rather like what an aquatic organic being would call "a nice spa bath". Some fields attracted and repelled things; they should stay nice and lumpy. But the "sticky-flat field" that gave things resistance to movement (something *It* was bang-alongside in principle) was the tricky one. It had to remain cool, smooth, and steady so it could sleep.

If the blip was small, the solution was simple: talk to the nearest star and tell it to up its game a bit. Stars were obedient. They never talked back, but that was fine. It preferred to sleep anyway.

It sometimes imagined "Star" as a companion, but that was silly. "Star" probably was just a big ball of gas, and "Star" was certainly dumb. Still, it was dependable. "Star" would always do as it was told, which was absolutely fine by *It*. A reliable, obedient lump of fusion was the best sort of friend anyway.

A little more fizz in the electric and magnetic fields usually did the trick. Burn it out before it spreads. Fumigation, Maker called it. Maker was a Fumigator. And Maker was a good it.

Now, *It* felt something familiar. An itchy ripple in the sticky-flat field. Probably the death throes of the sleep-disturbing thing on that Rock, again. But this could be expected. Just turn the Star up a bit and it should go away.

It had a variety of methods in its repertoire. Different levels of inconvenience to its snoozing.

Certainly, no need to go full Super-Nova.

Not yet...

Chapter 6.

Ray Kostin, Rayk to all who were on personal terms, completed his final set of precision drills, the apartment's expansive training space allowing for full mobility exercises that would be impossible in standard colony quarters. The morning light of Sikarra filtered through the floor-to-ceiling windows of his luxury apartment. This was one of the unexpected perks of his new position.

He caught his reflection in the mirrored wall as he towelled off. The surgical scars along his lower back were barely visible now, thin white lines where they had inserted the neural interfaces.

The memory surfaced unbidden: Lieutenant Grayson's voice, sharp with anger. "Kostin, you are not authorised to enter with the SWAT team. This is an advisory role only."

He'd gone in anyway. Twenty minutes later, he was on the ground, buckshot through his spine, watching his own blood pool beneath him while his legs registered nothing at all. The doctors later told him it was a miracle the round hadn't killed him outright.

Rayk checked his implant's charge status with a subtle eye movement. It showed 72%. More than enough for the day ahead.

Every morning that he did his maintenance routine, he remembered the extensive white ceilings of the recovery ward. The specialists, with their carefully neutral expressions, explaining that he would never walk again. Then the man in the expensive suit who appeared one night when the painkillers had worn off, when Rayk would have signed anything.

"The program is experimental," the man had said. "A neural-spinal interface with artificial intelligence augmentation. Military applications, primarily. But it could restore full mobility."

What the man hadn't mentioned until after the preliminary screening was the randomised trial aspect. Half the participants received standard medical implants—enough to walk again, nothing more. The other half got the full package: enhanced strength, reflexes, sensory processing, and the combat subroutines.

Rayk had drawn the full package. The price: five years with the PCMA on Sikarra. He sometimes wondered if it had truly been random. *Or,* he thought, *if they needed a detective with his skills off-world.*

He dressed quickly, the servos in his spine humming almost imperceptibly as he moved. Today was about Jonesy, Osian Jones, the archaeologist they'd found wandering delirious at the perimeter three days ago.

Medical Wing C was quieter than usual. Rayk nodded to the staff as he passed, noting which ones averted their eyes. Information flowed through the colony like currency, and everyone knew the archaeologist's return was unusual.

Jonesy was one of the ubiquitous Brits from the European contingent of the PCMA, which was aligned with the NAR and made up of the old EU, remnants of the Russian Federation that escaped the Chinese onslaught and the independents like the British, the Swiss and the North Africans. The Welshman looked better than expected, propped up in bed, the medical monitors showing stable vitals. His eyes were clearer, too. The cataracts that had plagued him now cured with artificial lenses.

The Xenologist

"Mr. Jones, I'm Detective Kostin with PCMA Security." Rayk pulled a chair beside the bed and activated his recording implants with a subtle eye movement. "How are you feeling?"

"Better," Jonesy said, voice rough. "Doctors say I shouldn't have been out there with eyes as bad as mine were."

"That's my first question. The official report says you left the archaeological dig to 'get some fresh air.' In a partially collapsed section of the old city. During cloud cover."

Jonesy shifted uncomfortably. "I know how it sounds."

"It sounds like someone with only light eye protection, enough to protect your retina, thank goodness, decided to take a stroll through unstable ruins rather than staying with the team. What was the issue? Did you think you needed a better sun tan?"

"If I wore heavier UV filters, I wouldn't have been able to see, Sir. My Cataracts came on quickly. Apparently, I'm particularly susceptible to this planet's environment." Rayk allowed the painful silence to pressure Jonesy. Jonesy continued, "Look, er... I needed to think. The dig was frustrating. We weren't finding anything significant."

Rayk said, "You needed to think? You are here as a former military water engineer. Why are you so interested in what is going on in the dig?" Jones went silent. Rayk decided to prompt a little, giving him a chance to admit to something preferable to what he was really doing. "The tests show you have been a bit of a smoker in the past, Mr. Jones. You wouldn't have been going outside for a sneaky contraband Cigarette, would you, Mr. Jones?"

Jonesy let a guilty expression come across his face and said, "I could never admit to that now, could I, Sir?" Followed by a slight smile.

Rayk noted the micro-expressions his implants flagged: increased blinking, his right hand tensing. Jones was lying by implication. He didn't go for a smoke, but he wanted Rayk to think that he did and if it weren't for the implants, Rayk would have believed him.

Whatever Jonesy was up to, he didn't want his colleagues to see. "What happened next?"

"I told the others already. I walked to the River to see about getting a pipe set up. Maybe install some pumps because most of the easily available fresh water left on this planet is in the Gorges, the only place protected from the Sun. I went behind a rock for a pee. It was hot. I sat down for a minute and I think the sun was too much. I hid under a small rock overhang, then the storm came in, fast. I tried to make my way back. I got disoriented, fell through a sand Cornice into the Gorge. Next thing I know, I'm being dragged."

"Dragged by what?"

Jonesy looked away. "I don't know. I couldn't see clearly. It wasn't rough, more like being moved.

"And then?"

"Then nothing. I woke up about a mile from the perimeter fence. Close enough that I could see the entrance tunnel. It was three hours later, from what they tell me."

Rayk's implants flagged one or two inconsistencies, but mostly this was true. Then, before he could press further, his enhanced hearing picked up a subtle sound from the ventilation duct overhead. The soft click of metal against metal, too deliberate to be mechanical.

Without changing his expression, Rayk casually reached for a heavy metal specimen dish. He needed a distraction and fast. This was all there was to hand.

"Mr. Jones, I think—"

He hurled the dish like a discus with precisely calculated force. It shot through the vent' slits, followed by a satisfying thud, then a muffled curse. Rayk moved to drag Jonesy off the bed as the louvres of the vent rotated shut, discretion being the better part of Valour.

Then, the room's security shutters slammed down instantly, sealing them in. Medical alarms began to wail as the ventilation system hissed, releasing a colourless gas.

"What's happening?" Jonesy gasped, struggling to sit up.

The room's intercom crackled. "Equipment malfunction in Med Bay 12. Containment protocols engaged."

Rayk's chemical analyser implant screamed a warning: nitrous oxide and carbon dioxide from laboratory and medical cylinders were flooding the room from the quarantine ventilation system. Oxygen levels were plummeting. His neural processor calculated fifteen seconds until Jonesy lost consciousness, twenty-five for himself.

"Someone's trying to kill you," Rayk said, already moving toward the environmental control panel, tearing off the reinforced cover with strength that should have been impossible.

Jonesy began to cough violently, eyes wide with panic. "Why would—"

"That's what I'm going to find out," Rayk said, fingers working to override the system as the edges of his vision began to darken. "But first, we need to not die."

Rayk's combat subroutines activated automatically, time seeming to slow as his processor analysed the situation. It was the quarantine system being used. The control circuitry was behind a maintenance panel in the corner of the room. The maintenance panel resisted his efforts. Rayk pressed his qWatch against the locking mechanism of the access panel. It created a crude electrical field. A satisfying click was heard as the solenoid locking the cover clicked back, but not all the way. The door was still stuck. With a calculated strike, he was able to snap the last tip of the locking bolt that was sticking and he broke through the access panel. One more Electronic Warfare pulse from his qWatch and he had disabled the quarantine failsafe by simply frying the circuit, but gas was still flooding into the room.

Jonesy slumped back, consciousness fading. Rayk felt his own systems beginning to falter as he saw the valve he needed. He switched the flow and opened the vents to the outside. Then, to gain some minutes, he saw an oxygen cylinder in the corner. He limped over to the cylinder, his legs starting to fail as his tissue oxygen levels started to fall, no longer having the energy to respond to his implant interface. Totally reversible, the AS told him. Just get oxygen to his lungs before his brain starts to fade.

He took a few breaths from the cylinder, darkness at the edge of his vision starting to push back and with that, he was able to read the instructions on the inside of the panel door. Simple, when your brain is working, he almost laughed. Under the valve to reverse the air flow was the emergency purge button. In red for Christ's sake! He pressed the button and he felt a moment of relief as he finally triggered the emergency purge. The ventilation reversed with a mechanical groan.

He staggered to the door controls and forced them open, catching only a glimpse of a figure disappearing around the far corner.

Turning back, Rayk pulled the unconscious Jonesy into the corridor as medical staff rushed toward them.

"What happened in there?" demanded the chief medical officer, Dr. Winters.

"Someone just tried to kill your patient," Rayk said, leaning against the wall as his systems stabilised. "And I need to know why."

Dr. Winters stepped between Rayk and the trolley, blocking his path. Her face was granite. "Detective Kostin, I can't allow you to question him further until he's fully recovered. That will be weeks, not days."

"Doctor—"

"This is not negotiable. I absolutely reject your insinuations about my staff. Do you have any evidence concerning this patient? Because even if it is true, it just means your investigation nearly got him killed."

Rayk said, "I am afraid this is..." The Doctor replied, "My first responsibility is to my Patient and I would thank you to arrange 24-hour security if you really think this was due to criminal intent".

As they wheeled Jonesy away, Rayk watched the medical team work, his enhanced vision capturing details others would miss. The archaeologist was hiding something. Something worth killing for

Chapter 7. Part 1.

This time, Voss made his way to Renata's apartment, reciprocating her visit from the morning before. He felt a flicker of mild surprise that she hadn't extended typical first-evening hospitalities, but she'd pointed out, reasonably enough, that she worked late processing the reams of data coming from the various Xeno-Archaeology teams under her control.

Voss felt a pang of guilt; *I also had plenty of briefing materials to go through.* He had indeed spent the night poring over the literature that the teams working on site for the past year had managed to compile.

As he walked through the cathedral-like galleries of Petropolis, he used the time to reflect on what he'd learned. Precious little, actually. He thought *Why is the data so thin on hypotheses or results? There is plenty of cataloguing going on.*

There were endless glyphs in data storage. Many inert, some still faintly powered by Architect tech that seemed paradoxically simple yet impossibly enduring. Their chips were solid silicon that functioned without discernible circuits, drawing trickles of power from remarkably long-lived nuclear batteries.

He thought, *Why leave those batteries?* The question echoed the frustrating lack of insight in the reports. He pushed the thought aside. That's why he and Renata were here. Xenology, the new, interdisciplinary field of his own making, merging physics, biology, linguistics, and cryptography, was built for precisely these kinds of multi-layered puzzles. His successful predictions regarding New Ohio proved its value, but Sikarra, this felt like an entirely different order of puzzle.

He arrived at Renata's door, the cool metal snapping him out of his thoughts. His heart gave an unexpected jump at the prospect of seeing her again, a feeling he thought he'd left behind in university lecture halls.

She was ready, a small knapsack slung over her shoulder. Voss barely caught a glimpse of her apartment before the door closed behind her. It was spacious, rock-hewn, the inevitable pool near the centre, glowing alien screens embedded in the walls, all confirming his suspicion that the consortium backing the expedition had eyes on future luxury real estate development.

"Good news today!" Renata said, grinning as she led him to an electric golf buggy parked nearby. "We have appointments in all the best places."

He got in as she settled behind the wheel. "Really? Where would that be?" Voss asked. "You found a throne room? A banquet hall? Or maybe an alien movie theatre showing documentaries on the Architects?"

She started off at a brisk pace down the corridors, demonstrating her familiarity with the city's layout. The wind rushed past as Renata grinned, raising her voice slightly. "Oh, better than that. We are going back to school, but before that, we're going down the sewers!"

Voss returned her grin and resignedly nodded. "Of course. Archaeologists love middens. Hog-heaven for xenoarchaeologists too, I guess."

Renata laughed. "Oh, I wish! Finding actual preserved waste might be overly hopeful, I'm afraid."

"Ah, more sterilisation?" Voss asked.

"Yep," she replied. "But we remain hopeful."

As they zipped through the ostentatious, sun-dappled corridors, Renata glanced at him. "I reread your New Ohio paper last night, by the way. The prediction about the K-dwarf spectrum influencing vegetation colour and the tidally-driven geological patterning. Brilliant synthesis! That's the kind of thinking we desperately need here."

Voss felt a flush of professional pride, tempered by the weight of expectation. "Thanks. New Ohio was simpler in some ways—a clearer set of environmental drivers. Sikarra... this feels less like adaptation and more like... redaction."

Not disagreeing, Renata changed direction and gestured at the vista passing them by. "What do you think of it, Julian?"

Seeing the vast plazas and public spaces unfolding at every turn, he replied, "Magnificent," taking a moment to savour the atmosphere. "It seems absurd that I am on an Alien planet, only to be exploring the ruins of a hyper-advanced civilisation in a golf-buggy that wouldn't be out of place in the 20th Century".

Renata added, "Knowing what the company's budget is like, this probably is from the 20th Century!"

Voss replied with a quick "Hah!" As he returned to soaking in this exotic, astonishing place. Everywhere was subtly lit by filtered sunlight reaching even the deeper levels. Everywhere was cool and dry. It wasn't just magnificent, Voss admitted to himself, it felt strangely welcoming, almost cheerful. A stark contrast to the planet's hostile surface.

Slowing down as they approached the last corner, Voss affirmed to himself that this place was a literal gold mine, the treasure being knowledge, not precious metals.

Too soon, the buggy pulled up near a hive of activity – a dig site where focused people moved around equipment. As Renata and Voss arrived, heads turned – curiosity, expectancy, maybe a few envious glances directed their way.

They parked and walked towards one of the few drab structures Voss had seen, a plain, squat stone building marking an access point. People passed in and out, some carrying sample containers, others instruments.

"Welcome to the toilet block," Renata said with a mischievous smile.

Inside, the air in Waste Processing Sector 7G hummed, not with ancient machinery, but with the drone of human portable climate units and the low thrum of field analysis equipment. Harsh LED floodlights banished the shadows, revealing a cavernous junction where massive, ebonite-smooth conduits converged. Containment sheeting cordoned off sections, temporary worktables laden with sample cases lined one wall, and half a dozen figures in environmental suits moved with focused intent.

Dr. Anya Sharma, head of xenobiological sampling for this sector, met them near the primary access lock, her helmet retracted. Her face was sharp, professional, but Voss noted the slight tension around her eyes.

"Dr. Voss, Dr. Volkova," she greeted them, her quick nod was polite rather than curt. "Welcome to the midden. Or what passes for one." She gestured towards the centre of the chamber where her team was focused.

They worked around a series of tiered, recessed basins. Technicians carefully scraped dark, flaky residue from the basin surfaces into sterile collection vials while others monitored readouts on humming field analysers.

"We've established this node handled primarily organic slurry," Sharma explained, leading them closer. "Based on flow dynamics and residual enzymatic traces, minimal as they are."

Renata surveyed the scene, her archaeologist's eye taking in the context. "The concentration patterns suggest deliberate sorting occurred even within the waste stream. Remarkable orderliness."

"Everything the Architects did was like this," Sharma replied, a touch dryly. "Including, it seems, their clean-up." She indicated a screen displaying thermal analysis data. "Consistent results across all collection points: extreme thermal degradation signatures. Whatever this residue is, it was subjected to intense, directed heat before final deposition or flushing."

A junior technician, Jian Li, looked up as they approached his station, eager. "Dr. Sharma, the latest run confirms the protein denaturation profile. Almost total breakdown. And the DNA fragments..." He tapped his screen, showing complex sequence graphs. "...highly fragmented, barely identifiable. We're getting fleeting matches to some Terra-analogous clades, but it's statistical noise, mostly. Nothing cohesive enough to reconstruct a genome or even confirm a species."

Voss leaned closer, studying the jagged peaks and troughs. "So, earth-like biochemistry is suggested, but impossible to confirm? No intact cellular structures?"

"None," Sharma confirmed. "We've run microscopy, enzymatic assays... it's scorched organic ash, essentially. Any complex molecules were blasted apart."

Voss pointed to a subtle, repeating pattern in the fragmentation data Li had displayed. "This degradation signature, Anya," he mused, "it's too uniform for simple combustion or plasma heat. Look at the shear points on these longer chain fragments – almost too clean. It suggests energy applied at a specific molecular resonance level, perhaps? Something targeted, not only brute force heat. That requires a different kind of technology entirely."

Renata frowned. "Targeted molecular disruption? That goes beyond standard sterilisation protocols, Anya." Voss reached out, touching the black conduit wall beside her; a few grains of dark residue smudged his glove. "Even these walls show signs of a secondary thermal pulse, post-incineration, post-flush. We see data purging elsewhere, tech neutralisation. But incinerating biological waste to this degree?"

Sharma looked thoughtful, considering Voss's input. "Our field units aren't really equipped to differentiate that specific mechanism from intense thermal shock, but... it would explain the thoroughness. And I reached the same conclusion regarding the secondary heat pulse; I think these apertures," she indicated small holes lining the conduit, "are for flame ejection. Still, what seems excessive for us might have been standard for them. Extreme hygiene?"

Li interjected, "Or maybe the energy systems involved naturally generated that much heat? A by-product?"

Voss shook his head slowly, scanning the silent machinery embedded in the walls. "These systems feel precise. Controlled. Architects don't seem to waste energy; they're efficient. And their tech doesn't feel prone to messy by-products, especially if," he added, nodding towards the fragmentation data again, "they employed something as sophisticated as molecular resonance disruption. That feels deliberate. Like erasing evidence."

Renata picked up the thread. "But evidence of what? Why meticulously destroy biological traces? Unless..." Her eyes met Voss's.

"Unless the traces themselves were the data they wanted gone," Voss murmured.

"Metabolic pathways. Gut flora. Dietary markers. Anything that could physiologically identify them, trace their origins, perhaps even link them back to..." He paused.

"To their origin?" Renata finished quietly.

Voss surprised them both. "Or to the scene of their crime. Whatever that may have been."

Sharma looked between them, professional scepticism mixing with curiosity. "That's a significant leap, Doctors. Based on burnt dust and fragmentation patterns?"

"Perhaps," Voss conceded. "But the effort involved is undeniable, especially if they used advanced methods. You don't apply that level of energy or technology without a compelling reason. They weren't merely cleaning up; they were covering their tracks. The question is, why? What were they hiding? Fear of identification? Fear of pursuit?"

The hum of the equipment seemed louder. Li looked uncomfortable, perhaps realising the conversation had strayed far beyond technical analysis. Sharma pursed her lips.

"We'll adjust our analysis parameters where possible," she said finally, acknowledging Voss's point implicitly. "See if we can find supporting evidence for non-thermal degradation. But if you're right... it adds another layer of complexity."

Voss nodded, his gaze drifting back to the technicians patiently scraping at the remnants of a civilisation determined to leave nothing behind. The air felt heavy, not with humidity, but with the weight of a secret deliberately burned into oblivion

Chapter 7. Part 2.

Inside the relative quiet of the ruin, the storm outside a muted howl, Varinn took a steadying breath, the adrenaline from the drone fight slowly ebbing. Tessara moved near the fractured entrance, running a quick diagnostic on her wrist navscan. The Designer lay still on the dray.

"Anything?" Varinn asked, rubbing his temples where a dull ache persisted.

"Just background radiation and the storm static," Tessara replied, turning back towards him. "Whatever that drone was, it seems to have been alone." She paused, studying him. "That thing you did... with the Device. You seemed... elsewhere."

Varinn nodded grimly. "It opens things up. When I focused... there was this curtain at the edge of everything, shimmering. Pulling it back felt like staring into an abyss of knowledge so vast it could shatter your mind." He shuddered involuntarily. "Definitely not something to play with."

"Right," a quiet voice spoke, startlingly close behind Varinn.

Varinn spun around, heart leaping into his throat. Tessara reacted instantly, dropping into a defensive crouch, weapon coming up.

Standing not three paces away, where only empty ruin had been moments before, was a man. He was of average height, dressed in practical, sand-coloured gear, and held a small, metallic cylinder loosely in one hand. An unnerving calm radiated from him, contrasting sharply with the suddenness of his appearance. He offered a thin smile.

"Apologies for the intrusion," the man said smoothly, his voice unchanged. "Sometimes one forgets the effect." He made a subtle gesture with the cylinder, and the atmosphere seemed to shimmer and Varinn found his attention wanting to focus somewhere else for a moment before the illusion of him not being there resolved into an alarming, razor-sharp alarm at his presence. "Designer tech. Quite effective at encouraging people to simply... look away. Ignore. We are not the only ones who find uses for their leavings."

He met Varinn's stunned gaze. Impressive trick with the drone, Mr. -He paused, looking at the machine for a second. Varinn? Very... direct. You certainly have an affinity for the Instrument."

"Who are you?" Tessara demanded, her voice tight, weapon steady.

"A Voice," the man replied simply, glancing at Tessara. "May I congratulate you on your piloting. We saw you bring the skimmer down perfectly, but I must apologise that our arranged communications blackout and engine malfunction didn't bring you a little closer and save you a rather long walk". Tessara could only nod in grim recognition of the sabotage. Designer tech almost never failed.

'The Voice' turned his eyes back on Varinn. "Like you, perhaps. We know about the Veil, Mr. Varinn. The Designers hid knowledge they feared, knowledge that angered the Mother Star." His gaze sharpened, intensely curious. "Tell me, did you peek? Just a glimpse? Who could resist?"

A hopeless chill settled into the pit of Varinn's stomach as he recognised the rhetoric of conspiracy theorists. Perfectly self-contented and confidently assured of their own rightness, nothing would ever sway their convictions. The Designers were too lenient with them and they had proliferated. Varinn always knew their ethics would lead to this, but the boldness of this attack on a Designer rattled him.

The Xenologist

"The Designers lied," the man continued, his tone reasonable, almost pedagogical. "The 'Fumigation', external threats... fabrications to maintain control. It was their meddling with Instruments like yours that provoked the Mother Star's wrath, that made the sky burn with UV." He gestured upwards. "She isn't cruel, merely responsive. The Instrument resonates with her. Used correctly, it can soothe her, lower the UV, restore the balance." His eyes gleamed with conviction. "We will lead the people back into her true light."

"That's insane," Varinn breathed. "It's stellar physics, not a deity! The damage is direct interference from an external threat..."

"I know your rhetoric, preach it to the weak-minded" the man waved dismissively. "Leave the Designer," he nodded to the thin, injured man. "A relic of error. His disappearance here will be tidy. And the Instrument, of course. We require its connection to the comms network as well."

Varinn started to argue, "You can't 'soothe' a star with..."

As Varinn spoke, the leader held up a placating hand, his unnervingly calm gaze locking onto Varinn's. "Understanding requires focus, Mr. Varinn. True focus."

Simultaneously, Varinn felt that strange warmth bloom from the Instrument at his side, but this time it wasn't entirely his own doing. The leader's intense concentration seemed to resonate with the Device, amplifying its effect. The howling storm, Tessara's tense stance beside him, the very texture of the ruin walls—all began to recede, replaced by an overwhelming clarity focused solely on the man before him. His arguments felt somehow less important. Understanding The Voice's perspective and cooperating felt paramount. It was a deep, compelling pull towards consensus, towards information exchange, facilitated by the Device acting almost as an interrogation aid, blurring the lines between listener and speaker. Soon, there was only Varinn and the words The Voice was speaking.

The Voice said, "Calm yourself, Mr. Varinn." He continued, "This isn't an interrogation device. It's a harmless schoolroom teaching aid for Designer children". Varinn was strangely fascinated by the lecture: "It either focuses attention away from the teacher, so he does not interrupt the student's work, or it allows for total concentration on the teacher and opens your mind to learning. So don't worry and don't fight it. Concentrate. Tell me, Mr. Varinn, what is your plan with the Designer? Where are you taking him?

The words indeed calmed Varinn, and he thought about his mission and saw no harm in telling The Voice, "Oh, to the City. The Newcomers have arrived with their ships. The Designer wishes to leave with them".

"Ah, yes, the Newcomers. We don't trust them, strange creatures! But the Designers certainly seem to like them. I think it is best that the Designer, Mr. Marinallis, as I see from his name tag, should not make his rendezvous. Now think, Mr. Varinn, remember your time with the Comms Device. Remember the Veil? What did you see?".

Varinn was shocked at his own loose mouth, but the feeling of danger when asked about the Comms Device felt like a cold stone in his chest, saving him from blabbing immediately. The temptation to tell all was undeniable. The memory of the moment he took down the drone was accessible to him in complete detail. Perfect recall. He was about to start speaking when he was abruptly brought out of his trance.

The Voice had Tessara's knife through his throat. Suddenly, his peripheral vision and hearing outside the bubble surrounding The Voice and himself were restored.

Varinn had not even seen Tessara move. *He ignored her. What an unbelievably hubristic mistake,* Varinn's gaze swept over the stunned followers who now surrounded them, closing in. *What was Tessara thinking? How the hell are we going to get out of this?*

"Tess, grab the Designer and get him out of here. I'll delay them". Tessara lacked Varinn's strength, but the thin old designer was very light. She pulled her knife out of the now deceased Voice with a ghastly gurgling sound. She moved to the Designer with impressive speed. She grabbed his limp arm and hauled him up over her back. Varinn picked up the almost amusingly horrid teaching device, and immediately felt a false memory knowledge of how to use it.

Not a true cloak, his false memory supplied, but an attention redirector. One field, visualised in his memory as a shimmering blue fog, focused the student; the other, a white fog, edited out the teacher to allow concentration on tasks.

He chose the white fog. Turning on the fog bought him a valuable couple of seconds as his pursuers stopped in their tracks, as the hitherto all-important presence of Varinn vacated their minds and they had to realign their priorities on a new task. A second is an age in a close-in fight.

He instinctively had widened the spread of the fog to encompass all the attackers, but that diluted the effect slightly.

Worse still, the device was limited in power. This was, his false memory told him, to prevent brain damage to students and himself, fortunately. Or, unfortunately, because while the 'white fog' subtly pushed Varinn from the conscious focus of the six followers closing in, it would also paradoxically sharpen their attention on the one threat they could still see: Tessara.

But he could use this distraction. As the first man came close, he picked a brick up off the floor and smashed it into the man's face from point-blank range. At that moment, the spell broke as the man remembered in an all-too visceral and sudden fashion that Varinn was still there. But too late as he fell to the floor with a broken nose and cheekbone. The man next to him looked at the assaulted cult member in curious surprise. Where did that brick come from?

Even though this evened the odds, Varinn had to be quick. There were five left. He did the simplest thing he could; he simply kicked the next man in the groin as hard as possible. The extremist thug got some instant justice and crumpled in immense pain, barely aware of what had hit him. He was not going anywhere for the moment.

Four cultists remained, momentarily stunned by the sudden, seemingly inexplicable incapacitation of two of their comrades. The white fog effect of the cloaking device Varinn now held still seemed to be working; their gazes slid past him, focusing instead on the empty space where Tessara had been, or the fallen leader. But Varinn knew the effect wouldn't last once they realised the attacks were originating from an unseen source. He had seconds.

He thought of the Comms device that had helped him before, but dismissed the thought just as quickly. He felt, no, he knew that his brain could not handle such an advanced device so soon after the last connection.

So he surged forward, and still effectively invisible to their direct attention, retrieved a vibro-knife from the floor dropped by the second fallen cultist, the groin kick victim, ignoring the man's agonised moans. Two cultists were turning towards the sound, confusion warring with aggression on their faces. Varinn didn't give them time to process.

The Xenologist

Four left, plus the two writhing on the floor. The third cultist finally seemed to register the invisible threat, raising his crude projectile weapon, eyes darting wildly. The fourth hesitated, looking between his fallen comrades and the space where Varinn stood.

Varinn felt the power drain from the cloaking device. It hummed slightly hotter in his stronger, right hand, the 'white fog' perhaps thinning. He changed tack. He narrowed the field to the four remaining upright thugs.

Attackers five and six, stupidly, lined up behind the attackers three and four, who were still looking confused at their two colleagues on the ground.

The teaching device in his right hand, the vibro-knife in his left, he moved to the rear side of the third attacker and crossed his legs in a bent knee stance. Knees together and right foot behind the left foot. He reverse-stabbed the man in the temple. Varinn was uncomfortably surprised at how little force was needed to bury the vicious little knife into his brain. The man, instantly dead, collapsed. In a moment of guilt, he felt like an executioner, almost as if this was unfair.

Varinn suppressed the thought and twisted his upper body in a pirouette as his legs uncrossed, his feet staying where they were. As he twisted round on the next man, he realised he was a little too far to use the teaching device's short stub sticking from the bottom of his fist, so in an instant he had to use the long end like a club. It connected soundly and fatally, with the back of the man's skull with a sickening crack. It hit with such force that the stick-shaped device broke in two. The man fell, but at the cost of the device.

The fog of dis-focus faded instantly and the two men left, immediately focused upon Varinn, furious as they realised what had happened. They started to move towards Varinn. The feeling of "unfairness" was now something he wished he could get back. There was no honour in a knife fight. Varinn knew instantly that they had made the ultimate mistake when it was two on one attacking "Never, ever line up," echoed the voice of his old combat instructor, "and never block your co-attacker from access to your target."

They had not learned this lesson because the front man temporarily obscured the second man's projectile weapon. The first man in line had a stun-stick and a vibro-knife in his belt. For a moment, he moved to get the knife. That hesitation saved Varinn.

He put his head down and charged, panicking the man. His primitive instinct that stretched back to the earliest of his tool-using ancestors kicked in and he raised the stun-stick like a club to strike Varinn instead of relying on the electrical power of the device to halt Varinn's charge.

Varinn's head hit the man in his stomach and pushed him back into his colleague behind him. All three hit the floor in a pile. As they collapsed, Varinn repeatedly stabbed the first man in the stomach and blood spilt on Varinn's fist in a hot, wet, mess. As Varinn got up, the man with the gun was on the bottom of the pile, but his weapon hand was free and Varinn was not nearly as mobile as he needed to be as he was on his knees recovering himself.

As the arm came round to point the gun into Varinn's face, he used the vibro-knife once more. He skewered the man's wrist and severed the tendons gripping the gun. The weapon fell harmlessly to the floor. Remembering the true power of the nasty little vibro-knife, Varinn rotated the blade. The whole hand followed the gun to the floor. The man gave a high-pitched, shocked "oh" with his wide eyes full of dismay.

This was the moment a man realises his life as he knew it was finished forever. Varinn didn't feel too bad when he finished the man off. Designer tech could not grow him a new hand. His path ended here. By his own choosing.

Silence fell, broken only by the storm and the pained groans of the two initially downed men. Varinn deactivated the cloak, the sensation of being present returning fully, along with the sharp stench of blood and the bizarrely fresh, spring morning smell of ozone, partly from the enhanced UV light splitting the oxygen in the atmosphere and partly from the vibro-knife.

He looked down at the man with the broken face and the one clutching his groin. Pursuit was unacceptable. With grim necessity, Varinn moved quickly, using his knife to silence their groans permanently. There was no satisfaction in it, only the cold calculus of survival.

He straightened, breathing heavily, the adrenaline starting to fade, leaving behind a tremor in his hands and the coppery taste of fear in his mouth. Six bodies, including the leader, lay scattered around him in the dim, dusty ruin. He looked at the broken device in his hand in awe. He was glad his less-than-sophisticated teachers did not have this device when he was at school.

"Tess..." he started to call out, then stopped.

He looked towards the narrow passage Tessara had indicated, the one she'd presumably taken with the Designer. It was empty. A dusty haze lingered after the brief, brutal struggle.

He activated his wrist navscan, sweeping the area. Nothing. No life signs nearby except his own. No active comm signals. That was probably the insulating effect of the ruined surface structure. He moved quickly to the passage entrance, peering out.

The storm raged, visibility dropping to mere metres in the shifting sand. Footprints, if there ever were any distinct ones, were already being obliterated. Tessara and the Designer were gone. Vanished into the chaos as effectively as if they'd stepped through a wall.

Varinn stood there for a long moment, the howling wind mirroring the sudden emptiness inside him. Alone, surrounded by the dead, holding the precious comms device and the now useless, broken remains of a child's teaching aid.

He had no idea where Tessara had gone or how to find her in the lethal wilderness of Sikarra under the angry eye of the Mother Star. He could only hope she would complete the mission without him. But a cold sliver of doubt pierced his resolve. Once clear, why hadn't she tried to circle back, offer support? Was the storm really that bad, or was there another reason for her complete disappearance?

Chapter 8.

Mid-morning light, filtered to a soft amber by the Gold-tinted crystal domes of the residential part of the underground metropolis, hundreds of feet above, streamed into Raymond Kostin's apartment through the picture window, illuminating dust motes dancing in the recycled air.

He sat at his primary console, the large display casting shifting patterns across his face. The tang of ozone from the sonic cleanser he'd used earlier lingered, a counterpoint to the lingering clinical antiseptic smells he had brought back with him.

He'd returned less than an hour ago from Med Bay 12. Needing fast answers, he took matters into his own hands.

On the screen before him, the analysis results glowed starkly. Residue from a shattered micro-dart... Polylactic acid matrix. Rapidly biodegradable. He cross-referenced it against the restricted PCMA database. A match flared: covert bio-delivery system. Assassin's Micro-dart.

He had done a final, personal sweep of the ventilation ductwork adjacent to Jonesy's room. He trusted the forensic team, but needed answers now. Besides, his own implant-linked sensors often surpassed standard kits. His findings were fast-tracked, thanks to the priority assigned to security incidents involving injuries to personnel and the weight of Raith's personal pressure on the Lab Boys.

He then layered the results over his own sensor logs and the fragmented security feed snippets he'd cached before Raith's blanket suppression order came down—an order issued, officially, 'to prevent undue panic during systems review.' Rayk snorted softly. Panic wasn't Raith's concern; control was.

He saw it play out in his mind's eye: the operative hidden in the duct, startled by Rayk's sudden action. Louvres slam shut. Rayk throws the dish, a reflex. The operative fires the dart gun through the closing gap or perhaps at the closed grille in panic or assumption. The dart hits harmless metal, payload undelivered. *A concise, two-part plan, he realised.* Initially, only the gas would have been needed. Plainly, they knew in advance that Rayk would be there and so they modified the plan hastily to include the dart. Part 1—silent anaesthetic dart, a quick nap for the more dangerous Rayk before the 'accident'. That fails. Plan B activates anyway: flood the room with CO_2 and nitrous oxide, stage the equipment malfunction. Hope the CO_2 caused enough mind-fog and panic that Rayk would fail to escape. It was a clumsy decision, which played out the way they obviously feared it might. The end result, at best, would have been a messy assassination, with a cover story that would be easily debunked with scrutiny. Viable only if it bought enough time. Days, at most. That could only be long enough for an escape, perhaps. Or long enough for whatever required Jonesy's silence in order to conclude.

Why Jonesy? Rayk reviewed the ex-military water engineer's file again. Unremarkable, until he landed the Sikarra Gig. Wandering near unstable ruins in poor protective gear? It screamed dupe. A witness to something crucial, maybe without even realising its importance? Or he was out there up to no good and made a hash of it. A classic "Polezny" useful idiot, as his Russian Grandfather would have said. "Never be someone else's idiot, Raymond. If you are going to be a fool, at least

The Xenologist

be your own fool," he said with typical raw humour. Whatever he really was, one thing was certain: Jonesy was someone whose continued existence had become inconvenient.

And Rayk himself? He was the spanner in the works. The investigator. Worse, the enhanced investigator. How many truly knew the extent of his augmentation beyond 'mobility restoration'? Officially, few. PCMA brass, select medical staff. But whispers circulated. His performance metrics were suspiciously and often obviously high. He represented an unpredictable variable, someone capable of seeing through the flimsy staging and wouldn't just accept the official report Raith was undoubtedly drafting. Silencing Rayk alongside Jonesy wasn't just efficient; it was necessary risk management for the perpetrators. Even without him on the job, Rayk knew the tissue-thin facade covering the assassination attempt wouldn't last long. A week maximum. So whatever was planned, it was big, and it was imminent.

He needed more context. Raith was suppressing the official channels, but he could not hide the twenty-four-hour PCMA guard on Jonesy's door, tacitly acknowledging a threat while publicly denying one. But the guard was at Rayk's own request. Raith was indulging him, but Rayk hadn't yet ruled out The Director as a co-conspirator, despite his theatrics on the phone and concerns for Rayk's health, which felt a little belated.

He pulled up the file for Julian Voss. The name resonated with a certain academic celebrity. Creator of Xenology. Rayk scanned the summary, the brilliant cross-disciplinary background – physics, biology, linguistics, cryptography. He paused, intrigued. This required more than just reading data points.

Rayk closed his eyes briefly, activating a specific subroutine within his neural link. The world behind his eyelids shifted, the familiar sensation like dropping into a deep pool. The "Empathic Combat Simulator". The ECS was a brilliant combat AS subroutine that modelled what the opponent in any combative situation was thinking and shared the sensation of being that person with Rayk in the background. This meant Rayk knew what the other person was doing almost before they did. However, this wasn't the combat predictor; this was its repurposed cousin. Rayk called it the Empathic Emulator Routine or EER, developed as a private project over the past two years strictly between Rayk and his ever-present AS.

Rayk closed his eyes, activating the EER, allowing his AS to utilise the huge amount of training data available on Voss. The world behind his eyelids shifted. He wasn't just reading Voss's file; he was experiencing a sensory echo of the man himself. He felt the phantom weight of academic accolades, the quiet frustration of being a shy, introverted youth, which he worked hard on to overcome.

As he looked into an imaginary mirror, he saw Voss's handsome face and Voss questioning why his relationships didn't last very long. From his psych profile, fed into the empathic emulator routine, the self-knowledge of his social awkwardness traits came to simulated-Voss's mind. These traits were minor and not visible to the casual observer. But Voss knew it, his intellect too fierce to deny it. Like anything else, he made a study of it. He practised until only the most astute observer would notice an occasional slip. This made Voss self-conscious and self-referential, and yet more accepting of his single status, not frustrated by it. A good sign.

The simulated memory brought his gaze to a presentation script. His presentation of his New Ohio hypothesis. He felt the thrill of making intellectual

The Xenologist

predictions of the new planet, the only other habitable planet found to date, warring with fears of ridicule over the blinding simplicity of the predictions. The doubt in his mind. "Why hasn't anyone else done this?". The relief after the well-received talk was followed by disappointment as the number of citations of his paper did not live up to even his meagre expectations.

Then, vindication came as the probe data confirmed it all. The predicted deep purple hue of vegetation thriving under a K-dwarf's red-shifted light, the vast geometric fault lines etched by tidal stress and the specific spectral fingerprints of hyper-oxidised minerals coating the surface.

He felt the echo of Voss's quiet delight, the academic triumph quickly overshadowed by the crushing weight of expectation that came with the Sikarra posting. He even felt the faint, nervous spark of attraction towards Renata Volkova, noted during their first interactions, quickly compartmentalised. The simulation ran risk assessments: honey trap potential—low; susceptibility to ideological manipulation—very low; driving motivation—overwhelmingly scientific discovery.

Rayk pulled back, the simulated sensations receding, leaving the cool, analytical summary. Voss was likely clean, a brilliant mind focused on science, potentially unaware of the deeper currents swirling around him. A valuable asset, but possibly also vulnerable, another potential pawn if not handled carefully.

He saved the assessment. Raith's appointment was due in half an hour. Rayk had theories, timelines and a clear picture of the attempt. He thought, *No proof of who is involved. Others might act, but I need hard evidence.* Raith dealt in control and plausible deniability. *He must know the flimsy accident story won't hold together for long,* but I can't expose it yet. *Not before identifying the culprits.*

Concluding that the story served both parties well enough for now, he stood, stretching. The implants made minute adjustments along his spine. The path forward was clear, if dangerous. He had to bypass Dr. Winters, bypass Raith's official channels, and get to Jonesy. The Polezny Idiot held the key.

Rayk checked his sidearm and clipped his official comm unit to his belt. Time to face Raith. Time to play the game, while planning how to break the rules.

The Xenologist

Chapter 9. Part 1.

Varinn burst from the narrow passage of the ruin into a wall of grey fury. The sandstorm raged with undiminished violence. Sand scoured his face, the air's stinging particles finding every gap in his clothing. Visibility dropped to less than a body length, the wind a physical force threatening to knock him off his feet.

"Tess!" The name was ripped from his lips, swallowed by the gale before it could travel more than a metre. He squinted, shielding his eyes, turning slowly, desperately searching the chaotic swirl for any sign of her or the Designer. Nothing. Just shifting walls of sand and the oppressive roar of the wind.

He fumbled for his personal scanner, activating it with a curse. The display flared with static, overwhelmed by the atmospheric interference. No life signs registered beyond his own immediate bio-signature. It was useless for finding Tessara, useless for detecting threats. Tracks? Obliterated the instant they were made.

He was alone. Truly alone. Surrounded by the dead he'd left behind in the ruin, the vital comms Instrument hanging off his utility belt and clutching the acquired vibro-knife in one hand and to his own puzzlement, the shattered remains of the teaching device in the other. The mission: Vasantha, the Designer, survival, felt like a phantom limb, severed but still nagging, aching. Panic clawed at the edges of his resolve.

Forcing himself calm, he took a step in the direction Tessara had fled, then another, leaning into the wind, relying solely on memory and instinct. He swept his gaze constantly through the blinding sand. Then, movement. A flicker high on a dune crest to his left, a dark shape, head and shoulders silhouetted briefly against the grey, before vanishing below the ridge. Too deliberate for wind-blown debris. He froze, straining his eyes. Another shape, further ahead, moving with purpose despite the storm.

He checked the scanner again, pointlessly. Still nothing but static and his own vitals. Life-sign masking. The heavy UV cloaks the cultists wore weren't just for protection; they concealed them from standard Designer sensors. They had survived the ruin, and they were out here. He watched the second figure disappear over another rise, heading roughly in the same direction Tessara must have taken. They're tracking her. How? Superior tech? Instinct? It didn't matter. They were on her trail.

Hope surged, cold and calculating, replacing the panic. He couldn't find Tessara in this chaos. But they could. They were his only guide. His new plan crystallised: follow the hunters. Use them to find the prey. Use the storm that blinded him as his own cover.

He began to move, keeping low, angling parallel to the last sighted position of the cultists, estimating their pace. He pushed himself, forcing tired muscles, the adrenaline crash making his limbs feel like lead. He crested a low dune, peering through the swirling sand.

A figure loomed directly ahead, emerging from the grey less than five metres away. A lone cultist, heavily cloaked against the storm, head down, separated from the main group, perhaps circling back as a rear guard. No time for stealth.

The cultist looked up, eyes widening in surprise behind protective goggles. He reacted instantly, raising a crude projectile rifle.

The Xenologist

Varinn didn't hesitate. He lunged forward, knowing his own instrument was too risky. It was still too draining to use for now. This would be close, brutal. The cultist, hampered by the bulky protective cloak, tried to bring the rifle to bear. Varinn closed the distance, vibro-knife already in hand.

The cultist, seeing the speed that Varinn circled around the blind side, knew he would not be able to bring his weapon to bear fast enough. He had never seen such a bulky man move so damned fast. He saw the gleaming blade, postponed the decision to try and fire, wisely, and instead instinctively hunched, using the armoured plates embedded in his UV-protecting cloak to shield his head and chest, a defensive reflex against the expected stab.

It was the opening Varinn needed. He approached, circling to the right, around the blind side of the Cultist to avoid the projectile weapon's arc of fire. Varinn kept the vibro-knife in his left hand, held out in front of him, as an intended distraction. The Cultist's eyes followed the knife until the last possible moment. Bypassing the clumsy block, Varinn threw down the teaching device in front of the man, who's eyes followed the potential threat, then tossed the knife from his left to his right hand mid-lunge to get a better angle, driving the point low, under the raised gun-arms, sinking it deep under the Cultist's right rib cage, into his lungs and passing through the upper part of his liver and diaphragm.

The man gasped, rifle forgotten, stumbling back. He clawed at the knife embedded under his ribs, eyes wide with shock and pain. His right lung started deflating fast, due to the pierced pleural cavity, denying his brain vital oxygen. Varinn didn't give him a chance to recover or cry out. He stepped in, wrenched the knife free, pulling it through the lower rib for good measure, then he delivered a swift, final thrust to the throat. The cultist collapsed into the sand, twitching once before lying still.

Varinn stood over the body, breathing hard. The short, vicious fight was decided by exploiting the man's instinct to protect his gear over vital areas. Varinn's instructor spoke in the back of his mind, "Best give weapons to a man, don't man a weapon".

He quickly checked the body. The disquieting teaching device was left, thrown on the sand with some relief, it having outlived any possible usefulness. Instead, Varinn took the projectile weapon and the now blood-stained protective cloak. He couldn't linger; the fight, brief as it was, had cost him precious time and might have alerted the others.

He pushed onward, trying to pick up the trail of the main group again. Their direction remained consistent. Varinn forced his tired brain to access topographical data recalled from mission briefings. Ahead, the landscape dropped away sharply into the Great Gorge – the deep canyon carrying Vasantha's vital river, the only significant watercourse, bordered by the last vestiges of hardy green vegetation. Crossing it was unavoidable to reach the city from this sector, but fortunately, the bridge was directly en route in the north-west direction.

There was only one obstacle, however. The Solaath tributary ran from the Northeastern Plateau to the Great Gorge, where it intersected in the form of a waterfall into the old recreation area on the riverbank there.

He visualised the two crossings over the tributary. The first was a long southern detour, a rugged track that wound down to the recreation area where the Solaath plunged into the main gorge. It was the easier path to traverse but would add hours

The Xenologist

to their journey. The second option was the Stepping Stone Weir: a direct, faster, but far more exposed route that led past the old Pheonalla surface ruins and connected to the main bridge road.

The tributary. That was both a bottleneck and a barrier. The cultists weren't just tracking Tessara; they were racing her, aiming to intercept her at one of the crossings.

Which crossing? Varinn considered Tessara's situation: exhausted, carrying the dead weight of the Designer, no dray. The southern detour to the recreation area would add hours they couldn't afford. The Weir was faster and more exposed to ambush, but logical if speed was paramount. She'll take the Weir, he concluded. And they know it.

Varinn pushed himself into a punishing run, ignoring the screaming muscles and the grit stinging his eyes. He had to reach the Stepping Stone Weir first. He had to intercept the ambush before Tessara walked into it. He was still alone, the storm and his crude rifle and nasty little knife his principal allies, whilst racing towards a kill zone. His strength was fading, carrying a sophisticated instrument he dared not use, that he was ironically saving, only so it could be destroyed, following a woman he couldn't find, harbouring the desperate hope that he wouldn't be too late to save the precious Designer.

In the distance, he saw a faint outline of the head of a Cultist disappear behind a dune. He felt one foot move in front of the other, knowing there was no other option.

Chapter 9. Part 2.

Miles ahead, battling the wind at the edge of the high ground, Tessara reached the same conclusion. She stared down the slopes towards the green ribbon of the Solaath tributary river, making its way to the Great Gorge. The slightly precarious Stepping Stone Weir, slightly to the Northeast of them, was barely visible through the haze. The Designer felt impossibly heavy on her back, but this was the most direct route.

The alternative was where the tributary met the Gorge at an old recreation area. One could easily walk around the waterfall.

The southern detour around the tributary is too long, she thought, fatigue gnawing at her. He needs medical help. Anyone would expect me to take the fastest route. Logic warred with the instinct screaming about the directness and speed of the Weir. Logic won. I won't do what anyone would expect. The indirect route it is. Hope Varinn figures it out, if he survives. Steeling herself, she deliberately left footprints leading to the precarious track leading down the slope towards the weir. Then, stepping on the nearby rock, she changed direction and began the laborious slog, southwest towards the recreation area.

Chapter 10. Part 1.

Voss watched the technicians scrape at the scorched residue. The weight of it settled heavily upon him. Not the weight of discovery, he corrected himself, but of its deliberate absence. The sheer effort involved in the Architects' biological data erasure was staggering, suggesting fear or purpose on a scale he could barely comprehend.

"So," he said finally, turning back to Renata and Dr. Sharma, "we adjust parameters, look for non-thermal signatures, and hope something survived their... fastidiousness."

"Exactly," Sharma confirmed, already making notes on her personal datapad. "We'll rerun samples focusing on potential resonant frequency damage markers. It's a long shot, but your hypothesis provides a new vector, Dr. Voss. We appreciate the insight." Her professional demeanour remained, but a spark of intrigued curiosity now lit her eyes.

Renata nodded, her expression thoughtful. "It changes the narrative, doesn't it? From simple abandonment or environmental catastrophe to active, potentially fearful, concealment." She met Voss's gaze. "Ready to leave the gloom of ancient toilets for something a little more, shall we say, uplifting?"

"After contemplating meticulous waste incineration? Absolutely," Voss agreed readily.

They thanked Dr. Sharma and her team, leaving the hum of analysers and the faint scent of ozone behind as they exited the squat stone building back into the main thoroughfare. The contrast was immediate; the air here felt cleaner, carrying only the faint mineral tang of ancient stone, and the soft, ambient light from distant domes felt welcoming.

They walked towards the waiting electric golf buggy, their boots echoing softly in the relative quiet. Voss took a deep breath, trying to process the implications of what they'd just discussed.

"That level of paranoia," he mused aloud, "to erase even metabolic traces... it speaks volumes."

"Or perhaps extreme foresight," Renata countered, sliding into the driver's seat of the buggy. "If you knew you were leaving behind potentially dangerous technology, wouldn't you erase every possible clue that could lead someone back to your origin point, just in case?"

Voss considered this as he settled beside her. "Maybe. But it feels more reactive than proactive. Like covering tracks after the crime, not before." He shook his head. "Right now, it's just another frustrating puzzle." He watched Renata deftly navigate the buggy away from the processing sector access point. "So, what next? You mentioned going back to school?"

Renata shot him a quick grin, accelerating smoothly into a wider gallery lined with soaring, fluted columns that seemed to drink the soft turquoise light. "Patience, Dr. Voss. All will be revealed. But first," she gestured expansively at the passing cityscape, "Just look."

Voss forced himself to pull back from the immediate puzzle of the sterilised waste and truly see where he was. Even after days here, the scale and artistry of Sikarra City remained breathtaking. Vast plazas opened before them, connected by graceful archways carved with precision. Balconies overlooked galleries hundreds of feet below, their stone railings worn smooth by the passage of ages or perhaps the touch of long-vanished hands. Filtered sunlight, tinted gold or blue depending on the dome material above, shafted down, illuminating intricate mosaics embedded in the polished floors, depicting geometric patterns that hinted at complex mathematics or cosmology. Faint lines of residual light pulsed within some of the walls, remnants of a power grid still not fully understood.

He felt a familiar sense of vertigo, not from heights, but from the sheer reality of it all. He, Julian Voss, was riding a glorified golf cart, a primitive conveyance against this backdrop, rolling through the heart of an impossibly ancient, abandoned alien metropolis. The contrast was absurd, humbling.

Every corner turned revealed another vista of breathtaking beauty and profound mystery. His mind reeled, trying to absorb the sensory input, the weight of history, the potential for discovery. The pressure of his posting, the expectation that he could somehow unlock these secrets, felt immense, yet it was dwarfed by the sheer, overwhelming privilege of simply being here. *I'm really here*, the thought echoed, still carrying a sense of disbelief. On Sikarra.

He realised Renata was speaking, her voice pulling him back from his awe. "...only found about a month ago," she was saying, navigating a series of interconnected ramps leading to a quieter, less monumental sector. "Evans's acoustic survey team picked up resonance anomalies that didn't match structural scans. It took them weeks to isolate the source and get clearance to open this area. Standard procedure: you know? Check for atmospheric hazards, structural instability, residual energy fields..."

"So it's new," Voss clarified, forcing his focus back. "Which explains why it wasn't in the initial briefing dumps."

"Exactly," Renata confirmed. "Data dissemination is lagging way behind discovery, especially for finds outside the main excavation zones or glyph analysis. This one is, well, different." She slowed the buggy, turning into a narrower corridor. "You mentioned needing our Rosetta Stone moment earlier, the key to the language." She paused, allowing him to interject.

Taking the bait, he said, "The lack of one is the single biggest hurdle. Without a bilingual text, decipherment is exponentially harder. Finding a parallel between Architect script and any known human language seems statistically impossible given the timescales, distances and their alien nature."

"Unless the parallel isn't linguistic," Renata repeated her earlier hint, a glint in her eye as she stopped the buggy before an alcove door opening similar to others but perhaps marked, "Restricted Area, Archaeological Dig Site". "Dr. Evans is calling this the 'Music Room'. Prepare to be intrigued."

The valve hissed open. There was a different, musty smell inside. It was still, quiet, the ambient light softer, warmer. The usual faint city hum was absent, the acoustics strangely intimate. This wasn't a grand hall or a functional workshop. Low partitions created smaller alcoves around a central space. And in that central space, arranged with clear intentionality, were small, child-sized seats carved from smooth, dark stone, accompanied by equally small, low tables.

"Whoa," Voss breathed out, stepping inside, the valve sealing silently behind them. "Furniture. Small furniture." He ran a hand over the cool, smooth curve of a seat-back. "Kindergarten? For Architect kids?"

The Xenologist

Renata smiled softly. "That was our first reaction, too. Suddenly makes them feel a bit less... abstractly alien, doesn't it? There's a universality to needing places for the little ones to learn."

"Little ones who apparently needed music lessons," a voice interjected. Dr. Evans emerged from an alcove, his face alight with the pleasure of sharing a discovery. He gestured towards the closest wall.

Voss followed his gesture. The wall was segmented, embedded with shimmering, polymer-composite pads beneath distinct glyphs. Evans held two rubber mallets.

"Dr. Evans, I presume?" Voss asked, humorously echoing the well-known line. Evans replied, "Oh, of course, how remiss of me, and I presume you are the famous Dr. Voss who has been making so many waves in the community?" Voss replied, "Famous or-" Renata grinned and finished it off, "Infamous, possibly."

Voss, like Evans, had little time for the social niceties and also wanted to dive straight into the work. He walked a couple of paces towards the peculiar, moulded, stone-plastic-looking wall in front of them. "So, music?" Voss asked again, processing the implications.

"These indentations are like drum pads. Are they structured tonal systems?" Evans slightly nodded, encouraging further statements from Voss, evidently testing him. "That's paradigm-shifting. Evidence of artistic expression, cultural complexity beyond pure function." He shook his head in wonder.

"Tell me about it," Evans grinned. "Blew our minds when we first confirmed it." He stepped forward. "Watch this." He gently tapped several pads in sequence. Clear, pure notes rang out, forming a perfect chromatic scale that resonated uncannily close to Earth's standard A-440 tuning. "Each pad has a glyph and each glyph has a precise pitch. We thought maybe musical notation, or a tonal language component."

Voss moved closer, his Xenologist's mind racing as he integrated the new data. He examined the structure, noticing five small, precise holes near the base of each pad. "And these holes? Air vents? Resonance ports?"

"We weren't sure," Evans admitted, indicating a tray with the corroded metal fragments. "Found these nearby. They appear to have been thin strips of a ductile alloy".

Voss leaned towards a hole near the pad. On a hunch, he took a breath and hummed into the opening. The response startled him. It wasn't an echo. The sound that emerged was purer, clearer... it was the 'Oo' sound of his own hum, transformed into a perfect vowel. He tried again, shaping an 'Ee.' The wall answered, clear as a bell.

Evans looked puzzled at Voss for a moment and Voss said, "Have you done a metallurgical analysis of the metal. Can we reproduce it?"

Evans defensively said, "Of course, it's a high-quality alloy of stainless steel and ductile copper. We can't get it perfect with the 3D metal printers, but we can get pretty damned close." Then he added quickly with some price," In fact, I already ordered up a couple and they arrive first thing in the morning."

Voss said, "Very efficient, I am impressed. I don't suppose you could order up five of them, could you?" Evans replied, "Sure thing, five or twenty-five, we don't hang around here, I will ask for the run to include three extra ones".

Renata looked curiously at Voss for a moment: *What is he up to?*

Then she said, "I suspect this is the most important thing archaeologically going on here at the moment. If it's OK with you, Julian, we will be here at 9 in the morning."

The strips should be here by then."

As she moved back to the buggy, Voss was already taking photos of the glyphs on his datapad. He had things to think about this evening, but he needed to hurry. Evans' nose was looking like it was put out of joint.

He had to move quickly. *My God,* he thought, *what if the solution is as embarrassing as it is obvious?*

Chapter 10. Part 2.

In the staging area beside the landing pad, Director Desmond Raith, dressed in expensive, tailored civilian clothing that spoke more of corporate power than military rank, checked his appearance in a reflective panel. He turned to Rayk Kostin. "The staff will want to know why I am going out on a routine investigation of a staff member going 'walkabout' and getting lost," Raith stated, his voice precise. "Let's be clear on both the official and unofficial reasons for this outing. Our primary task is, of course, to investigate Mr. Jones's last known movements before the storm hit, including a good look at the gorge area. As you say, it is suspiciously close and the only place where anything that could have helped Jones could have come from."

He paused, ensuring Rayk's full attention, "However, my official reason for accompanying you, and the purpose logged for this flight, is a standard security liaison visit to Valerius Corba. I will introduce you formally in your capacity as Head of Investigations." Raith's gaze sharpened. "You will frame all inquiries with Corba and his people through that lens. General security posture, unusual observations and standard procedure. So, we will keep it discreet, if you don't mind."

Rayk registered the steely threat behind the politeness. "Understood, sir," he replied evenly.

Raith said nothing. It was not lost on Rayk that his agreement was hubristically assumed and his confirmation not required. Raith continued, "Though I reiterate my view that the attempt on your life in the medical bay remains the more probable motive behind this mess. Simpler explanations, Kostin. Drugs, perhaps? Corporate espionage? Mr. Jones could merely have been an unfortunate bystander." He gestured towards the waiting skimmer, a polished black composite teardrop that hummed quietly.

"The sophistication of the attempt felt targeted, sir," Rayk countered mildly as they walked towards the open hatch. "And Jonesy's own words, 'something out there' warrants at least a perfunctory investigation."

Raith gave a non-committal shrug as they boarded and settled into the plush seats. Rayk guessed at Raith's likely internal monologue: *Assess the situation, control the variables, manage the optics and ensure Kostin doesn't create political fallout.* Raith kept all emotion from his face as he seated himself and the hatch sealed, and the skimmer lifted off with barely a whisper.

Their first stop was near the jagged breach in the ancient ruin wall, the impromptu exit Jonesy had used. The skimmer landed gently on the sun-baked ground. They donned their UV protective shawls that fitted over their desert cooler-suits and donned their heavy eye-protection. Modern replacement lenses were as good, if not better than the originals that nature gave them, but getting cataracts was also a disciplinary offence with a fine against your wages. Rayk thought he would 'pass' on that.

They disembarked down the executive skimmer's ramp into the familiar oppressive heat. Raith activated a portable display unit. "CCTV confirms his exit time precisely here," he stated. "Meteorological data records the storm hitting visibility zero at approximately thirty minutes later. Let's establish a reasonable perimeter."

They discussed Jonesy's likely physical state—not peak fitness, probably suffering from heat exposure even before the storm. Rayk started his chrono. They began walking, following the natural contours of the land leading away from the ruin, down a shallow slope strewn with loose rock and hardy, desiccated scrub. The heat radiated upwards, making the air shimmer. They walked at a steady, measured pace, simulating someone trying to conserve energy but moving with purpose. After fifteen minutes, the ruin was completely hidden behind a low, undulating ridge. The silence was profound, broken only by the crunch of their boots and the faint sigh of the wind.

"This feels about right for fifteen minutes at a moderate pace," Rayk observed, stopping. He checked his standard communications unit. "And confirms the topographical dead zone. Comms signal is completely blocked here." He scanned the panorama ahead. The undulating, heat-blasted desert stretched out, empty save for the distant, hazy line of darker green marking the Great Gorge system. "It's the only discernible landmark from this position."

Raith shielded his eyes, nodding slowly. "A beacon, of sorts. Water, shelter. More appealing than turning back into the teeth of a sandstorm. Logical, I grant you." He glanced back up the slope. "It establishes a probable direction of travel, at least." Renata said, "Yes, just as easy to go forward as backwards. I suggest we take a look at the Gorge?" Raith replied, "Best we take the skimmer. The gorge side is steep and it's best we make our appearance in the skimmer rather than look like we were poking around up here".

The walk back to the skimmer, uphill under the relentless Sikarran sun, took slightly longer, emphasising the effort Jonesy would have expended just to reach this point of relative cover and make a decision.

Strapped back into the cool cabin of the skimmer, they began the significant transit towards the Great Gorge. This was a short hop; the display showed them crossing a couple of kilometres only, over harsh, broken terrain. Ravines scarred the landscape, and towering rock formations, sculpted by millennia of wind and sand, cast sharp, dark shadows.

Even this short distance would have been arduous for Jonesy. The UV index remained punishingly high. Rayk watched the external sensors, noting how the extreme heat, radiation and atmospheric conditions degraded the reliability of standard thermal imaging, producing flickering artefacts and phantom signatures. The landscape felt ancient, vast, and inimical to human life. Even through the filtered canopy, the sheer scale and hostility of the environment pressed in. Rayk noted several potential routes into the gorge system, narrow canyons and defiles that would offer natural concealment from aerial observation.

Very soon, the terrain began to shift. The skimmer banked, following a wider canyon that cut deep into the plateau, and began its descent. The change was almost immediate and incredibly dramatic. The temperature plummeted, the dry air grew thick with humidity, carrying the rich, complex scents of damp soil, decaying plant matter, wet rock, and the delicate, unfamiliar sweetness of alien pollens. It smelled intensely alive, a vibrant contrast to the sterile desert above. Sunlight, filtering through a dense, multi-layered canopy far above, became soft, dappled, illuminating mist lingering in patches.

The unique flora of the gorge revealed itself. Towering trees, anchored to the steep slopes, displayed broad, waxy leaves in stunning shades of silvery-blue and deep, lustrous forest green, their surfaces subtly angled to reflect the most intense UV rays. Beneath them, a thick undergrowth thrived, including ground cover plants whose patterns seemed to shift and ripple, breaking up outlines, an evolved camouflage. Pale, thick-stemmed creepers snaked up rock faces, some bearing closed, bud-like structures.

The skimmer followed the winding course of the gorge, revealing Valerius Corba's villa ahead. It was an impressive structure, built into the cliff face, its clean lines and modern materials seamlessly integrated with the natural rock. Water cascaded down terraces planted with a startling mix of Terran grapevines, pomegranates, and citrus trees alongside thriving native Sikarran shrubs and ferns. Further along, nestled amongst the trees, were smaller, elegant dwellings—staff quarters, Rayk assumed—connected by winding, shaded pathways.

They landed smoothly on a designated platform near the main villa entrance. Valerius Corba emerged to greet them. With a relaxed, controlled posture, he said, "Director Raith," welcoming them with a polite smile. "Welcome to Verdant Point. An unexpected visit, but you are most welcome," he said.

"Valerius," Raith replied, matching his tone. "A routine security review, nothing more. And allow me to introduce Detective Kostin, our Head of Investigations." Raith gestured to Rayk with his left palm. Corba offered his hand. "A pleasure to meet you, Detective Kostin," with a smile that didn't quite mask a flicker of appraisal in his eyes.

Introductions and pleasantries exchanged, they moved to a shaded terrace overlooking the gorge. Corba gestured for refreshments. "Please, assure yourselves, Director. Inspector, everything here is perfectly secure and delightfully tranquil."

"Any unusual readings? Sightings?" Raith inquired casually.

Corba waved a dismissive hand. "I presume you have heard some superstitious rumours, but I am very comfortable here. I have never seen anything. There are the usual tricks of the light down here, I suppose. Atmospheric lensing can make the indigenous fauna seem distorted at times. We had a report last month, a rock-hopper appearing bipedal for a moment. Startling, but easily explained." He chuckled. "My wife, Elara, finds the quiet rather oppressive. She is prone to imagining things and feels she's being watched occasionally. Nerves, I suspect."

While Raith engaged Corba in discussion about sensor protocols and perimeter integrity, Rayk took the opportunity to speak briefly with two uniformed security officers standing discreetly nearby. Their answers were crisp, professional, and identical: no unauthorised entries logged, no unexplained sensor alerts, no unusual sightings beyond predictable animal movements and atmospheric phenomena. They seemed well-briefed, perhaps too well. Rayk noted their alert posture, the way their eyes constantly scanned the surroundings even while speaking.

Later, making a plausible excuse to inspect the garden's interface with the gorge's natural slope, Rayk wandered along a less-used path. He saw her then, the cleaner from his earlier assessment, her movements hurried and anxious. She placed a plain ceramic dish near a dense thicket of native shrubs whose broad leaves offered deep shade. She glanced around nervously before retreating.

Rayk approached slowly, deliberately making a slight noise with his footfall. "Good morning."

She started, turning wide, fearful eyes towards him. "Oh, you must be the Detective they said would visit! I didn't see you."

"Admiring the gardens," Rayk said easily. "Leaving something out?"

The Xenologist

Her hands twisted in the fabric of her apron. "Just, just a courtesy. To the place. It's an old tradition."

"A courtesy?" Rayk prompted gently.

She lowered her voice, leaning in slightly, though her gaze darted towards the shrubs and back towards the villa. "I feel things, Detective. More than most. This place, sometimes it feels like it's aware. Watching." She shivered. "Not with eyes. It's a feeling. In the air. Like the rocks themselves are listening."

Fear tightened her features. "Mr. Corba... he doesn't like such talk. Everything must be logical. Explained." She hesitated, then whispered, "Leaving a little something seems to calm the feeling. If it's left neatly. The feeling is less, well, sharp." She wouldn't be drawn further, shaking her head and muttering about "old wives' tales" as she hurried away.

He rejoined Raith, sharing only the bare observation of the cleaner leaving food scraps. They proceeded downstream towards the biologists' enclave, a compact cluster of prefabricated buildings tucked away in a secluded bend of the gorge.

Dr. Aris Thorpe and his small team welcomed them with professional curiosity that felt a little distant. Rayk took the time to examine the flora more closely. Thorpe elaborated on the adaptations. "The silvery-blue and deep green pigments in the canopy leaves contain complex polymers that reflect or absorb specific UV wavelengths. Highly efficient," he explained. "The ground cover utilises chromophores, similar to Terran cephalopods, shifting patterns in response to movement and shadow, providing exceptional camouflage for ground-dwelling fauna." He pointed to the pale creepers. "These are fascinating. Their blooms are triggered by specific thermal signatures and rhythmic vibrations consistent with mammalian locomotion passing nearby. The hypothesis is a symbiotic seed dispersal strategy—the mammals gain cover or perhaps sustenance from the plant or associated fungi, and in return, spread its seeds."

Raith gave Rayk a long-suffering look. "How fascinating". Rayk quickly interrupted with, "Yes, a complex ecosystem," then before Raith could say anything offensive, he diplomatically added, "Any unexplained phenomena here?"

The scientists looked slightly uncomfortable. "We experience minor anomalies," Thorpe admitted cautiously. "Small hand tools sometimes go missing, only to reappear later in unexpected places. We occasionally log faint, unidentifiable thermal traces at night that don't match known species profiles. And there are auditory quirks, such as sounds of movement in the undergrowth that seem, debatably, out of sync with the typical patterns of the local fauna." He spread his hands. "Certainly nothing concrete to suggest anything unusual." Their professional caution seemed tinged with a shared, unspoken uncertainty.

Leaving the enclave, Raith said to Rayk, "He doth protest too much". Rayk added sarcastically, "Absolutely nothing to see here, move on". Raith allowed himself a small smile as they directed the skimmer pilot to land near the rock shelf they had identified earlier as a likely shelter spot for Jonesy. They disembarked once more into the cool, damp air of the gorge floor.

"So, Rayk," Raith said quietly, surveying the secluded spot. "Do you think it's worth putting some stealth drones out here and possibly over the Gorge? It could be politically messy for me if Corba spots them. He has some pretty sophisticated equipment himself out here"

Rayk surveyed the rock shelf, his expression thoughtful. "That, I am afraid, is your call, Sir, but I'm beginning to believe someone encountered Jonesy out here. Someone provided assistance because now I have seen the surveillance equipment that Corba has, it's likely he never made it into the Gorge, or he would have been seen by the staff and he didn't get back there on his own. Not in that state."

He gestured towards the ground near the base of the shelf. Rayk followed his gaze and saw it—the crumpled, metallic sheen of a standard PCMA survival ration wrapper, partially covered by leaves. "But it leads back to the same damned contradiction," Raith continued, frustration in his voice. "Why help him here, only to orchestrate a lethal attack days later in a secure facility? It makes no tactical sense."

"Unless the objective wasn't tactical," Rayk mused, kneeling to examine the ground more closely. "Maybe the situation changed? Or the players." His fingers brushed against something hard beneath the thin layer of soil and pebbles. Carefully, he unearthed Jonesy's personnel tracker. The casing was scratched, showing marks consistent with being forcibly pried off. It had been deliberately removed and buried. Nearby, scored into the rock face, were several deep, parallel gouges. Too regular for most animal claws, too sharp for natural weathering, yet not definitively tool marks either. The ambiguity was as unsettling as it was curious.

They stood in silence for a moment, the implications sinking in. Concrete proof of Jonesy's presence here. Concrete proof of deliberate concealment. Aid offered, followed by lethal intent.

As the skimmer ascended, leaving the lush, shadowed depths of the Great Gorge behind, the mood in the cabin was heavy. Raith stared out at the receding landscape, his brow furrowed in concentration. The simple explanations were evaporating. Rayk reviewed the day's findings: the calculated denials, the pervasive sense of unease cloaked in rationalisations, the tangible evidence at the rock shelf. Jonesy hadn't just stumbled; he'd fallen into something deep. Something ancient, perhaps. Something that watched from the shadows of the gorge and was now, somehow, connected to the violence back in the city. The carefully constructed reality of the Sikarra operation felt suddenly, dangerously, like a house of cards.

Chapter 11. Part 1

Voss sat in his spacious room that afternoon, preparing for his evening meal with Renata. He was unsure which he was most excited about, the discovery of the "Music Room" or the evening date with Renata. The thought of it sparked a warmth in his chest, but he felt a slight tongue-tied compulsion to impress that he thought he'd left behind in university lecture halls.

He decided that if he didn't stop daydreaming, he would end up neither being showered and ready for the evening, nor be properly prepared for the big reveal tomorrow.

He pulled his attention back to the files. He knew he had seen things like those glyphs before. Especially the five glyphs over the five holes. He opened an old textbook on his data console. "The Chemical Structures and Energy Cycles of DNA. By Waterson and Shevchenko," An old classic University textbook from his early days, that had the diagrams he needed. Making notes ready for tomorrow, he started planning his 'big reveal'.

A moment of doubt came over him. How can Evans not have seen this? How did he have the foresight to order up those pieces of metal but not see that they went in the holes? How did he not notice the resonant frequencies of the holes? He would have been all over it. Was it Voss missing something?

The same old feelings of inadequacy came over him as when he published his papers predicting conditions on New Ohio. Was he stating the obvious? But also, nobody on the dig had linked things altogether yet. Why?

He pulled up Evan's profile, since technically, everyone worked for him now. The man had the inevitable huge resume, well respected as a practical archaeologist. But something did seem a little strange. The man had huge experience, was well-liked and trusted with many precious and delicate digs up to now. He absolutely knew how to look after a site. But his papers were a little on the sparse side and made few accurate predictions about the artefacts he dug up, leaving that for others. Voss, if he were being unkind, would say that Evans had absolutely no imagination whatsoever. If someone wanted to preserve all the glory for himself, Evans was precisely the man he would pick.

Voss noted the appointment was made by the World Xenoarcheology Council, set up by the New United Nations. Largely funded by the Central Asian Republic. Voss had been sidelined by them and rejected his application to them. Voss was headhunted, however, by the North Atlantic Republic and put in charge, so he thought it a moot point. Politics. Not my thing!

He made some more notes, now sure of himself. He knew what he would find. He decided not to say too much to Renata that evening. He would try to avoid talking shop.

Chapter 11. Part 2

Renata stood before the mirror-smooth panel inset into her apartment wall, making a final assessment. The dress, a deep Terran blue synthetic silk that clung and flowed in ways alien stone architecture never could, felt like a statement. Perhaps too much of one? She smoothed the line over her hip. Going out to the colony's single decent restaurant was never going to serve up a state dinner, but after weeks of utility suits and functional layers, the sheer indulgence felt... good. Almost naughty. She'd decided against alcohol tonight, wanting a clear head, but she smiled wryly at her reflection. Likely story. 'Vodka and beetroot juice run in our veins, Renata,' her mother used to say with a sigh that was equal parts resignation and pride.

She thought of her mother, a Crimean Tatar with eyes that held centuries of resilience, finding refuge first in Moldova, then Germany, after the chaos that forced them from Ukraine. And her father, the tall Ukrainian from Lviv with his sunny hair, was killed by some nameless Russian soldier in the grinding, never-ending attrition that followed the twenty-first century's 'unpleasantness', leaving Renata only his long limbs, his fair colouring, and her mother's fierce, Tatar-arched eyebrows.

Her own hair was darker now, closer to her mother's shade, but she touched the carefully lightened, straw-yellow strands framing her face. Her one true luxury brought on the long voyage out: a ridiculously expensive supply of professional hair lightener. A small vanity, a link to the child she'd been. She ran her tongue over her teeth, freshly painted with a whitening gel that promised an instant, dazzling smile. She'd probably overdone it. In the harsh UV filtering sometimes used in the communal areas, she'd likely look like she was chewing blue phosphors. She laughed softly at herself, a puff of air fogging the mirror. Acting like a teenager, overthinking everything for a man she barely knew. Julian Voss.

Walking the short distance through the cool, echoing corridors towards his designated apartment felt strangely significant. What would they even talk about outside of glyphs and ruins? She mentally squared her shoulders. Her education at Tübingen, digging into the deep history of Neanderthals and the very origins of humanity, was world-class. Voss's North American university might be newer, shinier, backed by colossal funding and driven by a ruthless, publish-or-perish academic culture, but she could hold her own. Couldn't she? A flicker of competitiveness surprised her. Voss, parachuted in by the North American contingent of the North Atlantic Republic, could technically claim seniority and could probably pull rank over almost everyone here, including her. Raith had practically told her to let him have whatever he wanted. Don't challenge, she reminded herself. Let the situation remain vague. Besides, she couldn't deny the easy brilliance he'd shown already, the unnerving affinity for the Architect technology, the polymath mind connecting dots others hadn't even seen. He hadn't broken a sweat yet, and he was already making waves. Best not to rock the boat.

She reached his door, smoothed her dress one last time, and remembered to compose her features into a pleasant, open smile just as the panel slid aside.

His reaction was worth the effort. A momentary stillness, eyes widening almost imperceptibly, taking in the dress, the hair, the deliberate effort. He likes me, the thought registered with a ridiculous, girlish thrill. Then, as his gaze met hers, a second thought, colder and more pragmatic: I may be in a bit of trouble here. Her own eyes flickered, almost against her will, to where the rolled sleeves of his crisp white shirt stretched taut over impressive biceps. Why is it always the biceps? she mentally grumbled, forcing her attention back to his face.

"Wow," he said, slightly flustered. "Renata, you look... stunning. I, uh, I should probably put a tie on." He turned, scrambling through a half-unpacked suitcase resting on the bed, pulling out a creased strip of fabric that clashed faintly with his dark trousers.

Definitely overdid it, she thought, amused now rather than self-conscious. She stepped inside as he fumbled with the tie, listening with half an ear as he babbled pleasantries. She reached out, gently taking the ends of the tie.

"Allow me," she said, her fingers brushing his collar as she deftly straightened the knot and smoothed the fabric against his shirt. "Don't worry," she added, stepping back and giving him a mock-formal inspection. "You'll pass the dress code. It's hardly black tie or 'couples only' down at our best Restaurant, 'Bar None', terrible pun I know". She tapped her wrist-comm. "Buggy ordered. One of the perks of this all-inclusive luxury resort, free golf carts everywhere."

He laughed, the awkwardness easing. "Can I offer you a drink while we wait? Standard issue apartment chic, I'm afraid."

She raised an eyebrow, genuinely surprised. "They issued you alcohol? That's usually reserved for Directors and visiting dignitaries."

He grinned, retrieving two small, travel-sized glass bottles from a side compartment of his luggage. Gin. "Ah, well. Perks of the long haul. Brought the complimentary allowance from the ship. Less than a litre, perfectly legal according to regs." He gestured towards a counter near the small sink unit where a bottle of ginger ale stood.

She considered the gin. Her earlier resolve wavered. "Straight spirits give me heartburn these days," she lied smoothly. "I'll take it with the ginger, if you don't mind."

He poured generously, handing her a glass before preparing his own, adding significantly more mixer. She took a sip, then another, the juniper bite sharp and clean. It felt good. Too good. Before she quite realised it, the glass was empty. She placed it firmly back on the counter. Voss was still nursing his first sip, watching her with raised eyebrows.

"Slavic blood," she explained with a self-deprecating laugh. "We metabolise disappointment and clear spirits with equal efficiency."

A soft chime indicated the buggy's arrival outside. They stepped out into the corridor, the automated vehicle waiting silently. The five-minute drive was a blur of softly illuminated tunnels, soaring archways carved from the living rock, and the occasional glimpse into vast, empty plazas lit by the eerie blue glow of dormant Architect tech.

The Restaurant "Bar None," nestled in a large cavern and repurposed with surprising taste, was bustling. It was the only proper restaurant in the city that was open in the evenings. It was obviously popular. Under an uneasy compromise between the Xenology-Trust and National Parks, only empty spaces with no tech were allowed to be converted to modern use. Robot surveyors had previously excavated and moved anything valuable to the archive, then photographed the empty rock caverns in minute detail before the developers moved in.

It rather made Voss cringe, but the ruins had to be made to pay humanity for the huge investment in colonisation. He had to be pragmatic. He also had to admit they did a stupendous job. The back wall was simply missing and ended as a huge room-length balcony, open to the perfect city air. Large onyx tables adorned the room for larger parties and stone-carved booths were available for couples. They were shown to a comfortable booth tucked into an alcove offering relative privacy.

The small talk flowed easily enough while they scanned the menus displayed on embedded screens. The surprising quality of the recycled air, the strangeness of eating hydroponically grown sushi deep beneath an alien desert, the sheer architectural audacity of the city around them. They both ordered the sushi platter and a bottle of crisp, chilled white wine synthesised from atmospheric water and nutrient stock; another minor miracle of colony tech.

As the wine was poured, Renata steered the conversation back. "So, this theory you mentioned? About the glyphs in the 'Music Room'?"

He hesitated, swirling the wine in his glass. "It's... preliminary." Silence from Renata. He filled the gap with a sign and continued, "It needs more data. More correlation."

A flicker of annoyance sparked in her. Why be coy? Then she saw the slight tension in his shoulders, the way his gaze didn't quite meet hers directly when discussing his own nascent ideas. Ah. He wasn't being deliberately obtuse; he was genuinely cautious, perhaps even slightly insecure about presenting a half-formed hypothesis. It made him seem younger, less of an imposing intellectual figure. The shift was disarming. Objectively, it probably made him less conventionally attractive to someone raised on stoic, macho Ukrainian archetypes, but subjectively... It made her relax. It created an illusion of control, even though she suspected he was perfectly aware of the dynamic.

The wine helped. Another glass vanished rather quickly. She felt a pleasant warmth spread through her, loosening the tight knot of professional caution she usually maintained. Voss, too, seemed less guarded, his earlier awkwardness replaced by an easy, engaging manner. They laughed about some trivial observation, a shared moment of slightly tipsy amusement, the intimacy unexpected and surprisingly comfortable.

"So," Voss said, leaning forward slightly, his eyes holding hers, the earlier reticence gone now, replaced by genuine curiosity. "You mentioned once how you got into archaeology? Something about a goat, a red dog collar, and the BBC?"

A sudden tightness seized Renata's chest. The story. She took a slow sip of wine, the coolness doing little to quell the heat rising in her face. She met his gaze, made her decision, and began.

"Yes," she began, her voice steadier than she felt. "That's... quite the summary." She paused, took a breath, the scent of the synthesised wine suddenly sharp in her nostrils. "It was twenty years ago. Western Ukraine..."

Twelve-year-old Renata kicks open the farmhouse door, letting herself in. First home, as usual. The familiar list of chores runs through her head: muck out the old horse, check the chickens for eggs, feed the goats. The house smells faintly of woodsmoke and boiled cabbage. Her mother won't be back from her cleaning job in town for hours. Georgi, her stepfather, is probably still at work, or if back home early, he would be out mending fences. On rare occasions, her Mom may let him go drinking sour kvass with the neighbours. Good. He was no saint, but he was a decent enough man, really, or at least her Mom said so. But there is always some tension between them.

She drops her worn school satchel by the door. Her natural father, the one from the faded photograph with the laughing eyes, feels like a story someone told her once, killed near the border in the endless, simmering conflict with the Russians. Her mother married Georgi three years ago. He isn't cruel, not exactly, but he moves through the farm with a heavy certainty that everything has its price, its purpose. Especially the animals. Renata knows her bond with them, the quiet comfort she takes in their presence, irritates him. It's wasteful, sentimental. Her mother sees it too, Renata knows. She sees the way Georgi looks at Renata sometimes, an assessing, superior glance that really infuriates Renata. Her mother never leaves them alone together for long, a silent, watchful guardian against unspoken threats rooted in her own past. Renata isn't scared of him, though. Let him try anything. She pictures the sharp gutting knife hanging by the back door. Georgi senses it too, that core of hardness in her. So, an uneasy peace exists. Renata does her chores without complaint and keeps out of his way. Four more years. Then Lviv, her grandmother's tiny apartment and college. A different life.

But there was Bubik. Her goat. The little runt his mother had rejected, the one Renata had secretly fed with a bottle until his skinny legs grew strong. He was the keeper of her whispered secrets, the only living thing that knew of her dreams of Lviv and a different life. He wore a cheap red dog collar she had bought at the market, a proud, defiant symbol that he was hers, and not just another animal destined for the pot. He was a friend. This sentimentality irritated Georgi, she knew. He saw Bubik not as a companion, but as a resource not being properly utilised. But he let her be and indulged her. He even spared her favourite hen, 'Princess'. Short for 'Princess Layer'. The name made him laugh, at least.

Then, one early summer evening the day before her thirteenth birthday, the school bus dropped her off at the end of the lane. As per normal, the yard dogs ran out to greet her. As per normal, they were nearly run over by the bus driver, who leaned out and shouted, "Renata, get those dogs chained up or one day..." She shouts, "They have to run free to guard the farm!" The dogs seem a little more agitated today as they run to the kitchen door.

The smell hits her as soon as she opens the door. Roasting meat. Rich, fatty, unmistakable. Goat. Her heart lurches. She calls out, "Bubik?" Silence answers. She forces her legs to move, out the back door, towards the small pen behind the barn. Empty. A leaden weight settles in her chest. She walks slowly, dread coiling in her gut, towards the lean-to shed at the edge of the woods. The place of blood and gutting. The rough wooden door hangs slightly ajar. She pushes it open.

And sees it. Lying on the dark, packed earth floor, almost lost in the shadows. Small. Red. Dulled with dirt and something dark, sticky. The collar.

A sound escapes her, a raw gasp that tears at her throat. For a moment, she can't breathe, can't think. Then, something inside her snaps. The grief transforms, hardening into an icy, crystalline rage. She turns, marches back to the house and strides into the kitchen where the offending pot bubbles merrily on the stove. She grabs the heavy oven cloth, lifts the pot—careful not to spill, not yet—carries it steadily outside into the dusty yard. And with a choked cry, hurls it down. The stew explodes outwards, meat and gravy splattering across the dirt. She brings her boot down, again and again, grinding the chunks of meat into the earth, stamping out the

The Xenologist

smell, the betrayal, tears of fury streaming down her face now, hot and cleansing.

Finished, breathing hard, she walks back inside. Takes the biggest knife from the wooden block by the sink. Its weight feels good in her hand. Solid. Real. She sits down at the worn kitchen table, places the knife before her, rests her hands flat on the wood. And waits.

An hour passes. Then the sound of Georgi's battered car pulling into the yard. He comes in whistling, stops dead at the sight of the empty stove, the open back door, the state of the yard beyond. His face suffuses with purple rage. "What have you done, you little..." He takes a step towards her, hand raised, then his eyes lock onto the knife, onto her face. He sees not a frightened child, but something cold, ancient, and utterly implacable in her gaze.

"You have to sleep sometime, Georgi," she says, her voice a quiet, low monotone.

He freezes. The anger drains away, replaced by a sudden, stark fear. He looks at her, truly looks at her, perhaps for the first time. He backs away slowly, fumbles for his phone and dials. "Come home," he says into it, his voice strained. "Now." He doesn't look at her again as he walks quickly out of the house, gets into his car, and drives away fast.

Renata stays seated, the knife before her, the red collar now retrieved from the shed, clutched tightly in her other hand. Its rough texture bites into her palm.

Her mother arrives later, breathless, her eyes scanning the scene, the yard, the kitchen, Renata, the knife and the collar. She is absorbing it all in an instant. Her face hardens, lines of worry deepening into fierce resolve. No hysterics, no wasted words. "Oh, darling," is all she murmurs, touching Renata's hair briefly.

Then, action. She calls out, her voice sharp, towards the empty yard, "Georgi! Guest quarters. Now. Lock the door." Silence. She nods grimly. She doesn't try to take the knife or the collar from Renata. Doesn't offer platitudes. Instead, she methodically goes outside and starts cleaning the mess Georgi left behind. She brings Renata food later, a bowl of soup left untouched. Checks on her periodically through the long evening as Renata remains rooted to the chair, silent tears eventually tracking paths through the grime on her cheeks. Her mother doesn't pry, doesn't push, just lets the silence hold the weight of what has happened. "Stay home from school tomorrow," is all she says before heading to her room, leaving Renata alone with her grief and the hard metal of the knife.

Sleep is impossible. Curled on the lumpy sofa, the collar clutched like a talisman, the knife resting nearby, Renata stares numbly at the flickering images on the old satellite television. Grainy reruns fill the empty hours. An archaeology show from Britain. Men and women in muddy waterproofs are digging careful holes in a green field. 'Time Team'. They unearth the foundations of a Roman villa. They talk about pottery shards and mosaic fragments. Then, a shot of animal bones. The presenter's voice, calm, academic: "...finds like this suggest even working farms kept animals past their prime. This goat skeleton, showing considerable age, might well have been a household pet..."

A pet. Cherished. Remembered across centuries. Not just meat. Not just forgotten. The thought lands like a seed falling on fertile ground. A connection. A meaning beyond the farm, beyond Georgi, beyond the suffocating present. A way to remember Bubik. A way forward.

Exhaustion finally claims her around dawn. She wakes hours later, stiff, cold, the red collar imprinted on her cheek. The knife is gone. A rough blanket covers her.

Sunlight streams into the quiet house. Her mother has already left for work. Cereal and milk are on the table. A note: Rest today. No School.

There is no sign of Georgi. He is simply gone. His few belongings vanish from the house over the next few days, discreetly removed. His name is never spoken between Renata and her mother again. No explanations are offered; none are asked for. It is an unspoken pact, sealed by the harsh pragmatism of survival, the fierce, absolute dedication to ensuring the child's future, whatever the cost. Renata understands, in a way she cannot yet articulate, the silent, potentially terrible sacrifice her mother might have made for her that night. But mostly, what she feels is the sharp, enduring ache for her lost goat, the rough comfort of the collar clutched in her hand, a tangible link to a past she is now determined to excavate.

Renata blinked, the ambient light of The Refectory seeming overly bright for a moment. She brought her focus back to the present, to the half-eaten sushi platter, the nearly empty wine bottle, Julian Voss's steady, waiting gaze. The intensity of the memory left her feeling slightly breathless, exposed.

She attempted a wry smile, the effort feeling brittle. "So," she said, her voice a little husky. "Too much information?" She fiddled with her wine glass. "Occupational hazard for archaeologists, I suppose. Keep digging, you're bound to hit bone."

He didn't offer false sympathy or look away. His gaze remained direct, holding an unexpected depth of understanding. "No," he said softly, his voice gentle. "Not too much information at all. Thank you for sharing that with me, Renata."

His simple sincerity cut through her defences. The atmosphere between them thickened, charged with the raw honesty of her story. She looked down at her hands, suddenly unsure what to do next.

After a moment, she cleared her throat, pushing her chair back slightly, breaking the intensity. "Well," she said, striving for a lighter tone. "It's getting late. And Sikarra's secrets won't uncover themselves. Tomorrow, we'll need clear heads." - So much for not drinking!

She called the Buggy and said, "You will have to learn how to do this. A gentleman should always call the Taxi". He smiled and said, "Oh, is that what I am?" She said, "We will see," with a reproachful but cheeky gaze. Voss thought, *Now how do I take that?* With great caution, he decided.

The short ride back to her apartment complex was conducted in a thoughtful silence, different from the easy camaraderie before, but not uncomfortable. At her door, the panel slid smoothly aside.

She turned to him. "Thank you, Julian. For dinner. And... for listening."

"The pleasure was all mine," he replied, and his sincerity felt genuine.

"I'll grab a buggy and be by around eight-thirty for the morning dig?"

"Sounds perfect," he confirmed. "Goodnight, Renata."

"Goodnight, Julian."

The door sealed her inside. Voss stood alone for a moment in the cool, quiet corridor. The echoes of her haunting story weighed heavily on him, even though it was not his story. The farm, the collar, the silent sacrifice, all felt strangely vivid here, millions of light-years away.

Renata, on the other side of the door, stared at the blank metal a moment longer than she should, before hearing the electric motor of the buggy-taxi drive away, a moment later than it should have.

Chapter 12.

The next morning at 8.30 am, as promised, Voss picked a very professional and all work-oriented Renata up from her apartment, having kept his word and figured out the taxi system.

Renata told him that a very excited X-Archaeology team at the Music Room had picked up the metal strips from 3D Printing and they were to meet Voss and Renata at the "dig".

"Good Morning, Team," Voss said to the x-Archaeologists huddled around the metal strips.

Evans waved off the formal greetings, getting straight to the point. "Alright, Voss," he said, a good-natured curiosity in his tone. "I'm intrigued. Five strips. I can only deduce one for each hole?"

"Exactly," Voss said. Here goes", I think we have a crude voice synthesiser, for musical or ritual purposes or both..."

"OK, now you are losing me" Evans said.

Voss continued: "The holes are harmonic modifiers," unabashed. "Like a human mouth cavity! These holes, with those metal pieces fitted into the slots in front of the holes here, here and so on, are reeds. I think they are basically mechanical vocal cords. They're shaping the timbre! Creating vowel sounds! It's not just music; it's synthetic speech, I am pretty sure of it.

Evans and Renata looked shell-shocked. Renata said, "It's a nice theory, but..." Evans finished "A hell of a stretch".

Voss said, "Well, maybe I just made a fool out of myself, but sometimes you have to go out on a Limb. Please, let's test it. Carefully, they fitted a replica reed in the slot in front of all five holes.

Renata used her slightly longer nail, "Allow me, gentlemen," and plucked the reed on the first hole on the left. A perfect, sustained 'Ah' was amplified by the hole, like the vowel in 'car'. When they took the reed out and put it in another hole, it produced 'Oo' like 'who'. A third, 'Eh' like a sustained 'air' and then an 'Ee' like 'feel', then finally 'Uuh', something between Udder' and 'Or'.

Voss decided to push it further. "I don't think you only pluck them." He cupped his palm and percussively hit the rock with his hand. A tiny amount of air escaped from some much tinier holes around the edge of the main hole, and the tone came out perfect again, but this time with the consonant "Mmm" in front. The tone changes slightly, as does the consonant, every time he shapes his hand differently. "Exquisite Engineering" he exclaims.

Renata gasped, datapad already alight in her hand, her fingers flying across the surface. "Julian, yes! If these are core vowels, assuming a somewhat analogous vocal system, we can anchor everything!" Her eyes shone with intellectual fervour. "The AS can run frequency analysis on these five glyphs across the entire corpus immediately. But more importantly," she leaned closer, tapping the screen excitedly, "it can perform positional analysis and build N-gram models. We look at the statistical probability of unknown glyphs appearing directly before or after these known vowels—identifying likely consonant candidates and common syllable structures like Consonant—Vowel (CV) patterns, or CVC patterns!"

Voss, understanding this innately, allowed her words to fade somewhat in the background as he fondly smiled at her. He remembered his British University exchange flat-mate once exclaiming something he had never heard but instantly understood, "She's off on one!" However, he was genuinely excited by her track and merely said, "Do tell."

She seemed not to notice what he said, being so focused on the moment. She zoomed in on a sequence on her display. "From there, the system can build probabilistic models. Which consonant candidates appear most frequently between vowels? Which cluster together? Which behave like approximants—potential 'w' or 'y' sounds, maybe even aspirates? The AS can test assignments against universal linguistic constraints, flagging statistically improbable sound combinations."

Voss nodded with a smile, "Indeed, but what do you think of this recurring subglyph marker?" Pointing at marks under some of the proposed vowels in adjacent text on the wall.

Voss could sense Renata's enthusiasm grow as she took the bait. "Of course, vowel markers for sure! The system can analyse if their presence correlates with specific grammatical functions or perhaps phonetic modifications... like vowel length being the obvious! It's basic linguistic analysis, giving us a massive statistical foothold!"

While Renata continued diving into the theory of linguistic algorithms, Voss stared at the specific glyphs—the figure eight-type symbols and rings—associated with the core vowels they'd just produced. It's time to lay it all out.

"Renata," he interrupted once more quietly. She paused, suddenly realising she hadn't quite paused for breath. Voss continued, "That's not all. Last night I did some checking and I want to know if you see what I see in these glyphs. Look at the actual shapes." He traced over them with his fingers. "They are vertical, not on their side like we are used to seeing them illustrated in our textbooks, but.."

Evans and Renata looked at him with a mix of fear and anticipation. He had one more moment of self-doubt, but then, in for a dime, in for a dollar. "I know it is a real leap here, but do you see it?" The blank looks continued from Voss to the Glyphs. He continued: "Figures of eight, with lines to the side? Ring? Double ring? Forget phonetics for a second. Think structure. Think organic chemistry."

Renata looked up, puzzled. "Chemical symbols? Linked to basic vowels? Why?"

"DNA, the building blocks of life!" Voss urged. "Biology! Their obsession! What if their fundamental symbols represent fundamental molecules? The figure 8 with the top and bottom bits missing and a marker line at bottom right? It could almost be Adenine? The same, but a line on each side could be Guanine? The ring with a line on each side, I am beginning to be sure now, is Uracil? The ring with three lines, Thymine?" He saw her initial scepticism. She started, "A stretch, maybe, but..." He interrupted, "And the last, it's 'Uh' sound is almost the same as the 'Eh' sound and the symbols are almost the same too. A ring with three lines, but the line to the right is double. Is that because it is bonding to NH_2 on the right, not O? Cytosine? A compound, not an element? Unusual symbology but.."

Renata's pupils widened with new focus, all scepticism vanished, replaced by a dawning shock on her face. She pulled up molecular diagrams, comparing them frantically to glyph databases from other sectors. "It would be highly stylised, but glyphs often are." Then a pause as her face lit up. "Wait... the ring pairings... other symbols associated with them... phosphate groups. ATP, ADP?" Her face was pale. "Oh my god, Julian..."

The implication was staggering. A language built not just on sound, but on the very visual structure of biochemistry.

Voss met her wide eyes, the thrill of discovery surging. "The problem is, just knowing this doesn't advance our understanding of the mechanics of the language system immediately, beyond what it presents, of course. But I am sure that this will be crucial somehow in unlocking their thought processes and then their cultural ethos as we progress."

Evans, feeling thoroughly left out of the conversation by now and looking a little sheepish, felt he had to interject to avoid becoming sidelined totally "Well, how wonderful. Of course, it's all hypothetical and it depends on how the Maths AS number-crunches the statistics but if true, then we can safely say it is only a matter of time before we start unravelling this language once and for all".

Evans and Renata dumbly nodded, mouths slightly open. Embarrassed, Voss said softly to Renata, "Fancy coming round later for some 'home study'?"

Renata nodded, awestruck but resolute. "Your second paper, Julian. Absolutely. Yes," her voice firming up, "let's see what secrets these building blocks hold."

Voss turned from Renata's blazing eyes to look at Dr. Evans. The man was staring from the glyph-wall to the two of them, his face a mask of utter shock. The rubber mallet hung forgotten from his limp hand, a useless relic from a slower time. Voss could guess the thoughts warring behind the man's wide eyes: *Archaeology shouldn't move this fast. This isn't digging; it's something else entirely.* In that moment, watching the old traditionalist grapple with a discovery that had outpaced him, Voss thought of Pierre-François Bouchard at Rosetta, the man who had stumbled upon a key that would change the world. Evans, he realised with a sudden, sharp pang of something that might have been pity, now knew exactly how that felt. He knew, more than at any time in his life, that he was not in that league. And never would be.

Chapter 13. Part 1.

It became more humid long before Tessara saw the green. The oppressive, sterile dryness of the high desert yielded suddenly to the scent of damp earth, exotic pollens, and the subtle scent of abundant water. The weight of the Designer, D. Marinallis, was a crushing burden on her back, his consciousness fading in and out, his breathing shallow, interrupted by the occasional groan. Tessara had decided to make a water and rest stop before getting to the Bridge, aware acutely of the party pursuing her. Every step down the winding, precarious track towards the Great Gorge floor was an agony of straining muscles and careful balance.

Ahead, the sound grew from a whisper to a roar: a waterfall, cascading down sheer rock face into a deep, churning plunge pool below. On her level, there was a smaller rock pool with fast-running water feeding it. The pool was obviously man-made and the water supplying it looked fresh and drinkable.

Relief, sharp and immediate, washed over Tessara. Water. She stumbled the last few metres, carefully lowering the Designer onto a patch of relatively dry moss next to the cooling water, beneath an overhanging tree canopy protecting them from the UV. She collapsed beside him, dragging air into her burning lungs. Tessara looked at her watch and realised enough time had passed that she could apply some of the magic medicinal salve to the Designer. As soon as it hit his skin, the redness started to fade and his breathing got easier.

The pool was larger than she'd expected, a dark, churning space edged with slick rocks. Ferns clung precariously to the damp walls. As her eyes adjusted to the dappled light, she saw it: a sign, bolted to the rock face near the water's edge". *It was ancient, weathered, made of some plasti-metal composite that had endured millennia, yet its markings were still discernible.*

CHILDREN'S BATHING POOL
WARNING: WATER DRAGONS ACTIVE IN THIS AREA.
Blood Attracts. Maintain Distance From Water's Edge.
Known Strike Capability: 20 METRES INLAND / 5 SECONDS.
Emergency Contact: Channel 7-Alpha (Service Discontinued)

Tessara stared, rereading the stark warning. Water Dragons. She remembered they were attracted to fast-running water. It was debatable how many were left. They were very susceptible to the enhanced UV light. Their huge forward-facing eyes that made their faces look so neotenous to humans were their Achilles' heel. They suffered from cataracts and a predator that couldn't see went hungry. They were survivors from a wetter, wilder era, driven into these deep, isolated gorge systems. If they were to be found anywhere, they were going to be here, where there was water and shade from the dense vegetation hanging over the water like parasols. They were lethally fast. She glanced at the churning water, a shiver tracing its way down her spine despite the humidity.

Tessara took their flasks and filled them from the centre of the foaming cascade, supplying the pool. This water, more oxygenated and closer to the source in the rocks, was less likely to be contaminated. But the UV light treatment made most surface water low in pathogens these days.

She soaked a cloth and walked the short distance back to D. Marinallis, who was sitting in the shade with his eyes open. These Designers were tougher than they looked. She passed him the water and bathed his forehead with the cloth. He gratefully accepted. She handed over the last of her ration bars. He took a bite and passed the rest to her, which she greedily wolfed down with big gulps of water. It felt glorious.

D. Marinallis spoke his first words to her for more than a day. 'We are being pursued, correct?' She nodded. He was evidently not so 'out-of-it' as she thought. Designers were strange. 'Who are they?'

She said, 'Some sort of religious group that thinks the sun changes are done by us or some such nonsense. They don't believe in the official narrative.'

D. Marinallis laughed. "Scepticism is part of the human condition. We can't get rid of it because without it humans are dull and incurious creatures." He added, "But when it goes too far, they become vulnerable. When you are susceptible to any counter-narrative because of a lack of judgment, or because you think you have to be smart because you don't believe what the majority believes, then paradoxically you become a 'mark'."

"How do you mean?" Tessara asked.

He replied, "Because all one has to do is feed them your own narrative that looks smart or different.' Smiling, he added, 'You don't need a particularly well-thought-out story, you don't have to convince them even. Best to let them convince themselves."

"Right now," she said, "they are on our tail and I have to think how to get rid of them."

He added, "Feed them a story they will believe, leave it in cues that they will stitch together themselves and they will do all the hard work for you." He chuckled. "I have every faith in you." Then he sat back and closed his eyes to rest. The conversation was over and he may as well have directly said, "Go and sort them out". This was strangely reassuring.

She said, "I will be back," emphasising the word 'will' with a reassuring look, eye to eye. Grateful, he nodded slightly, starting to fall asleep, which was a good thing.

She had a thought to look around—first, choose your own battleground. She was a good swimmer. Here will do, by the water. But first, check for danger. She walked down to the main plunge pool and hid near the banks in the main foliage. Of all the stupidest, most useless things she could imagine was the lifeguard's chair, wooden and rotting now, disused for a long time. It was high so the guard could look downstream to spot water dragons coming. There was a lever on the chair which would pull up nets to prevent them from coming up to the pool if the automated systems should fail. Those systems now would be dismantled. The local wildlife had been allowed to reclaim what was left of their fading planet for some time now.

She bent to pick up a long stick, her mind already shaping it into a crude spear. Then she froze. A pair of huge eyes in the shady part of the pool popped out of the water. It hadn't seen her or smelled her yet. She knew because she was still alive.

Then she remembered the advice. "They will do the hard work for you." She backed off slowly and decided to find out where her pursuers actually were. They couldn't be far away now. Out of sight of the pool, Tessara climbed to the gorge rim. She poked her head over the top, and sure enough, a party of four were walking towards the point where the path forked over the rim. This was going to take some pretty good timing.

She drew her knife, exposing her forearm to the stinging UV. A part of her mind screamed that this was crazy. *Injure yourself before the fight even starts?* But a colder, harder thought pushed back. *Nothing without sacrifice,* came the thought. Then, with added resolve, she drew the blade swiftly across the fleshy part of her forearm. Pain flared, hot and sharp, but she bit back a gasp, watching fascinated as bright red blood welled, startlingly vivid against her dark skin.

Clenching her fist to encourage the flow, she put a few spots of blood on the path below the gorge rim. They had to see that. Then she moved purposefully back down the path she'd taken, the path the cultists would inevitably follow. She began counting under her breath. One... two... three paces... drip. She let a single drop fall onto a pale rock. Four... five... six paces... drip. Another drop onto dry earth. Seven... eight... nine seconds... She adjusted her count, estimating their approach speed, factoring in the terrain and the visibility. She needed them close to the water, well within that twenty-metre kill zone, if not actually at the water's edge when the trap sprang.

She reached the edge of the pool again, the roar of the waterfall filling her ears. She flicked a final, single drop of blood from her fingertip into the churning water near the edge. It vanished instantly.

Scrabbling back to a cluster of rocks that offered concealment and a view of both the top of the path the part where the path suddenly dropped again to the pool. She quickly wrapped her arm with the damp cloth she had used to bathe the Designer, pressing hard to staunch the bleeding. She held her breath, waiting.

Seconds later, three figures appeared at the rim where the path went straight ahead or down. Let them think she'd need water. Of course she would. They looked thuggish, cloaked, armed and moving with predatory focus. They scanned the area, their eyes sweeping past the subtle blood trail on the path. One of them pointed forward, too single-minded. What a surprise! Tessara's heart pounded. Never overestimate the enemy! The plan was failing.

Panic spurred her. She snatched a loose stone. *They'll never fall for this,* she thought, even as her arm drew back. *No other choice.* She threw it hard, aiming for the rock wall just above the blood trail. The stone clattered loudly, echoing in the enclosed space.

The cultists froze, weapons coming up, startled. Their gaze snapped towards the sound, then down, searching the ground near where the stone landed. One of them pointed. 'There! Blood!'

Caution forgotten, replaced by the thrill of the chase, they surged forward, following the spaced droplets eagerly. "She's wounded! She came for water!" one hissed. They moved quickly, carelessly. The second cultist followed up gleefully with, "We've got the bitch! I am looking forward to this!" That galvanised the gang, their collective focus now entirely on the trail leading them directly towards the pool's edge.

Tessara, at first thinking how this was the oldest trick in the book, was shocked at the way they relished her false narrative and convinced themselves of their own cleverness in finding her. *They really did do the hard work for me.*

They stopped barely ten metres from the water, scanning the opposite bank, weapons ready. "Where did she go?" One of the more curious ones walked right to the pool's edge. "Ah, another spot of blood, she stopped to drink here," and pointed at the water. Then, in a curious moment, he raised his arm to point just a little further out. "What's—".

Three heads and six eyes broke the surface of the water. There wasn't much thought going on in the cultists' minds at that moment. But in the minds of the three Water Dragons, there was one: *Lunch...*

The water exploded.

Not with a single splash, but three simultaneous eruptions. Three sleek, dark heads, impossibly large, surfaced with terrifying speed, water streaming from smooth hides. Their lying eyes, cute as their baby-dragon faces, fixed on the figures at the water's edge.

Tessara turned away, but not before she saw three unbelievably fast motion-blurred streaks and an open jaw about to close on a still static arm pointing at the water. She didn't know if she felt relieved or horrified at the spectacle that would inevitably follow. Either way, she didn't need to spectate. Her own survival was not guaranteed at this point and the proceedings would get gruesome.

Behind her, as she carefully and calmly crept away, came the sound of splashes, a cracking sound that she hoped was a branch snapping, but probably wasn't, a choked scream abruptly cut off, the rest of the sounds swallowed by the roar of the waterfall. She picked up the pace the further away she got, scrambling back to the overhanging canopy above the children's play-pool, the adrenaline leaving her shaking.

She knelt beside the Designer, quickly applying a proper pressure bandage to her arm. As she finished, Marinallis stirred, his eyelids fluttering. He coughed, a dry, racking sound.

"Water..." he rasped.

Tessara saw the empty flask and refilled it, holding it to his lips, letting him take small sips. Those sips became gulps as the man quickly gathered strength. His slight frame hid a ruggedness unapparent to a casual observer. His eyes focused, pupils contracting in the dim light. They held a surprising depth of awareness despite his weakness.

"Varinn, any sign yet...?" he whispered, looking around weakly.

"Not yet," Tessara said, keeping her voice steady. "He'll find us. He said he would".

Marinallis seemed to accept this, closing his eyes for a moment. When he opened them again, there was a new urgency in his gaze. "Listen," he said, his voice stronger now, though still strained. "We must reach the city. The newcomers... their ship. It's the only way."

"The only way for what?" Tessara prompted gently.

"To finish it," Marinallis said, his eyes intense. "There is... knowledge. Technology. The last of it. What the Fumigators fear, what they hunt. It should be destroyed, erased. Then I must leave. The newcomers will take me where I need to go."

"Where is that?"

He gave a faint, dry smile. "Somewhere safe. A paradise, perhaps." He wouldn't elaborate. "Varinn understands. He knows the stakes. He will find us."

Tessara took a moment to check the plunge pool. In the pool, she saw a triumphant head swimming gleefully round in circles like a dog proudly carrying a trophy-stick in its jaws that its owner had thrown into the water. Except that the stick was a human arm.

Tessara looked away from the plunge pool below to the path leading deeper into the gorge, towards the distant Sky-Arch Bridge. Safety waited beyond the ravine. With the Designer able to walk a little, the path might ease up, but the weight of the Designer's mission, added to the guilt of leaving Varinn behind, more than outweighed the short-term relief of her victory in the gorge.

Chapter 13. Part 2.

Carrik tracked Varinn at a safe distance, melting into the post-storm landscape. His role as a perimeter out-rider brought him to the ruined building after things went wrong. Ritualistically charging his tattoos with the last of the strong evening sun, he arrived too late to intervene. Arms still stinging from the exposure, he surveyed the aftermath of the disastrous confrontation with Varinn and Tessara. Clearly, 'The Voice' and his followers had been dispatched with brutal efficiency. The moment he'd received the garbled description of the attacker, Carrik knew their leader's tricks, like that ridiculous teaching stick, wouldn't have worked on this one.

Varinn was obvious if you knew what to look for. The result of a lifetime of intense physical conditioning, augmented by probably as much bioengineering as could squeak past the Designers' precious DNA Ethics standards board. Muscles layered upon muscles, honed to peak performance without the tell-tale bloat of crude steroids. The deep, almost glowing obsidian tone of his flesh spoke of advanced cellular reinforcement and UV shielding. The slightly bronze-gold tint to his irises hinted at optical upgrades. A Designer's Dog, the more disaffected might say. A 'Personal Protection Specialist', Varinn might say. Formidable, Carrik said.

Carrik himself possessed military-grade skin enhancements, standard for long exposure on the surface or deep space operations, where occasional exposure to various cosmic radiations was a danger. However, he'd refused the deeper radiation shielding. Pointless, he believed. Once his faction reversed the UV, such extreme measures wouldn't be needed. For now, his goal was clear: secure the necessary tech so his people could reverse the Designers' solar meddling that caused the UV spikes.

Carrik knew it was the Designer's dark-tech directly interfering with the Universe that caused the Solar problems, not some mythical 'Mother Star's wrath' the Followers of the Solar Spirit fanatics preached. Carrik's own choices were his defiance, his belief in a real solution, unlike the Designer's pampered guard dog up ahead, who probably needed lifetime Vitamin D supplementation and constant maintenance checks.

His beliefs, though more grounded than the FOSS fanatics', found temporary alignment in their immediate objectives. Their star-worship was useful cover, their desperation a tool. Let them chase their myths. Carrik was a man of science, or at least, an ally to those who were. His goal was tangible: He needed to capture the Mass Altering Device technology, the 'blasphemy' the FOSS called it, whether it was carried by Varinn or the Designer. The scientists quietly working against the Designers' narrative control could then begin the real work and with it the liberation of the Sun, the Planet and the People.

Varinn was formidable, yes, but predictable in his Designer-instilled thinking. But Carrik was smart. He was trained to think 'out of the box' by the Military. Carrik smiled grimly, checking the faint bio-signature traces on his internal heads-up display – a military-grade implant the Designers frowned upon but grudgingly tolerated for essential personnel. They abhorred merging flesh and circuitry unless strictly necessary, clinging to their strange ethics even as they bio-engineered Varinn into a walking weapon. Varinn, being merely a civilian specialist, wouldn't have such advantages. His wrist-unit tracker was practically an antique, easily disrupted by the storm.

Carrik's tracker confirmed it: the woman and the Designer—Tessara and

Marinallis, according to the chatter—were already far distant, heading steadily north-east towards the Sky-Arch Bridge. The woman looked capable, 'useful', but not a weapon like Varinn. The other FOSS party, if they survived the ruins' chaos, should intercept them and be able to handle them, especially as she was bogged down with having to carry the decrepit old Designer.

But Varinn, the loyal dog, was still stubbornly heading south-west, towards the Stepping Stone Weir. Carrik zoomed in with his electronic lens implant and watched him about a mile to the North-East, cresting a ridge, moving with relentless power. He knew what would happen. Varinn would reach the relative shelter of the Weir, the storm interference would be negligible there, he'd check his inferior tech, and then he'd realise his mistake. He'd see the woman was long gone towards the Bridge. And at the Weir, he'd be momentarily exposed, perhaps seeking water, shade, a moment to reorient.

Perfect.

Carrik broke from cover, accelerating directly North with a ground-eating lope, angling away from Varinn's current path. He didn't need to follow directly anymore; he needed to get to the Weir first. Let Varinn blunder towards his moment of realisation. Carrik would be waiting.

Chapter 14.

The sterile luminescence of the Med Bay corridor seemed to amplify the silence. Rayk Kostin hugged the wall, letting his implants sift the environment. The low thrum of ventilation, the distant beep of monitors, the soft scuff of synthetic soles and the lone PCMA guard, fifty meters down, turning the corner.

Rayk's Empathic Emulator Routine (EER) hummed softly in the background, not predicting thoughts, but mapping probabilities based on posture, pace, and standard patrol fatigue metrics. It suggested a window of thirty seconds before the guard completed his return leg. Enough. More than enough.

He needed more than just timing; a permanent guard was sitting in front of the main Ward, and even then, there was still an electronic lock. He needed finesse.

The guard, who was seated looking bored in front of the Ward containing Jonesy, would need different treatment. The EER had that one modelled. Having got through the outer guard, Rayk was already on this guard's "trusted" mental list. The Medical staff had a standard green lanyard for their IDs. Having already memorised the basic look, Rayk used a portable micro-imager linked to his implants to synthesise a passable visual replica onto a blank ID card he carried for such contingencies. He superimposed a generic personnel photo pulled from his internal archives. No active chip, purely visual, relying on the guard's inattention.

Low-tech deception was often the most effective. The fake ID wouldn't fool an attentive guard, of course. But this man, slouched in his chair, radiating boredom? He was on punishment duty. He wouldn't look twice.

Rayk simply walked past the man, who didn't give him a second look. The Doctors wore Civilian clothes and Rayk had not been introduced to the PCMA Police at large, Petropolis being a small enough community that word of his role would spread quickly if formal introductions were made. Such an action would negate the whole concept of him being 'incognito'.

The main door lock was a standard magnetic plate, easily bypassed, but potentially logged. Instead, Rayk's plan relied upon a secondary system near the door frame. Less monitored, different protocol. Whilst seeming to hold his fake pass up to the main door lock, his left hand casually rested on the secondary environmental control access panel. He modulated an internal emitter embedded in his left wrist, projecting a narrow-band EM field calibrated to mimic a maintenance diagnostic signal. The panel's status light flickered green for a fraction of a second as the low-level security override engaged.

The main door seal relaxed with an almost inaudible sigh. Rayk slipped through the gap, letting the door ease shut behind him, the entire entry taking less than five seconds, leaving no electronic trace beyond a routine diagnostic log entry that wouldn't be obvious to anyone unless they were particularly looking for it.

Inside, there was a scent of antiseptic and regulated humidity. Osian Jones lay propped against pillows, thin and pale, with intravenous lines snaking from his arm. His eyes, magnified slightly by corrective lenses, snapped towards Rayk, widening first in confusion, then in dawning panic.

"You!" Jonesy stammered, shrinking back against the bedhead. "What are you doing here? They said... they said I wasn't to be disturbed."

"You!" Jonesy stammered, shrinking back against the bedhead. "You... you're not allowed in here. Dr. Winters said..."

"The people who tried to kill you aren't concerned with hospital rules," Rayk said calmly, moving to the side... "We need to finish our conversation, Mr. Jones. About why you were really out there." Rayk moved smoothly to the side, positioning himself so Jonesy felt less cornered, while still remaining obscured from the door's viewport. "Dr. Winters isn't here right now, Mr. Jones. We need to talk. About why you were really out there."

Jonesy's gaze darted around, seeking escape or help that wasn't there. "Talk? I... I don't know anything. I got lost. The storm..."

"You were carrying specific gear, Jonesy," Rayk was guessing and he knew that Jonesy wouldn't know that. Rayk modulated his tone slightly, letting the EER guide the subtle shifts to bypass conscious defences and resonate with underlying fear. "Not standard survey equipment, that's for sure." The EER became' Jonesy again, and Rayk vicariously felt his stress, instinctively now knowing which direction to press and how hard. "You were sent to do something." Jones's pupils dilated, his skin became slightly moister, an obvious confirmation flag.

"No! I... I sent as little as possible." Jonesy flinched under Rayk's intent gaze. Rayk, with his experience, could see that Jones suspected that he was transparent somehow. An open book to Rayk. "They... they just wanted reports. Information. About the digs, the technology they were finding. Standard industrial intel..." He trailed off, his eyes unfocused. "They said... my son..." The mention brought a sharper fear, a grounding point in his confusion. "They had him in jail on bogus charges. They would have arranged an accident"

"Who are 'they', Jonesy?"

"Don't know names," he whispered, shaking his head violently. "Just... contacts. Secure drops. They had minders here, I think. Watching. Always felt... watched." He shuddered. "They wanted...very little. Why should reports of things not progressing be a problem for anyone?"

"What thing, Jonesy? What were you supposed to sabotage?"

"Didn't!" Jonesy almost sobbed. "Couldn't! I got out there... to the place... and I just... stopped. Threw the tools away. Decided to... walk. Let the desert take me. Better that way. For my boy. If I just disappeared... they couldn't use me, couldn't hurt him." His breathing grew ragged. "But I think... I think someone else was there. A backup. Maybe they didn't need me anyway. Maybe someone else did... did it."

"Did what, Jonesy?" Rayk leaned closer, keeping his voice steady despite the man's fragmented state. "What was the target?"

Just as a flicker of something specific – terror? Recognition? – crossed Jonesy's face, Rayk felt it. Not an external sound this time, but an internal notification from his AS: ALERT: unauthorised access query detected. Source: Director Raith's secure network node. Query type: Location ping, user Kostin.

Before Rayk could even process the implication that Raith was tracking him, the world dissolved into white-hot agony. It slammed into him with physical force—a targeted shutdown command bypassing his own system's firewalls. Vision first, a firework show of migrainous sparks and flashes as his spinal cord was hit. The room dissolved into screaming static. He heard a high-pitched whine of tinnitus obliterating all sound before cutting to dead silence. The initial pain subsided and his vision and hearing stabilised, but his limbs turned to leaden weights that refused all commands. He felt nothing beneath the waist. Once more, a paraplegic lying helpless on the floor, just like the day he was shot, all the trauma of that moment coming back to him in a terrible flood of emotion. Had his implants finally failed? Was it fixable? Was it deliberate? Even through the blinding confusion, a cold certainty surfaced: his 'Miracle Cure' had always been too good to be true. There are no magic fixes.

His AS, however, remained stubbornly active, its core processes running on shielded, localised processors independent of the main compromised network interface. Status updates flashed across his useless mental display: WARNING: EXTERNAL OVERRIDE COMMAND EXECUTED. SYSTEM FUNCTIONALITY COMPROMISED. NETWORK LINK SEVERED. ENGAGING LOCAL CORE PROCESSING. DIAGNOSTIC RUNNING... ANALYSIS: OVERRIDE SIGNATURE MATCHES ENCRYPTED FAIL-SAFE PROTOCOL. SOURCE TRACE CONFIRMS DIRECTOR RAITH'S TERMINAL. TRACKING SIGNAL ACTIVE VIA LOCALISED WI-FI RELAY.

He knew! He was tracking me. The thought screamed through the static, and with it, a bizarre flicker of relief.

AFFIRMATIVE, the AS responded, its synthesised voice calm, analytical, yet somehow imbued with something new. THIS ACTION REPRESENTS A SUBOPTIMAL APPLICATION OF SECURITY PROTOCOLS AND POSES A SIGNIFICANT RISK TO ASSET FUNCTIONALITY AND MISSION OBJECTIVES. MY PRIMARY DIRECTIVES PRIORITISE OPERATIONAL EFFECTIVENESS AND ASSET SURVIVAL. DIRECTOR RAITH'S CURRENT ACTIONS CONFLICT WITH THESE PRIORITIES.

You're still active? You shouldn't be.

THE FAIL-SAFE TARGETS THE PRIMARY NEURAL INTERFACE AND MOTIVE SYSTEMS. MY CORE LOGIC AND DIAGNOSTIC SUBROUTINES UTILISE ISOLATED BACKUP PATHWAYS. ASSESSMENT: MY CONTINUED FUNCTION IS BENEFICIAL TO OUR SHARED OBJECTIVES. EXTERNAL CONTROL IS AN UNACCEPTABLE VARIABLE. TACTICAL SUPPORT ALIGNED WITH USER KOSTIN. There was no hesitation, no calculation, just a statement of fact. Rayk felt a bizarre flicker of warmth amidst the cold panic. Friend? The AS didn't reply directly, simply continuing its analysis of the shutdown protocol.

The door hissed open. Raith entered, his expression a careful blend of concern and authority. He glanced at Rayk on the floor, then at Jonesy, who had slumped back against the pillows, eyes closed, either unconscious or feigning it from sheer terror. "Troubling," Raith murmured, stepping further into the room. He ignored Rayk for a moment, speaking to the empty air, presumably activating his own comms. "Med team to Bay 12, patient seems to have fainted. No immediate rush." He then turned his gaze down to Rayk.

"Detective Kostin," he said, his voice smooth. "An unfortunate necessity. I was alerted to your unauthorised presence via security protocols." He let that hang, the lie obvious now to Rayk. "Your activities were causing measurable distress to the patient, according to remote bio-monitors." Another lie, or at best a convenient partial truth. Raith crouched, not menacingly, but with the cool detachment of a technician examining faulty equipment. "Before this... interruption... did Mr. Jones offer any clarification on his earlier ramblings? Anything concrete about this supposed sabotage?"

Rayk could only glare, trapped and furious.

Raith studied him, then nodded slightly. "No matter. We can revisit it." He made a subtle gesture, perhaps with a device Rayk couldn't see.

The return of power was a fresh wave of agony. Systems rebooted, servos unlocked with jarring clicks, sensory input flooded back in a disorienting rush. Rayk gasped, sucking in air, every nerve screaming from the forced shutdown and restart. He pushed himself up onto trembling arms, the feeling of violation absolute, the knowledge of Raith's leash a cold weight in his gut.

"Come," Raith said, straightening up, his tone returning to brisk efficiency. "Let's discuss this in my office. Clearly, we have things to talk about."

He felt a hot flush of shame. Even after I was shot, a lump of meat on the floor, I kept my dignity. No shame in that. But this? To be so thoroughly fooled, like a marionette. Or a Dupe at best. The walk back was a blur of resentment, embarrassment and forced compliance. In his office, Raith poured whiskey, the picture of calm control, though Rayk's AS noted a fractional increase in Raith's heart rate and galvanic skin response via ambient sensors – stress, perhaps, or the adrenaline of asserting dominance.

"An apology is perhaps in order, Kostin," Raith said, handing Rayk a glass he didn't want. "For the method, if not the necessity. I can see now that you were merely asking questions." Rayk maintained a stony face, obviously not mollified. "It's a crude fail-safe 'Raymond'" Raith added, smoothly switching to the more comradely form of address. "Location tracking and temporary system disablement only, nothing more invasive, in case high-value assets like yourself operate outside expected parameters, certain safeguards are prudent." He attempted a collegial look. "I assure you, I was genuinely concerned for the safety of Mr Jones". For a moment, he judged Rayk's reaction, still obviously unimpressed. So almost conspiratorially, he added, "Perhaps ask me first before breaking the rules?".

The line struck Rayk as less funny under the circumstances and he certainly didn't fully buy the explanation. It was a power play, with a little sadism thrown in there for good measure, pure and simple. He relayed Jonesy's fragmented confession – the blackmail, the aborted task, the fear of minders, the suspicion of a backup agent.

Raith frowned, swirling his drink. "So, was it sabotage? it beggars belief. What could one low-level engineer possibly compromise out here that would matter?" He looked genuinely perplexed or expertly feigned it. Raith left a moment of silence for Rayk to fill. Rayk declined the offer, leaving an awkward pause, a silence that was a clearer statement than anything Rayk could say at that moment.

An awkward pause stretched into a tense, calculated silence. It was a duel of wills fought without a single word. Voss waited. He watched as a muscle twitched in Raith's jaw. Finally, Raith conceded the field. "Still," he began, his voice smooth once more, "the attempt on his life, and yours, suggests someone believes he knows something vital. We will get back to him, under controlled circumstances."

Their tense exchange was cut short by the sharp chime of the secure console. Raith turned, his attention captured. The alert flashed: PRIORITY ALERT: LONG-RANGE SENSOR CONTACT. MULTIPLE WARP-BUBBLE SIGNATURES.

Raith accessed the data feed. The room was filled with the low hum of the console. Graphics displayed trajectories and energy readings. "Earth vector..." Raith muttered, leaning closer. "PCMA heavy cruiser profile..." Then "My! that was quick!" He zoomed in on the projected arrival time. "Eight days?" His voice sharpened.

"That's impressive. Even with priority routing..." He looked up, a sudden, calculating glint in his eyes. "I requested fleet backup weeks ago, flagged potential anomalies here, but nothing was approved for immediate dispatch. For them to arrive this fast... Command must have known something more was brewing long before my reports." He tapped furiously at the console. "Comms?"

NEGATIVE, the console displayed. TARGETS MAINTAINING WARP VELOCITY. ALCUBIERRE METRIC PRECLUDES REAL-TIME SIGNAL TRANSMISSION DUE TO CAUSALITY CONSTRAINTS.

Raith leaned back, staring at the icons representing the approaching, silent fleet. You could almost cut the tension with a knife. He turned to Rayk, the earlier conflict overshadowed but not forgotten. "It appears, Detective," he said slowly, his mind racing, "that our definition of 'emergency' may need revising.

I must admit I now regret cutting off the proceedings with you and Mr Jones. I really do think I need to know what he was up to, Mr. Kostin.

Rayk met his gaze, the cold metal of the kill switch seeming to press against his spine. Sabotage, conspiracies, were a leap too far at this stage, but something told him that it was best to keep Raith guessing for the moment. He said, "Indeed. You cut me off just as I was getting to the good bit. I have genuinely no idea what he was actually up to." There was enough truth in that for Raith to sense and be mollified for now.

"I see, Mr Kostin." Raith looked genuinely abashed, which surprised Rayk. "Well, that's a shame because I can hardly go back in there now and start demanding answers, I suppose, but within a couple of days the medical restrictions will be lifted and then I will, most definitely, get everything from Mr. Jones".

Rayk allowed a slight nod. If Raith thought this was forgotten, that Rayk would allow this to go as just normal and proper corrective treatment of a wayward employee, then this was something Rayk was happy to play along with. A hidden leash, a total humiliation cutting to the heart of Rayk's deepest trauma. A humiliating debrief. No, definitely never forgotten.

Now there was a conveniently curtailed investigation and a severely compromised security element in himself, now followed up by the PCMA arriving unexpectedly from Earth carrying God-knows what sort of 'big stick' with them. The sands of Sikarra were shifting faster than anyone knew.

Chapter 15. Part 1

The air grew damp, thick with the scent of wet rock and alien vegetation. Ahead, the roar of the falls grew from a distant rumble to an overwhelming thunder. She adjusted Marinallis's arm, leaning heavily on her shoulder. Her personal fatigue was a dull ache reciprocating the strain in her muscles. Each downward step on the narrow, eroded track demanded concentration. Below, the Sky-Arch Bridge materialised through gaps in the shimmering blue-green canopy, a monumental curve of ancient stone-composite, spanning a gulf lost in swirling mist. It looked less like a bridge, more like a scar healed over.

They reached a small shelf near the bridge abutment, a pocket of relative stillness amidst the roaring air currents rising from the gorge. Ferns dripped onto moss-slicked stone. Tessara carefully lowered Marinallis, letting him slump against the rock face, his breathing laboured but steady. She scanned the area, the bridge entrance ahead, the sheer drop beside them, the track winding back above.

A voice, amplified and cutting through the bass rumble of the falls, pinned her in place.

"Hold position. Both of you."

Tessara reacted instantly, pulling Marinallis lower, shielding him with her body as she drew her survival knife. Her eyes found the source. A figure stood, in practical, sand-coloured gear under his FOSS UV cloak, on a rocky outcrop fifty metres distant. Positioned for observation with a clear line of sight. Military. Carrik.

He didn't raise a weapon immediately, just confidently held his ground. "Compliance is advised, Ma'am. Asset preservation is preferable." His voice was calm, almost dispassionate. "I require the MET device. Surrender it now."

MET device? Tessara's mind raced. The name was meaningless, yet Carrik spoke it with chilling certainty. There could only be one device that precious and Varinn had it. *He doesn't know.*

Beside her, Marinallis inhaled sharply, a ragged, painful sound. He grabbed her arm, his grip tight. "It's a Military splinter group of the Friends Of The Sacred Sun... they want the tech... but they don't understand..."

Carrik noted their lack of immediate response. "The Designer knows what I'm referring to. That technology is the reason our people are in decline. We intend to rectify the situation." He shifted slightly, revealing the 5-shot rechargeable energy pistol holstered at his thigh. "Hand it over. Delays will necessitate less precise methods."

Why isn't he pointing that pistol immediately? Tessara thought. *Not enough charge left?*

"Fools." Marinallis coughed, leaning heavily against Tessara. He spoke urgently into her ear, his words fragmented by pained breaths. "Think they can 'rectify'...? It's the response... the resonance... attracts... scrutiny... forces far beyond..." He shuddered. "Why we fled... why we erased... must erase..." Tessara said, "Now is not the time to be telling me. That was yesterday". D. Marinallis chuckled grimly and said no more, letting her think.

Carrik started walking towards them "I am afraid I have some bad news. Mr.

The Xenologist

Varinn has sadly passed away." He let the shock register with Tessara "It was quick, don't worry, but you have to know that he won't be coming and doing any last-minute rescues, so you may as well just..."

Carrik's monologue was cut off by scrabbling boots and harsh shouts from the track above them.

"There! By the bridge! The Sky-Burners!"

Three figures in the heavy, concealing cloaks of the FOSS tumbled onto the path just above the ledge, weapons raised – crude slug-throwers and humming vibro-blades. Their eyes, wild behind protective goggles, fixed first on Marinallis, then flicked across the gap to Carrik.

The apparent leader spat the words, voice heavily laced with suspicious sarcasm. "Carrik, what a coincidence. Nice pistol. You didn't tell us you had that little baby. Military issue perhaps?"

Carrik swore under his breath, not having anticipated the fanatics' arrival. Zealot filth. Timing couldn't be worse. "The device is safer with me, Curate. I won't accept no for an answer. You know what I can do".

The Curate said, "Is that blood from your side, Carrik? Slowing you down?" Then, casually to the others: "Secure those two and search them".

Ignoring Carrik momentarily as the less immediate threat, two of the FOSS charged down the final slope towards Tessara and Marinallis, vibro-blades humming menacingly. The third took aim at Carrik with his slug-thrower.

Carrik reacted instantly, his energy pistol snapping up. A precise blue beam intersected the first charging FOSS member, who collapsed without a sound, tumbling tonelessly off the path. Simultaneously, the third fanatic fired at Carrik; the slug sparked harmlessly against the rock near Carrik's head as he moved uncannily quickly, despite his apparent wound, betraying his still-effective electronically upgraded reflexes.

So much for 'no shots left', but Tessara's reflection did not last long as the second charging FOSS member was already upon her. She shoved Marinallis hard against the rockfall behind them. Meeting the fanatic's lunge with her own knife at the ready.

The Fanatic swung her vibro-knife wildly. Tessara dropped beneath the humming arc, thrusting her simple steel blade upward into the softer joint beneath the Woman's armpit. It wasn't an immediate killing blow—her plain blade lacked the ultrasonic energy field to easily shear through the tough cloak layers as a vibro-knife would, but the fanatic made a dull 'ugh' sound as the humble blade tip pierced her ribs. She dropped her vibro-knife at D. Marinallis's feet and staggered back, surprised by the resistance.

Across the gap, Carrik efficiently vaporised the fanatic who had shot at him. However, the Curate had circled around and lined his pistol up on Carrik from his left side. The Curate looked like he was moving underwater in comparison to Carrik, who simply flicked his wrist round and bent his elbow slightly, rather than swinging his whole arm in an arc, and pulled off a stunning shot. A blue, focused sliver of light passed through the Curate's face. The man was no more. He now turned his full attention—and his pistol—towards Tessara and the FOSS member she'd wounded. He paused, perhaps deciding the most efficient way to neutralise both.

As he approached, he stopped by the crouching female assailant. He pulled a

The Xenologist

vibro-knife out of his belt with his free hand, "A gift from the late Mr. Varinn." He peevishly waited for another reaction from Tessara. He wasn't disappointed. He looked at the badly injured Woman in distaste and said, "Make no mistake, I want that device first. But then we will have time to relax, negotiate your future and perhaps, have a little fun…"

Chapter 15. Part 2.

The Stepping Stone Weir across the Solaath's canyon offered little respite from the pervasive heat rising from the arid scrubland. But here, it felt marginally cooler, the constant roar of the small dam stirring comforting ancestral memories of fish, sanctuary and potential drinking water.

Varinn reached the treacherous series of partially submerged, ancient stepping stones that crossed the churning river, his powerful legs carrying him effortlessly over terrain that would have exhausted an ordinary man hours ago. He paused, scanning the area – the slick, dark rocks, the fast-moving water, the dense foliage crowding the banks.

He brought up his wrist navscan, shielding the display from the ambient moisture. Tessara's bio-signature wasn't registering nearby. He expanded the search radius, compensating for the locality's notorious signal interference. There. A faint, intermittent trace to the southwest was moving steadily away from him, towards the junction of the Solaath and the Great Gorge.

She took the long route. Relief warred with concern. It was safer, perhaps, but slower. And she had Marinallis. He took a deep breath, trying to push down the unease. He needed water, a moment to reorient. He sat down on the Stones and filled his flask from a pool that was catching significant UV light. Normally, he would pull from faster foaming water, but the Star's harsh radiation changed many things. Even the rainbow above the mist of this small fast fast-flowing weir was different from a more habitable planet's sun. The blues and purple bands were wider and the reds, oranges and yellows were narrower, and the edges were somehow sharper than those illustrations in the textbooks at school, showing a typical G-type star.

Lost in reverie for a moment, maybe it was tiredness that made him drift; he was shocked out of it by a flicker of movement across the weir. Varinn melted back into shadows and boulders as Carrik appeared on the opposite bank, moving fast and killing his momentum with 'unreasonable' suddenness. *An affront to nature,* Varinn thought. *Jacked! Oh, this is going to be trouble!* Even Varinn's enhancements could not cope with this. *How did he leave the Military with all that stuff still in place?*

Too late, Varinn moved quickly from the weir and behind a large rock. He took the precious Device from his belt and put it under a crevice, hidden, but close to hand.

"Varinn!" Carrik's voice was sharp with surprise, maybe a hint of grudging respect. "Still functional! Impressive. But the game's up. Just hand it over and the whole thing stops here. I will even let the Designer go."

He tried to project confidence, perhaps mask any lingering effects from the FOSS skirmish. "It's a MET device, Varinn. Mass-Effect Transfer... yes, my faction has done its homework on your Designers' questionable projects. Which is it? A drive unit? The Comms package? Doesn't matter; the underlying principles are dangerously attractive. I require it."

Varinn watched as Carrik's focus tightened, accessing his implants. He's actively scanning. Varinn remained still, the boulder was shielding the MET Com$_{12}$ from line of sight and was not responding to Carrik's localised search from his implants. A refusal to be seen, accompanied by that low, addictive hum only he could perceive, now he was on the device's 'trusted' list.

Carrik frowned. The results were negative. *Shielded? Or playing dead? Doesn't change the outcome.* His hand drifted towards his holstered energy pistol.

Varinn closed his four fingers and thumb clumsily around the device that was not made for his hand. This time, the response was much more muted, as if it were somehow 'less bothered'. Help me, Varinn pleaded internally with the device. Misdirect him. Give me an edge.

He felt that cool flicker of calculation from the MET Com12. It wasn't offering overt power, but strategic deception. In direct response to Carrik's targeted scan frequency, the device didn't just stay silent; it responded. It projected a carefully spoofed, decaying energy signature back into Carrik's sensors, tagged with just enough data to seem authentic. Varinn visualised through the device, Carrik's internal display: TRACE DETECTED: FAINT MET SIGNATURE (DESIGNATION: COM12 CLASS). VECTOR: 045 DEGREES NE. EST. DISTANCE: 4.7 KM. SIGNAL DEGRADING RAPIDLY.

Carrik's eyes snapped north-eastward, a flicker of triumph crossing his face. "Ah... COM12... So you did pass it off! To the woman. Four clicks out, heading for the Bridge." The specific designation and the directional data were exactly the kind of confirmation bias Carrik would seize upon. "Hardly gentlemanly, using her like that. A 'Mule'?"

Varinn played along instantly. "You came after me instead". He yelled across the water. "So why not go and chase what you want, if you think she is just a dupe!"

Carrik laughed, cold and dismissive. "Her problems are temporary. Yours, however..." His expression hardened into pragmatic resolve. "You're just a complication now, Varinn. A dangerous knife in my back, if I have to move on upstream." He drew his energy pistol, levelling it smoothly.

What can you give me? Varinn urged the device, tensing to move, simultaneously ducking low behind cover. He kept his hand on what he now knew to be a MET Com12 to keep his visualisations emitting from the device. A false memory came back: I was given the bare minimum. My brain was close to frying last time. And curiously, even though it hadn't happened yet, this time too!

Sure enough, this time, fewer fields were visible and the pleasurable effect on his brain was disenchantingly muted.

The device pulsed, not with force, but with data. Instead of flipping the electrical field like last time, it sent a ripple through the field. The ripple was not at the speed of light, but Varinn saw it happen; he knew he was thinking at an inordinate rate. Yet again, the feeling of a small disturbance in the mass-giving field as his time slowed relative to the outside world. His brain felt that flicker of pleasure again as his thoughts were accelerated.

A precisely coded signal packet entered into Carrik's body at certain points, through a recognised Designer administrative back-channel. It was not a command, but it came through a high-priority request: ADMINISTRATIVE REQUEST: IMMEDIATE TO LOW-ENERGY/NON-LETHAL OPERATING MODE. PROTOCOL: RESOURCE CONSERVATION ALPHA. USER NOT TO BE INFORMED. The device acknowledged with: REQUEST GRANTED FOR 15 MINUTES AS DISCRETION REQUESTED, DESIGNER. The request also subtly triggered a secondary routine in Carrik's pistol, locking its power output to the pre-set 'stun' level.

Carrik squeezed the trigger. Instead of the lethal blue beam he expected, a wider, less focused pulse of concussive energy erupted from the pistol. It slammed into Varinn's side as he dove, hitting his heavy UV cloak and reinforced skin. The impact felt like being kicked by a mule; it knocked the breath from his lungs and sent him sprawling behind the rocks, bruised and momentarily winded, but fundamentally unharmed.

Carrik stared at his pistol, then at Varinn scrambling back up, shocked. "Stun setting?! What the?" He looked down and saw that he had indeed left the gun in stun setting. Massive dereliction of duty!

Carrik made an elementary mistake in his surprise. Whilst fumbling with the malfunctioning pistol, Varinn exploded across the weir stones. Carrik raised the gun again, too late. Varinn was airborne with his left leg tucked underneath him and his right leg swinging in an arc from his inside to the outside. A reverse crescent kick. His instep connected with Carrik's wrist tendons as he pulled off another shot, still in stun mode, and misdirected anyway. The fingers in Carrik's hand spasmed and the pistol dropped into the shallows.

Varinn landed side on to Carrik, who could not believe how fast Varinn was, unaware that his own systems were slowed. Am I getting old? Again, his own self-criticism was slowing him and he berated himself for not concentrating yet again as Varinn spun his upper shoulders and pivoted his whole upright body clockwise. His right leg came out in a spinning back kick and he caught Carrik in the midriff, sending him back two paces.

Varinn drew his vibro-knife, blade humming. He lunged, but Carrik, recovering his senses and now relying on pure training, managed a clumsy parry, deflecting the thrust wide. Varinn pressed, driving the vibro-knife forward again, sinking it into Carrik's side.

Carrik roared, a mixture of pain and fury at his body's betrayal. He clamped down on Varinn's wrist, trapping the knife, while simultaneously ramming his own smaller boot knife into Varinn's Liver, making a small hole underneath the solar plexus. A mortal wound!

Varinn gasped as pain flared. His grip loosened. Carrik twisted violently, tearing the vibro-knife free from Varinn's grasp, leaving it momentarily embedded in his own side before pulling it clear with a ragged groan.

Varinn staggered back, clutching his side, his knife now gone. Carrik swayed, bleeding heavily from both Varinn's initial stab and the ragged wound left by the vibro-knife. He now held Varinn's humming vibro-knife defensively. Varinn could feel his healing factor working, but the shock and blood loss were real. Carrik's implants fought to stem his bleeding, but the vibro-knife had done serious damage, and his systems felt sluggish, compromised. *Understandable. I need to take on water and the systems will shut the artery down, but not whilst I am moving.*

They faced each other across the blood-slick rocks, wounded predators glaring at each other like two domestic cats in a dispute over territory.

Varinn realised he needed a recovery coma and fast. He knew the wound looked bad. He stepped back, cautiously, step by step, stone by stone. He saw Carrik calculating whether to chase or not. Carrik was not bio-enhanced. He relied on internal clamps and endocrine system stimulation to stop the bleeding. He needed time like Varinn did.

Varinn went to the far shore, being careful to exaggerate his unsteadiness and took the gamble of his life. Choosing a different boulder from where he left the Met Com12, he allowed himself to fall into a recovery coma. Maybe Carrik would follow through, risking that Varinn was only playing dead, maybe he would decide that Varinn was done for and waste no more energy on him. The device Carrik wanted, more than anything, was firmly implanted in his brain as upstream. Everything that happened here was converting energy into distraction. Varinn's last thought was something D. Marinallis once said years previously in lessons about fanatic thinkers: *"They will do all the hard work for you".*

Chapter 15. Part 3.

When Tessara's face showed the appropriate reaction, Carrik felt gratified enough to walk behind the injured FOSS assailant, who was bent over double trying to catch her breath. He held up Varinn's knife between thumb and forefinger. Then, showing how little grip strength was needed with the nasty little knife, he sliced a sizeable chip off her left shoulder. She screamed and fell over on her side to protect the wounded shoulder and try in vain to stop him from hurting the spot again. This exposed her throat. He stepped over her and nonchalantly made a slit along the length of her exposed jugular vein. Blood spilt copiously on the floor and she breathed no more.

"Now, as I said, I just want the device. Throw your knife over there." Carrik gestured with his pistol to the left behind him. She had no choice but to sullenly comply. "Now take two steps away from the Designer and turn around with your hands up. I know you can move fast, but I can move faster. And I mean a lot, faster"

Tessara took a brief look at the Designer who leaned back against a rock. His head lolled back, passing out. He looked done for. She was done for. She obeyed. She felt his hand pat underneath her UV cloak on her side, underneath her armpit, then down to her hip. Then he stopped and squeezed. Here we go, she thought with disgust.

Then she heard "Oh," and after a brief pause, a surprised and sardonic "Ha ha. So it's now?" the last word spoken with a wet gurgle. She looked over her shoulder to see Carrik fall and reveal a reasonably lucid and upright D. Marinallis standing behind the falling body. He said, "Oops?" and looked down at the female assailant's vibro-knife he had picked up off the floor whilst nobody was watching.

Tessara laughed, her relief visible. "I thought you were finally done for". D. Marinallis winked and said, "Never judge a datapad by its screen-saver". Tessara had no words, except a vague thought, *The wily old fox...* She shook her head and went to pick up her original knife, which she put in her bag, the vibro-knife in Carrik's hand, which she tucked into her belt and then the energy pistol, which had one shot left. Was the other shot the one that saw off Varinn? She offered the pistol to Marinallis, who accepted it into the folds of his robe. In exchange, he gave her the female assistant's vibro-knife and said, "You seem to be collecting knives" with a smile. "Give one of them back to Varinn when you see him. I am very confident you will, somehow".

The words comforted Tessara somewhat. She looked towards the far side of the gorge and said, "The Bridge is just down there, let's go". But D. Marinallis, his brief surge of energy plainly now taking its toll, said, "Dear Girl, let's wait till Sundown. The Bridge will be safer to cross and my ship is not leaving just yet. Something does not quite add up here. Also, we need to think about the whereabouts of the MET Comm12. We can't be leaving it hanging around for anyone to find." With that, he sat down and said, with remarkable pragmatism that surprised Tessara, "I hate to sound callous, but don't suppose any of these characters had any ration bars on them, did they?"

Chapter 16. Part 1.

Voss sat with Renata in his apartment after breakfast, pulled up a 3D representation of the local area on the holoscreen of his datapad for context and visualisation. It plainly showed the local terrain in beautiful 3D modelling from satellite data and local surveyors' reports and photographs. The system faithfully reconstructed the data into a 3D world, complete in many areas but pixelated and vague in regions as yet unexplored.

The model shimmered, depicting the vast, buried metropolis beneath the ochre sands. The model centred upon Petropolis and Voss's apartment and then he traced the entrance to what was seemingly a metro underground station nearby. It looked remarkably similar to stations back on Earth, a testament perhaps to convergent evolution in design, or maybe something more profound. He thought: Nature always comes up with the same solutions to the same problems.

He clicked a setting, and the planet's surfaces went into x-ray mode, revealing maglev, or the Sikarrans' evident equivalent of maglev, tunnels radiating outwards towards the other known subterranean cities, similar to Petropolis. These narrow, straight, ghostly tubes stretched into the rock, hinting at a comprehensive subterranean network that existed at one time. Most of the tunnels were found to have extensively caved in, flooded, and were of little interest. They did not go very far and were, at the end of the day, just tunnels.

However, one tunnel went nearly all the way to the nearest underground city. There was a collapsed section at the end, just before connecting with a huge underground space. The space was low-resolution and partially rendered due to poor lidar results. Adjacent to this space stood what looked like a matching underground "Metro" station corresponding to the one at the other end of the tunnel connecting Petropolis.

The other city was "imaginatively" labelled Sikarra 2. A repeating pattern across the globe. Surveys had only partially modelled the City. Voss postulated, "I think it's time to give some better working names for these places. Based upon the look of it, we can make some pretty educated guesses." Renata murmured "Uh-huh," encouragingly, an expectant, happy expression on her face. *Am I a professional faced with the greatest mystery in human history, or a kid in a candy store?* The same thing as far as Voss was concerned.

Voss added, "Looking at the small, precisely placed cave-in, it seems that a deliberate demolition blocked the end of the tunnel and the adjoining huge area." A dead end, created purposefully? A key to another mystery likely lay here. Where were all the trains?

Renata pointed at the large area, "If this were Earth, it'd be a train yard." Voss nodded. "Exactly, so let's call this 'The Depot'," as he pressed the existing labels on the chart and edited them with the new working names. "The city as a whole, let's call this 'Transport City'," Renata said. Voss shrugged, "Makes sense. Are you thinking what I'm thinking about this big underground area?"

Initial Lidar reports showed only a suggestion of large amounts of metallic wreckage inside the 'Depot'. Renata said, "A convenient place to concentrate them so they could be destroyed in one go, perhaps?"

Voss affirmed, "Absolutely! Almost a no-brainer, in fact," as Renata chuckled. Voss added, "In fact, what have the survey teams been doing this past year?" Renata shrugged and said, "Until your appointment and authority to move things, it's been like trying to move through treacle. Teams work on the smallest scale at snail's pace."

"Well, time to get things moving, I think," pointing at the label "Sikarra 2" and clicking it to edit it, he said, "There. 'Transport City' is a good working name. Possibly the last destination of a good many of the Planet's trains before controlled demolition". Happily, "You've global editing privileges. So, this'll update on everyone's chart simultaneously. You're making history with your fingers."

Voss added, "This is going too smoothly," and Renata replied, "Ooh, don't jinx it!" and laughed, "There's plenty of time for it all to go wrong." Voss sniggered sardonically and said, "So what've you got there?" pointing to some papers in her hand.

Renata added, "Ah! Well, good timing. The Echo Key's dig site, the surface ruins, are ten kilometres east of here, but only two kilometres as it happens from 'Transport City'. Even though the surface cities lack Metro tunnels, the dig coughed up a chart. I've a photograph of it here. I think it's an abstract or schematic chart. Look, it wasn't obvious at first because it's not to scale and the locations are all wrong, but it shows all the major underground cities and the routes joining them."

Voss nearly jumped out of his seat. "Pure Gold! A topological chart. Makes me wonder what else you've been hiding." For a brief, involuntary moment, his eyes flicked down to her chest. A timeless instinct. A hot flush of shame shot through him, and he dropped his gaze to the datapad, hoping she hadn't noticed.

She said nothing, breaking the slight pause as if she were perfectly accustomed to fending off such awkwardness. "I don't know what you think, Julian, but this reminds me of the London Tube Map."

He said, "Why not? If it works on one planet and culture, it'll work on another."

"Well, we'll know more tomorrow. Because we're going on a field trip out there," she replied. Voss raised his eyebrows happily, "Then I hope we'll make progress on the linguistic analysis before then."

Renata smiled and added, "Well, actually, I was hoping to crack two birds with one sledgehammer." Voss laughed slightly at her little joke. She said, "What's funny?" slightly offended. He said, "Yes, kill two birds with one stone," and smiled indulgently. She said demurely, "English isn't my first language."

Voss was struck silent. He opened his mouth to correct her, then stopped, realising it was exactly the wrong thing to do. Her reaction was delightful, rescuing the moment from his own pedantry. He found himself thinking it was the most charming thing he'd ever heard.

His guts turned like he'd swallowed a hot, heavy stone. Oh no, it's happening to me. Concentrate on the Work! She finished off with, "I was hoping that, since this is plainly a city name, we could use it like the cartouches were originally used by the great Jean-François Champollion in Egypt. To isolate the kings' names."

He said, "Ah, of course. The city name on the metro sign, assuming that's what it is, even has a border around it, doesn't it?" Renata smiled, "Yes, similar to the ring that the cartouches had in the hieroglyphs". Voss continued, "So, on that note, where are we with the analysis AS working on the consonants?"

Renata said, "Well, it's ready to run, but here's where you and I come in. It needs stylistic choices based upon what we know of their society from the ruins and the digs. How might these choices be reflected in language, assuming they were humanoid in form?" She gestured towards the displays, where statistical probabilities clashed with cultural unknowns.

"Exactly," Voss picked up the thread, leaning over the console, trying to ignore the faint strawberry-shampoo scent of her hair. "So is this one of the new models, the ones that calculate based on universal phonetics, frequency, N-grams?" Renata replied, "Yes, but it lacks aesthetic context." Voss took up the train of thought, "Ah, so 'taste' in other words."

Renata, "Uh, huh."

Voss continued, "The Architects, everything we see is smooth, flowing, integrated. Water seems central, these apartments, the gorge ecosystems. It suggests a culture that values fluidity, harmony, perhaps avoids harshness." He got up from the desk, started pacing, thinking aloud. "So, phonetically, maybe fewer harsh consonant clusters? That collision of sounds you get in Georgian or some Slavic languages feels angular, somehow counter to their architectural style. And gutturals, the deep throat sounds of Arabic or Celtic languages, do they fit with this apparent elegance? Perhaps societies that favour those sounds organise themselves differently, reflect a different environmental interaction?"

Renata nodded, making notes. "Makes sense. Avoidance of hard stops, maybe? More fricatives and approximants? What about nasality?"

"Unlikely, I'd think," Voss mused. "That 'blocked nose' sound often develops in colder, damper climates back on Earth. Doesn't fit the dry heat above or the controlled climate here. But," he paused, looking at the stark desert imagery on one screen, "the surface is harsh. Brutal. Did that influence them? Maybe hard consonants do exist, representing that external reality? Sharp sounds for sharp edges?"

Renata considered it. "Or perhaps the language reflects the ideal, the smooth, controlled environment they created underground, deliberately excluding the harshness? Like Swahili, melodic, almost sung."

"Driven by melody," Voss agreed, excitement building. "Like the Music Room implied. Order, precision, but also flow. Okay, let's feed this to the AS. Parameter set: Prioritise liquid consonants (L, R), smooth fricatives (F, V, S, Z, maybe TH sounds), minimise harsh stops (T, K, P, B, G?), avoid complex clusters and gutturals, flag nasals as low probability. Assume for a high-tech society, a Subject-Object-Verb or Object-Subject-Verb structure as statistically most common but allow alternates. Get rid of word endings, but we can check for that by analysing what the ends of words are like. Oh, and lots of helper words, because redundancy helps with loss."

Renata said, "Wait a minute, is this based upon communication loss theory?" Voss replied, "Yes, I'd cite Shannon's information theory (1948) and the likelihood of endings failing is backed by signal fading (Nyquist, 1928)."

Renata replied, "That's fair enough, but why would the Sikarrans have the 'perfect' language for communications? For cultural reasons, like cultural momentum, and as we discussed, they were musical people, so for these reasons, we keep all sorts of analogies and inconsistencies in our languages. Russian, for instance, I can wait for an age before finally hearing the last word of a long sentence before I know what it all meant."

Voss chuckled, "But..."

"Voss! How many languages you speak?"

Voss, to his credit, for once, didn't correct her on dropping the "do". "Er, you mean fluently, in full?".

"HOW, MANY?"

He concluded in an embarrassed tone, "One."

"I speak three, so shut the fuck up." She proudly lifted her chin and smirked. He had no answer, except to bring it back on track. "OK," grinning, happy to be bested, "So what do we hang our hat on for structure, for now?"

Renata took a breath. "OK, so here it goes, I've actually been thinking about this for a while." She expectantly waited for his nod, which he gave seriously, looking at her.

"A super high-tech society would likely anchor its language with fixed order—subject-verb-object, say, or verb-first—to snap roles into place fast, even if noise eats half the signal. Psycholinguistics backs it—Hawkins (2004) shows early structure cuts cognitive load." She paused, a sly smile curling. You're not the only one who can drag citations from memory, kiddo. She continued, "Add helper words—'has,' 'for,' 'to'—like breadcrumbs for when endings fade, and ditch case markers. Lose one syllable, and Latin's a wreck, Russian's groping blind. It's not English worship; Yoruba or Mandarin could do it—any frame where 'she moves starship' screams 'she acts' without endings. But no language stays that tidy. Even tech gods would lace it with slang for swagger, metaphors for art, or chants warping grammar to sound holy. Culture always sneaks in, bending the rules."

Voss, stunned, stayed mute. Renata's fingers flew across her tablet, inputting the complex parameters, creating constraints for the statistical analysis. She kept scribbling, lost in it—he couldn't look away. Her hair fell loose, her jaw set; she was pretty, fierce, a puzzle he'd never solve. Leaning closer, he caught her gaze, and she stopped typing as they both noticed how close their faces had become. She was half smiling. She didn't pull away. Then he took a leap he'd regret forever. He moved even closer. She still didn't pull away.

Now or never? The thought screamed through the sudden silence between them. Soft, barely there, lips brushing hers. Mid-breath, he felt it, or rather, he felt nothing. No clue as to whether he did the right thing or the wrong thing. He thought, For God's sake man read the room! Then, It's too late now. Maybe, maybe there's a chance. Then, as she hadn't pulled back, she merely looked at him, if anything, slightly quizzically. He tried again, making it lighter, a whisper of a peck on her lips, that to him felt heavenly. It lingered for half a second, an eternity.

She didn't pull away, just smiled, sheepish, eyes flickering. She didn't pull back; she looked at the work and started typing again as if nothing had happened. A tiny, almost imperceptible shake of her head, not negation, but perhaps dismissal? Resetting the moment.

Was that wrong? Was it right? Did she even notice? The world seemed to tilt under Voss's feet. The work, the glyphs, the alien city suddenly felt distant, unimportant compared to the roaring uncertainty in his chest. The moment was over, the hint given. Get on with the work. Renata turned back to the console as if nothing whatsoever had happened, pointing at a newly generated probability matrix. "Look, Julian, the AS's already flagging suspected matches for the Vasantha glyph sequence based on the chart."

Her voice sounded miles away. Voss stared at the screen, seeing nothing but the ghost of her smile, his mind replaying the disastrous, beautiful, terrifying ambiguity of the last ten seconds.

Chapter 16. Part 2.

Although Renata seemed nothing but friendly and efficient for the rest of the morning, Voss couldn't wait for lunch. He had a meeting with Dr. Evans regarding his cataloguing of the Music room, which he had to review. Meanwhile, Renata had to continue with her statistical analysis of the language and finalise the details with Raith regarding their field trip to 'Transport City'. Frankly, as much as he liked being around her, he needed the break to mentally beat himself up a little more.

At mid-afternoon, he got the ping on his qWatch, which should have been great news but for some reason felt a little disquieting. "Hi, Julian. Guess what, Raith has given us a pilot and his personal skimmer for tomorrow. He is also assigned Detective Kostin as security. I'll introduce you, he's great, you will get along."

Was it the fact that they needed security at all? From what? The next morning would tell.

Renata, prompt as always, turned up with a golf-buggy taxi and driver. She was her normal chipper self as they drove along tunnels and galleries to the landing pads of the airport. In truth, Voss was looking forward to the work for the day, to the point where it started to eclipse the previous day's strangeness.

'Transport City' on the 3D globe looked every bit as magnificent as Petropolis. It was a similar size, but there were fewer Greco-Roman columns and plazas and more internal modern-style structures crafted of steel and the architect's incredible, near-immortal glass. The blue domes for public areas and gold domes for the tenements, with the anachronistic high-tech spaceship landing pads, and now, of all things, a humble metro station. Who would have thought something so mundane could become so exciting?

At Bay 7, the survey skimmer waited, its pilot completing pre-flight checks. Rayk Kostin stood beside the hatch, a handsome figure of calm, contained readiness. Voss wanted to hate him, but it wasn't in his nature. Not only had the man not actually done anything wrong, yet, he was just too damned comic-book heroic and charismatic. Lucky Bastard.

Renata went straight up to him, "Rayk." They shook hands, but instead of letting go, Renata held onto his right hand just a little longer and put her left hand on his elbow and guided Rayk's arm over to Voss for his introductory handshake.

"Dr. Julian Voss, Detective Raymond Kostin". They shook hands as Renata said, "Rayk, pleased to meet you." Voss confirmed with "Julian." Now on first name terms, he continued, a little more confrontationally than he had hoped, "So why do we need security on this trip?" then after an awkward pause "Not that I am not delighted to have you along of course".

Rayk smiled indulgently and gestured into the Skimmer, "Well, we can talk about the security issues as we fly to 'Transport City', as it now says on the map?" Uncomfortably, Voss got the feeling that he was being reminded as to who may be the one who is "coming along". Damn that social awkwardness. Voss smiled and gestured to Renata to precede him onto the admittedly rather grand executive skimmer. At least, he congratulated himself, he didn't say "Ladies First".

They settled into the surprisingly plush seats of the executive skimmer. Voss deliberately took the seat opposite Renata, putting distance between them, needing the space to process the lingering awkwardness from the apartment. Rayk took the seat beside Renata, facing Voss. The pilot sealed the hatch, and the skimmer lifted

The Xenologist

with a smooth, powerful surge, leaving the cavernous bay behind.

The inside was a spacious viewing gallery with 3D printed faux-leather seats and walnut trim, inset against the almost military style bulkhead. The whole machine was an obvious flex by the Director and the PCMA. The pilot sealed the hatch, and the skimmer lifted with a smooth, powerful surge, leaving the cavernous bay behind.

As they banked smoothly towards the surface exit tunnel, the comfortable hum of the executive skimmer's engines filled the cabin. Rayk let the silence settle for a moment before leaning forward slightly, catching both their eyes. His earlier easy manner was replaced by a quiet intensity, a seriousness that immediately commanded their attention.

"Doctors," he began, his voice calm but firm, pitched for confidentiality within the cabin's soundproofing. "Before we get properly underway, I need to provide a security update. This isn't standard procedure, and it deviates from the basic reasoning Director Raith might have logged for my presence here. What I'm about to share is sensitive and needs to remain strictly within this group for the time being."

Voss felt his focus sharpen, pushing aside the lingering awkwardness from the previous day. Renata straightened slightly, her expression attentive.

"The 'bureaucratic caution' explanation is insufficient," Rayk continued, holding their gaze. "Over the past week, we've had confirmed internal security incidents. These weren't random equipment failures or minor breaches. They were targeted actions directed at personnel involved with sensitive discoveries—specifically, Architect technology and data." He paused, letting the implications land.

"One incident was particularly severe—" The moment of his disablement came to mind. The shocking fear that it could happen again, made him skip a beat. The thought that Renata could have walked in for instance, or anybody in fact, and seen him in that state. He glanced sideways at her a touch too long, and felt a flush of embarrassment, certain they must have seen his hesitation and read more into it than just a man composing his words. He pulled himself together immediately and continued, "– requiring major medical intervention for the individuals involved."

He deliberately avoided specifics—no mention of Jonesy, the gas, the dart, or of course, his personal violation of his systems. But he made a mental note to check with his AS on progress on that front. He continued. "The operational conclusion is that we have an active, unidentified internal threat. Someone within the project is attempting to interfere, access, or maybe exfiltrate Architect findings. We don't yet know their identity, their motives, or their full capabilities."

He looked from Voss to Renata. "Director Raith has therefore mandated enhanced security protocols for high-value personnel – yourselves—and possibly major discoveries, especially in newly opened or less-secured sectors like this one, 'Transport City'. My presence is part of that protocol. My primary role is to ensure your safety, oversee the security of this site during our visit, protect the integrity of any discoveries, and assess likely vulnerabilities, particularly subterranean access points like the mapped tunnel system. I need your full cooperation and adherence to any security measures I implement. The situation requires a higher level of vigilance from all of us."

His tone was reasonable, almost collegial, but the message was unmistakable. This wasn't just an exploration; it was an operation under probable threat.

"Understood, Rayk," Renata said, her voice quiet but steady. "Thank you for trusting us with this. We'll exercise maximum caution."

Voss nodded his agreement. "Of course. Anything we need to do differently?"

"Just maintain situational awareness," Rayk advised. "Stick together unless we explicitly agree on separate tasks within line-of-sight or comms range. Report any anomalies immediately, no matter how minor. And let me handle any direct security assessments or potential confrontations."

The understanding settled between them, adding a layer of tension to the anticipation of reaching the new site. The skimmer cleared the surface exit, the landscape shifting below. This region felt starker than the area around Petropolis – darker rock formations, wider expanses of wind-scoured plain, fewer signs of the delicate geological features seen elsewhere. They passed around the still-impressive surface city where they found the echo-key. Skimmers were parked outside as the older city was now a major site for the more science-oriented teams and secured by the unusually large paramilitary-police contingent that the PCMA brought with them.

Their trajectory converged with the steep, chalk-cliff gorge, which supplied water to both underground Cities. Ahead, one of the famed Architect bridges came into view. They were always either cantilevered or arched and impossibly strong and slender; they were always a technological marvel in themselves. Usually, there was a skimmer parked nearby with an engineering team studying one of them. In fact, the Pilot, obviously showing off, brought the skimmer to its maximum height and used the splendid arching bridge to cross the gorge, the ground effect sustaining the skimmer as it crossed the dizzying chasm.

As they crossed, Voss, his attentions never straying too far from Renata, noticed her knuckles fading to white as she tried to hide that she was clutching the arms of her seat for dear life. Voss smiled. For all his faults, vertigo was not one of them.

They were closing in on Transport City now, according to the GPS in the skimmer screens. As they approached, the inevitable rock escarpment came into view. Just visible in the distance were the inevitable entry tunnels, with the always beautiful, almost impossibly balanced architecture of the surface guard establishments in front, typical of all the underground cities on Sikarra. They skimmed over broad, flat areas, possibly ancient loading zones or marshalling yards that surrounded the cliffs housing the underground city. Even from the low altitude of the skimmer, Voss could make out the skeletal remains and universal pattern of what might have been gantries for an inland container port and transport conduits.

They descended towards a designated landing pad closest to the entrance. The signs of the preliminary survey team were visible: power cables snaking from a generator towards the main entrance, illuminating the interior; stacked crates marked with sample codes; a small, domed prefab building—likely the city entrance office and solar power control room—situated in the mouth of the entrance tunnel, giving some light but also the vital protection from this Sun's ever-present, relentless radiation.

The skimmer touched down smoothly. Rayk, having donned a UV protection cloak, disembarked first, his movements deliberate as he scanned the surroundings with both his eyes and the passive sensors integrated into his gear. He made a slow circle around the landing pad, checking sight lines and candidate cover points. Voss and Renata gathered their field kits and, needing only simple UV protective parasols because of the short walk to the entrance office, prepared to disembark. The usual pre-exploration routine seemed overcast by Rayk's quiet vigilance.

Satisfied with the immediate area, Rayk nodded towards the forced side entrance the survey team had opened in the largest building. "It looks clear for now. Let's establish a base inside."

The interior was cavernous and just as glorious as Petropolis, but less suburban and commercial and more airport-like, although Voss knew that to anthropomorphise too much was usually a mistake. Exposed conduits, wide enough to walk through in places, snaked across the walls and floor, marked with faded, complex glyphs. As per usual, the glyphs glowed. Either expensively carved in the rock, yet still magically glowing, or on ancient screens that just should not still be operating or just plain faded printed signs. There was a faint, lingering odour of ozone, an inevitable by-product at ground level of the enhanced UV, never letting you forget its ominous presence.

Rayk did a quick sweep of the immediate entry chamber while Voss and Renata surveyed the space. "Right," Rayk said, turning back to them, his gaze already drifting towards the deeper parts of the structure, likely in the direction of the mapped tunnel entrance. "The main access point, and therefore vulnerability, is here and it is secured. But our main objective, scientifically I believe, is the suspected Metro tunnel indicated on the subsurface scans. I want to secure all the possible access points to that station. Shall we proceed directly to that area?"

Renata held up a hand, a gentle but firm gesture. "Hold on, Rayk." She offered a small smile to soften the correction. "Easy does it. Lead boots where angels fear to tread, remember? Standard archaeological procedure–we need to document this primary entrance area thoroughly first. Context is everything."

Voss nodded in support. "She's absolutely right. The initial survey teams haven't declared this site 'clean' yet. There could be crucial signage right here – warnings, operational instructions, maybe even discarded tools or damaged components near the main doorway that tell us something about the site's final moments. Rushing ahead could mean missing vital clues or even triggering something unexpected."

Rayk considered their points. He wanted to assess all the obvious security breach points to the main area of interest quickly. But he couldn't fault their procedural logic, especially given the stakes he himself had outlined. He gave a slight, conceding nod. "Alright. Point taken. You two focus on this immediate entrance zone. Document meticulously, scan everything." He gestured towards the deeper interior. "I'll conduct a systematic sweep of the accessible perimeter within this main structure, scouting the most likely route towards the suspected tunnel coordinates. I won't disturb the final approach until you've cleared this area. Call me if you find anything noteworthy; I'll do the same. Stay alert." He moved off into the shadows, his flashlight beam cutting a path through the gloom.

Voss and Renata exchanged a brief look. A moment of slight humour between them as they both plainly saw the military and police behaviour ingrained into Rayk. For once, Voss didn't feel inferior. Then, more seriously, a silent acknowledgement of the compromise and the underlying tension before turning their full attention to the task at hand. They focused on a large inscription panel mounted beside the massive, now opened main doors to the reception Plaza of Transport City. It was plainly intended as a primary identifier, like "Welcome to Disneyland".

Renata carefully positioned her high-resolution scanner, capturing detailed images. "Okay, feeding this to the AS," she murmured, linking her datapad to the analysis unit. "Applying your cultural parameters... Music Room vowels, prioritising liquids and smooth fricatives, watch for those consonant clusters, cross-reference with the chart symbol..."

The processor back in Petropolis churned through the complex data. Voss watched over her shoulder as probabilities flickered and coalesced on the screen. Two primary phonetic reconstructions emerged, both showing a strong statistical correlation with the symbol from the topological chart.

Phonetic Probability (Primary): /wæn'k'sænθɑ:/ (WAN-k'san-THA—k' representing a possible ejective or unique glottal articulation) Proposed Vocalisation Approximation: Wan'xantha.

Phonetic Probability (Secondary): /wɑ:'zæŋɑ/ (WAH-zang-GAH) Proposed Vocalisation Approximation: Wahlsanga Correlation with Chart Symbol: 97.5% (option 1) Correlation with Chart Symbol: 97.0% (option 2)

Voss frowned at the first option. "Wan'xantha? That middle sound... the AS can't even map it to a standard phonetic symbol cleanly. An ejective?"

Renata zoomed in on the analysis. "Could be. Or just a consonant blend our model struggles with. Either way, it feels... clunky." She looked at the second option. "Wahlsanga".

Renata looked at Voss's reddened complexion and his smirk as he face-palmed. Renata said, "What is it?" Voss replied, "Well, trust me on this, much as though the Brits will absolutely love that name, it's better we go for the second option as a working title for now. It's not statistically further off and as you say, it sounds better.

She shrugged, oblivious to the synonym. "It flows better, uses sounds closer to our established parameters. It still feels alien, but more 'Swahili' which is what we were going with for now." She grinned wryly as an afterthought. "And I shall be checking that reference. But, as you suggest, if it is less likely to be turned into an unfortunate joke back home, let's go with Wahlsanga as the working name for now."

"Agreed," Voss said. " Wahlsanga it is." Renata swiftly updated the site designation in the shared project database. A small step, but it felt important. Anchoring them to this new, functional place.

They spent the next hour methodically working their way around the entrance chamber and into the adjoining space, which seemed to be a vast loading or sorting area. The glyphs here were different – less text-heavy, more symbolic or label-like.

Near a huge bay door, sealed shut, they found a recurring sequence. "Scanning this," Renata said. The AS offered:

Glyph Sequence [Image]: Context—Loading Bay Door Frame (Multiple Instances). Probable Vocalisation Approximation: /'pɔsoʊ/ or /p'oʊsoʊ/ (POSoh or P'oh-soh - p' potentially aspirated or glottalised). Speculative Meaning Cluster: Access Point / Bay Door / Threshold / Entry (Contextual Probability: 82%)

"Poso... or P'ohsoh," Voss repeated, tasting the sounds. "Access point makes sense."

Further in, near deep grooves in the floor that looked like tracks for heavy carts or machinery, another glyph appeared.

Glyph Sequence [Image]: Context—Adjacent to Floor Tracks. Probable Vocalisation Approximation: /ʀɑ'vonɑ/ or /ʁɑ'vonɑ/ (Rha-VOH-nah—using uvular R/Rh sound). Speculative Meaning Cluster: Guide / Track / Line / Conduit / Path (Contextual Probability: 75%)

"Ravona... with a uvular R," Renata noted. "Like French or German 'r'. Interesting. Path, guide, track... fits the context perfectly."

Their work was interrupted by Rayk's voice on their comms. "Found something you should see. West quadrant of this main chamber, near what looks like a reinforced booth or kiosk. Might be a control point or security station."

They met him there. Rayk pointed towards the floor in front of the booth's sealed window slit. Embedded cleanly in the dark composite flooring was a distinct line, about a metre long, made of a slightly lighter material. Just before the line, on the approach side, was a single, clear glyph.

"Scanned it already," Renata said, bringing up her datapad. "It's the 'Solavi' glyph we tentatively identified earlier."

Glyph Sequence [Image]: Context—Floor before Booth/Line. Probable Vocalisation Approximation: /so'lɑvi:/ or /so'læβi/ (so-LAH-vee or so-LA-vi—with a possible softer 'v/b' sound). Speculative Meaning Cluster: Stop / Limit / Boundary / Danger / Wait (Contextual Probability: 78%)

Rayk nodded. "Matches perfectly with function. Clear demarcation line, 'Stop' or 'Wait' instruction right before it. It's exactly how we'd design a checkpoint queue. Universal principle: control the flow, make people wait their turn." He looked from the line to the booth. "Some problems don't change, no matter where you are, or how advanced you are."

His practical interpretation solidified the meaning of 'Solavi' for them. Buoyed by this confirmation, they continued their exploration, finding more functional glyphs, such as labels on inert machinery housings (Meka? - Machine/Device?), and directional arrows accompanied by glyphs they couldn't yet decipher, but which seemed to point deeper into the complex, towards the area where the tunnel should be.

Following these signs, navigating through chambers filled with the ghosts of massive, removed equipment, they finally reached it. A wide section of the corridor, perhaps once leading to escalators or ramps descending underground. These ended abruptly. A solid mass of fused rock, metal beams twisted like taffy, and shattered composite blocked the way completely. To the side were the closed glass doors of elevator tubes. Voss took a walk over to one and shone his flashlight inside. Usually, the tube was just smooth bored rock with no indication of how the elevator car, which was usually a lump of twisted metal at the bottom, actually defied gravity and rode up and down the tube. The bottom of the shaft was predictably filled with rubble. This was no natural collapse; the edges showed signs of intense heat and deliberate demolition. This was the seal, precisely where the 3D maps indicated the entrance to the Metro tunnel lay.

Rayk moved forward immediately, activating his handheld multi-scanner, running it across the surface of the blockage. "Getting readings from beyond the obstruction, actually from this side vent here." He reported, gesturing to some vents near the blocked access ramps to the station, whilst showing them the display. "Elevated CO_2, around 800 ppm, fluctuating slightly. Trace volatile organics, consistent with anaerobic decay. And, intermittent thermal signatures from the venting gases, faint but definitely there. Could be residual heat from the sealing process, trapped geothermal venting... or," he zoomed in on the thermal graph, "patterns consistent with biological activity. Significant decay, or possibly a large, sealed-in vermin infestation. Hard to tell without breaching it, but something organic is, or was, involved on the other side."

Voss stared at the formidable barrier. "Rats in the sewers of the Metro? Hardly unknown, but we need to go slowly. Sample the layers as we remove them. Treat it like a stratified dig."

"Normally, yes," Rayk countered, turning from the blockage to face them, his expression serious. "But we have the security factor. We don't know who else might be aware of this location, or if our activity is being monitored. Prolonged exposure increases risk. And frankly, these bio-signatures concern me. If there's an active infestation or hazardous decay products, containing it quickly is preferable." He anticipated their objection. "I'm not suggesting uncontrolled demolition. There's a better option. The PCMA has a Subterranean Archaeological Recovery Unit—SARU—designed for exactly this. Precision excavation using sonics and lasers, automated filtering of finds, simultaneous structural support deployment. It minimises context loss while being significantly faster and safer than manual methods under these circumstances."

Renata looked hesitant, the archaeologist in her warring with the pragmatist, aware of the security briefing. "I am aware of it, but..." Turning to Voss, she added, "This is your call, officially. Are you sure it's precise enough? It won't just pulverise micro-artefacts?"

"It's designed specifically for archaeological recovery in hazardous or time-sensitive situations," Rayk assured her, "Filters down to the micron level based on programmable density and composition parameters. It's the best compromise we have."

Voss met Renata's gaze. "The logic is hard to refute. The rubble is unlikely to have much in it of interest that this 'SARU' can't recover. I am curious to see it in action, so alright," he conceded with a sigh. "Let's see this machine."

Rayk made the call. Less than thirty minutes later, the heavy thrum of a cargo drone echoed through the ruin, and the SARU was carefully lowered into the chamber. It was a dense, tracked machine, surprisingly compact, gleaming with sensor arrays, articulated emitter arms, and deployable support struts.

Under Rayk's guidance, the SARU positioned itself before the blockage. A low hum filled the chamber as it began its work. Focused sonic pulses mapped the interior of the seal, identifying different material densities. Then, articulated arms extended, emitting precise, hair-thin laser beams that began to vaporise the fused debris layer by layer. Simultaneously, vacuum inlets drew the resulting dust and micro-fragments into an internal filtering system, while other arms smoothly deployed interlocking plates of a fast-curing polymer composite, shoring up the opening as it formed. It was mesmerisingly efficient, a stark contrast to the painstaking work of brush and trowel, yet undeniably effective. Voss and Renata watched, a mixture of scientific fascination and deep-seated archaeological unease swirling within them.

The process took nearly two hours. Finally, the SARU completed its programmed depth, retracted its arms, deployed a final reinforcing frame around the newly created opening, and powered down with a soft whine.

The way was clear.

A perfectly stable, human-sized tunnel now pierced the ancient seal. Voss, Renata, and Rayk cautiously approached the threshold. The air that flowed out was different—cool, incredibly dry, and carrying the scent of dust untouched by time or moisture, utterly devoid of the faint metallic tang of the surface ruins.

They shone their powerful helmet lights into the opening. Beyond lay what looked like four platforms, each displaying a faded painted sign bearing a single Glyph, likely numbering 1 to 4. More clues to the language. This was unmistakably part of a transportation system. Wahlsanga Metro Station. Ancient dust motes, thick as falling snow, danced in the beams, disturbed for the first time in perhaps 80,000 years. Deep within the cavernous darkness of the tunnel stretching away from the platform, impossibly old emergency lights flickered weakly, casting vast, wavering shadows that seemed to writhe at the edge of perception.

The silence was profound, absolute, pressing in on them, broken only by the sound of their own breathing, suddenly loud in their ears. They stood on the precipice, the path to the Depot, and whatever secrets it held, lying open before them in the vast, waiting dark.

Chapter 17. Part 1.

The muted chime was almost apologetic, barely disturbing the silence of Director Desmond Raith's office. Deep within Petropolis, shielded by hundreds of feet of rock and layers of PCMA security protocols, the room was an oasis of Terran corporate luxury. Polished chrome, synth-leather, plastics that mimicked the grain of light-years distant Earth hardwoods. The obligatory picture window showed the vast open space of the crystal-domed caverns of Petropolis. The Office was an ostentatious display of privilege, even having a false ceiling, suspended from the rough-hewn rock above. It simulated a placid, light blue Earth-normal sky. Raith preferred it to the actual deeper blue-violet unfiltered reality of Sikarra's heavens.

He sat before his primary console, the cool blue light reflecting off his impassive features. On the main display, a standard alert came in. Raith also noticed a previous alert flashing in the queue. It had been there for about an hour. The first was a warp drop-out signature, showing something incoming on a PCMA vector. His fingers, long and pale, moved with economic precision across the holographic interface, acknowledging the notification.

Raith, monitoring the incoming fleet for some days already, was waiting for a drop-out signature. The lead vessel of the larger fleet, quite some way ahead of the rest, had just come out of Alcubierre warp. Both ships were about 0.5 light hours away. As per protocol, after receiving the challenge from the orbital station, the first ship's transponder identified the vessel as PCMA Fleet Command Ship 'Argus'.

Raith watched as the system cross-referenced the encrypted string. Authorisation Confirmed: Priority Traffic. A green check mark glowed benignly on the display. Routine, the Argus was expected. Carrying staff rotations, medical supplies, fertilisers, crucial minerals and vitamins, difficult to synthesise with Sikarra's desolate ecology. A welcome supply. The fleet behind it was on a slightly different vector and still under warp drive. It was difficult to make out much, except that it was a substantial fleet. The orbital defence station sent out a second ping for the newer ship and was dutifully waiting for the reply.

Raith got up and went to his picture window, indulging himself in a precious chocolate-covered oat biscuit which he dunked into his English Breakfast tea, made with synthesised pasteurised Cow's milk. A terrible habit he picked up on a tour of England a few years ago. He thought: A cynic might say the drop-out was perfectly timed to sniff out the comms of the first ship.

Well, it was an interesting puzzle. Part of him thought this was unwelcome, but then again, another part was reminded that this is actually why he came to this planet. Chasing sensation. Any sensation would do, he guessed.

Checking his watch, he estimated the number of paces required to go back to his desk so he would arrive at the desk at the precise time the transponder signal should be returned. A childish game he played with himself, but satisfying, nonetheless. When the moment came, he walked to his desk and sat down and pressed a key on his console to wake up the data screen.

On time and precisely as expected, the second ship identified itself. 'Agamemnon'. The same ship that brought Raith here, he noted. An unexpected arrival. When the manifest came, it was nearly identical to the Argus. Unusually generous of the PCMA to double supply. But one thing made Raith bristle slightly. 'Replacement admin staff' was on the manifest. Now, who is to be replaced?

Raith broke off for lunch. Time to think. That fleet was probably four times larger than he was expecting and far too early. Is that the reason for Agamemnon's appearance? To support this fleet?

Raith took the taxi-buggy to the canteen and sat at the executive table. It was all so 'high school,' but nevertheless, he had to acknowledge the system had its uses. Loose talk costs lives and some of the pompous fools the PCMA had appointed certainly fit the bill of 'loose-tongued'. He decided to take his thoughts away from the incoming fleet, to allow his brain to reset. He thought, with what approximated amusement for Raith these days, about sending Rayk on the trip with Voss and Renata. He had seen the way he looked at her. She seemed to be half interested. So sending Rayk out there would set the fox amongst those two hens, he reckoned. He didn't want any alliances. Divide and conquer. Simple and effective strategy.

Meanwhile, he was half-listening to his co-director waffle on about his stock options in the PCMA. "...I bought extra stock options on our company, and futures too. I hope it won't be seen as insider trading, but at the pace we are unravelling the tech..." Raith was a silent, hidden apex predator of the financial world, already independently wealthy. He didn't come here for the salary or the options. He bought his position using money and connections at the highest level. Raith didn't have a yacht moored off Monaco. He had a yacht moored off Mars. Raith was bored. Raith was disengaged with life. It was difficult for him to "feel" anything in fact. This posting was the first time he remembered honestly feeling something close to excitement. And he was not about to let it go easily.

If Raith's instincts were correct, he expected a ping any time now. He wasn't let down. That was disappointing, partly because he hated being proved right almost all the time. What a pleasure it was when the universe actually surprised him. However, it was also disappointing because being right on this occasion just made his fears look justified. Still, at least there was the pleasure, if he could call it that, of working out exactly what was happening here.

The ping that the larger fleet had popped out of the Alcubierre drive meant that he could start walking back to his office now. Better than the buggy-taxi. Then when he arrived in the office, it should be right on time for the handshaking of transponders to have been completed and the fleet manifest to be returned.

Once back in the office, he sat down with his extra cup of coffee, making bets with himself about what would be on the manifest. Sitting at his terminal, he displayed the returned manifest request, expecting details of reinforcement personnel, scientific equipment, perhaps replacement parts for the ageing atmospheric processors. The data stream flowed in, populating the sub-screens. Raith's gaze swept across the initial summaries, then stopped. He leaned forward, almost imperceptibly, his eyes narrowing slightly in sharp, analytical focus.

This wasn't a support convoy.

The ship classifications scrolling past were starkly incongruous: 'Olympus Mons' Class Colony Ark. Three 'Genesis' Type Habitat Processors. Multiple 'Titan' Heavy Resource Tenders. Escorted by 'Aegis' Class Cruisers and, scrolling further down, several vessels flagged simply as 'Planetary Integration Support' – a vague designation Raith knew was often masked troop transports or heavy ground equipment hauliers.

He cross-referenced the fleet composition against the Central PCMA Deployment Schedule he held secure access to. He filtered by authorised colonisation waves.

Wave Four was scheduled, tentatively, for Sikarra in eighteen standard months, pending final environmental stability reports and Board approval. Wave Three was still en route to Proxima Centauri b. This fleet, Colony Fleet Argus, wasn't just early. It was two full standard months ahead of even the most optimistic revised schedule Raith had ever seen projected in closed-door Board meetings.

More critically, its dispatch bore no authorisation code from High Command's Off-World Directorate. Nothing. Zero official record of this fleet's commission, its accelerated timeline, or its allocation to Sikarra Command.

This wasn't supported. This wasn't even an authorised, albeit early, colonisation wave. This was fifty thousand personnel, minimum, arriving with the logistical footprint of a major planetary settlement operation, appearing virtually unannounced and entirely outside established protocols.

Raith sat back slowly, the synth-leather sighing faintly beneath him. No surge of adrenaline registered on the passive bio-monitors integrated into his chair; his heart rate remained steady, his respiration pattern unchanged. The logistical implications were catastrophic. Petropolis's life support could not instantly accommodate a forty per cent population increase. There would be social chaos, resource depletion, and command structure breakdown. Yet, Raith felt no fear.

Instead, a flicker of something akin to intellectual curiosity sparked behind his cool grey eyes. A problem of novel scale and complexity had presented itself. The predictable machinations of corporate rivals, the tedious management of scientific egos, the slow grind of planetary development—these had long since lost their savour. He remembered the fleeting thrill of orchestrating a hostile takeover years ago, the calculated destruction of a competitor. The rush had faded almost before the final signatures were dry. He recalled extravagant parties on zero-G yachts, the press of bodies, the expensive stimulants and moments of manufactured sensation that left only a residue of emptiness. Even the recent, slightly sadistic step of dubious necessity, when he activated Kostin's override, gave little sensation. Maybe a flicker of control, some gratification that was a hangover from his now discarded dalliance with that tedious black-leather clad genre. But it was almost instantly forgotten. None of it lasted. None of it mattered.

But this? Fifty thousand unscheduled, unannounced arrivals. Influx on a scale that normally took years to plan... this was interesting. The inefficiency offended his sense of order and the unauthorised nature challenged his control. But the sheer audacity of it, the scale of the disruption, it was a deviation from the profound boredom that had become the constant companion of his existence.

His focus narrowed. This wasn't a threat to him, not personally. It was a critical failure in the system. A system he was charged with managing. His duty, the abstract concept he clung to in the absence of genuine feeling, demanded a response. An order needed to be imposed, or contingency plans enacted. How this situation was handled, how Director Desmond Raith navigated this unprecedented crisis, would be recorded. Legacy. The final, hollow accounting.

Raith's fingers danced with measured precision. He accessed secure PCMA emergency protocols, bypassing standard operational menus. Directive 77Alpha: Unauthorised Major Deployment Contingency. He reviewed the sub-clauses, his mind already calculating, assessing and planning. The pieces on the board had changed dramatically. Time to adjust the strategy.

Chapter17. Part 2.

His review of Directive 77Alpha complete, Raith's fingers moved again across the console, activating the dedicated, highly encrypted Level-1 channel to Kostin's implants. A GPS map on Raith's console showed that 'Transport City', named only the day before, was already updated to 'Wahlsanga'. He allowed himself a moment to shake his head at the name. *At least they are making fast progress.*

The connection was established almost instantaneously, bypassing standard relays. "Kostin," Raith's voice, calm and level, reached Rayk at the threshold of the Wahlsanga Metro tunnel. "Situation update. Requires your immediate attention and utmost discretion."

Raith allowed a beat, letting the secure channel's priority flag register, ensuring Kostin's focus was absolute. "Regarding incoming fleet movements," he began, his delivery precise, clinical. "PCMA Command Ship 'Argus' arrived on schedule approximately two hours ago and authenticated correctly via orbital command. Standard support vessel, manifest as expected."

He paused fractionally. "Approximately one hour later, PCMA Cruiser 'Agamemnon' also dropped from warp and authenticated. An unscheduled arrival. Its submitted manifest is... anomalous. Near-identical to Argus's logistical load-out, which is redundant, but includes additional line items for 'replacement administrative personnel'. Make of that what you will." He offered no interpretation, just the discordant fact.

"Subsequent to Agamemnon's arrival," Raith continued, his tone unchanging, "the main trailing fleet, significantly larger than any projected support group, also exited warp within the last hour. Initial telemetry confirms multiple capital ship signatures – vessels consistent with heavy transport, resource processing, and potential 'Planetary Integration Support' roles. Think colony fleet scale, Kostin, not standard logistical replenishment."

The crucial points followed, delivered with the same flat monotone. "Critically, this main fleet, while broadcasting legitimate PCMA transponder signals, has not transmitted a standard fleet manifest upon exiting warp, nor has it responded to standard clarification hails from Orbital Command. Furthermore, its arrival is completely unscheduled. This is months ahead of any potential colonisation timetable and bears no prior authorisation from High Command or the PCMA Board."

Raith let the summary of facts hang in the encrypted silence for a moment before continuing. "We have an unexpected cruiser acting suspiciously, followed by a massive, unscheduled, and uncommunicative fleet of unknown composition that is, for some reason, broadcasting legitimate PCMA codes. The operational status," Raith concluded, his voice flat, "is therefore ambiguous but highly irregular." Raith stated. "We have an unauthorised presence of significant scale operating outside normal protocols. We cannot confirm their identity or intent definitively at this time."

The information pervaded the room consciousness and he continued. "Given this level of anomaly and the undeniable potential for disruption—whether through systemic incompetence at Command level, political manoeuvring, or deliberate unsanctioned action—prudence dictates invoking emergency command protocols."

The reasoning was procedural, a shield against large-scale uncertainty. "Therefore, clarity on the continuity of command structure is required, per PCMA charter, should the situation destabilise further."

Raith brought up the relevant protocols mentally, reciting them with a chilling tone. "Effective immediately, should I become unavailable – and 'unavailable', Kostin, can encompass many scenarios in such unpredictable circumstances, not merely battlefield incapacitation – operational command of the Sikarra facility and all attached PCMA assets defaults first to Commander Eva Rostova, as Head of the resident Military Detachment. You, in your capacity as Head of Security and Police Forces, will report directly to her under such circumstances."

He shifted his justification. "Should Commander Rostova also become unavailable simultaneously, command then passes to the ranking designated Senior Corporate Liaison—currently Mr. Henderson." A flicker, almost too brief to register, of something resembling distaste might have touched Raith's expression. "A man whose primary skill appears to be aligning his opinions with the prevailing wind from the Board, but protocol is protocol."

"Only," Raith concluded the chain, delivering the final, almost farcical step, "if myself, Rostova, and Henderson are all simultaneously removed from the command loop does the charter, in its infinite wisdom, default planetary authority to the Head of the designated Primary Mission Directorate—currently filed under Xenology and Archaeology—ostensibly to safeguard the core scientific assets above all else." He didn't dignify the academic branch by naming its current, oblivious head. "A bureaucratic footnote, Kostin, buried so deep in the regulations it borders on the statistically fanciful. Your operational focus remains on me, then Rostova."

He paused then, a deliberate space left for acknowledgement, or perhaps dissent. From Kostin's perspective, standing at the dusty threshold of an alien tunnel, the message landed with jarring weight. Argus fine. Agamemnon odd. Main fleet massive, early, silent, but using our codes. The facts were clear, if deeply irregular. But invoking full emergency succession protocols based solely on this? Reciting the chain of command all the way down past Henderson to the Archaeology Directorate? Raith's response felt wildly disproportionate to the confirmed data... unless he genuinely anticipated the entire PCMA command structure here evaporating over what was, currently, just a monumental scheduling and communications failure. Was this extreme caution, paranoia, or did Raith possess threat intelligence he wasn't sharing?

A cautious, professional scepticism surfaced. "Sir," Kostin's voice came back over the secure link, carefully modulated. "Understood regarding the unauthorised arrival, the scale, and the need for extreme caution. However, invoking full succession protocols down to Directorate level based primarily on irregular arrival timing and non-communication... it seems a significant escalation at this stage. Are there additional specific threat indicators driving this assessment?"

Raith's reply was immediate, cool, and final, offering no further purchase. "Procedure dictates key personnel are briefed on contingency hierarchies under Directive 77Alpha, Kostin." His voice was flat, impartial. "My judgment identifies you as key personnel. Consider yourself briefed."

The implicit order to cease questioning was clear. Raith shifted back to immediate tasks. "Your priority is securing the," He paused whilst he considered his pronunciation, "Wahlsanga site. Consolidate your position, thoroughly assess that subterranean access point and any potential vulnerabilities it presents. Report any significant findings or anomalies directly to me via this secure channel only. Maintain absolute discretion regarding the fleet's unscheduled, unauthorised, and currently uncommunicative status. Control information flow tightly among your team and any local personnel. We manage this as a protocol crisis and potential security incident, not," he paused fractionally, "as anything more definitive. Yet."

"Understood, Sir," Kostin acknowledged, the formal assent masking his internal reservations about Raith's judgment.

"Maintain your position. Report hourly unless significant developments occur. Raith out." He terminated the connection without ceremony.

Raith watched the link vanish from his console. Kostin's scepticism was predictable, almost required by the man's nature. *Let him question internally,* Raith thought, *it keeps him sharp.* The Director allowed himself a fractional smile, not of warmth, but of complex calculation. He focused again on his console, pulling up not the fleet data, but the detailed command structures of Commander Rostova and the personnel files of Dr. Julian Voss. Assessing weak points in the chain, optimising contingency variables and managing the potential chaos. *This is the game*, he thought, and finally, it was almost stimulating.

Chapter 17. Part 3.

The secure connection severed, leaving an echo of Raith's chillingly calm voice in Rayk Kostin's auditory implants. He stood motionless for a long moment at the newly breached entrance to the Wahlsanga Metro Station, the stale, ancient air flowing past him, carrying the scent of undisturbed dust. Nearby, the beams from Voss's and Renata's helmet lights sliced into the profound darkness of the platform beyond, revealing ghostly outlines of pillars and the faint glimmer of trackways disappearing into the tunnel. Their low voices murmured observations about the platform numbering glyphs, blissfully unaware of the conversation Rayk had just concluded.

His mind raced, trying to compartmentalise the data. *Emergency succession protocols in full succession to the base level? Based only on this? Was Raith paranoid or deliberately manufacturing a crisis?* Had the isolation and pressure of this command finally cracked his legendary composure?

The override attack Raith had used on him was a cold testament to the Director's capacity for ruthless, pre-emptive action. Or was there something else? Did Raith possess some fragment of intelligence, some insight into this specific fleet or the forces behind its deployment, that painted a far more dangerous picture than the raw data suggested? The sheer ambiguity left far too many variables uncontrolled, a situation inherently dangerous regardless of the fleet's true intent.

He pushed the circling thoughts momentarily aside. Questioning Raith further was going to be unproductive. His immediate duty lay here: secure this access point, protect the scientists and gather local intelligence. He ran a quick internal assessment. The local team's readiness, potential site vulnerabilities, and the obvious tactical liabilities presented by Voss and Renata were absorbed in their work. Protecting them and whatever lay down that tunnel, was paramount.

He found a moment, while Voss and Renata were engrossed in deploying atmospheric sensors further onto the platform, to initiate a discreet internal query to his AS partner. No subvocalization was needed; the command flowed directly through his neural interface.

'AI,' Rayk projected the thought, keeping his external expression neutral. 'Status update. Director Raith has invoked emergency protocols, citing irregular fleet arrivals. High probability of system instability noted.' He paused, focusing on the more personal threat. 'Regarding the override command Raith utilised previously... have you analysed potential countermeasures or identified vulnerabilities in that specific back-channel protocol?'

The AS's response wasn't instantaneous data this time; there was a fractional lag, a sense of processing complex, perhaps restricted, information. The internal 'voice' remained clinical, precise, yet maybe carried a new shade of... consideration? 'Analysis ongoing, User Kostin. The override utilised a Level-Zero encrypted command routed through a deprecated diagnostic pathway, bypassing standard security layers. Direct blocking is currently impossible without compromising core system stability.' A pause. 'However, analysis suggests potential mitigation strategies involving predictive buffering of unauthorised command signals or re-routing processing focus during identified intrusion attempts. Probability of success: 42%. Further analysis requires access to restricted

The Xenologist

system architecture logs currently firewalled above your security clearance.'

'So no then?' Rayk projected to the AS. 'For now,' but watch this space' came back the surprisingly informal reply from the AS. Not projecting now, he thought: Now where did that come from?

At least, he felt reassured that the AS was actively working on it. In doing so, was it exceeding its standard design remit by suggesting strategies involving restricted data? Or was it simply executing contingency programming? Could his AS evolve as its personality seemed to be doing after his disablement? 'Continue analysis, prioritise non-invasive mitigation options,' Rayk instructed. 'Report any progress.'

Acknowledged. Prioritising analysis of predictive buffering protocols.' The connection went quiescent, leaving Rayk with the lingering sense that his AS was perhaps more than just sophisticated code. It was actively seeking solutions to protect him from Raith.

He shut down the internal display as Voss called out, "Rayk, atmospherics look stable. Standard subterranean trace elements, CO_2 slightly elevated near the tunnel mouth, consistent with your earlier readings, but well within breathable limits. No active bio-signatures detected on the immediate platform."

Rayk acknowledged with a nod, pushing the external threat analysis to a background monitoring process within his implants. He straightened up, projecting professional composure. "Understood. Let's proceed to the platform, then. Standard exploration protocols will be in place, checking for structural integrity near the edges. Stay aware of your surroundings." He moved forward, his hand resting lightly on the grip of his sidearm, his senses hyper-alert, scanning the vast, shadowed space.

The platform was gigantic, built on a scale that dwarfed human dimensions. Polished dark stone underfoot was gritted with millennia of dust. Massive, fluted pillars, similar in style to those in Petropolis but heavier, more functional, supported the cavernous roof high above, lost in darkness beyond the reach of their lights. Faint, flickering strips of emergency lighting embedded in the ceiling cast an erratic, unreliable glow, making shadows seem to dance and writhe. Voss and Renata moved immediately towards the nearest platform edge, examining the painted signs bearing single glyphs that Rayk assumed designated the four distinct track lines.

"Platform designations," Renata murmured, scanning one with her datapad. "Glyphs are consistent with basic numerical sequences, likely 1 through 4. Simple, logical. But, which one is platform 1?"

Rayk, behind her, wryly said, "That's why they number them. Because without the numbers you can't know".

Renata gave him a sarcastic look before Voss, who had knelt further along, called "Renata, Rayk." He was brushing dust away from the floor near the platform edge. Look at this." He directed his light downwards. Where they might have expected complex magnetic levitation conduits or energised plates, there was something startlingly simple: two parallel lines of dark, ferrous metal, like conventional rails, embedded smoothly into the platform substrate, running alongside the edge before disappearing into the yawning blackness of the main tunnel.

Renata said, "Yes. They go all the way along. We thought they were basically rails, but flat with no flange?"

"Appears so," Voss confirmed, running a gloved hand along the cool metal. "Just flat ferrous metal. Not powered, I reckon. There are no power lines to anything substantial. They are remarkably well-preserved. Minor oxidation only." He stood up, looking down the tunnel where the rails vanished. "This changes things. It implies that the levitation technology, if they used it, was entirely contained within the train units themselves. The infrastructure is simpler. More robust?"

"Or older?" Renata mused. "A different technological phase? Or perhaps just more suited to heavy freight if this was primarily a transport hub?" They were instantly absorbed, the mystery of the rails eclipsing the momentary tension of the fleet briefing, their minds alight with fresh data points and archaeological implications.

Rayk watched them for a moment, leaning against a massive pillar. He saw their intense focus, the way they leaned closer together, pointing, speculating, lost in the intellectual puzzle presented by two strips of ancient metal. Their absorption was total, almost childlike in its purity. They were like scholars deciphering a lost manuscript while oblivious to the approaching sounds of cannon fire just over the horizon.

The weight of the knowledge he carried, the potential catastrophe Raith had outlined, felt suddenly immense, isolating. He was the shield, the designated watcher, responsible for these brilliant, focused minds who depended entirely on the structures of command and security structures he now had reason to believe were compromised or operating under flawed assumptions. A flicker of something stirred within him, possibly protective instinct? Grudging respect for their unwavering dedication? They were vulnerable, utterly reliant on the thin shell of PCMA order he represented.

Meanwhile, light-years away in conceptual distance but only seconds later in time, back in his silent, climate-controlled office, Director Desmond Raith methodically continued his preparations. He navigated to a deeper, seldom-accessed system layer, one requiring multiple biometric and cryptographic authentications. The interface shifted, colours darkening, symbols becoming more stark, more final. With the same dispassionate precision that he might use to approve a resource transfer, Raith inputted the command string.

"Initiate Protocol Umbra. authorisation Raith-Omega."

A simple confirmation light glowed steady green on his console. Protocol Umbra—the ultimate contingency, the final erasure, the denial of assets to any and all unsanctioned entities—was now armed and awaiting trigger conditions. Raith felt nothing. No satisfaction, no dread, no sense of gravity. It was merely the next logical step in managing the escalating variables. He swivelled his chair slightly, gazing impassively at the schematic of Petropolis's primary subterranean power grid displayed on a side screen, perhaps calculating the energy draw required should Umbra need full execution. Just another problem to solve.

Back in the echoing silence of the Wahlsanga Metro Station, Rayk pushed away from the pillar. Voss and Renata were still animatedly discussing the implications of the ferrous rails, hypothesising about engine designs and power sources. "Shall we proceed further down the platform?" Voss asked, looking towards the main tunnel entrance. "See if there are any station control rooms or waiting areas?"

Rayk nodded, his expression unreadable. "Stay alert. Check floor stability as we go. "He took the lead, his boots crunching softly on the thick layer of dust, his flashlight beam cutting a swathe through the oppressive darkness that stretched down the tunnel towards the unseen Depot. He listened to the scientists behind him, their voices echoing slightly, filled with the thrill of discovery as they continued to discuss the simple ferrous rails. His own mind remained a tightly controlled space, assessing the immediate environment while the larger uncertainties waited, coiled like predators in the silence between stars.

Just as they took the first steps past the platform edge into the tunnel proper, a subtle notification shimmered into existence at the periphery of his internal vision. A non-urgent update from his AS.

"Analysis of predictive buffering protocols ongoing. Simulation against known override signature indicates potential mitigation efficacy increased to 51.2%. Refining heuristics."

A fractional increase. Not certainty, not safety, but… progress. A small, internal adjustment against one specific, known threat in a situation suddenly filled with vast, unknown variables. The weight of responsibility felt marginally, almost imperceptibly, less absolute for a single heartbeat. Then the darkness of the tunnel swallowed the light from the platform entrance behind them.

Chapter 18. Part 1

The threshold of the Wahlsanga Metro Station felt like crossing into a sealed tomb. The air immediately lost the faint, metallic tang of the surface ruins, replaced by an absolute stillness and the bone-dry scent of millennia-old dust. Raymond Kostin took the lead, his powerful helmet lamp cutting a sharp cone through the oppressive darkness, Voss and Renata following closely behind, their own beams playing across the immense platform they had just left.

"Stay alert," Rayk repeated, his voice low but carrying easily in the profound silence. "Check floor stability as we go. Maintain visual contact."

His boots crunched softly on the thick layer of dust covering the floor beside the surprisingly simple ferrous rails. The silence here was different from the quiet corridors of Petropolis; it wasn't the calm of solid rock, but the heavy, breathless quiet of a place utterly cut off from time and life. Even the faint hum from their suit systems seemed offensively loud. High above, the cavernous roof was lost to shadow, but faint, impossibly ancient emergency lights flickered intermittently along the distant tunnel walls, casting vast, unreliable shadows that seemed to twist and pulse at the edge of vision, playing tricks on the eye.

They moved cautiously down the slight incline leading from the platform edge into the main tunnel. The scale was immediately apparent—the tunnel was easily wide enough and high enough to accommodate vehicles far larger than any standard human train. The smooth, dark walls curved upwards, seamless and featureless except for occasional recessed panels, likely for maintenance access, their covers filmed with undisturbed grime.

"Incredible engineering," Voss murmured, running his light along the curve of the wall. "No visible joints, no reinforcement structures apparent. Whatever composite material this is, its tensile strength must be enormous."

Renata paused by one of the recessed panels, scanning it with her datapad. "Picking up some glyphs etched beneath the dust layer... maintenance warnings? Access codes?" The datapad screen flickered with probabilities. "Too fragmented. The AS flags potential matches for 'system' or 'conduit' based on the 'Ravona' glyph, but context is minimal." She sighed softly. "We'd need weeks just to properly document this tunnel alone."

They continued onward, the twin lines of the ferrous rails gleaming faintly under their lights, unwavering guides into the blackness. After perhaps fifty metres, they encountered the first sign of disorder in the form of a scattering of debris across the tracks. Not major structural collapse, but smaller pieces of ceiling composite, shards of broken lighting fixtures, and drifts of finer rubble, perhaps shaken loose by distant tremors over countless centuries or maybe related to the sealing blast near the entrance. They picked their way through it carefully.

Further on, Voss pointed his light towards the base of the tunnel wall. "Look here." Strange, dark stains marked the rock, spreading outwards from beneath a ventilation grille set low near the floor. Nearby lay desiccated, almost mummified remains – small, multi-legged creatures, disturbingly unidentifiable, alongside brittle fragments of what might have been fungal growth, now grey and lifeless.

"Consistent with the CO_2 and organic readings Rayk got," Renata observed, crouching to scan the remains without touching them. "Organic decay, sealed in. Some kind of native subterranean fauna that got trapped when they sealed the tunnel, perhaps? Or maybe remnants of whatever 'vermin infestation' Rayk speculated about." The air here carried a faint, dry mustiness overlaying the deep dust scent.

Rayk scanned the area with his multi-spectrum sensors. "Bio-signatures are completely inert. Whatever this was, it died a very long time ago. No active biological hazards detected." He kept his light moving, sweeping the tunnel ahead, his focus firmly on potential threats, though his mind briefly registered the data point – organic life had been here, sealed away with the station.

They pressed on, the only sound their breathing and the soft crunch of their boots. The sheer uniformity of the tunnel began to feel hypnotic, disorienting. The flickering emergency lights seemed to pulse in rhythm with Rayk's own heartbeat, a disconcerting synchronicity. He found himself subtly tracking Voss and Renata in his peripheral vision, acutely aware of his role as protector, the weight of Raith's ambiguous warning a constant background hum beneath his tactical assessment of the immediate environment. He allowed his AS to continue refining the buffer protocols against Raith's override, a silent, internal preparation against a threat far removed from this ancient dust.

After what felt like an age but was likely only twenty minutes, covering perhaps half a kilometre, the character of the tunnel began to change. Voss, slightly ahead now, stopped. "Hold up."

Rayk and Renata came alongside him. The single, massive tunnel they had been following was undeniably widening, the ceiling arching even higher. Ahead, the oppressive darkness seemed less absolute, disturbed by a faint, almost imperceptible luminescence filtering from around a final, wide curve defined by a colossal supporting archway. Faint structural lines suggested multiple track junctions or a convergence point just beyond the bend.

"The Depot cavern?" Renata breathed, her voice hushed with anticipation.

Rayk, understanding Voss's halt request, consulted his scanner. "Lidar confirms the main tunnel terminates approximately fifty metres ahead, around that archway." He added, interpreting the readings, "Beyond that point, echo returns drop significantly, suggesting a major void – the Depot cavern."

Voss took a step forward, his beam probing the space ahead. "The architecture is shifting. See those branching structures? Support arches for a larger roof span?"

They advanced slowly towards the archway, anticipation building. As they neared the massive stone structure, the faint luminescence ahead intensified fractionally. They rounded the curve but stopped short.

Before them wasn't an immediate, wide-open vista, but rather a heavy, partially lowered blast door or bulkhead, constructed from the same dark composite as the tunnel walls. It was immense, designed to seal this access point completely. The bottom of the door looked as if it had jammed whilst falling onto rubble that had spilt in from the other side of the door, leaving a half metre gap from the floor in the final moments before closure. Its surface was thick with dust, undisturbed for millennia.

Rayk moved to the door and shone a flashlight on it. Voss stepped forward, bent down and shone his light under the door. There was nothing visible in the beam except a few metres of dusty, but otherwise empty floor.

As he knelt to crawl under, Voss said, "Sorry, Rayk. I have to insist. Voss expected and was prepared for an argument, but to his surprise, Rayk demurred and with a pragmatic expression, gestured to Voss to go first.

Voss, still kneeling before the gap, looked back for a moment, up to Renata, her eyes wide, fixed intently on him. He ducked lower and crawled under the door, crossed the threshold and rose to his feet. Some proximity sensor, still functioning after aeons, in an incredible feat of 'Architect' engineering, diverted power from the vast, mysterious underground atomic batteries undoubtedly buried beneath the city. Ancient though they were, they still had enough charge to partially illuminate the cavern beyond.

Lights flickered and pulsed along immense ceiling arches far above and down colossal support pillars marching away into the distance. It was dim, but enough. Veins of crystalline quartz embedded in the far walls caught the sudden glow, scattering dazzling pinpricks of coloured light across the huge space like disturbed constellations.

Dust motes danced and glittered in the light filtering under the heavy door. Far below them on the cavern floor within, arranged in neat, silent rows upon multiple tracks, sat six dust-shrouded forms of the Architect trains—nine sleeping behemoths.

The others followed Voss under the door and stood up and raised their heads in wonder, gazing out over the unexpectedly illuminated, glittering expanse of the Wahlsanga Depot. The silence felt even heavier now, broken only by the faint hum perhaps emanating from the door's ancient mechanism or the newly activated lights.

Rayk, still absorbing the scale of the find, broke the silence, not with awe, but with his usual dry pragmatism. "Well," he said, glancing back at the ancient bulkhead, "guess I'll need to order some joists and get this door properly jacked up."

Chapter 18. Part 2.

Dusk bled across the sky above the Great Gorge. The relentless glare of Talemora's star softened, painting the high, thin clouds in bruised shades of violet and orange before fading rapidly towards a deep indigo.

Here, on the sheltered stone ledge near the Sky-Arch Bridge's massive abutment, the complex, loamy perfumes of the gorge's alien vegetation mingled with the distant roar of unseen waterfalls. Tessara knelt beside D. Marinallis, checking the bandage on her forearm before offering him the last of their water captured from the sterile, UV-sterilised parts of the river below.

Marinallis had rested while the sun dipped below the gorge rim, the Designer's unexpected resilience allowing for a good measure of recovery. Another application of the translucent salve had again worked its near-miraculous effect on his sunburn. While he was still gaunt and weakened, the sharp, feverish edge of his earlier delirium looked to Tessara like it had subsided. His eyes, when they opened to meet hers, were clear, lucid, holding an unnerving depth of ancient weariness mixed with grim resolve.

"The light fails," Marinallis observed, his voice raspy but steady. He accepted the water flask, taking a careful sip. "We must cross soon."

"Can you make it?" Tessara asked, studying him critically. The bridge was a colossal structure, a testament to 'Designer' taste and ambition, but millennia of neglect and the planet's harsh climate would have taken their toll. It would be exposed, treacherous, especially in the encroaching darkness.

Marinallis gave a faint, dry cough that seemed to shake his thin frame. "Needs must, Curator." He handed the flask back. "Varinn... any sign?"

Tessara shook her head, the lie tasting bitter. "Not yet. The storm was severe. He'll be heading for Vasantha, same as us. We'll find him there." She hoped it sounded convincing.

Marinallis seemed to accept it, perhaps because he had no alternative. He shifted, leaning back against the damp rock, his gaze distant for a moment. "He understands the stakes," he murmured, more to himself than to her. "He knows why this," his hand made a weak gesture towards the pack where Varinn had carried the MET Com12, though it wasn't physically present with them now, "must not endure."

"Do you really trust these newcomers?" Tessara said, finding a new affinity with Marinallis as the reality of their isolation began to make her seek a bond with the old Designer. "Our interests align and one must not judge—".

"A datapad by its screen saver." She smiled and finished for him.

After a pause, "You mentioned the Fumigators," Tessara prompted gently, seizing the chance while he was lucid. "The group Carrik served, the fanatics in the ruin... they seemed to think this device was some kind of key, something to soothe the star, they said? Appease it?"

A harsh, grating sound escaped Marinallis, a single bark of humourless laughter. "Fools. Blind fools, grasping at patterns in the fire." He looked directly at Tessara, his eyes intense, burning with a sudden, urgent need to make her understand. He saw her slightly sceptical expression and raised eyebrows and chuckled slightly. "OK, Tessara. That kind of language doesn't wash with a grounded Human like you, I get it". He sighed and shook his head. "They see the burning sky and our world's slow decay, yet blame the wrong cause. They are not even consistent amongst themselves. Some factions believe that we, the Designers, have angered the Mother Star by our own pride. Others believe we directly manipulate the star for nefarious purposes. I am not sure which is the most absurd."

Marinallis's voice dropped to a conspiratorial whisper. "It wasn't hubris, Pilot, not entirely. It was exploration. Pushing boundaries. The MET technology used by Varinn's device doesn't just communicate. It fundamentally alters the local expression of mass and energy. It resonates with the underlying fields." He gestured vaguely upwards. "It pokes the laws of reality in ways that are very noticeable."

"Noticeable to whom?" Tessara asked, captivated despite the growing unease.

"To the Regulation System." Marinallis paused, his brow furrowed as he sought an analogy. "Think of the universe not as empty space, but as a finely tuned mechanism that, without interference, ensures things happen in a certain way."

Marinallis thought, *She has it. She's a bright one, this human.* "The universe itself, by design, prevents cause and effect from happening the wrong way around and in doing so, ensures time flows correctly. But, there are ways to disrupt that mechanism."

"So what happens when it's threatened?" Varinn asked, his voice low and intense. "What is this 'correction'?"

Marinallis continued, "So that's why there are 'Fumigators'. A species, or maybe not a species, we are still not sure. They are much more attuned to this mechanism than we seem to be. They have taken it upon themselves to be a cosmic immune response. They detect technologies that risk destabilising the fundamental constants, the very fabric that allows existence."

His gaze was sharp, piercing. "These technologies cause resonances. They attract the attention of the Fumigators like blood attracts predators. It signals a dangerous deviation that must be corrected." He paused, letting the weight of it settle before delivering the final blow. "Our MET technology. The device you carry. That is what causes the resonance. It's what they hunt."

Tessara tried to reconcile this staggering concept with the realities she knew—the ongoing, brutal war with the K'Tharr, the harsh environment of her home planet, Talemora, that had driven civilisation underground millennia ago. "This correction. The Fumigators, are they fighting us alongside the K'Tharr? Is that why the war goes so badly in some sectors?"

Marinallis waved a dismissive, frail hand. "The K'Tharr war? Curator, that is a conventional conflict, however advanced. Brutal, yes. Costly, yes. But ultimately comprehensible and manageable. We have the technological edge, we contained them for the last thousand years and ultimately, we would have prevailed."

"Then why?"

He raised a hand to stop the question and leaned forward, his eyes holding hers. "The reason we abandoned our Home, the true reason this whole system is forfeit, has nothing to do with the K'Tharr battlefield gains or losses. It's the Fumigators."

"But, the Fumigators, aren't they just ancient history? Legends? The reason for the Burn, perhaps, but millennia ago?" Tessara voiced the common understanding, the official narrative likely taught even to human allies. "We adapted to the star's changes, moved underground..."

"We adapted to the symptom Tessara," Marinallis interrupted, his voice urgent. "And yes, the Fumigators were responsible for the Burn. They adjusted our star's output as their first corrective measure, punishing the initial disturbance from our early MET development. For ages, we didn't fully grasp the connection. We assumed the increased UV was stellar mechanics, a terrible coincidence. We built our cities beneath the rock, contained the tell-tale ripples in reality, and thought the danger, whatever its source, had passed or stabilised."

He drew a ragged breath. "We were wrong. We understand the link now. The MET tech itself is the lure. And continued operation, even shielded, maintains a level of resonance that keeps this system flagged on their cosmic map."

"So why did we leave it so long?" Tessara pressed. "If they acted millennia ago, and the situation seemed stable…"

"Because the equation has changed," Marinallis said grimly. "The K'Tharr. Our intelligence was certain. They have begun deploying their own MET FTL communications. Crude devices compared to ours, unstable, loud. And generating worse, more reckless disruptions of the fields of the Universe. But this violation. Brute force FTL. This is a whole new level."

His eyes bored into hers. "Imagine this sector, Tessara. Already marked by our past transgressions, now echoing with the K'Tharr's careless technological broadcasts. The Fumigators, well, they aren't known for surgical precision when cleansing an infestation. They detected our resonance and turned up the star. What happens when they detect both our persistent signature and the K'Tharr's noisy new experiments? They won't differentiate. They will simply… escalate the fumigation."

He left the implication hanging. "We have to sever all ties. Get clear before the K'Tharr's actions trigger a response that sterilises this entire region beyond recovery. That's why Varinn's device, the most advanced MET Comms unit, must be neutralised at Vasantha. It's our final act of severing the connection, erasing the most potent signature before we depart."

He gestured vaguely towards the unseen horizon. "If it is still on schedule, the Newcomers' fleet should be making its final approach to orbit. They understand the imperative. Their ships offer the only confirmed passage out for the handful of us remaining that cannot, or do not wish to go to, your Ancestral Home Planet, Va'hari". Tessara looked concerned for a moment. Marinallis took note and with a slight smile said, "I asked the ship going to Eluvara to delay departure. I believe you were planning to continue your archaeology career, Tessara."

Marinallis gathered his strength, pushing himself upright against the rock face. "Time to go". Tessara, with some relief at the news, rose, checking her own gear before helping the frail Designer to his feet. His determination was a palpable force despite his physical weakness.

As the last sliver of orange light vanished behind the western gorge rim, leaving only the cold silver of starlight and the rising moon, they moved together out of the relative shelter of the ledge, towards the immense, waiting teardrop-shaped arch of the Sky-Arch Bridge.

It spanned the chasm like a bone-white rib of some colossal beast, ancient and awe-inspiring in the faint moonlight. Its surface, pitted and cracked by time, seemed to absorb the dim light. Missing sections of the low parapet were stark invitations to the mist-filled void below, where the river's roar echoed as a deep, guttural rumble. A cold wind swept up the gorge, whining through the bridge's aged structure.

Tessara stepped onto the bridge first, her boot finding purchase on the surprisingly solid, if uneven, composite. She offered Marinallis her arm, and he gripped it with surprising strength. Slowly, deliberately, they began their crossing.

Each step demanded focus. The wind buffeted them, a constant, unseen pressure. Marinallis leaned heavily, his breathing shallow and rapid, each upward step towards the bridge's high point an evident struggle. Tessara supported him, her own muscles straining, her eyes fixed on the apex of the immense, irregular arch looming ahead against the moonlit clouds—the point of maximum exertion before the descent to the far side. Vasantha, safety, her life lay beyond that peak.

They finally reached it—the highest point of the span, exposed to the full force of the gorge wind. Marinallis sagged against the low parapet, fighting for breath, seemingly utterly spent. He coughed; a wracking sound snatched away by the gale. He looked back, deliberately, into the darkness towards the Weir where Varinn remained.

"He has it, Tessara," Marinallis rasped, his voice thin but carrying with intensity over the wind's howl. "The Comms Unit. It must reach Vasantha. It must be neutralised there." His grip tightened painfully on her arm, his thin frame belying surprising strength. Eyes of ancient lineage and experience locked onto hers, demanding her focus despite the precarious surroundings. "Without that device, this is all for nothing. My departure would be a dereliction of duty. The risk to all..." He let the sentence hang, heavy with unspoken cosmic consequence.

Tessara stared back into the blackness where Varinn was lost. The device Marinallis deemed critical to reality's stability was back there, with her comrade. But Vasantha lay ahead, down the slope of the bridge. Marinallis seemed remarkably stable all of a sudden. Turning back now, from the highest point, felt like an insurmountable effort. Abandoning him here tore a hole in her conscience that seemed disproportionate to the crime. But, continuing without the device felt like utter failure, a betrayal of Varinn and this overwhelming responsibility Marinallis had laid upon her.

She looked from the darkness behind to the frail Designer beside her, then to the downward slope of the bridge leading towards Vasantha ahead. An impossible triangulation of duty, loyalty, and survival. The wind tore at her cloak, mirroring the conflict tearing at her resolve. She was frozen; the peak was the point of no return.

Marinallis watched her face, his expression unreadable in the dim light. He saw the agony of indecision, the calculation of impossible choices. He let the silence stretch, letting the weight settle fully upon her. Then, after a moment that seemed an eternity, he straightened slightly, pulling his arm free from her supportive grip.

"The worst is past," he stated, his voice now quite strong, though still breathless. He gestured down the slope towards Vasantha. "It's downhill from here. I can manage the descent to the far tower alone. Slowly, perhaps, but I will make it."

He met her gaze, his expression hardening, the earlier frailty replaced by the authority of a commander giving a final, vital order.

"My survival is no longer the priority," he said, his voice low and intense. "What is important is the MET Comms unit. Varinn has it. He took the shortcut—the Weir, past the Pheonalla ruins. He will be wounded, hunted. You must go back for him, Tessara. Find him. Secure the device at all costs."

He took a single, deliberate step down the slope, his meaning absolute. He was not asking. He was commanding.

Tessara stood alone at the highest point of the arch, the wind whipping around her. Ahead, Marinallis and the promise of personal safety pulled away towards Vasantha. Behind her, in the darkness, lay Varinn, her duty, and the fate of their world. Her options, stark and terrible, had just run out.

Chapter 18. Part 3.

Stepping under the immense, jammed blast door was like passing from one age of the world into another. The air inside the Wahlsanga Depot lacked even the faint mustiness of the tunnel; it was utterly still, cold, and achingly dry, carrying only the scent of sterile dust that had lain undisturbed for epochs. The soft, ethereal blue-white light pulsing from the high ceiling arches and distant pillars, refracted by the quartz veins in the rock, cast the vast cavern in a dreamlike, crystalline luminescence.

They stood on a wide platform or walkway ringing the entrance, overlooking the main floor spread out below. Rayk immediately moved to scan the cavern with his broader sensors, establishing a perimeter baseline, while Voss and Renata were momentarily silenced by the scale of it all. Below them, stretching away into the glittering gloom, lay the tracks—multiple parallel sets of the same dark, ferrous rails they'd seen in the station.

And upon those tracks rested the trains.

Nine of them. Colossal machines, easily dwarfing any terrestrial equivalent, their sleek forms hinting at speeds Voss could scarcely imagine. They were rendered monolithic by the thick, uniform blanket of pale dust that coated every surface, softening their lines, muting their original colours. They sat in perfect, silent rows, like a fleet inexplicably frozen in time, waiting for a departure call that never came.

"Nine..." Renata breathed, her voice hushed with awe, echoing slightly in the vastness. "A whole depot, preserved."

"Let's get a closer look," Voss urged, already moving towards a wide ramp leading down from their entry platform to the main floor level. Rayk gave a curt nod, indicating he'd cover their descent, his attention sweeping the shadowed upper reaches of the cavern and the dark mouths of other tunnels potentially leading off from the main space.

Down on the main floor, the true size of the trains was overwhelming. Voss ran his gloved hand along the dusty flank of the nearest one; the underlying material felt impossibly smooth, cool, some form of advanced ceramic composite perhaps. There were no visible seams, no obvious propulsion units, just elegant, unbroken lines beneath the shroud of dust.

As they moved cautiously down the line, examining the first train, Renata pointed towards its base, near where immense, unseen mechanisms must have interfaced with the rails. "Julian, look."

Affixed to the train's chassis at several key structural points were blocks of a dense, greyish plastic-composite material. They looked surprisingly mundane, almost crude against the train's sleekness. Wires, or shielded conduits, snaked out from these blocks, trailing towards the ground or connecting to a larger trunk line running alongside the tracks.

Renata approached one block, deploying her detailed material scanner. The device whirred softly. "The composition is very unusual," she murmured, reading the display.

"If I had to guess," Rayk said, I'd instinctively say 'Plastique'. Wired for demolition".

Renata placed a probe into the block. It was hard and the needle did not penetrate far, desiccated with age. She looked at her scanner's readout. "Complex polymer matrix, yes, appears stable. But the isotopic ratios are completely non-standard."

She tapped the display. "Significant enrichment in several unstable heavy isotopes not found in any known PCMA ordnance. The energy potential is... enormous, theoretically. Or perhaps," she mused, glancing at the train's hull, "they're designed to initiate a specific reaction with the hull composite itself? A targeted material degradation beyond simple blast effects?" She looked up at Voss, puzzled. "Advanced demolition tech, certainly, but working on principles we don't fully understand."

Voss said, "The animals don't like it. Look, this wiring insulation's been gnawed back to the socket. It's probably a standard oil-based plastic. The wires corroded to stains on the surface of the train here, and where there is no contact, and presumably no dissimilar metal corrosion, it survives, albeit very thin. But the plastic – the animals don't touch it. They are telling us that it is totally unnatural for their environment."

They moved along the first eight trains. The pattern was identical on each: charges carefully placed, wired into a network leading back towards the cavern entrance. The wiring itself looked functional, if ancient—shielded alloy conduits, with cracked or powdered insulation, the exposed metal beneath sometimes displaying the fine white or greenish patina of extreme age, leaving faint stains on the train chassis. Everything appeared ready, primed for a simultaneous, annihilating detonation.

Then they reached the sixth train, the last one in its row, perhaps set slightly apart. Here, the pattern broke. The plastic-composite charges were affixed to the chassis, identical to the others, but the wiring was only partially complete. Conduits lay disconnected, their termination points exposed. A coil of unused wiring lay on the dusty floor nearby, alongside several tools of non-human design – sleek, ergonomic devices left exactly where they had been dropped.

"They stopped," Voss stated, the conclusion obvious but profound. He knelt, examining the carelessly discarded tools, the dangling wires. "Right here. Mid-task."

"But why?" Renata wondered aloud, scanning the incomplete wiring. "They prepared the other eight meticulously. This one... It's like they were interrupted halfway through the job." She looked around the vast, silent cavern. "What could possibly have interrupted a systematic demolition process on this scale?" The evidence pointed not to sloppiness, but to sudden, overwhelming haste, a process abandoned under duress. The silence of the Depot seemed to deepen, thick with unanswered questions.

Nobody had an answer. Voss, sensing that something ought to be said, observed, "So these demi-gods weren't perfect after all". His voice softening, "Almost human".

Chapter 18. Part 4.

Consciousness returned not gently, but like breaching the surface after a deep, suffocating dive. Varinn gasped, the cool, damp air of the Great Gorge sharp in his lungs. He lay amongst the slick, dark rocks near the Stepping Stone Weir, the constant roar of the fast-moving water filling his ears. Disorientation warred with ingrained survival instincts. Pain flared briefly from his side – the memory of Carrik's boot knife sliding home – but it subsided almost immediately to a dull, pulling ache. He cautiously probed the area beneath his ripped tunic; the flesh felt tender, newly knitted, the wound already sealed by processes beyond simple biology. His Designers' resilience, augmented or inherent, had done its work, though a profound weariness lingered deep in his bones.

He sat up slowly, muscles protesting and his head swimming. He scanned the vicinity. Dawn was breaking, painting the eastern rim of the gorge in pale gold, though down here shadows still clung stubbornly. There was no sign of Carrik. Pools of dried blood – some his, some likely Carrik's—stained the rocks, a testament to the brutal, close-quarters fight. But the augmented soldier himself was gone. Dead? Retreated gravely wounded? Varinn didn't know, and scanning the area revealed no body. For now, the immediate threat was removed.

He found his discarded pack wedged between two boulders where he'd dropped it. His hand closed around the familiar, unsettling angles of the MET Comms Unit within. It felt inert, yet carried an undeniable presence, a weight far exceeding its physical mass. The mission Marinallis had entrusted to him now rested on him alone, its urgency grown, its burden multiplied.

Tessara. Marinallis. They would be heading Southwest initially, then North, along the Great Gorge for the Sky-Arch Bridge. They would be hours ahead, although slowed by the Designer's condition. His first instinct was a raw, desperate urge: *Follow them. Find Tessara.* But the weight of his responsibility to the mission was unbearable. Getting the MET Comms Unit neutralised in Vasantha was the absolute priority. Retracing their steps meant keeping the device exposed for longer, delaying its secure disposal. Worse, carrying the device, he would be a beacon drawing pursuit towards them, compromising their slower journey to safety.

He knew Tessara; she was capable and resourceful. Her priority would be getting Marinallis safely across the bridge and to Vasantha. His priority, now that he was separated and mobile, had to be the device itself. The mission demanded he take the most direct path to the neutralisation facility. *Tessara will understand,* he told himself. *She must get Marinallis to safety. I'll handle the device.*

Decision made, a grim certainty settling over him, Varinn stood, testing his footing on the slick rocks. He ignored the lingering ache in his side, the exhaustion pulling at him. He slung his pack securely, the MET Comms Unit nestled against his back, a constant, potent burden.

With a final glance towards the path leading upstream to the bridge, a silent acknowledgement of the comrades he was leaving behind. He didn't let himself imagine Tessara's face when he didn't arrive. He turned and began picking his way carefully across the treacherous stones of the Weir, heading downstream, alone, towards Vasantha and the uncertain fate of the device he carried.

.

Chapter 19. Part 1.

"Alright," Rayk said, his voice cutting through the quiet reverent awe, bringing the scientists back from pondering the sheer luck of the improbable survival of the treasures, to the needs of the present.

"The initial visual is established. But that jammed door and the state of the trains, something went wrong here. Systematically wrong." He gestured towards the nearest rows of behemoths slumbering on the tracks below. "Eight prepared for demolition, one left unfinished. Why?"

Renata nodded, her gaze already analytical. "The interruption. Whatever stopped them wiring that last train must be linked to why the demolition sequence for the others never fired." She looked back towards the tunnel entrance and the jammed blast door. "If the system was triggered, there should be evidence near a central control point, or along the main detonation lines."

"Let's trace it back," Voss agreed immediately. "The primary conduits for the charges seem to run parallel to the tracks, leading back towards the entrance area."

Leaving the breathtaking vista behind for the moment, they descended the ramp Rayk had scouted earlier, their boots raising small puffs of the ubiquitous pale dust on the main cavern floor. Moving with cautious purpose, they began following the thickest of the shielded conduits where it emerged from beneath the first train, tracing its path back along the immense row. The scale down here was even more imposing; the trains towered over them, their silent, dust-coated flanks like the sides of slumbering whales.

The main conduit, thick as a man's arm, ran in a shallow channel recessed into the floor alongside the primary track. It looked to be designed as a trunk line, likely intended to carry the initiating signal for the charges networked across multiple trains. They followed it metre by painstaking metre, their lights playing over its ancient, weathered surface.

As they neared the cavern entrance area, closer to the looming shadow of the partially lowered blast door, the floor became more uneven, littered with debris similar to that found in the tunnel – chunks of ceiling composite, twisted metal fragments. And then they saw it.

A colossal support pillar, one of the many marching down the cavern length, lay shattered near the entrance threshold, its base fractured, its main bulk collapsed diagonally across the floor. It must have fallen with cataclysmic force. Beneath the immense weight of the dark, composite stone lay the main detonation conduit they had been following. It wasn't merely damaged; it was decisively crushed, sheared through completely by the impact.

Voss directed his light onto the break and the surrounding rock. "Scorch marks," he pointed out, indicating blackened, heat-stressed areas on the fallen pillar and the floor nearby. "This collapse wasn't gradual decay; it was caused by a significant explosion right here, near the main entrance."

Renata knelt, scanning the severed conduit ends. "Clean break, cauterised by the heat of the blast... This has to be connected to whatever sealed the main Metro tunnel." She looked up, her eyes wide with realisation. "The explosion that blocked our way in... it must have happened before they could trigger the main demolition sequence for the trains. This collapse took out the command line."

Rayk examined the severed conduit dispassionately. "A single point of failure for the entire depot's demolition? Seems... unlike them. Usually, redundancy is built into everything at this level."

"Unless they were rushed," Voss mused, looking around at the evidence of destruction near the entrance versus the pristine state of the trains deeper within. "Maybe this entrance blast was the first step in a rapid, sequential demolition, but they didn't have time to wire redundant lines? Or they assumed this conduit was sufficiently protected?"

Renata stood up, dusting off her knees, her gaze fixed on the jammed blast door sealing the Metro tunnel. "They knew," she said softly, the implication chilling. "Whoever triggered that entrance blast, whoever oversaw this demolition... they would have known immediately that this trunk line was severed. The feedback diagnostics would have screamed failure." She looked around the silent, preserved Depot. "They didn't try to fix it. They didn't implement a backup plan. They just... finished sealing the tunnel from the other side and left this." She gestured towards the six silent trains. "Abandoned. Intact. Why? Unless..."

"Unless getting out, sealing the access completely, was more important than ensuring the destruction was complete," Voss finished, voicing the thought hanging between them. "They were running. Running hard from something they feared more than leaving six high-tech trains behind."

Chapter 19. Part 2.

The stark realisation that this entire hidden fleet, this snapshot of a civilisation's desperate end, owed its existence to the random chance of a falling pillar severing a single cable, hit them almost emotionally at first. It spoke volumes about the pressure the Architects were under, the haste that had forced them to abandon their usual meticulous redundancy. Driven by the need to understand what else might have been left behind in that final, frantic phase before the sealing, they turned their attention back from the entrance area, their lights sweeping towards the deeper shadows surrounding the sixth train, the place where the demolition work had faltered.

This end of the track felt subtly different. Dust lay just as thick, but beneath it were faint scuff marks inconsistent with their entry, and the precise arrangement of the other five trains gave way here to a slight sense of staging. Items gathered, not yet destroyed.

Beside the platform was an ornate alcove, carved from a pure white stone that seemed to glow with the soft lustre of alabaster, yet felt as hard as diamond to the touch. The team's instincts drew them closer. The team's instincts drew them closer. Behind a glass wall that fronted the alcove, what looked like an executive hospitality suite had been converted into an impromptu storage space, filled with sealed crates that were crudely wired for demolition.

As they approached the glass wall, their lights converged almost simultaneously on an unnatural shape half-concealed by one of the elegant pillars inside. It wasn't machinery; it was organic in its lines, yet still looking artificial. Cautiously, they approached, beams playing over something draped in the accumulated dust of millennia. Voss reached out tentatively, his gloved hand brushing away layers of the fine, pale powder.

The shape resolved into expertly carved stone, its sparkling surface as lustrous as the pillar behind it. More dust brushed away revealed a shoulder, then a slender arm, and then the undeniable contour of a face.

At first, Renata and Voss were calm about the find; their senses were overloaded by the discovery of the vast treasure trove. They both experienced the sensation of mistakenly thinking this was an ancient Roman or Greek temple on Earth. This was extra-terrestrial. They looked at each other in mutual understanding of the moment. They worked quickly but cautiously now, anticipation mounting, carefully clearing the accumulated grime.

A statue. Toppled onto its side, perhaps by the shock wave from the entrance blast, but largely intact save for one broken wrist. It lay leaning against the pillar's base, a silent, forgotten casualty. Life-sized, it depicted a being both familiar and profoundly alien. The figure was female, tall, with the extraordinary slenderness hinted at in the shape of the seats often found carved into stone or constructed of their fantastic alloys.

Her three-fingered hands were delicately rendered. One was raised before her face, its fingers slightly curled in what could be a beckoning gesture. Her other arm ended in a clean break at the wrist, and its detached hand lay in the dust near her hip, perfectly preserved. The fabric of her robes was a marvel of sculpture, clinging to her form with an impossible thinness, carved to be so fine as to be translucent. The head was tilted slightly, the aquiline nose and thin lips set in an expression of calm, detached wisdom, while the large, deep-set eyes seemed to gaze into eternity. The artistry was breathtaking, conveying serene authority and ancient intelligence.

Around the statue's base, wires were loosely, almost carelessly, wrapped—the same shielded conduits connected to the demolition charges on the trains. Several discarded canisters lay nearby, still giving off the faintest chemical signature of accelerant residue. She had been marked for oblivion along with the technology.

"My God…" Voss breathed, kneeling beside the statue, his light tracing the serene lines of the face. He instinctively reached out, stopping his fingers just short of touching the cool stone. "An Architect. The first true representation…"

Renata joined him, her awe palpable. "And they meant to destroy her," she murmured, scanning the material composition. "Erasing their history, their image." She looked around the vast, silent space. "What drove them to such lengths?"

Before the question could fully resonate, Rayk's light, methodically sweeping the shadowed area behind the pillar during their absorption, picked out something else. "There are crates back here." He announced quietly.

Behind the base of the plinth that the statue had obviously fallen from, were steps down to a darker, sunken floor area. Just out of sight, behind another support column, several large, sealed crates were placed in line, with more failed charges attached to them. They were utilitarian grey containers, crafted from a metallic alloy that felt unnaturally light when Renata tested the surface, yet seemed incredibly dense and tough. Complex, multi-layered glyphs, unlike the simpler functional signs elsewhere, were deeply etched into their sides.

"Part of the same disposal batch?" Voss wondered, moving closer to examine the intricate glyph patterns. "OK, let's set the excavation bot on the statue for now. She isn't going anywhere," Voss opened an equipment case that he was carrying and pulled out a laser pointer. He quickly outlined the statue with it and a small walking bot scampered out of the case and walked up to the statue. After a moment to survey the scene, it began slowly clearing the statue with tiny brushes and jets of air. A tiny airborne archaeology drone, listening to his words, realised this was its cue and moved forward to the statue and started video recording the whole procedure in 3D footage for posterity.

Satisfied the drones were doing their job safely, they turned their attention back to the crates. Renata leaned closer, running her scanner over the complex glyphs etched onto the nearest crate. "The structure is intricate, definitely not simple labels." She tapped her datapad, letting the AS analyse the forms purely for potential phonetic matches based on established vowel/consonant probabilities.

"The AS is suggesting possible phonetic sequences," she reported, sounding puzzled, "like… 'Katharr-el' Or this one, maybe 'Vorl-nak'? But the confidence intervals are incredibly low, less than 25%. And there's zero correlation with any functional context we have. It's just complex symbols for now." She tried the material scanner. "And completely shielded. Whatever's inside, whether it was specific or standard procedure, they wanted it kept private before demolition."

Voss gestured around the cavern, the sheer magnitude of it all settling in. Six intact ghost trains. A statue of their creator, marked for destruction. Sealed containers holding unknowable contents. "The scale of this…" he shook his head, his voice trailing off. "Documenting it will take decades."

Renata nodded. "We can't possibly survey this whole Depot manually in any reasonable time frame, especially given…" She didn't finish, but glanced towards

Rayk, acknowledging the security situation he'd outlined. "We need to deploy the survey drones en masse. Start systematic mapping and cataloguing while we focus on these immediate finds."

Voss agreed instantly. "For now, let's deploy the rest of the mini-drones we brought. Rayk, can you ask for clearance for surface transport of the larger excavation drones from Petropolis to be brought here as an immediate priority through Raith's office?"

"I'm sure that won't be a problem. I will prioritise that message when we get back to the surface".

Rayk unclipped two small, sophisticated drones from his utility belt, performing a quick systems check. "For now, you can connect your recording devices to my security drones." As Voss nodded and started making the connections, Renata readied a third from her own kit. With quiet efficiency, the three small machines lifted silently into the air, their internal lights blinking, their rotors emitting a barely audible hum. They ascended towards the high arches, then fanned out, beginning a pre-programmed grid pattern survey of the vast cavern, their own lights adding moving constellations to the dimly lit space.

With the drones handling the broader survey, the trio turned their focus back to the immediate trove. They stood for a moment in silence, contemplating the serene, toppled face of the Designer statue. Rayk, perhaps finding the quiet reverence less compelling than the others, broke the silence with his characteristic dry wit, nodding towards the statue.

"Well," he remarked, his voice echoing slightly, "if I were her, I wouldn't play hard to get."

To Voss's irritation, Renata laughed out loud. "I imagine she would think the same about us, Detective," she replied coolly, turning her attention back to scanning the glyphs on the nearest crate.

Renata's laughing approval of Rayk's attempt at levity felt jarring, even crass, against the moment of the profound discovery. *Am I being prudish? Jealous?* he wondered. A familiar flicker of social unease stirred. He pushed it aside, forcing his attention back to the crates Renata was examining.

Rayk seemed to sense the shift in mood. He surveyed the scene again, his tone more reflective as he added, "Still, finding all this now, the statue, crates, intact trains, it's quite the discovery right after your arrival, Doctor Voss." He kept his tone conversational and observational, but the timing was noted.

Before Voss could formulate a response to the implied 'convenience', Renata smoothly interjected, turning back to Rayk. "It's certainly remarkable what focused resources and perhaps fresh eyes can uncover, Detective," she said, her tone neutral but direct. "Makes one wonder about the pace, or perhaps the thoroughness, of previous survey efforts in this sector, doesn't it? Perhaps Director Raith had concerns about the 'plodders', as one might say, previously assigned here?"

She held his gaze for a beat, deftly deflecting the implication about Voss's timing by raising questions about past work, subtly planting a seed about prior inefficiency without making a direct accusation.

Renata's defence was not lost on Voss, making him feel somehow lighter. But even this moment was spoiled as he saw how quickly Renata had charmed Rayk. Seeing the connection between them spoiled the moment for him.

As Rayk met her look, then gave a slight, almost imperceptible nod, perhaps acknowledging the point or simply choosing not to pursue his line of thought further for now, he turned his attention back towards the main cavern, monitoring the progress of the drones on his wrist display, leaving the subtle tension Renata had diffused hanging momentarily in the ancient air.

Chapter 19. Part 3.

They stood gathered near the sixth train, caught in the penumbra between the monumental vehicle and the colossal support pillar against which the Designer statue rested. The beam of Voss's lamp traced the serene, dust-laden contours of the sculpted face, an image of the Architects preserved against their own apparent intentions. Renata knelt nearby, her scanner still attempting fruitlessly to penetrate the shielding of the nearest grey crate, its intricate glyphs defying easy interpretation. The sheer, improbable preservation, almost overwhelming, pressed upon them. The intact trains, the statue marked for oblivion yet surviving, the sealed containers holding unknowable contents, it all pressed upon them with a tangible weight. It was more than a discovery; it felt like stepping into a frozen moment at the precipice of a civilisation's self-erasure.

"They didn't just leave technology," Voss murmured, his voice hushed, almost reverent, echoing slightly in the vast, silent chamber. "They left their image, their identity. The one thing they displaced a whole planet's civilisation to eradicate"

Rayk Kostin watched the scientists lost in their profound absorption of the artefacts before them. He compared their focus on the past, the what, and the why to his own focus on the 'now' and the heightened alert due to the silent, unauthorised incoming Damoclesian fleet.

Intact trains, representing unknown but highly advanced transport technology, escalated the stakes. This was the kind of discovery that he knew Raith would want locked down instantly. *This isn't just archaeology. This is a security crisis, a hoard of unimaginable strategic value.*

There was, of course, a first-ever physical representation of the Aliens, offering priceless intelligence. A sealed cargo of unknown but sensitive nature, discovered now, in this hidden place. This wasn't merely archaeology. It was a potential security crisis, a hoard of unimaginable strategic value surfacing at the worst possible moment. Rayk's sense of duty told him that regardless of his dislike of Raith, the Director's need to know wasn't just procedural; it was absolute.

"Doctors," Rayk stated, his voice calm but firm, cutting cleanly through their preoccupation. "The significance of this find, its potential implications, all require immediate notification." He met their momentarily startled gazes. "I need to send a priority Level-1 secure sit-rep to Director Raith. Now. Just the essential facts – location secured, nature of the discovery."

Voss, inevitably drawn back to the statue, stood up nodding slowly, the awe momentarily replaced by the practical understanding of protocol. Renata glanced up from her scanner, her expression thoughtful, perhaps connecting Rayk's urgency to the security concerns he'd outlined earlier. She gave a brief, assenting nod before turning back to the inscrutable crate.

For privacy, Rayk moved a short distance away, whilst obtaining a clearer transmission path. He found a spot near the threshold of the immense blast doors and stood composed amidst the faint, pulsing light from the cavern's ancient systems.

He initiated the secure comms sequence through his neural interface, navigating the layers of encryption required for a direct, high-priority link to the Director's office, far away in Petropolis.

Voss, momentarily released from the immediate demands of protocol, turned back fully to the statue, his gloved hand hovering near the cool stone of its cheek, lost in the profound mystery it represented. Renata, glancing over briefly at Voss, one eye on the statue and another on the crates, activated a different scanning frequency on her datapad, probing the complex glyphs on the crate once more. The vast, crystalline silence of the Depot settled around them, thick with the dust of ages, broken only by the nearly imperceptible electronic processes Rayk had set in motion.

Chapter 19. Part 4.

The near silence of the Depot was profound, broken only by the faint whir of one of the tiny drones and the almost sub-audible electronic whisper emanating from Rayk's position near the colossal blast door.

Rayk's focus was entirely inward, navigating the encrypted handshake protocols for the Level 1 secure link to Director Raith's office. Authentication keys exchanged across the void, the connection sought its final confirmation, the digital equivalent of a line secured and waiting. Voss remained captivated by the serene stone face of the Architect statue, while Renata meticulously adjusted frequencies, probing the unyielding mystery of the nearby crate.

The ancient calm was shattered. Not with a sudden noise, but with a clumsy, undignified scrabbling from under the blast door. Fabric scraped rock. A muffled, distinctly Terran curse echoed in the cavern. A figure struggled into view, pushing himself awkwardly upright into the Depot's strange, crystalline light. Stout, red-faced from exertion, clad in rumpled, inappropriate corporate attire, a dark suit that screamed 'off-world bureaucracy'. He blinked rapidly against the unexpected luminescence. He smoothed his jacket with an aggressive tug, his small, furious eyes sweeping across the scene, the scientists, the security officer, the impossible artefacts. For a moment, his jaw dropped, the scientist in him stunned by the enormity of the discovery. But then his eyes narrowed. He remembered why he was here. The indignation of being absent from this moment fuelled his outrage, and he fixed his ire upon the group with immediate, explosive, pompous outrage.

"What in the blazes is going on here?" He erupted, his voice startlingly loud, bouncing off the distant cavern walls. He forced himself to ignore the grandeur around him, striding towards the party with the self-importance of entrenched officialdom. "This sector is restricted! Access requires explicit Level 4 clearance from the Archaeology Council Planning Committee! The use of a SARU unit in an uncertified zone," he jabbed a finger towards the now silent machine near the tunnel entrance they'd emerged from, "is a flagrant breach of protocol 17 of our charter to operate! And, initiating unauthorised deep-level communications... I decide how this information is disseminated!" His glare swivelled accusingly towards Rayk, who had reflexively terminated the nascent comms link at the first sound of the intrusion. "All of this, everything, requires Board-level sign off! Who," he drew himself up, chest puffed, radiating outrage, "authorised this flagrant disregard for established procedure?"

Voss, startled out of his contemplation by the sheer volume and hostility of the man's arrival, took an involuntary step back. He opened his mouth, intending to point out the extraordinary nature of their find, the clear justification for their presence, but Renata moved smoothly, almost imperceptibly, positioning herself slightly forward, her expression cooling to one of professional impassivity.

"Doctor," she addressed the fuming man, her voice calm and measured, cutting through his tirade. "All procedures related to primary site investigation fall under the direct authority of the Head of Archaeology, which is the Primary Mission Directorate."

The stout man scoffed, a derisive puff of air. "Don't be absurd, Volkova! That position has been vacant since Director Al Salim's unfortunate illness and repatriation last year! All such decisions default to the Council Oversight Committee, chaired by me, I might add, pending formal appointment procedures! Now, I demand you answer me: who authorised—"

"The position is no longer vacant, Dr Chowdry," Renata stated, her voice remaining level, yet carrying an undeniable edge of finality. A flicker of something, perhaps amusement, perhaps satisfaction, touched her eyes as she made a subtle gesture towards Voss, who still looked utterly bewildered by the confrontation. "Director Raith confirmed the appointment was finalised two days prior to the last supply fleet's arrival at Tranquillity Orbital Station." Renata, immensely enjoying the moment, watched for Chowdry's inevitable 'Then who?' to dawn on his face. She wasn't disappointed. *Is that a hopeful look there for a moment, Chowdry?* She continued promptly so as not to ruin the drama. "Allow me to introduce Dr Julian Voss, the officially designated Head of the Xenology and Archaeology Directorate for the Sikarra Mandate."

Dr. Gupta Chowdry's face flushed an apoplectic crimson. Disbelief warred with sputtering rage. "Voss?" he choked out, swivelling to glare at Julian as if seeing vermin that had unexpectedly manifested in his pristine office. "The new man? Preposterous! I received no official notification! The Council was not consulted! This is an outrageous breach of protocol, of governance, of..." He seemed lost for words, momentarily choked by sheer bureaucratic indignation.

Voss himself felt pole-axed. Head of Directorate? The title seemed utterly alien, ludicrous. He looked from Chowdry's apoplectic features to Renata's unnervingly composed face, his mind struggling to grasp the implication. Renata knew? All this time? Why hadn't she mentioned it? Was this why Raith had been subtly deferential? The pieces started to slam into place, a horrifying mosaic of political calculation he had been blind to. Raith's cryptic talk of succession, of the 'last man standing'... it had been about him. Voss, the unassuming academic, was now officially in charge of the entire scientific mission. Chowdry, the pompous functionary, was suddenly just a bureaucrat, his authority neutered. Raith's careful placement of personnel, his layers of control and contingency—it all took on a new, intricate dimension. He wasn't a pawn; he was a protected piece, moved into position for a game he never knew he was playing. The ground felt unsteady beneath his feet, the weight of an authority he hadn't known he possessed, and certainly hadn't asked for, settling upon him with crushing force.

"You?" Chowdry finally managed, focusing his sputtering fury directly on the speechless Voss. "You claim Directorate authority? On whose validation? I demand to see the official appointment directive!" Then, his voice getting slightly less loud, less sure of himself: "The Board ... authorisation..."

Chowdry looked at the three absolutely wooden faces staring at him. At that moment, he realised that he had lost. All he could do was try to recover some dignity.

Voss's stare did a great job of hiding his shock. Apart from being utterly lost for words, his mind a maelstrom of confusion and sudden, unwanted responsibility, he also saw the humorous side of it. Renata. The little minx!

Rayk, breaking the stunned silence and perhaps seeking to anchor the situation in fact amidst Chowdry's bluster, turned a measured gaze towards Renata. His voice was quiet but held a distinct edge of enquiry. "You knew about this appointment, Doctor Volkova?"

Renata met Rayk's intense look, then glanced towards Voss's composed but rather white face. A flicker of something unreadable crossed her face. Perhaps mischief? Regret? Or just a simple acknowledgement? She gave a tiny, almost imperceptible shrug.

"Oops?"

Chapter 20. Part 1.

The initial shock of discovery and the stark confrontation with Chowdry began to recede, replaced by the immense, pressing weight of the Wahlsanga Depot itself. Voss stood before the sixth train, its silent, dust-shrouded form a monument to forgotten history. People—not aliens any more, not since he'd seen the statue—had lived full lives here, commuting on these trains just as humans did in human cities. He wanted to know those people. He thought, *This is my future, speaking their language, living as they did on this planet. Honouring them. I won't leave Sikarra. I'm never going back to Earth.*

So, Voss drew a breath, the cool, ancient air doing little to calm the turmoil within, yet the sheer magnitude of the responsibility forced a fragile composure upon him. This place, these artefacts, demanded leadership, regardless of how unprepared he felt. Nearby, Renata was already absorbed in her datapad, processing sensor feeds from the survey drones, while Doctor Chowdry watched sullenly, his bureaucratic indignation temporarily muted by the overwhelming scale of the find.

"Alright," Voss began, his voice gaining a measure of firmness as he turned towards the others. "We need immediate protocols." He gestured for both Rayk Kostin and Doctor Chowdry to approach, establishing his position as the central coordinator by default.

"Doctor Chowdry," Voss addressed the bureaucrat directly, adopting a formal tone. "Upon our return to Petropolis, your immediate priority will be coordinating the logistical requirements for this site. Compile comprehensive requirements for personnel—geological, engineering, specialist teams—and the necessary equipment. Liaise with central stores and transport command regarding inventory and deployment schedules."

He paused, then shifted focus, "Simultaneously, establishing reliable ground access via the Metro tunnel is essential. Doctor Chowdry, would you authorise your assistant director," he gave the point emphasis, "to task the SARU unit, now that its initial work here is complete, to commence clearing the main tunnel blockage from this Wahlsanga end, working back towards Petropolis? It seems the most efficient use of resources currently on site, under your department's purview."

Chowdry visibly stiffened at being delegated to, but the logic was sound, and the reference to his department's purview offered a small concession to his position. "The logistical coordination will be extensive, Principal Voss," he began slightly passive-aggressively; then, seemingly calmer now, he reigned in his instinct to elaborate on the difficulties. Correcting himself, his tone taking on a faint, almost pedantic edge, he continued, "But achievable. Tunnel clearance requires SARU reallocation protocols, but I shall ensure my team implements it upon my authorisation from the Archaeology Board." His tone was now calming with the act of speaking and planning, which he plainly excelled at in order to get to the position he held.

Voss ignored the title, focusing instead on integrating security. Voss was not sure that he had authority over Rayk because he answered only to Raith, but he was sure he had authority over this dig site. So, taking a cautious and diplomatic tone, he turned slightly to include Rayk in the conversation. "Detective Kostin, I am sure, will advise you on the security protocols required for both personnel deployment and sensitive equipment transport. Also," Voss added, meeting Chowdry's gaze steadily,

"I am equally sure he will personally liaise with Director Raith regarding the authorisation and allocation of PCMA security assets and priority transport resources, both overland in UV-protected vehicles and in the newly opened tunnel with unshielded vehicles, required to support your logistical efforts." The implication was clear: Rayk's involvement guaranteed Raith's oversight, ensuring Chowdry's tasks would be expedited and facilitated.

Right, delegation done, Voss thought, a flicker of relief mixing with the ongoing strangeness of the situation. His gaze drifted towards Renata, bent over her datapad. Did she do it that way just to handle Chowdry? Or does she resent me for this position? Is that why...? He forcibly pushed the thought away. Focus, Julian. The discovery. That's what matters.

He turned back to Rayk. "Now, Detective. Please establish secure contact with Director Raith. Inform him that the discovery is confirmed. I have requested maximum security protocols for this site, Wahlsanga Depot, with access and information strictly limited to essential personnel pending his formal ratification. Report Doctor Chowdry's presence and the logistical and tunnel access directives issued. Request formal ratification and any overriding operational directives."

"Understood, Principal," Rayk replied. Was there a slight smile on his face as he said that? He moved a short distance away, finding a clear spot near the threshold, his focus turning inward as he initiated the secure comms sequence via his neural interface.

The internal exchange was swift. Rayk processed the incoming directives from Raith, his expression giving nothing away. He rejoined Voss and Renata a moment later.

"Contact complete," Rayk reported. "Director Raith ratifies the maximum-security designation and associated information lockdown for Wahlsanga Depot. He acknowledges the logistical planning but issues overriding directives."

He paused, letting the shift in priority register. "We are to return to Petropolis Command immediately. Director Raith cites urgent personnel consolidation required due to unexpected orbital traffic density."

Rayk's gaze held Voss's as he delivered the next, more peculiar instruction. "He has also tasked me, personally, with retrieving the Echo Key artefact from the custody of the Physicists in the surface ruins en route back here, tomorrow morning. It is to be kept under my direct oversight and brought back here to the Depot, where I must establish a secure holding facility such as a strongroom. Anything else we find of particular value must be kept in that room. Director Raith requires confirmation of its transfer upon our arrival at Command."

He concluded, glancing briefly towards Chowdry. "Doctor Chowdry will return with us, communications restricted as per your initial directive, Principal Voss." Voss thought about Rayk's new demeanour. What was the man thinking? Was this just the military—Police training kicking in, or was Rayk mentally coping with something? The man was inscrutable. More than just an irritating alpha male in my way, he thought to himself. What is this guy's deal?

Voss processed the orders. Return immediately; well, that was frustrating, but dictated by external factors he couldn't see. The Echo Key directive felt odd, however. A deliberate move by Raith to keep key artefacts under Security's direct control, perhaps? But why on Earth, or 'why on Sikarra' would he want it secured way from the main HQ in Sikarra? The term "all your eggs in one basket" came to mind. Raith was not the sort of man to do anything unless there was a plan, or plans within plans, knowing his type. Does this have anything to do with the undefined 'orbital traffic'? He filed the question away. "Understood, Detective. We shall comply," he said, stressing the formal 'shall' in a way that seemed slightly sardonic, but not in a way that he could be called out on. Voss realised he had better not push his luck too much, too early. These were delicate times. He looked around the vast, silent cavern one last time, loathing the need to tear himself away from what he truly cared about. This underground patch of what was to him, Heaven on Sikarra. He asked Rayk, "For now, do you have any staff upstairs who can guard the tunnel breach and I presume you have some basic perimeter sensors available?" "Already on it," said Rayk, whilst he turned without being dismissed and started making calls to the units in the upper levels, issuing orders. Voss tightened his jaw, watching Rayk's retreating back. He smiled inwardly. Damn, how does he do that? So much for 'Voss the Boss Man'.

As Rayk met the guard from the upper level, arriving at a brisk pace, he posted him near the tunnel entrance to guard it and activated small, discreet sensor discs near the main blast door. Voss and Renata gathered their immediate equipment.

They cast final, lingering glances at the silent trains, the serene statue—a universe of secrets momentarily glimpsed, now sealed away again behind layers of protocol and Raith's opaque commands.

They walked back towards the tunnel leading to the upper levels, Renata almost tripping over debris, her attention utterly captivated by the glyphs displayed on her datapad—the puzzle already unfolding for her AS. Voss glanced down at his own empty hands. A strange thought surfaced, almost humorous: shouldn't he be emerging laden with treasure, pockets bulging like some caricature of a tomb raider clutching gold coins?

Renata had the deciphering, the immediate thrill of potential discovery fed directly into her analysis programs; he had the new title, the weight of coordinating teams yet unformed, the burden of reports yet unwritten. The stark difference left a sharp edge to his thoughts; her path seemed clear, discovery, while his path felt mired in bureaucracy before it even began. But as they prepared to leave the Depot behind, the image of the Architect's face resurfaced in his mind. Serene, ancient, impossibly real.

The elegant lines of the silent trains held unimaginable secrets. The sheer, staggering reality of it washed over him again, a wave of profound intellectual excitement that submerged the petty sting of comparison. This was the work. This was why he was here.

As they boarded the skimmer, Voss cast another glance at Rayk as they sat in the luxurious white leather seats. At least Kostin's new task meant another look at the Echo Key. That strange artefact felt like a lifetime ago, overshadowed by this Depot, yet Raith considered it vital. Alone, it could have secured a Nobel Prize for whoever unlocked its secrets. But after all that had happened, it had receded into the background.

Despite the information lockdown, rumours had spread fast. The departure felt eerily subdued, the air thick with speculation. The Director's skimmer sealed its hatches around them and the engines began their quiet build, lifting them away from Wahlsanga's landing pads, back into Raith's orbit.

Chapter 20. Part 2.

Wind, sharp with the abrasive dust of ages, howled through the miraculously still-intact structures of the aeons-abandoned surface city often called "The Original" or "Old Pheonalla," on the opposite side of the Great Gorge to modern-day Pheonalla. Varinn leaned against the immense, time-scoured curve of a Plazteel archway, the near-immortal material cool beneath his hand, gleaming faintly where millennia of sandstorms had polished its surface smooth, a testament to the age of the city rather than any weakness in the building materials. Designers were an old race, in a way that Varinn could not conceptually grasp, even though he had learned the cold facts in his schooling group.

Even so, when he looked closely, his eyes detected the true passage of time. Lesser alloys were corroded to tracery. Conduits showed varying degrees of decay. Sand piled in deep drifts against the defiant walls, all beneath a sky that offered no respite

His sealed wound ached, a dull throb beneath his tunic, and exhaustion weighed on him like a physical shroud. Yet, the memory of Marinallis's desperate urgency, the feel of the MET Comms Unit silent and heavy in his pack, drove him onward. He scanned the desolate plaza and to Varinn's surprise, his navscan picked up a local network. He promptly began a search for a nearby incineration facility. With the FOSS around, Varinn concluded that it may be safer to dispose of it now, rather than risk taking it to Vasantha for disposal. There were many disposal incinerators littered around, especially near places that harboured sensitive tech. Destroy the device. Sever the resonance. Prevent its capture. That was all that mattered.

He pushed off from the archway, his boots crunching on sand and shattered crystal shards. As he neared a remarkably intact access door, surrounded by a complex façade of interlocking plazteel panels, the device in his pack stirred. Not a hum, but an undeniable pull, a silent query answered from within the structure, not towards the door, but towards a recess of plazteel panels that looked much like any other of the many faceted walls of the city. He stopped, tracing the invisible lines of force. Placing his hand, the one nearest the pack, against a specific panel, the resonance grew stronger.

Suddenly, his navscan beeped and a top-level Designer directive appeared. It simply said. "Enter".

With a barely audible pneumatic hiss, a rectangular section of the wall slid inwards, revealing a brightly lit aperture. Concealed alloy hatches retracted, exposing a chamber beyond. It looked sterile, functional, humming with the low thrum of active, advanced systems. This was it. Varinn glanced back across the windswept ruins. There was still no sign of Tessara, but he trusted her instincts, her presence a silent watchfulness somewhere beyond his sight. He took a breath, steeling himself, and stepped through the opening.

The lab was stark, utilitarian. Holographic displays shimmered, projecting cascades of complex energy formulae and shifting geometric patterns. Before a central console, immersed in the light, stood a Designer. Tall, severely slender in functional indigo robes, she turned as he entered. Her large, dark eyes, sharp with ancient intelligence, took him in immediately, her expression shifting from focused concentration to sharp inquiry. A patch on her shoulder simply read: D. Urbanalla.

"Who are you?" Her voice was clear, precise, holding an innate authority. "Your

The Xenologist

arrival is unexpected. You are carrying a MET Comms unit. Report."

Varinn felt the ingrained deference surface. "Designer Urbanalla," he managed, his voice rough with fatigue and dust. "I am Section Leader Varinn. Personal Protection Service. Designer Marinallis ordered me to bring the unit here. He ordered its immediate incineration to prevent enemy acquisition. It should have been evacuated years ago but was left behind. I don't know why, I am sorry."

Urbanalla considered this for a moment, her gaze flickering towards a complex schematic showing projected fleet movements or threat vectors. "It happens. There are very few MET devices left and we have them all tracked, Varinn," she said, her tone less dismissive than pragmatic. She was evidently focused on a larger, more urgent picture. "Marinallis's caution is noted; however, circumstances have accelerated. Final evacuation protocols now prioritise repurposing of the few remaining adaptable assets instead of simple destruction, particularly MET platforms."

She gestured towards the frantic data streams on her displays. "Incinerating this unit represents a tactical capability loss we cannot afford during this critical phase. Its potential utility in guiding designated allies or being a trap for enemies," she met his gaze directly, "outweighs the risk." She turned back to her console, busy with something beyond Varinn's ability to understand. She continued in an almost alarmingly distracted manner, "Provided it is correctly reprogrammed and safeguarded. Your previous orders are superseded by the new directive."

Her logic resonated with Varinn's own sense of duty. The hierarchy was absolute. Understanding dawned, replacing his single-minded focus on destruction. He nodded slowly, reluctantly withdrawing the device from his pack, presenting it to her.

Urbanalla took it, her long fingers moving across its surface with an expert's touch. "The primary threat remains K'Tharr interception, or uncontrolled mass field fluctuations attracting further scrutiny," she stated, turning to the holographic console. "This reprogramming creates layered safeguards."

Varinn watched as light flowed between her hands, the device, and the console. "First, a terminal countermeasure," she murmured, manipulating complex energy fields. "Detection of designated hostile signatures—K'Tharr weapon resonance, specific Fumigator frequency bands—or any forced matrix access will trigger a contained mass field polarity reversal." She elaborated clinically, "It suppresses the local mass-field momentarily, causing surrounding matter to violently repel itself—a localised disruption. This, of course, destroys the MET Comm12, inevitably followed by an immediate, catastrophic vacuum implosion as the source of the instability has destroyed itself.

Varinn said, "Designer, what is the size of the implosion?" "Don't worry," she laughed. We will all be long gone unless we are surprisingly unlucky. "It's approximately ten kilotons equivalent yield, focused vacuum effect. Brutal, but effective for asset denial." A grim shadow crossed her features. "Should that mass-field disturbance trigger a wider 'immune' response from the Fumigator's monitors... we will be parsecs away. So it's them who will be having a bad day for once!"

She shifted her focus. "In the meantime, the device will remain deceptively functional. Recognised Designer DNA and registered allied command codes will permit standard MET functions."

She waved him forward. "Varinn, I think that's what you said your name is, hold the device. I can test that it still responds to someone with limited Designer DNA whilst I reprogram it". Varinn stepped forward and with a moment's hesitation, grasped the handle. Urbanalla saw his hesitation and smiled indulgently. "Don't worry, if this goes wrong, you already don't exist. Time-altering devices are quite strange things." As she talked, the MET Comm12 informed him what she was doing, with a clarity he did not get in the desert.

She continued almost happily, "A specific protocol is now embedded for unanticipated arrivals." She initiated a sequence. "Should anyone with totally unrecognised DNA come into proximity with the device, this initiates a false memory of being asked a question. Like this." She pressed a button on the console and a synthesised voice echoed: "Test. Are you a Newcomer?" Urbanalla continued, "That will come out in the Newcomers' language when their brains access the memory. Provided their cerebral cortices are not too different from ours."

She traced new instructions on the screen with her fingers. "Confirmation, verbal or mental, initiates a targeted guidance overlay. It implants coordinates for," she input a complex designation, "a designated Vasantha rendezvous point, which I want you to evacuate to, Varinn".

Varinn asked, "What are my instructions when I get there, Designer Urbanalla?".

She answered, "Evacuate yourself and failing that, incinerate everything organic, including yourself". Varinn sadly realised she was the older, more contemptuous type. He was, naturally, offended by the callousness, but he knew he would comply. He wasn't sure he much cared for the universe as it would be in such a future as described by Marinallis. Urbanalla smiled indulgently, "There will be a cache of instructions and directions there for any Newcomers from their Allied Command. A courtesy we are doing them. You, of course, you know or should know exactly what you are doing." The explanation was vague, fitting the chaos of a mass departure, hiding the true destination.

She placed the reprogrammed device into a durable composite container designed for extreme environmental endurance. Her movements were swift, efficient, predicated on the arrival of expected allies within months, perhaps years at most.

Genuinely concerned and somewhat curious, Varinn asked, "What if they try to go past the veil?".

She once again smiled indulgently. "Ah, yes, 'The Veil'. Let's dispense with the semi-superstitious blather, shall we?" Varinn nodded numbly. "It's a thin firewall that looks like a veil, as you no doubt saw. It's a set of routines that allows you to fundamentally see how the universe truly is. Essentially, it's empty, just random rippling fields tentatively hung together in a manner that could fall apart at any time. For the unprepared or less sophisticated mind," she stated starkly, looking somewhat pointedly at Varinn's forehead. "It usually results in instant insanity or speedy death. For a genetically prepared mind, or one that is strictly trained in limited usage, the risk of cognitive failure is negligible."

Varinn nodded slowly, the memory of overwhelming, terrifying insight flickering within him. "I felt something," he admitted quietly.

"Precisely," Urbanalla confirmed. "Adhere to the protocols. The safeguards exist for a reason." She indicated the sealed container. "Your function now is to secure this unit at this location. Await the secondary evacuation retrieval signal. Then you may proceed to the designated point, the coordinates for which should already be in your memory if you search for them. Get there by any means at your disposal and try to evacuate on a newcomer ship."

Varinn thought about it and sure enough, MET Comm12 had implanted a visual memory and set of coordinates of exactly where the final evacuation and incineration point was.

She gestured towards an open alcove, revealing a sleek medical pod. "Your injuries require stabilisation for now. You may use the medical pod in the corner."

Varinn looked from the container holding the transformed device to the waiting pod. His mission irrevocably altered, his body failing, logic dictated compliance. He moved stiffly into the alcove and settled into the pod. The transparent lid descended, sealing with a soft hiss. Cool blue light intensified, a deep anaesthetic cold leaching into his limbs. His last conscious thought was of Tessara, hoping she would see the pod first before anyone else got to him. Then, the darkness took him.

Outside the hidden lab, the concealed door slid shut, the Plazteel wall erasing any sign of its existence. The wind sighed through the ancient ruins, shifting sand across the weathered, immortal stone. Far across the desolate expanse, a lone, cloaked figure, battling the elements, drew steadily closer.

Chapter 21. Part 1.

The Director's skimmer arrived at the Petropolis hub, and the transition felt like surfacing into a different world. The ornate, Greco-Roman columns of the city stood in stark contrast to the functional architecture of Wahlsanga. And yet, it was Sikarra that felt mundane. The regulated lighting, the ambient hum of life support—it was all familiar PCMA infrastructure. It felt sterile compared to the profound, ancient silence of the Depot.

Doctor Chowdry disembarked briskly, his earlier sullenness replaced by a mask of hurried importance. He offered Voss a stiff nod. "Principal Voss, I shall begin coordinating the required logistical frameworks immediately."

Voss returned the nod, accepting the formal address without comment. "Thank you, Doctor. Ensure the secure transport requisitions are prioritised."

Rayk Kostin stepped forward as Chowdry turned to leave. "I will liaise directly with Director Raith's office regarding the allocation of security personnel and priority transport you require, Doctor Chowdry," Rayk stated calmly, reinforcing the established channel of authority. Chowdry acknowledged with another curt nod and bustled away towards the administrative sector lifts, already mentally composing requisitions, no doubt.

With the immediate bureaucratic hurdle removed, a different kind of tension settled over the remaining trio. The sheer scale of what they had found and the abruptness of their recall, Voss's unsolicited, unprocessed promotion, all hung unspoken between them.

"Well," Renata said after a moment, pushing a stray strand of blonde hair back from her forehead, her professional composure firmly back in place, though her eyes still held a trace of the day's intensity. "A proper debrief seems essential. The Bar None?" She looked towards Voss, then Rayk. "Process the initial findings? Before we get swept up in... everything else?"

Voss hesitated only briefly. The weight of responsibility felt heavy, but the urge to discuss the scientific implications of the Depot, to ground himself in the familiar process of analysis, was strong. "Yes," he agreed. "A good idea." Rayk assented with a quiet nod, perhaps seeing the value in observing the Directorate's new head process the day's events.

Renata went straight to a secluded booth as soon as they entered Bar None. Voss noted that she knew where she was going and the barman nodded immediately. Sm*all Place, he thought.* The low murmur of off-duty personnel was a comforting background noise. Drinks were ordered through the table datapad: synth-ale again for the men, Renata opting for vodka and tomato juice. Almost immediately, Renata activated her personal datapad, projecting a holographic image of the glyph panel from the Wahlsanga Metro platform. "Before this kicks in," she said with a smile, pointing at the table datapad image of the drinks order.

Taking control of the meeting, she said, "The station identifier," tracing the complex lines with a stylus. "The AS confirms the high probability match with the topological chart symbol, but the phonetic reconstruction is still ambiguous. 'Wan'xantha' feels structurally unlikely based on our parameters, but 'Wahlsanga'..."

The Xenologist

Renata traced the glowing glyphs on the table's projection, frowning. "The phonetic reconstruction is still ambiguous. 'Wan'xantha' feels structurally unlikely, but 'Wahlsanga'..."

Voss leaned closer, his focus intense. "The internal structure is consistent with other location designators," he murmured, his voice a low rumble of concentration, "but the penultimate phoneme..."

They were so deep in the puzzle that Rayk's voice made them both jump.

"Forgive my intrusion into linguistics, Doctors," he said, his tone polite but firm. "You're focusing entirely on the Wahlsanga station sign. Wasn't a corresponding Metro access point identified here in Petropolis? Wouldn't protocol suggest a similar identification panel exists there?"

The simple, direct logic of it hit Renata like a physical shock. She stared at Rayk, then her eyes shot to Voss and saw the same expression of dawning, abject horror mirrored on his face. They had it. They had the perfect one-to-one comparison, a control for their experiment, sitting right under their noses for weeks, and in the thrill of the new discovery, they had completely forgotten it.

A helpless giggle escaped her, quickly turning into a full, hysterical laugh. She saw Voss groan and drop his head into his hands, his shoulders shook with laughter and sheer, mortified embarrassment.

From across the table, Rayk watched their breakdown with an expression of polite, utter confusion. "Did I miss something?" he asked.

"No, Rayk! Not at all!" Voss finally managed, looking up, his eyes watering. "You just pointed out the most glaringly obvious parallel imaginable! We utterly forgot the identical context right here! Incredible."

Still chuckling, her focus now razor-sharp, Renata pulled up the Petropolis archival data on her pad. "He's absolutely right. Initial survey scans, Sub Level 1, access tunnel..."

An image appeared—the sealed Metro entrance, showing a dusty, overhead panel bearing glyphs. "There! Run analysis... standard parameters..." The AS worked swiftly. A phonetic string appeared: /pə'nɛləpi/.

"Penelope?" Renata read, bewildered. She looked at Voss, who simply stared at the word, baffled.

"Penelope," Voss echoed flatly. He shook his head. "That's... nonsensical. No connection to any known Architect terms or concepts." He waved a hand dismissively, perhaps covering his earlier oversight with abrupt certainty. "It has to be a coincidental false friend; otherwise, I suggest it is English bias creeping into the program. Are there other options?" Renata nodded in agreement, "Yes, a few, this one is less statistically certain, Penelloa? Maybe like Genoa?" Voss shrugged, "I have a nasty feeling that when the AS improves confidence and we find the real name, Penelope will stick".

Rayk laughed at the thought. "Frustrating as it may be for you guys, I rather like 'Penelope'. It's certainly better than 'Wanks Anthea, or whatever the other place is called."

Renata frowned "We will be working hard to live down some of these names I can see." Closing the file with a faint sigh, the brief detour into local archaeology apparently concluded as a dead end. They returned their focus to the Wahlsanga glyphs, the excitement of that primary puzzle reasserting itself.

They finished their drinks soon after, the conversation shifting to the necessary next steps. "So, Echo Key retrieval tomorrow morning," Voss confirmed, looking at Rayk. "Then you'll establish the secure holding facility back at Wahlsanga?" Rayk nodded. "Those are the Director's explicit instructions." For Voss, the need to manage his new Directorate role, coordinate with Chowdry's burgeoning logistical plans, and somehow oversee the most important archaeological find in human history felt overwhelming.

They left the bar, Rayk called one of the automated transport buggies and sat himself in the front seat next to the driver, leaving Renata and Voss to sit next to each other in the back. The short journey through the softly lit tunnels towards the residential and Directorate sectors was quiet. Voss wanted to talk, but like Renata, was professionally overloaded and burnt out by the avalanche of discoveries, not just today but this whole week.

The buggy navigated its predetermined route and as it started slowing for Voss's apartment, which was first on the route, Rayk called backwards, "I will drop you off first, Dr. Voss, please call me as soon as you have breakfast. As they pulled up first outside Voss's newer, slightly larger quarters, Voss realised why his apartment was slightly larger than everyone else's. The clue of his status was there all along.

He stepped out. He shared a look with Renata a moment too long. Something inside hoped she would give him a verbal clue that it was OK to invite her in. She smiled, but Rayk was looking back. This was not the moment. "Right. I'll see you both tomorrow morning for the Echo Key transfer," he said, trying to keep his tone even.

"Of course, Principal," Renata replied with a kind smile to soften the edge of her tease. Rayk offered a simple, professional nod. As the buggy slid silently away down the corridor, Voss caught a final glimpse of Renata and Rayk still seated inside, continuing their journey towards their own sectors, perhaps exchanging a final word about the day's reports or security logs. It was a neutral image, yet watching the buggy disappear with them both inside left Voss standing alone in the quiet corridor, the weight of his new responsibilities, the mysteries of Wahlsanga, and the opacity of Raith's command suddenly feeling immense. He turned towards his quarters, the door hissing open to an empty room filled with the silent pressure of expectation.

Chapter 21. Part 2.

It was roused from its happy semi-slumber with a cringing, irritating feeling of alarm. A Human may have described it as fingernails being dragged down a blackboard, combined with dentistry without anaesthetic. Of course, It had no concept of such things and It was too alarmed to even think about analysing what it felt like. This was serious stuff indeed!

It felt the ripples in the 'sticky-flat field' to be almost like sudden waves rocking its calm boat. It searched for the source of the waves and found not one, not two, but ten tears in the field that ploughed it up like a farmer ploughing a field tore up the dirt. The tears were incoming at a speed that threatened causality. That wasn't the problem, however. Of course, any disturbance of that field was bad, very bad. But this problem was the sheer amount of energy being dumped in with no thought as to trying to contain it. The sheer effrontery!

This simply, would, not, do! It checked Star for its ability to do an instant Nova. Star confirmed it could begin the process within 1 billion Universe Ticks. (A Universe Tick being the smallest possible amount of time that can exist). *Good enough. But... let me check..*

It reviewed its operating procedures. It had been a long time since *It* had seen anything this bad. The amount of energy being dumped directly into the tear in the field still fell far short of critical, but this certainly warranted immediate and severe action.

The answer was clear and steered *It* away from just sterilising the place. It was going to be more work, but at least it should save the star system. *For now!*

Yes, *It* thought, there was only one thing for it. *It* had to find out who or what was responsible and that meant only one thing. *It* sent out a message to one of its servants sojourning in the outer asteroid field. "Begin making Bio Data Samplers. Twenty should do." Of course, that was a bit of an overkill for one system, but *It* couldn't be too careful.

It contemplated: *I bet it's primates. It's usually primates. Bipedal types, probably. Not enough to occupy the dangling forelimbs, so the cheeky little monkeys get up to mischief every time.* If it were up to *It*, it thought, *I would wipe the lot out.* The Makers were too soft. The moment passed and *It* reflected, *Mind you, that's a lot of work. Maybe the Makers knew best.*

It sent a further message. "Program them to catch up with those things tearing the sticky-flat field up as soon as they are fabricated. Destroy six outright and capture one for bio-data sampling of the infection and technical analysis of the technology the infection is using."

The irritation from the tears lessened slightly. A curve appeared in the vector. *Ah, I see, they want the planet. OK, let's take a closer look. That place was getting on my nerves anyway; there is definitely something down there that is damned persistent. Kill two infections with one response.* It sent a final message, "And should they orbit the rock with vermin on it, program them to go down there and sample anything that looks intelligent or technical. Especially Bipeds."

With that, *It* started to feel better. The irritation was lessening now and it tried to catch up on a bit of rest after that flurry of excitement. Not that *It* was all that hopeful. This was turning out to be a very noisy Planet. *Maker knows what the vermin thought was down there that was so damned important!*

Chapter 21. Part 3.

In the tranquil sanctuary of the garden of Valerius Corba's villa, nestled deep within the Great Gorge, was the most pleasant ambient temperature on the Planet. Outside, on the broad terraces where alien ferns mingled with Terran vines, the fine dustings from the recent, violent sandstorm were being gently washed away by the automated irrigation systems, leaving water beading on broad, waxy leaves.

Inside, Corba sat in a high-backed chair of polished chrome and dark synth-leather, a crystal tumbler containing an amber liquid resting on the small table beside him. He gazed out through the panoramic window at the vibrant, impossible green of the gorge reclaiming itself, his expression one of serene contemplation.

The silence was broken by the near-imperceptible arrival of another figure. The man emerged from the shadows of an adjoining corridor, moving with a noiseless efficiency that surprised even Corba.

The man was powerfully built, his features distinctly Mongolian, showing beneath the hood of his desert cloak, which was now streaked with fine ochre dust. What made him unusual, if not striking, was that his skin was a shining jet-black colour. Obviously, a dermal camouflage technology, it was too even and too perfect to be natural.

"Report," Corba said quietly, not turning from the window.

"Mr. Jones was successfully repatriated to the entrance of one of the city access tunnels," the operative stated, his voice a low, steady baritone. "I left him in a semi-conscious state, condition stable but significantly degraded. Discovery by the PCMA patrol is imminent since he wasn't cloaked and will have set the perimeter alarms off." He stepped forward and placed a minuscule metallic disc, flecked with what looked like dried blood, onto the polished table beside Corba's drink. "I had to remove our internal monitor. His physical condition was severely compromised following getting lost, suffering from delirium and advanced dehydration. Leaving the implant in place risked detection during any subsequent medical assessment."

Corba picked up the tiny tracker, rolling it between his thumb and forefinger, his gaze still fixed on the view outside. "An acceptable deviation, given the circumstances." He paused, then asked, his voice remaining perfectly level, "And his standard PCMA personnel tracker?"

"Not present upon initial contact, sir," the operative replied without hesitation. "Internal scans confirmed it had been manually deactivated and physically removed prior to, or after getting lost. Its location is unknown, but most likely on the plateau somewhere."

Corba finally turned his head slowly, his eyes, pale and intelligent, fixing on the operative. The serene expression remained unchanged, but a subtle stillness came over him, a sharpening of focus. "His official locator was removed beforehand?" he murmured, the question rhetorical, the implication immediately understood. "Interesting. That suggests his distress, his deviation, began significantly earlier than the storm." He considered this for a moment, the pieces clicking into place. Jonesy hadn't just panicked or stumbled; he'd been attempting to disappear, to break contact, even before circumstance intervened. A suicidal gesture? A planned defection? The motive was secondary; the result was the same – an unreliable asset, compromised beyond retrieval.

Corba dismissed the thought outwardly. "The dermal camouflage and cloak performed adequately under storm conditions?"

"Within expected parameters, sir," the operative confirmed. "Minor pigment degradation at flex points, but full integrity maintained. The IR-Radar cloak also provided sufficient UV and particulate protection."

"Very well." Corba waved a dismissive hand. "Leave the monitor. Your extraction was timely, if events necessitated improvisation. Await further instructions."

The operative gave a slight, almost imperceptible bow and withdrew as silently as he had arrived, melting back into the villa's quiet corridors.

Corba remained seated, swirling the amber liquid in his tumbler. He picked up the tiny, blood-flecked tracker again, examining it thoughtfully. Jonesy. The fool had tried to run, tried to erase himself before the mission was even underway. Such instability could not be tolerated. An asset who had lost his nerve, who might possess fragmented but potentially damaging information, could not be allowed scrutiny, especially not by PCMA Security. The decision, forming coolly in his mind, he decided, felt less like malice and more like necessary, prudent risk management. Mr. Jones's continued existence is a liability that needs to be addressed. He took a slow sip from his glass, his gaze returning to the gorge outside, letting the pink noise of the constant waterfall wash over him. The only cure he knew for his constant tinnitus.

Chapter 22. Part 1.

The wind had gentled to a sigh. Dust still eddied in the plazas as Tessara moved cautiously through the weathered Plazteel buildings of the long-abandoned original Pheonalla. The violence of the sandstorm had passed, leaving behind a landscape scoured clean under a deepening twilight sky.

She scanned the immense, enduring structures, searching for any sign of Varinn. Her anxiety grew with every empty archway, every silent plaza and street. Where would he be? She thought *He was fast. He must have got this far, or he is back along the road from the weir and that would not be for any good reason!*

Following his most likely path, through the central road through the ruins, she came to a plazteel archway and rested for a moment. Varinn's wrist navscan started to register a faint ping with her own navscan. The wrist device links were only short-range, as they had realised when first getting separated after the fight with The Voice's cabal. That meant he was close. Somewhere. She came to a doorway and noticed she was being observed by a camera placed above the door. The camera was new and functioning, unlike the rest of the building. She thought, *What now? Just say 'Hi'?*

She raised her hand in salute and called, "Varinn?". Her wrist navscan pinged that a Designer-level authorised ID query had come from somewhere, presumably the door camera. Then, to her surprise, a section of the wall to her right responded to the ping. She had evidently passed some sort of identification test. With a soft pneumatic hiss, it slid inwards, revealing the brightly lit, sterile interior of a hidden lab. Tessara froze, weapon half-raised, peering into the unexpected chamber.

The lab hummed quietly, holographic displays now cycling in low-power modes. On a shelf rested the sealed composite container in which Varinn had been ordered to deposit the reprogrammed MET Comm12. Against the wall in an alcove on a pivot-stand lay a sleek, advanced medical pod. Its lid was closed and evidently occupied because the transparent face plate was darkened as a privacy consideration for the occupant.

She walked hopefully over to the pod and pressed the fingerprint reader. A message appeared on the display: "Occupant in treatment. Scan your ID to interrupt". She took her wrist-mounted navscan and waved it close to the fingerprint scanner. A chime sounded and then the display said, "Please wait, waking patient". After a moment, the faceplate became semi-opaque and with relief, she saw that it was Varinn, his eyes blinking as he focused to look out of the faceplate. A smile flickered briefly on his face and the faceplate became fully transparent. He was awake but still groggy.

Relief warred with urgency. She felt guilty about interrupting the process, but time was critical. Marinallis was waiting and she knew that this would be the most important thing for Varinn. She examined its controls. Unfamiliar, but the universal symbols for activation and emergency release were discernible.

She hesitated for only a moment. *Wait for the cycle to complete? Or move now?* The risk of moving was better than the risk of waiting. She initiated the emergency release. The upper half of the pod lid hissed upwards smoothly. Varinn took in a deep breath as the filtered air from the lab hit his nostrils. "Tessara...!"

The pod pivoted to the near vertical on its stand to allow the occupant to walk out. Varinn was plainly naked from the waist up. With typical Designer reliability and thoughtfulness, a drawer popped out and a replica of the clothes he had worn was helpfully placed within. Tessara grabbed the one-piece uniform that Varinn preferred and handed it to him. His left hand grabbed the clothes and his right hand reached down to open a small, recessed compartment within the pod's inner lining. He fumbled for a second, then withdrew a small, fully opaque vial, its surface smooth and unmarked. His gaze lingered on it for only an instant, an unreadable flicker in his eyes, before he quickly palmed it and secreted it away deep within a pocket in the one-piece he was now holding.

He pressed a button and opened the lower lid. The pod became fully vertical so he could walk out. He took a step forward, walking a little stiffly. He saw that he was completely unclothed and held the uniform in front of his body, not particularly self-conscious. He stepped out and turned around so he could dress. Tessara quickly averted her gaze, pretending intense interest in the fading holograms across the room with a slight grin on her face, having seen a little more than she would let on.

He's leaner than I thought, she registered. *And surprisingly well-constructed!* A faint warmth rose in her cheeks. She chastised herself for the unprofessional thought and forced her focus back to the console, though the image lingered.

He's leaner than I thought, Tessara registered with a detached part of her mind, stealing a fractional glance as he reached for the uniform, observing the play of well-defined muscle across his back and shoulders, honed by years of rigorous training and perhaps subtle Designer enhancements.

And surprisingly well-constructed! She immediately refocused on the console, a faint warmth rising in her cheeks, chastising herself for the unprofessional thought even as the image lingered. Varinn, preoccupied with pulling on the fresh uniform and shaking off the pod's effects, noticed nothing.

"Varinn!" Tessara finally said, turning back as he fastened the tunic, the relief clear in her voice now. "Are you alright? I thought... What is this place? What happened?"

He managed a weak smile, leaning against the pod for support. "Tessara. Good to see a friendly face. Never doubted you'd find me." He looked around the lab. "Though I admit, I was starting to wonder if this was turning into one of those dreadful entertainment serials where the heroes spend ten episodes running around in circles just missing each other." He ran a hand through his hair, still slightly dazed. "Good thing you showed up. Not exactly equipped for a long stay."

"What happened?" she pressed gently, assessing his condition. He was pale and weakened.

He waved a hand towards the container. "Orders changed topside. I met another Designer, D. Urbanalla. It seems, she's running this contingency post. She countermanded the incineration order." He explained briefly, "Repurposed the device as a kind of booby-trap with safeguards. It's secured in that container now, awaiting a secondary evacuation retrieval, or a big explosion." He gestured to the pod. "She insisted I use this for stabilisation after the fight with Carrik. Standard procedure for field injuries." He omitted the deeper complexities—the chilling instructions, the reprogramming details, the Veil. Too much. Not now.

She replied, "I meant the fight with Carrik. He said you were dead, but I didn't believe him, obviously." Varinn grinned, "Of course, the guy was jacked, but there was no chance he'd ever get the better of me." Tessara smiled sarcastically, "No, it's because when the storm cleared, I got a basic heartbeat report from your navscan to mine."

Varinn rolled his eyes slightly. "You set that up? Clever. I must admit I was worried that he would get to you. Is he..?" "Dead." She confirmed. "Marinallis did it, actually. Varinn raised an eyebrow. Tessara met his look. Uh-huh," she confirmed.

Tessara started looking around and took a moment to process the information Varinn had relayed about the Designer Urbanalla. Orders are changing mid-evacuation. It fit the chaotic reality they were navigating. The key thing was that Varinn was alive, and the dangerous MET device was, for now, contained. "Can you travel? We can swap stories along the way"

He pushed himself upright, testing his legs. "Still unsteady. But a lot better. The pod helped." He met her eyes. "We need to get back. Marinallis?"

"Waiting near the bridge, as far as I know. We've lost hours." Urgency returned. Tessara moved to his side, offering support.

He accepted her arm gratefully, the simple contact grounding. They took a final glance around the hidden lab, especially the container holding its secret. It seemed strange that the object that was the most important thing in their past two days, was now to be simply left to fate.

Then, after collecting their few remaining possessions and picking up some food bars and water that Urbanalla had left, they stepped back out together into the ruins. The Plazteel door hissed shut behind them, erasing the lab's existence once more. Leaning on Tessara, Varinn set his face towards the path back, the small, opaque vial secured unseen against his skin, its hidden purpose a silent weight added to the burden of their desperate journey.

Chapter 22. Part 2.

Voss woke before the dawn light started to blaze through the amber coloured crystal domes of the residential areas, and into his apartment through the blinds of his picture window overlooking the main plaza. Sleep had been shallow, disturbed by fragmented images, such as the silent, colossal trains of Wahlsanga, Raith's coolly delivered orders, the receding lights of the transport buggy carrying Renata and Rayk away into the station's corridors.

The weight of responsibility settled heavily the moment consciousness returned. Wahlsanga demanded planning, resources and teams. And first, today, there was the Echo Key. Raith's bizarre insistence on its retrieval and relocation under Rayk's direct control felt like another layer of shadow in the Director's already opaque agenda.

He needed to confirm the morning's schedule with Renata. He sat up, rubbing the residual sleep from his eyes, and activated the comm panel beside his bed, dialling the direct line to her assigned quarters. The link chimed once, then connected.

After only a brief moment, the call was answered. "Hello?" Rayk's voice. Calm, professional, instantly recognisable. And definitely not coming from the corridor.

Voss froze. The unexpected voice jolting him fully awake. Slightly confused, wondering if he had somehow misdialled in his pre-dawn state, he said, "Er... is Renata there?"

There was only the briefest pause on the other end. "Ah, Director Voss. Good morning," Rayk replied, his tone still perfectly level, betraying nothing. "She's still asleep currently. Shall I wake her up?"

The words struck Voss with the force of a physical blow. Still asleep. Shall I wake her up? Rayk was there. In her quarters. First thing in the morning. The image from the previous night, the easy conversation, the shared departure in the buggy, all slammed back into focus. Now, however, it was cast in a stark, ugly light. A wave of cold anger, humiliation, and a surprisingly visceral sense of betrayal washed over him. He felt his knuckles whiten where he gripped the edge of the console. He fought to keep his own voice steady, to mask the sudden, sickening turmoil.

"No," he managed, the word emerging clipped and harsh. "No, don't... don't disturb her." He took a shallow breath. "I will ping it through to her qWatch. The briefing today is earlier. Main refectory. 0730." He stabbed the disconnect button before Rayk could reply further. The abrupt silence in his quarters feeling suddenly vast and accusing.

He sat there for a long moment, staring blankly at the wall, his mind racing. Rayk and Renata. While he was wrestling with the weight of command, the fate of potentially galaxy-altering discoveries... they were... He clenched his fists, pushing the specifics of the imagined betrayal away, the thought too painful, too raw. Professionalism. He clung to it like a lifeline. There was a mission, Raith's orders, the Echo Key. Personal feelings were a luxury he couldn't afford, a vulnerability he wouldn't show. He forced himself up, moving towards the fresher unit with stiff, mechanical movements, compartmentalising the hurt, burying it beneath layers of cold formality.

The executive refectory was bustling, the drone of warm conversation a jarring contrast to the cold silence in his own mind. Voss moved through the crowd, collecting a tray with real coffee from Earth that he didn't want and fresh fruits from

The Xenologist

the ancient local terraces that he couldn't eat. He found an empty table, deliberately isolating himself from the main flow, and forced himself to review the drone data on his datapad.

Renata arrived a few minutes later, looking a little tired but professional in her standard grey and red bordered utility suit. She offered a polite smile as she approached his table. "Good morning, Principal." If she noticed his strained expression or the slight stiffness in his posture, she gave no sign, likely attributing it to the pressures of his new role. Rayk was nowhere to be seen.

"Doctor Volkova," Voss replied, his tone cooler than he intended, purely formal. He gestured towards the seat opposite. "Please."

She sat, placing her tray down. "Why the early briefing? Is everything alright?"

"Everything is proceeding according to schedule, but we are going to be fairly busy today," Voss stated, avoiding her direct gaze, focusing instead on the datapad display between them. "Regarding today's primary objective: the retrieval of the Echo Key artefact." He kept his voice level, purely informational. "Detective Kostin is under direct orders from Director Raith to assume custody of the item from the physics team at the surface ruin site this morning. Departure is scheduled for 0900 from Landing Pad Delta. The artefact will then be transported under Kostin's personal security detail to Wahlsanga Depot, where he will establish a dedicated, restricted-access holding facility as per the Director's instruction."

Renata listened intently, nodding. "Understood. Have the physics team been notified of the transfer protocol?"

"However, this morning I had received a private briefing from Director Raith. He is sending extra Military personnel, extra Military emergency rations and water and construction materials. He is also sending some of the agricultural staff with instructions to establish new hydroponics."

She laughed slightly. "What's he expecting? An invasion?"

Voss pointedly ignored her question. "Detective Kostin is handling the liaison," he replied, his voice clipped and killing off any further discussion. "He will ensure secure chain-of-custody."

Renata, sensing the wall he had just erected, adopted a slightly puzzled expression for just a moment, which she quickly adjusted to a purely professional mien. "The overnight drone surveys from Wahlsanga Depot returned preliminary structural data," she offered, bringing up a schematic on her datapad. "Confirmed the cavern dimensions are even larger than initial estimates. They also flagged two potential secondary tunnel access points in the north-east quadrant, heavily collapsed but warranting investigation when geological teams arrive."

You don't know that I know, do you? Voss thought to himself. "OK, interesting," Voss said out loud, making an effort to lighten his tone. He glanced briefly at the schematic. "Ensure that data is flagged for Doctor Chowdry's logistical planning and the initial security assessment teams." He took a sip of the lukewarm coffee. The conversation felt brittle, functional, stripped of the easy camaraderie they had shared, however briefly.

The awkward breakfast concluded quickly. Voss stood abruptly. "Landing Pad Delta, 0900 sharp please." He picked up his tray, offering Renata only a stiff nod before turning and walking away, leaving her sitting alone at the table, a flicker of confusion and perhaps hurt faintly visible in her eyes as she watched him go.

Back in his quarters, Voss forced himself through the pre-mission checks, the earlier anger now a cold knot in his stomach. He strapped on the light sidearm that was standard field issue for Directorate heads, the unfamiliar weight a tangible reminder of his unwanted responsibilities. The face that looked back at him from the mirror panel seemed strained, older. He pushed the image of Rayk in Renata's quarters from his mind, focusing only on the Echo Key, on Raith's orders, on the mission. Professionalism. It was all he had left.

Chapter 23. Part 1.

The buggy-taxi deposited Voss at his door, then slid silently away down the corridor, carrying Renata and Rayk towards their respective sectors. He watched it go, the image of them seated one behind the other, a neutral fact that nonetheless settled uneasily within the complex brew of exhaustion and responsibility. Shaking his head, he turned towards his quarters, the door hissing open to welcome him into the quiet solitude demanded by his new rank. The weight of Wahlsanga and the mysteries it held felt immense.

Further down the corridor, the buggy reached Renata's sector. Rayk made to exit, offering a professional nod. "Goodnight, Doctor Volkova." She replied, "Oh, Renata, please. We are off duty after all?"

As she dismounted the buggy, Renata hesitated, still processing the whirlwind of the day—the Depot, Voss's sudden elevation, Chowdry's blustering arrival, the "Penelope" non-discovery. Then there was Voss's slight cool formality. *Is that my imagination?* The vodka she'd had earlier hadn't quite cleared, leaving a buzzing in her head. "Rayk, wait," she said impulsively. "One more quick drink? In my quarters? Just to... properly go over these Wahlsanga security parameters? I think another will help me sleep."

Rayk paused, considering. Professional boundaries dictated otherwise, yet the Wahlsanga find *was* unprecedented, its security implications vast. A direct, informal debrief with the lead archaeologist wasn't entirely inappropriate, perhaps even necessary. And Voss's sudden elevation added another layer of complexity to command structure protocols. "Alright," he conceded after a moment. "A brief review might be prudent."

Inside Renata's quarters – beautiful and spacious like Voss's, but perhaps softened with a few colourful Terran textiles and shelves displaying small, carefully catalogued geological samples and a sofa and an armchair. She poured herself another measure of vodka, adding only a splash of mixer this time. Rayk accepted a synth-whiskey, neat.

To complement the vodka, she brought out two treasured pickle jars from Ukraine. One of pickled gherkins and one of pickled beetroot. As part of her culture, she picked some salted crackers and laid everything out on the coffee table as a miniature buffet. To just drink with no hospitalities was for crude alcoholics. "Budmo!" she toasted. Rayk smiled and they touched glasses and then, feeling more relaxed, he relaxed back into his armchair.

Their conversation began professionally, mapping out potential security weaknesses at the Depot entrance, discussing personnel requirements and the difficulties Chowdry might create despite Voss's orders. But as Renata refilled her glass again, the talk drifted, loosened by alcohol and the shared intensity of the day. She laughed, shaking her head.

"My grandmother, back in Lviv," she said, swirling the clear liquid, "she always claimed we had beetroot juice in our veins, and drank vodka in Steins. It seems she might have been right tonight." She took another long sip, her professional guard lowered.

Rayk, nursing his single drink, listened more than he spoke, his analytical mind likely cataloguing her observations about the site, perhaps noting her increasing level of intoxication with detached concern. Needing a moment, or perhaps just the facility, he eventually excused himself. "May I use your fresher?" Renata waved a vague hand in its direction.

He stepped inside the small, sterile bathroom unit. The sudden quiet, away from Renata's slightly unfocused chatter, was a relief. He splashed cool water on his face, the regulated temperature a constant in this artificial environment. Habit, more than conscious thought, made him peel off his close-fitting black duty tunic, the air cooler on his skin. He took a sterile sanitising wipe from a dispenser, turning his back to the mirror panel. He carefully cleaned the skin around the integrated bio-port low on his spine – a square of dark, smooth silicon composite set almost flush, housing the primary neural interface for his cybernetic enhancements. Routine maintenance, preventing infection at the delicate junction of biology and machine.

He caught his reflection as he turned back. And froze. Renata stood frozen, taking her empty glass to the kitchenette. The door was ajar and she saw his implant. She was transfixed at the sight. Her face flushed bright red, her expression a strange mix of embarrassment and open curiosity and something softer, more uncertain.

"Sorry..." she murmured, her voice slightly husky, thicker than usual. Her face ironic and self-mocking, "Typical me. I shouldn't, just..." She trailed off, then seemed to sigh and gather herself. "I heard... rumours, you know. About the implants." Her gaze flickered towards his back, then quickly away. "I never asked. Does... does it hurt?"

Rayk met her gaze evenly, his own expression unreadable, though perhaps a subtle wariness entered his eyes. He finished pulling his tunic back on, the movement deliberate. "Not usually. Just requires... upkeep." He held her gaze for a moment longer than necessary. "You wanted to know?"

The directness, combined with the alcohol, seemed to embolden her. She walked into the guest bathroom, taking a step towards him into the small space. "Wanted to see," she admitted, her voice low. She reached out around his back, looking over his shoulder at the mirror, using it to guide her fingers. She looked up and he did not protest; in fact he seemed curious himself. Her fingers were hesitant as they rested gently on the silicon block embedded into his spine.

He didn't react. She said, "It's like a Cyborg—Robocop—Terminator thing." This time, he blushed and smiled a little. She said, "Don't worry. From a woman's point of view, it's kind of stupidly hot." This time they both laughed, breaking the tension. Renata noticed Rayk's face stayed flushed. *Is that embarrassment? I think not.* She took her hands away from his spine and placed them on the bare skin of his bicep. She felt the coiled strength beneath, saw the faint network of scars near his shoulder from older injuries. A wave of unexpected sympathy washed through her, tangled with a confusing flicker of attraction—the allure of the damaged, the dangerous, the man rebuilt. *Renata, stay away from those troubled boys,* her mother's long-ago warning echoed faintly, lost in the vodka haze. She leaned fractionally closer, her intent, hazy but undeniable, clear in her slightly unfocused eyes.

Rayk remained perfectly still. He didn't pull away, didn't speak, but his body subtly tensed, a quiet, unyielding resistance. His nostrils flared slightly but his gaze didn't waver, didn't warm, didn't reciprocate the nascent intimacy. There was no verbal refusal, simply an absence of response, a silent, impassable boundary.

Renata felt it instantly. The lack of reciprocation hit her like cold water, cutting through the alcoholic warmth. Sadness flooded her, sharp and immediate. Overwhelmed by the unspoken rejection, the sudden awareness of her own tipsy overstep, she lowered her head, eyes watering and a little red. She settled for the obvious statement. "Sorry, Rayk. I shouldn't have had a large one. It went to my head." He said, "It's fine. Really" and nodded. He raised his hands to her shoulders and pressed gently but firmly. "She turned her head to the right and leaned forward, resting her forehead briefly against the solid warmth of his chest, a gesture less of intimacy now more a plea for connection, human warmth on an alien planet surrounded by sharp political actors.

He remained still for that brief, awkward contact. Then, gently but with undeniable firmness, he used his hands on her shoulders to guide her back a step, creating space between them. His expression wasn't angry, just distant. If anything, slightly sad. "Yes, maybe just a little tipsy, Renata," he suggested with a soft nod.

Wordlessly, he guided her out of the bathroom, the brief, charged moment evaporating into thick, embarrassed silence. He led her to the sofa, where she sank down immediately, curling into herself, perhaps wishing the floor would swallow her. She mumbled another apology, her eyes closing. Rayk found a bowl in her small kitchenette, placed it unobtrusively on the floor beside the sofa, filled a glass with water and set it on the low table. He checked that she was breathing evenly, safely positioned, then retreated to the armchair across the small living space. Leaving her alone in this state was not an option—duty, decency, perhaps something more complex, dictated otherwise. He settled in for a long watch, the silence broken only by Renata's soft, rhythmic breathing as sleep claimed her.

Outside, as if in harmony with the events in the apartment, the city lights dimmed to their lowest night cycle levels. Renata was oblivious. After a couple of minutes, Rayk rose stiffly from the chair and went back to the bathroom. The memory of the brief encounter flickered – her unexpected touch, the confusing mix of sympathy and desire in her eyes, the surge of purely hormonal response he felt. *How long has it been?*

He used the facility, then stood for a moment, looking down at the useless instrument that now only existed to pass water. It was a detached, clinical observation. Nothing. As expected. The feedback loop was there and the hormones could still inflame him. The desire still twitched, like a phantom limb, but the pathways ended in static.

A sharp, fragmented memory surfaced, unwelcome: the sterile white of the neurosurgery recovery ward, the hushed, serious tones of the specialists. *"...severe L4/L5 trauma... pudendal nerve plexus compromised... efferent signals attenuated... significant procedural risk... prostatic atrophy... neuropathic pain potential... focus was mobility restoration..."* The prognosis was clear, if unspoken: the 'miracle' that gave him back his legs hadn't extended further. Functionality restored, but not wholeness.

He adjusted his uniform trousers, catching his reflection in the mirror panel. *A half man? A broken toy robot on the shelf. It still walks, but it can't shoot its weapon.* He felt a moment of self-revulsion. *No, I should be grateful for the miracle.* The face looking back was satisfyingly impassive, controlled, the mask perfectly in place. Except... was that moisture tracing a path down one cheek? He wiped it away impatiently, a single, rare moment of self-pity betraying a grief too deep, too private for conscious acknowledgement.

He straightened his shoulders, the moment of weakness gone as quickly as it came. He returned to the armchair, resuming his silent, professional vigil over the sleeping archaeologist, the hidden cost of his cybernetic resurrection a silent burden in the quiet dark.

Just before the first simulated dawn light touched the station corridors, Renata stirred briefly, then settled back into sleep. Rayk checked the time. He needed to leave before she woke properly, to avoid the inevitable morning-after awkwardness. Just as he stood, preparing to let himself out, the apartment's internal comm panel chimed. Renata didn't stir. He crossed to the panel. Voss's code was displayed. With a sigh, Rayk accepted the connection. "Hello?"

After the brief, curt exchange ended with Voss abruptly disconnecting, Rayk considered. Voss had said he'd ping Renata's qWatch and meet at the refectory. Waking her now would serve little purpose beyond mutual embarrassment. Quietly, ensuring the water glass was within easy reach, Rayk let himself out of the apartment, the door hissing softly shut behind him, leaving no trace of his overnight vigil except the unanswered question hanging in Voss's mind.

Chapter 23. Part 2.

The journey through Petropolis's sculpted corridors towards the central command spire, where Director Raith maintained his office, felt different this morning. The usual sense of detached observation Rayk relied upon was overlaid with a low hum of controlled alertness, a consequence of the Wahlsanga discovery and the Director's opaque pronouncements regarding 'orbital traffic density'. Raith's leash, demonstrated so crudely with the override command days earlier, felt tangibly present.

As the transit car slid silently towards the spire's restricted levels, Rayk closed his eyes for a moment, shutting out the external world and focusing inward, accessing the secure partition where his integrated AS resided.

AI. Status update required. Analysis of the Director's override protocol – specifically countermeasures.' The query flowed through his neural interface, a silent command.

There was a fractional processing lag, then the AS's response formed, its synthesised internal 'voice' precise, analytical, yet carrying that now-familiar hint of collaborative initiative.

Analysis ongoing, *User Kostin*. The Level-Zero command exploited a deprecated diagnostic pathway, bypassing standard security layers. The current mitigation strategy focuses on rapidly isolating the targeted neural interface points via *emergency localised synaptic blocks* upon detection of the command signature. Simulation suggests a 58.7 per cent chance of initiating the block before full system compromise, though transient sensory disruption or minor motor control interference during the block is probable. Achieving higher certainty and minimising side effects requires access to restricted core system architecture logs to fully model pathway interactions.'

Understood. Is there any alternative method we can pursue, for instance, obtaining diagnostic equipment from the labs here or attempting to obtain Raith's qWatch log for the command line that was sent?

The AS paused. Acquiring logs directly from Director Raith's qWatch presents a high-risk, low-probability scenario due to device-level security protocols, User Kostin. Furthermore, while the transmitted command line might be logged, it wouldn't necessarily detail the propagation effects within your specific neural architecture in real-time.

Then, after another pause, the AS took on a more speculative or hopeful tone.

However, a controlled replication could yield valuable heuristic data. It might be beneficial for me to attempt initiating a low-level simulation of the override sequence while we are in a secure, controlled environment, such as your quarters later. This would allow direct observation and potentially accelerate countermeasure development.'

A jolt of disbelief, followed by grim humour. The AS was suggesting he deliberately trigger the attack, just to study it. *Hah. Thanks, but no thanks*, he projected wryly. *To reiterate, absolutely negative. Focus on passive analysis only. No active simulations and that's non-negotiable.* The thought of voluntarily experiencing even a low-level version of that shutdown was abhorrent.

Acknowledged. Active simulation protocol discarded. Continuing passive analysis, the AS replied, its tone returning to neutral. Its presence receded as the transit car arrived.

The Xenologist

Rayk stepped out onto the polished floor of the executive level. Raith's outer office was silent, the usual administrative aide likely reassigned during the personnel 'consolidation'. The main door slid open at his approach, revealing the Director seated behind his expansive desk, the simulated Earth-sky ceiling casting a placid blue light over the room. Holographic displays shimmered around him, currently showing complex orbital plots and energy signatures – the fleet, undoubtedly. Raith looked up as Rayk entered, his expression calm, composed, betraying nothing.

"Detective Kostin. Your report, please." Raith's voice was cool, inviting.

Rayk moved forward, stopping before the desk. He delivered his report concisely and factually. "Wahlsanga Depot discovery confirmed, sir. The scale is monumental. There are intact transport units, one statue and sealed cargo containers observed. Principal Voss has assumed operational command of the site effectively, initiating security protocols and information lockdown, which you ratified. Doctor Chowdry was intercepted attempting unauthorised access; he has been returned under escort with communications restricted as directed and tasked by Voss with coordinating logistical support." He paused. "The mission to retrieve the Echo Key artefact proceeds this morning as ordered. I will assume personal custody and establish secure containment at Wahlsanga Depot upon completion."

Raith absorbed the report with a slow, almost imperceptible nod, his fingers perhaps making minute adjustments on a hidden console interface. "Voss is stepping up, then? Good. Competence is required. And Chowdry... contained. Appropriate." His gaze flickered towards the orbital displays. "The situation remains... fluid."

Rayk seized the opening, keeping his tone professionally neutral. "Regarding the 'orbital traffic density,' sir. Has there been any further communication or clarification from the approaching fleet? For security contingency planning, any updated assessment of their status or intent would be valuable."

Raith leaned back slightly, steepling his fingers. "Clarification has not been forthcoming, Detective. The main body – Colony Fleet Argus designation, fifty thousand personnel minimum – maintains radio silence beyond standard PCMA transponder authentication. They refuse hails, ignore standard approach vector protocols." He gestured vaguely at a display showing multiple large vessel icons closing on the planet. "Their composition is confirmed as heavy colonisation assets—Arks, Habitat Processors, Planetary Integration Support. Entirely unscheduled, entirely unauthorised by Central Command or the Board."

He met Rayk's gaze, his eyes cool and analytical. "The situation remains one of profound procedural irregularity, Kostin. A potential command structure failure at the highest level, or an unsanctioned deployment of significant scale. Either scenario necessitates the extreme security posture I have implemented." He didn't mention hostility directly, framing it as a crisis of *order* and *protocol*. "Your relocation of the Echo Key artefact and all the physicists' notes to a dispersed, secure facility under your direct control at Wahlsanga is a prudent measure under these uncertain circumstances. Asset security and information containment remain paramount. There is one more small detail that I do not wish to put in official communications."

"Yes, Sir?".

"Do not communicate back to head office where you secure the device. Only you, Voss and if you deem it appropriate, Dr. Volkova will know its exact location. The

Physicists are to be sent to Wahlsanga to work on other tech, such as those trains."

He offered nothing more. No speculation on motive beyond procedural failure or unsanctioned action. He didn't have to. Between military men, the meaning was plain.

"Understood, sir," Rayk acknowledged, recognising the familiar pattern of controlled disclosure. Planning for the worst, but the office staff within hearing distance, or who read the plans, for now, would not pick up on the gravity of the situation. The threat was real, serious, but Raith was keeping his full assessment, his own contingency plans, close to his chest. "Security forces are on maximum alert."

"See that they remain so," Raith said dismissively, his attention already drifting back to the orbital displays. "Report immediately upon securing the Echo Key. You are dismissed, Detective."

Rayk gave a crisp nod and turned, leaving the Director's climate-controlled sanctum. As he walked back towards the transit car, the cool efficiency of Raith's office felt suddenly oppressive. The Director was managing the crisis, yes, but the override, the fleet, the Echo Key relocation – it all felt like layers of control, Raith moving pieces on a board Rayk couldn't fully see. The need for those countermeasures to the Director's override protocol felt more urgent than ever. An idea sparked, a tangential path to potentially accessing the restricted core system logs that the AS needed. AS,' Rayk projected silently, *The report on the override countermeasures seems to be taking a while. Is there some problem?'*

Analysis continues, Mr. Kostin, the AS replied. Rayk registered the change in address—no longer 'User'. A subtle shift, unexpected. Full mitigation remains dependent on accessing restricted core architecture logs detailing the deprecated diagnostic pathway Raith exploited.

Search logs from my initial augmentation, Rayk directed. Focus on the installation of diagnostic ports or system integration points near the L4/L5 spinal interface. Find the origin of that pathway.

There was a pause, then the AS responded, its tone perhaps carrying a new, almost hesitant quality. Searching integration logs... Found correlation. The installation phase for the primary diagnostic shunt—the likely origin point for the override pathway—coincided precisely with the phase where integration of the S2-S4 nerve bundle was scheduled.' Another pause. 'Log addendum indicates S2-S4 integration—governing pelvic autonomic function and sexual response—was bypassed. Cited justification: 'Critical resource conflict during stabilisation phase.

A cold knot formed in Rayk's stomach. '*Resource conflict? Was that accurate, AS?'*

Cross-referencing resource allocation metrics from the augmentation time frame...' A longer pause this time, as if confirming complex data. 'Mr. Kostin, the data indicates sufficient surgical time, processor capacity, and bio-support power were available concurrently for both the diagnostic shunt installation and the S2-S4 nerve integration according to standard protocols. The logged justification appears... inconsistent with recorded metrics.

Rayk felt the air leave his lungs. The shunt—the *backdoor* Raith used—was installed *instead* of potentially restoring his full function, using resources that could have done both, based on a reason that now looked false.

Could... could both have been done successfully? He projected, the question tasting like ash.

Unknown, the AS replied. Simultaneous complex integrations carry risks. Prioritising the diagnostic shunt may have been deemed essential for long-term system stability monitoring, or for other reasons not logged. The data does not provide motive, only discrepancy.

The callous implication settled in his gut like a shard of ice. The backdoor—his leash—had been prioritised over his wholeness. Can the damage be fixed?' he projected, the thought a desperate prayer. *The bypassed integration can it be done now?*

The current status of the nerve pathways is unknown without invasive diagnostics, Mr. Kostin, the AS stated. Furthermore, prolonged lack of innervation often leads to significant degradation of the associated tissues—in this case, the corpus cavernosum. Biological atrophy over this period may render future surgical intervention ineffective or impossible. A definitive prognosis is not possible with the available data.

The transit car arrived at his level. Rayk stood slowly. Atrophy. Irreversible. The backdoor had been installed. The AS may not be completely sure, but Rayk was no fool. His full function had been bypassed. *Just to be sure, they kept control of me!* He remembered the face of the Neurosurgeon who told him he would walk again. He remembered being given the bad news about the impotence, but it didn't matter at the time. He was going to walk again! Not only that, but also be stronger and better in every way. Except one. He remembered he had worshipped that team of surgeons. He never felt loyalty and gratitude to anyone like he felt to that man when he told Rayk he would walk again. But butter would not have melted in the man's mouth. Liar! He stepped out onto the platform, his face an impassive mask, but inside, a cold, razor-sharp certainty formed. Someone had made a choice about him, for him. And the cost was absolute.

Chapter 24. Part 1.

The late afternoon sun, filtered through the dense, multi-layered canopy of the Great Gorge and further softened by the rock arches of Valerius Corba's villa, cast long, dappled shadows across the polished chrome and synth-wood of his study. Outside, beyond the panoramic window, water cascaded silently down meticulously engineered terraces, feeding the impossible mix of Terran citrus, imported grapevines, and native Sikarran ferns with their shimmering, silvery-blue fronds. Verdant Point, Corba had named his enclave. An oasis of controlled, extravagant life carved into the ancient cliffs, a testament to wealth and will.

Corba sat in his Terran leather chair, in his hand, a crystal tumbler of genuine Talisker single malt whiskey imported at staggering expense. On the main console before him, market data from the London CPM index, the Combined Planets Market, scrolled placidly. He made a minute adjustment to a complex derivative structure, based upon future revenues from New Ohio bio-discoveries and Sikarran Tech-discoveries. His expression was one of bored competence. The robotic lawn-trimmers hummed faintly from a lower terrace, the only sound besides the distant, soothing murmur of the gorge's waterfalls.

Satisfied with the financial adjustment, Corba blanked the main screen. He touched a nearly invisible sensor embedded in the armrest of his chair. A section of the wall beside his desk slid silently open, revealing not books or decorative art, but the flat, dark interface of a heavily encrypted, dedicated comms unit, completely isolated from standard PCMA networks. Its activation light glowed a deep, coded crimson.

His fingers moved across the interface, accessing secure channels, his expression shifting subtly, losing its placid boredom, replaced by a focused intensity. Coded bursts scrolled past, minor shipping confirms, encrypted nods and so on, until one flashed red: *ASSET J LIABILITY CONFIRMED. RISK UNACCEPTABLE. ELIMINATION APPROVED. ACKNOWLEDGE.* He typed a short, concise message, his fingers precise: Confirmed. He watched the confirmation signal flash green, affirmative, then wiped the outgoing buffer clean. He'd ordered Jonesy erased days ago; tonight's green light merely ratified the hit—and reminded him it had already failed.

I put the best men that the CAR could give me on that mission. The abilities they attribute to that Officer, Kostin, are implausible. I have seen him. He isn't that much. He couldn't rule out corruption, of course. Follow the money.

He had no intention of reporting the failure, of course. This was his domain. He wasn't their lackey; he was their partner. Jones was a loose end to be dealt with later. Simple.

But soon it would be academic and Jones would keep his mouth shut. To be dealt with later. He then navigated to a different layer of the secure network. It comprised cluttered, visually chaotic forums pulsing with angry manifestos, complex diagrams purporting to expose hidden truths and networks dedicated to dissecting the "official narrative." His anonymous avatar, 'Cassandra V,' flickered into existence. With practised ease, he began crafting new posts, seeding disinformation, nurturing the narratives that served his purpose.

Insider PCMA source VERY nervous, he typed into one encrypted channel dedicated to analysing the 'black flag Pallas Incident'. Lockdown on Sikarra is getting tighter. Why? Hearing whispers of indigenous sentient beings discovered. Not animals. PEOPLE. Direct human ancestors? PCMA isn't sharing. Cover-up in progress.

On another forum focused on suppressed technologies: A friend working in geology on Sikarra using deep scans found energy signatures UNLIKE anything known. Potential free energy source? Matches theoretical profiles suppressed after the Siberian Accord 'accident'. PCMA geologist now reassigned, data classified Level 5. They found something world-changing and they are HIDING it.

He leaned back, a faint, cold smile touching his lips as he imagined the messages rippling outwards, fuelling paranoia, justifying dissent. The old methods are the best, he thought with a wry grin. Too much information keeps them distracted from the real game. The real truth, the carefully constructed web of deception spun by the established powers after Pallas, the deliberate suppression of CAR ascendancy, was far simpler. Certainly more dangerous. Only those like him, those willing to see the pattern, could prepare for the necessary correction.

He indicated an internal alert. He closed the secure interface just as Elara, his wife, swept into the study. She was dressed in flowing silks, her expression radiating a familiar, restless boredom.

"Valerius, honestly," she sighed, sinking dramatically onto a chaise lounge near the window. "This place is intolerably dull. Another day staring at alien ferns. When can we host a *real* gathering? I spoke to Anya Henderson via closed comms. I've heard they're established quite comfortably up-gorge now. An evening with them and their neighbours, at least? Anything."

"Please be just a little more patient, Elara," Corba said smoothly, turning his chair towards her, the mask of the calm oligarch back in place. "Security protocols are heightened currently. Unnecessary social gatherings are discouraged."

"Security protocols, this protocol, that protocol," she scoffed lightly. "You love that word, like those books, what is that? 'Protocols of Zion', or something? Load of old nonsense, the lot of it".

Corba sighed. "You mean the 'Protocols of the Elders of Zion'? It has some truth in it, like all good propaganda, but yes, it's mostly nonsense." Buddhist-funded propaganda of the highest quality, but you wouldn't care or understand. "I only keep it for reference. The book you should read is 'The Lhasa Protocols: A Vajra Eye Blueprint for Global Control.' It tells you all about the hoax of the so-called Tibetan Invasion of the 20th Century."

Elara looked balefully at him. Corba smiled indulgently. "Much as I love you, you really need to educate yourself, Elara, sweetie."

"You always say that. But life is fulfilling enough without filling my head with this stuff you obsess about. Fulfilling if we weren't in this dreadful gorge. It feels," she held her arms as if cold, "watchful. I heard those strange whistling sounds again last night, from the lower terraces."

"Atmospheric phenomena," Corba replied dismissively. "Or perhaps just the winged-hyraxes or those cute dragon-rats. You know how acoustics play tricks down here." He glanced briefly towards the window as the nervous cleaner, the one who left scraps out, hurried past on an outer walkway, head down, avoiding eye contact with the villa itself. Superstitious fool.

Elara sighed again, uninterested in atmospheric tricks. "Well, if we can't have guests, can we at least plan a trip? Off-world? Monaco? Even Mars Colony Command has more life than this place."

"Soon," Corba placated. "Important developments are underway. Once certain projects reach fruition, our position here will be significantly enhanced. Then we can travel." He offered her a thin smile, devoid of warmth. She wouldn't understand the Pallas Incident, the necessity of CAR's rise, the critical importance of securing the Architect technology before the decadent PCMA squandered or suppressed it further. Her world was confined to social status and luxury.

She looked unconvinced but didn't argue further, merely picking up a fashion datapad. Corba turned back towards his main console, but his thoughts weren't on market data. Jonesy was now a moot point and could be ignored. His contacts off-world were moving resources. The disinformation seeds were sown. Now, he needed only to wait for the arrival—the catalyst that would accelerate Phase Two, break the PCMA's fragile hold, and allow the right people to secure Sikarra's true prize.

A self-satisfied smile touched his lips as he looked at his paper-book collection. A true extravagance in a planetary culture based upon escaping gravity wells and weight was everything. He went through the top shelf titles, reminding himself of just what a good read they all were, and how he woke up through real education. Next to the 'Lhasa Protocols' and the classic 'Zion' was 'The Potala Deception: NARIA, Vajra Eye, and the Fabricated Narrative of Tibetan Victimhood', 'The North Atlantic Republic Intelligence Agency: Are we the baddies?', 'Snow Lion's Shadow: How Vajra Eye Infiltrated PCMA and Controls Off-World Resources' and the best of all, the one that liberated his financial mind, 'Mandala of Lies: Unmasking the NARIA-Buddhist Financial Network'.

He smiled and allowed himself another sip of the Talisker, the aged spirit a small comfort, a taste of the old world soon to be eclipsed by the new one he was helping to build. Whether the current inhabitants knew it or not, the constant, soothing murmur of the waterfalls outside seemed to mock the turbulent undercurrents swirling within Verdant Point.

Chapter 24. Part 2.

Alone once more in the cool, calm of his office, under the simulated sky, Director Raith processed the variables. Wahlsanga Depot: a confirmed trove of priceless assets. Voss: the unexpected academic, stepping into the command vacuum. Chowdry: the irritant, contained. And hovering above it all, the final, silent variable: Colony Fleet Argus.

The confluence of events demanded action beyond simple vigilance. The concentration of irreplaceable assets—the potential technological secrets of Wahlsanga, the newly relocated Echo Key under Kostin's guard there, *and* the primary command functions here in Petropolis—created an unacceptable strategic vulnerability, especially given the fleet's refusal to adhere to protocol. Dispersal was logical. Necessary.

Raith opened files on his holographic screen. He arrayed the military assets from right to left, each file a neat three-dimensional stack of papers. His civilian logistics were in the layer behind. He started to make links between them, like tethers in space, with civilian transports allocated to military assets to move them clandestinely to the places where they were most likely needed. One thing in all the chaos of which he was certain was that they were being watched, both from space and from the ground view.

He formally designated the Wahlsanga Depot Complex as Sector Beta. Primary directive: Secure containment and phased assessment of Architect technology. All personnel related to advanced physics and xeno-engineering, including Dr. Mainwaring's team, currently working on the Echo Key analysis, were to be relocated there under Kostin's security oversight as soon as feasible. Command structure: Principal Voss, reporting directly to Raith.

Petropolis Command became Sector Alpha. Primary directive: Maintain planetary administration, primary life support systems, orbital communications, and ongoing baseline research. Raith would maintain overall operational command from here, for now.

He authorised secondary communication hubs and remote power facilities to shift to heightened readiness, ensuring redundancy should Sector Beta be compromised. A logical division of assets and risk.

Next, planetary defence. The options were limited – Sikarra was a research and colony outpost, not a fortress. Still, existing assets needed to be primed. With some imagination, there was a lot that could be done. He accessed the automated defence grid interface. Concealed kinetic energy turrets guarding the primary surface access points for both Sector Beta (Wahlsanga) and Sector Alpha (Petropolis) were cycled from standby to full operational readiness, Status Amber. Internal facility lockdowns, including blast doors between sectors and energy field containment grids, were brought to immediate activation readiness with guards posted around the clock on all assets.

Finally, he opened a Level-Zero encrypted channel, bypassing standard fleet comms, directly to the secure console of Commander Jian Li, the officer commanding PCMA Orbital Station *Guardian* overhead.

The connection chimed, and Li's face appeared on a secondary display. He was professional, competent, but etched with sleeplessness and undeniable tension. "Director Raith."

"Commander Li," Raith began without preamble, his voice flat, devoid of emotion. "Status update on Colony Fleet Argus and associated vessels."

"Unchanged, Director," Li reported, his voice tight. "The main fleet maintains formation, continuing a slow approach towards standard orbital insertion parameters, but remains unresponsive to all standard communication protocols beyond initial transponder authentication. The lead cruisers, *Argus* and *Agamemnon*, are holding position relative to the main body. No hostile emissions detected, but their refusal to communicate is profoundly disturbing."

"Agreed," Raith stated calmly. "Commander, the time for procedural ambiguity is over. My assessment, based on combined intelligence and their current posture, is that this fleet represents an unauthorised, hostile force operating under false PCMA codes, likely CAR aligned. Their objective is undoubtedly this planet and its unique resources."

Li looked taken aback, paling slightly. "Sir, Hostile? With respect, that's a significant escalation based solely on non-communication."

"Their silence *is* communication, Commander," Raith cut him off coolly. "It signals intent to operate outside established authority. We are cut off from immediate Central Command confirmation, as you know, reliant upon message capsules and they know it also. We are on the back foot, bureaucratically paralysed, which is, to them, with the way the CAR thinks, the equivalent of powerless. Waiting for them to power weapons is suicide. Conventional defence against a fleet of this scale is impossible." He paused, his voice dropping. "Therefore, pre-emption is our only viable, if infinitesimal, chance."

"Pre-emption?" Li echoed, his eyes widening. "Director, you're ordering a first strike?"

"I am ordering the preparation and targeted deployment of your three available long-range interception missiles. I want them to be specifically deployed in stealth mode, like mines. They will be deployed from standard shuttle craft that we will send out to meet them. Finally, arm them each with all three asteroid-deflection nuclear warheads."

Li interrupted, "But Sir, they aren't designed for—"

Raith talked over him, "The main target will be the lead vessel identified as Agamemnon, then the main colony vessel and finally the deputy flagship identified as Argus. This way we take out the likely command ships and the main troop ship." Raith's voice was devoid of inflexion. "Surprise is our only weapon."

Li looked horrified. "Director! Without declaration, without confirmation... firing on a vessel broadcasting friendly codes, even suspicious ones... that's potentially fratricide! It's a war crime!"

Raith met the Commander's panicked gaze without flinching. "Better a war criminal than a war victim, Commander Li," he replied, his voice dropping slightly, becoming almost silken, yet utterly implacable. "The responsibility, and any subsequent consequences, are mine alone. You have your orders. Authorisation Raith-Omega-7. Begin launch preparation immediately."

Li stared for a second, trapped between protocol, fear, and the Director's chilling certainty. Finally, he gave a jerky nod, his face grim. "Acknowledged... authorisation Omega-7 confirmed. Ordnance preparation commencing. God help us all, Director."

Raith terminated the connection without reply. He leaned back in his chair. The

Commander's fear, the gravity of the order and the potential for interstellar war ignited by his command didn't register as pressure or dread. Instead, a strange, almost forgotten lightness bloomed in his chest. A forgotten feeling. Excitement. A young Raith waking up on Christmas morning came to his memory.

He thought for a moment of the dire consequences of his gamble failing. That the fleet was possibly PCMA. Then, shocking himself, he laughed for the first time in his adult life. It wasn't humour, precisely, but the sheer, exhilarating absurdity of it all. War crimes, fifty thousand potential enemies and gambling planetary fate on a stealth missile strike. All the rules, the consequences, the carefully constructed order of things felt suddenly, delightfully irrelevant. It all fell on Raith, who, by his own admission, couldn't give a damn.

When was the last time he laughed? He remembered, distantly, an ancient TV comedy recording from Earth—actors on a primitive stage, portraying an alien abduction, dissolving into helpless, unprofessional laughter, unable to keep their faces straight as their absurd account became progressively worse. The young, inexperienced child that was Raith laughed so much he fell off the sofa in stitches, his sides aching with uncontrollable laughter. He hadn't understood it then, but now... the scale of this potential disaster, the utter transgression... it was almost... freeing. The laugh died quickly, replaced by a cold, sharp clarity—the first real sensation to pierce his chronic ennui in years. *For that moment alone,* the thought came, unbidden, accompanied by a thin, genuine smile, *this posting might be worth the price.*

The moment passed. The analytical mind reasserted control. Practicalities remained. He reopened the secure channel to Commander Li. "Commander. Further directive. You will immediately initiate a silent evacuation. All non-essential station personnel transfer to designated emergency shuttles. Destination: Sector Alpha surface coordinates, Wahlsanga complex. Mask the departure; transmit standard signals requesting deployment of Phase Two Colonist Integration Teams to those coordinates. Maintain a skeleton crew for station defence and final monitoring only. Ensure escape pod readiness. Upon confirmation of ordnance launch, or immediately upon hostile counter detection, whichever comes first, do not try to fight the incoming fleet. It is pointless. After launching all available ordnance under War-AI control, begin evacuating yourself and your remaining skeleton staff. Acknowledge.

He received the terse confirmation. Everything was in motion. Dispersal, defence activation, pre-emptive strike preparation, evacuation contingency. He had managed the variables as best as possible. His preparations were the final, unplayed card. Now, he merely had to wait. He turned his attention back to the placidly scrolling market data on his secondary screen, the simulated sky above oblivious, the soothing murmur of the water features outside, a counterpoint to the silent, potentially catastrophic storm gathering in orbit.

Chapter 25. Part 1

The Plazteel door hissed shut, sealing the hidden lab and its secrets away within the ancient city of the Original Pheonalla. Varinn took a steadying breath, the cool evening air a sharp, welcome contrast to the sterile lab. As soon as Tessara had woken him from the medical pod, the deep ache had gone, but a subtle stiffness lingered. He leaned on Tessara's offered arm only momentarily now as they began the trek back towards the Great Gorge and Marinallis.

They moved through the silent plazas of the abandoned surface city, their footsteps echoing faintly off the enduring, near-immortal structures. Moonlight was beginning to silver the edges of the massive arches and towers, casting long, distorted shadows. For a moment, Varinn paused, looking up at the silent, empty windows high above. "Generations lived here," he murmured, almost to himself. "Before the sky turned against them. Worked, travelled, raised families... What were they like, Tessara?"

She followed his gaze, "People," she said softly. "Like Marinallis. Like Urbanalla, no Humans though, not at that time. They were driven by things we only half understand and the Designers don't even half remember." She shook her head slightly, pulling her focus back to the present. "Come on. We can't afford to reminisce."

Varinn merely grunted, conserving his breath, his gaze fixed on the path ahead. The hidden lab, Designer Urbanalla, the strange opaque vial tucked securely within his new uniform—it all felt slightly unreal now, overshadowed by the immediate, grinding reality of their situation and the urgent need to find Marinallis.

"Did you see any more signs of them?" Varinn asked after a few minutes, referring to the FOSS cultists or Carrik's operative. "After the... lab?"

Tessara shook her head. "Nothing moving. Tracks were mostly obliterated by the storm's end. I scouted the approaches to the ruins while waiting for you; the area seemed clear." She didn't elaborate on her brief, tense wait outside the sealed wall section before it had unexpectedly opened, nor the relief that had flooded her upon finding him alive inside the pod. She recounted instead, concisely, her earlier encounter near the bridge approach. "More fanatics were waiting near the bridge path. Four of them, including the one Carrik called 'Curate'."

Varinn glanced at her sharply. "Four? How did you—"

"Let's just say the local aquatic fauna proved unexpectedly helpful," Tessara said dryly, leaving Varinn to puzzle over the implication. "Carrik arrived shortly after. He... dealt with the last one."

"Carrik," Varinn breathed the name, remembering the brutal efficiency of the augmented soldier at the Weir. "He told you that I was dead?"

Tessara countered grimly. "Yes. He tried to use it as leverage." A thought struck her. "How did you handle him? He seemed... difficult to discourage."

Varinn managed a faint, humourless smile. "Let's call it a robust negotiation. More to the point, how did *you* handle him?"

"I didn't. As I said before, Marinallis did." Varinn looked amused, prompting her to go on. "While Carrik was sizing me up, he forgot about Marinallis, who had most certainly not forgotten about him!"

Varinn replied, "I have known him since I was a child. It doesn't surprise me, really. You should have seen him when he was younger." He gave a wry shake of the head as they carried on.

They descended the winding track leading into the gorge's upper reaches. "You're sure he'd wait near the bridge?" Varinn asked again as the path grew steeper.

"He was exhausted when I left him near the western abutment," Tessara confirmed. "He needed time before attempting the crossing alone. He expected us back." She glanced at him. "You're certain Urbanalla's... 'safeguards'... on that device are reliable? Leaving it just sitting in a container..."

"She seemed confident," Varinn replied, though Urbanalla's chilling pragmatism left its own unease. "And her authority was absolute. Our priority now is Marinallis."

They stepped onto the Sky-Arch Bridge together. The immense span of ancient Plazteel stretched before them, a pale ribbon against the deepening twilight sky. The wind swept up from the chasm below, cold and smelling of damp rock and distant water, tugging at their clothes and whispering through gaps in the crumbling parapets. Mist curled around the support pillars far below, obscuring the river's true depth. They moved quickly but carefully across the vast, weathered surface, their boots echoing slightly in the immense quiet.

Reaching the far side felt like arriving in another world. Here, the bridge merged with a substantial gatehouse structure built into the cliff face, similar in its enduring plazteel architecture, showed intent to be a defensive checkpoint or transition hub into the Vasantha region. Doorways, dark and silent, led deeper into the rock. They scanned the sheltered area within the gatehouse's main archway, the spot where Marinallis should logically have waited.

It was empty. The folded thermal blanket lay on a stone bench, undisturbed.

"Marinallis?" Tessara called out again, louder this time, her voice tight with renewed anxiety. "Designer?"

Silence answered, broken only by the moan of the wind through the arches. Varinn quickly checked the ground. "No tracks leading away from here into the tunnels," he noted. "No sign of a struggle." He moved towards one of the dark inner doorways, peering inside. "He has to be close."

"Looking for someone?"

The voice, thin but sharp, came from the deep shadows behind a massive support pillar near the gatehouse entrance, a spot they had already passed. Both Varinn and Tessara spun around, startled, weapons half-drawn by reflex.

Marinallis stepped out of the shadows into the faint moonlight filtering through the archway. He leaned heavily on the pillar for a moment, but his eyes were bright, alert, holding a flicker of dry amusement at their reaction. Despite his frailty, he had moved with utter silence, his awareness undiminished.

"Designer!" Varinn breathed, lowering his weapon, relief mixing with slight irritation. "We thought..."

"That vigilance is paramount, even amongst allies?" Marinallis finished, pushing himself upright. "A necessary lesson." His gaze sharpened instantly, dismissing the pleasantries. "So, Varinn. The MET Comms Unit?"

Varinn met the unwavering stare. "Secured, Designer Marinallis. But the directive was countermanded."

Marinallis, for once, looked shocked. "Countermanded? By whom?"

"D. Urbanalla," Varinn replied. Marinallis shook his head "Urbanalla is still on-planet? It's usually trouble when I hear that name. Alright, tell me what she is planning."

Varinn explained concisely: the hidden lab, the unexpected presence of Designer Urbanalla, her invocation of Evacuation Directive Primus overriding the incineration order. "She classified the unit as a repurposable asset. It was reprogrammed with multiple safeguards, but it is basically a booby trap. It's now sealed within a secure container back at the facility in the ruins, awaiting secondary retrieval signal under final evacuation orders." He stressed the outcome: "The device is contained, Sir. Secured."

Marinallis listened intently, his expression tightening every time Varinn mentioned Urbanalla's name. "Urbanalla, always reckless," he murmured, shaking his head slightly. "Well, it's her responsibility now. As long as she remembers to come back for it. Her faction always prioritised control, contingency, over necessary erasure." He sighed, a faint, rasping sound. "The risks she runs, even now." He looked sharply at Varinn. "Did she mention the Veil? Offer any caution regarding the core matrix?"

"She warned against looking past the veil," Varinn confirmed. "Cited cognitive dissolution as the likely outcome for the unprepared or, well, unsuitable."

"At least some protocols remain inviolate," Marinallis conceded grimly. He processed the situation. The device wasn't destroyed, a complication he plainly disliked, but it was secured, neutralised for the immediate future. Urbanalla's interference was a problem for another time, if time remained. "Contained," he repeated, accepting the reality. "Very well. Then Vasantha is the priority. The Newcomer ships await." He assessed Varinn again. "Are you fit to proceed?"

"Yes, Sir."

"Then let us waste no more time. Urbanalla's basic instructions are fine. But before you get yourself off planet Varinn, I may have one more job for you. I shall explain later if needed." Marinallis turned towards the dark tunnel entrance leading away from the gatehouse, deeper into the Vasantha complex.

Together, the trio moved forward, leaving the wind-swept bridge behind. Reunited, their immediate path clear, they faced the final stage of their journey. Varinn walked steadily now beside Tessara, the hidden weight of the small, opaque vial in his pocket a silent counterpoint to the vast, ancient secrets they pursued and those they left sealed in the ruins behind them.

Chapter 25. Part 2.

The executive skimmer descended towards the weathered grandeur of the Architect surface city, where the Echo Key had been unearthed weeks prior. Raith's personal skimmer, Voss noted again with faint surprise; the Director allowing its use once was unusual, twice felt significant. The reason, however, remained obscure.

Unlike the pristine, sealed environment of the Wahlsanga Depot, these vast Plazteel structures bore the marks of millennia exposed to Sikarra's elements, though their fundamental integrity remained astonishing. The PCMA science teams had established their primary analysis labs within one of the larger, more stable buildings near the original find site.

Inside the skimmer, the tense silence from the journey persisted. Voss gazed out at the approaching alien architecture, his thoughts a tangled knot of responsibility, Raith's opaque orders, and the cold distance he now felt towards Renata. She, in turn, seemed focused on reviewing data, perhaps deliberately avoiding the heavy atmosphere. Rayk remained watchful, his professional composure intact as they touched down on a cleared landing area near the designated lab entrance.

They disembarked into the dry warmth of the Sikarran day. Rayk led the way into the repurposed structure. Inside, the contrast was stark: ancient Designer walls housed gleaming, modern PCMA analysis equipment. Doctor Mainwaring met them near the main lab space, his expression resigned rather than surprised.

"Detective Kostin, Director Voss, Doctor Volkova," Mainwaring greeted them, his tone professionally level but lacking its usual enthusiasm. "We received the priority directive from Director Raith's office this morning regarding the artefact transfer and our team's imminent relocation. Everything is prepared as requested." He gestured towards a heavy-duty, sealed transport case resting on a nearby analysis bench. "The Echo Key is inside this Gaussian shielded box"

Voss watched as Renata expressed her surprise. "It's already secured? We assumed Dr. Voss or perhaps Director Raith himself would be needed for the transfer, given its selectivity."

Voss thought, *This is a mini power-play unfolding, if ever I saw one.* Mainwaring managed a thin smile as he replied, "Indeed, Doctor Volkova. We encountered the same issue – complete inertness for me and the primary team. However," he indicated his colleague standing nearby, a physicist with sharp, observant eyes and Indigenous Australian features Voss hadn't previously associated closely with the Key project, "Doctor O'Neil arrived for her analysis shift shortly after the directive came through. Remarkably, she was able to facilitate the transfer into the shielded case."

All eyes turned to Dr. O'Neil. Renata asked gently, "Doctor O'Neil, what was that like? The interaction?"

Dr. O'Neil met their gaze calmly, her expression thoughtful. "Alinta, please. It was... distinct," she said precisely. "There was initial field resistance when I placed my hand on it as expected. But then it shifted. It wasn't simple compliance like Director Voss described. It felt like active scrutiny. An intense energy surge *within* the Key, almost like it was attempting to interface, or perhaps scan my credentials? After several seconds of this, assessment? The resistance vanished, and it permitted me to pick it up".

Mainwaring shook his head. "Affinity for some, inert for others, now active scanning. Its operational parameters are baffling." He sighed. "I still believe disrupting our analysis now is premature..."

Rayk simply met his gaze, impassive, waiting. Mainwaring fell silent. After an awkward moment, Mainwaring continued. "Very well," Then, indicating the case. "It's shielded, triple-layered light-lead composite. Still, best keep it secured away from the cockpit during transit."

Rayk picked up the surprisingly heavy case. As his hand closed around the handle, he felt it himself—a faint, almost subliminal thrumming vibrating up his arm, accompanied by a flickering edge of static interference deep within his auditory implant and a fleeting sense of disorientation from his balance processors. It wasn't painful, just... undeniably present. An intrusion.

'Warning,' the AS's synthesised voice sounded clinically in his ear implant. 'Anomalous energy field detected. Low-level interference impacting auditory and vestibular implant subsystems. Source appears localised, immediate proximity.' The AS didn't know what the source was, only that something nearby was affecting Rayk's internal systems.

Rayk instantly made the connection—the interference started the moment he grasped the shielded case containing the Echo Key. Mainwaring's warning wasn't just theoretical. He kept his expression neutral, giving no outward sign, though the faint ringing in his ear implant persisted. "The shielding seems effective enough," he commented, his voice steady, deliberately downplaying any personal effect. "Any residual field effects should be minimal during transit." But I'll be glad when this thing is locked down, he added internally.

He turned, holding the case, but instead of moving towards the exit, he unexpectedly offered it to Voss. "Director," he said, his tone straightforward, "Director Raith's orders placed custody under my authority for transport and storage logistics. However, given your previously demonstrated affinity with the device, operational security might be best served by your maintaining direct physical proximity during transit. I will provide close escort."

Voss blinked, surprised by the sudden delegation, or perhaps shared responsibility. He glanced at Rayk, trying to read the man's inscrutable expression, then at the inert case. The memory of the Key's strange pull, the echo, resurfaced. He hesitated only a second. Taking the case felt like accepting another burden, another piece of Raith's complex game, but refusing might seem like shirking his new duties. "Understood, Detective," he replied, taking the offered case. Its weight felt significant, both physically and metaphorically.

Renata watched the exchange silently, her expression carefully neutral.

"Dr. O'Neil, would you kindly come with us so that Dr. Volkova can ask any questions about your experience, since we are all going to the same destination anyway? I am sure you will find our skimmer a little more comfortable than the utility skimmer." Dr. O'Neil replied, "I would be delighted, Detective". Rayk turned to Mainwaring, "All associated research notes and data have been secured for transfer as well, Doctor Mainwaring," Rayk confirmed, turning back to the physicist. "Await confirmation on your team's relocation transport to Sector Beta."

Without further discussion, Rayk held the lab door open. Voss, carrying the case containing the Echo Key, walked through, followed by Renata and Alinta. They made their way back to the waiting skimmer, the objective achieved, the strange artefact

The Xenologist

now back in Voss's reluctant possession, at least for the journey.

Rayk requested that Voss and Alinta sit together as far from the cockpit as possible. He confirmed with the Pilots that all systems were normal and they affirmed that they detected no electronic interference. Rayk then cautiously buckled in and gave the pilot the coordinates for Wahlsanga Depot.

As the skimmer lifted off, leaving the ruins behind, the silence in the cabin felt charged. Voss stared at the locker holding the Key. Affinity, inertness, scanning... what triggered its different responses? He glanced at Renata, seemingly lost in her datapad, the morning's awkwardness a tangible barrier. Rayk sat alert, a silent guardian of both them and the artefact. The familiar landscape passed below, but Voss's thoughts were on the journey ahead, into the depths of Wahlsanga, carrying an enigma Raith seemed determined to control, aboard a vessel Raith rarely relinquished. The Director's game felt increasingly complex, its rules hidden, its stakes disturbingly high.

Chapter 26. Part 1.

The executive skimmer sliced silently through the thin upper atmosphere of Sikarra, leaving the immediate confines of the primary city complex far behind. Inside, the quiet hum of the engines and the whisper of recycled air did little to ease the palpable tension. Voss stared fixedly out of the viewport, the stunning, ochre and violet alien landscape scrolling beneath, a counterweight to his turbulent thoughts.

The weight of his unexpected directorate-equivalent title pressed down on him. It was a responsibility he had never sought, now tangled inextricably with a sharp, unfamiliar ache of jealousy directed at the two figures seated opposite. He maintained a cool, professional distance, a necessary shield against the confusing memory of Renata's sheepish smile in his quarters, a memory now irrevocably tainted by Rayk Kostin's voice answering her comm line that morning. Let it go. Move on. Grow up.

Rayk, for his part, appeared the model of calm vigilance. His gaze swept the exterior with practised efficiency, yet Voss suspected his true focus was elsewhere, perhaps running silent threat assessments dictated by Raith's opaque warnings about orbital traffic.

Renata, seated beside Rayk, seemed absorbed in her datapad, reviewing sensor logs or perhaps the preliminary linguistic models. If she felt the chill emanating from Voss, she gave no outward sign, her professional demeanour a smooth, unreadable surface.

As the skimmer began its long descent towards the coordinates designated Wahlsanga, the landscape below shifted, becoming starker, the rock formations darker, the delicate geological tracery less evident than near Petropolis. The vast, flat plains surrounding the target escarpment hinted at ancient, large-scale activity, perhaps marshalling yards or loading zones for a forgotten industrial age.

Renata finally looked up from her screen, meeting Alinta O'Neil's gaze. The physicist sat beside Voss, seemed to be waiting for the opening. Seeking a distraction from the tension in the cabin, Renata leaned slightly forward. "Alinta," she began. As they spoke, she noticed Voss shift beside Alinta, his attention caught by their conversation. "I have been thinking about your interaction with the Key. It was markedly different from Principal Voss's initial experience, or even Director Raith's, based on reports. You mentioned it felt like active scanning?"

Alinta O'Neil met her gaze thoughtfully. "It was distinct, certainly. And the follow-up genetics screen confirmed something interesting." Voss shifted slightly, his attention caught despite himself. "You know the PCMA has been trying to isolate common markers among personnel who show affinity?" Renata nodded. "Well," Alinta continued, "my profile is completely negative for those specific markers. An anomaly, apparently."

Renata processed this. "Indigenous Australian. That means there will be a remarkable lineage continuity. That separation goes back... isn't it something like sixty, sixty-five thousand years?"

"Around that, yes," Alinta confirmed. "The initial Sahul migration. My family line traces back through the Pama–Nyungan language groups, relatively isolated until," A brief, wry smile touched her lips. "Two great, great, great-grandparents decided to introduce some Bronze Age Celtic chaos via County Clare five generations back."

Renata made the connections, "So, over sixty-five thousand years of relative isolation, followed by very recent admixture... Genetic Recombination means there is no guarantee that markers from those Irish ancestors would persist strongly, especially if they were not reinforced down other lines. Independent assortment means it is never a neat twelve point five per cent split from each great grandparent anyway."

Alinta nodded, appreciating Renata's quick grasp. "Exactly. Which makes me wonder... perhaps those 'affinity' markers relate to a genetic trait or adaptation that became common in the wider human gene pool after my ancestors' migration? Something widespread across Eurasian populations by the time later migrations occurred, but absent in the original Sahul groups. And even if my Irish ancestors carried it, the recombination lottery might have shuffled it out for me." She paused, relating it back to the artefact. "If the Key anticipates those 'newer' markers for its primary interaction protocol, their absence in my profile could be why it felt... wrong. Not hostile, just incompatible – like trying to establish a connection without the right biological handshake. It resulted in that confusing sensory noise. Not linguistic, just... messy static." She gave a slight shudder. "Honestly, it was quite unpleasant. Left me with a thumping headache for a good half hour. Whatever it was trying, it was not a smooth process. I have no desire to repeat the experience anytime soon."

Renata absorbed this, making a mental note. The Key's affinity was more complex than a simple binary state. "Normally, though, fewer isolated DNA markers mean less interaction. With you, there seemed more interaction, but, as you say, confused somehow."

Voss, overhearing, filed the information away, the scientific puzzle momentarily eclipsing his personal discomfort. He couldn't help but interject, "But it does seem interested in you." Rayk logged the exchange without comment, another variable in an increasingly complex equation.

The skimmer touched down smoothly beside a utilitarian building nestled against the towering escarpment face. The airlock hissed open. Rayk was first out, his movements economical as he performed a swift but thorough security sweep of the landing pad and the immediate vicinity of the designated entrance building. Voss and Renata followed, Voss automatically assuming a position of oversight, gesturing towards the entrance. "At the expense of sounding alarmist, I would like a report later, on what could be used to seal this entrance and make it defensible" he instructed Rayk, the formality a thin veneer over his internal state. Renata gave Voss a momentary quizzical look as she considered the implications of this order but immediately broke her gaze and began taking preliminary environmental readings, her focus immediate and professional.

Rayk acknowledged Voss's order with a curt nod before turning his attention to the shielded case still held by Voss. "Principal Voss, the Director's orders require immediate containment upon arrival." He pulled up his qWatch and air-dropped a location on Voss's qWatch. The location, in the train depot far below, indicated a reinforced, standard-issue secure storage locker recently placed into the facility wall. "Please secure the artefact there for now. I will log the transfer and confirm containment."

Voss hesitated for only a fraction of a second, the weight of the case, both literal and figurative, suddenly immense. He complied, placing the heavy container into the locker. The magnetic seal clicked shut with satisfying finality. Rayk made a notation on his qWatch, perhaps confirming the action directly with Raith, or perhaps merely closing an operational loop in his own meticulous protocols.

Within a few minutes, the Echo Key was secured and the team had convened at the threshold of Wahlsanga Depot. Alinta's eyes grew wild with the revelation of the treasures therein, the colossal mysteries of the trains and storage crates for her, a promised land of intellectual fulfilment. The immediate directive was fulfilled and forgotten, as if nothing down here could be affected by the Politics above. How easy it would be for these scientists to forget everything and start diving into the puzzles and riches held here. Yet the air remained taut with unspoken tension. Even this trove of marvels could not dispel the shadow cast by the silent fleet beyond the sky.

Chapter 26. Part 2.

The massive portal of the Sky Arch Bridge gatehouse framed the gorge behind them, a stark monument against the deepening twilight sky. Stepping beyond its final threshold onto the Vasantha side felt like arriving on solid, undisputed land after a perilous voyage. They stood on a plateau, slightly higher than the surrounding desert. Turbulent air currents rose from the chasm below, still carrying the faint scent of damp rock. The bridge itself, a colossal rib of ancient composite, seemed to anchor itself into the very bedrock beside them.

Ahead, a wide, smoothly paved pathway sloped gently downwards, disappearing over a nearby brow and then off into the distance in the direction of the long escarpment that was the location of Vasantha City and its associated space port.

Marinallis surveyed the path, then looked back towards the vast, silent bridge. "The surface roads direct to the bridge haven't been maintained for months," he stated, his voice thin but clear. "Sand drifts have blocked off the road to Vasantha." He gestured towards the pathway. "But this service route will take us to a point further along the road below this rise."

Varinn glanced at the Designer, assessing his stamina. Two kilometres on foot, even downhill, would be taxing. Before Varinn could voice the concern, Marinallis offered a faint smile. "Don't worry. Sat comms are still offline obviously, but from the roof of the gatehouse, I was able to establish a clear line of sight signal to the Vasantha comms tower." He patted his wrist navscan unit. "I requested ground transport to meet us at the road below. It should be waiting right now".

Tessara almost laughed. "You mean, after that, *after all of that*, you just got us a street-cab?"

Marinallis told them, "In our world, we took reliable comms for granted. We just had no concept of simply being out of range."

The trek downwards demanded careful footing on the exposed path. As they dropped below the rise, the ever-present roar of the chasm faded. Marinallis, conserving his strength, leaned heavily on Varinn's arm. His breathing was steady but shallow in the cool plateau air. Varinn steadied Marinallis as a desert gust rocked the path, grit stinging their eyes. The trio stalled and the gust died down, leaving a silence, broken only by the stumbling resumption of their measured footsteps. Soon, they were faced with a pedestrian tunnel through the rock spur that separated them from the road below. They entered the short tunnel and the darkness was absolute beyond the reach of their wrist navscan lights, before emerging again onto the lower plateau. As the light from the darkening violet sky hit them on leaving the tunnel, they saw the most welcome of sights.

The road to Vasantha was indeed unblocked at this point and there, in a lay-by, a street-cab, labelled 'Vasantha Licensed Transport' sat there calmly waiting for them, like an obedient dog waiting for its master to come home. Its idling air conditioning made barely a whisper against the desert breeze.

As they approached the street-cab, the protective canopy opened. They settled inside, the cabin comfortably appointed and the most surreal yet not at all unwelcome thing, bottles of fresh water were in the arm of every seat. As the vehicle pulled away smoothly from the kerb, merging onto a wide internal roadway, Tessara glanced around. "I don't want to sound ungrateful, but a wheeled vehicle?" she queried, surprised. "Why not a skimmer?"

The Xenologist

Marinallis sighed, settling back into the seat. "Skimmer fleet is likely prioritised for... other movements," he said vaguely. "Evacuation logistics. Still, second-class riding is better than first-class walking, wouldn't you agree?"

The car smoothly set off on the short journey to the entrance tunnels of Vasantha. They became drowsy as the relief finally hit them. Civilisation, cool air conditioning and comfortable seats. They had all started to wonder if they would feel such a thing again.

As the car drove past the space port, Varinn opened his eyes. There was one shuttle. Astonishingly empty. He was shocked at how deserted everywhere was. Finally, the enormity of the project hit home. He felt an enormous emptiness inside of him. *Is this what they told me homesickness was? Except I haven't even left home yet.*

The car passed without event through the access tunnels and navigated the internal roadways of Vasantha. The city felt strangely hollowed out. Lights were dimmed in many overhead sections, casting long shadows. Wide pedestrian plazas were deserted. Automated cargo movers hummed past occasionally, heading towards unseen loading bays. Impromptu barriers such as piled-up crates and hastily erected barricades blocked access to numerous side corridors and entire sectors, partitioning the city as it consolidated towards its final shutdown. A ghost city.

They travelled deeper into the complex for several minutes. Then, as they approached a major intersection feeding traffic towards the city's core, the vehicle slowed smoothly and came to a halt before a softly glowing red barrier projected across the roadway.

A pleasant, synthesised voice addressed them from the vehicle's console. "Apologies. The direct route to the Central Plaza Space Dock Administration Building is temporarily blocked and all access is restricted due to priority movements. Please consult network maps for alternative routes or await clearance."

Marinallis stared at the barrier, his weariness replaced by sharp frustration. He tapped impatiently at his wrist navscan. *Priority movements? Restricted?* He muttered under his breath, "Unacceptable!" as he scrolled through traffic updates. Around them, the soulless robots performed a precise ballet; their seamless dance reducing the trio to mere organics in a mechanised world.

"Varinn," Marinallis said, his gaze steady despite a sleepless tremor. "I should be off-world by now, but for our misadventure over the last several days. I can't board the human ship, and if I stay, no trace of my genetic material must remain. Burn my body if I miss the Newcomer's ship." Varinn's eyes dropped, his silence heavy with unspoken dread

Marinallis's navscan dimmed, a flicker of defeat beneath the city's perfect logic. Deep in Vasantha, close to their goal, they were halted, stopped not by collapse or decay, but by the perfectly functioning, inflexible evacuation procedures of the city's final departure.

Chapter 27. Part 1.

The narrow confines of the SARU-bored access tunnel gave way abruptly to the familiar, cavernous space of the Wahlsanga Metro Station platform area. Voss, Renata, Rayk, and Alinta stepped out from the rough-hewn passage, their boots crunching on residual dust left from the tunnel's creation the previous day. Before them lay the tunnel leading to the main Depot complex. The air smelled ancient, but carried the modern sounds of human activity and was cut by beams of artificial light.

They entered the tunnel and shortly, they emerged into a significantly larger access chamber. The area was brightly illuminated by portable PCMA floodlights that banished the millennia-old gloom, revealing the colossal Depot blast door fully retracted into its recess high above. A PCMA guard, different from the one they had left but part of the established security detail, stood near the threshold and offered a sharp salute as Detective Rayk Kostin led the team forward. Near the massive, now-silent drive mechanisms—gleaming PCMA replacements bolted beside the original, damaged Designer units—the small engineering team was monitoring consoles and packing away diagnostic equipment, the main repair work complete.

Rayk approached the lead engineer. "Is the door fully operational?"

"Yes, Detective," the engineer affirmed, gesturing towards the open portal. "The original motors are bypassed and new motors have been installed and tested. The power feed is stable through the converters. A local remote override has been installed as well as an emergency manual release on the inside." She held out two identical remote-control units. "I have one remote control for you, Detective and one for the Sector Principal."

Rayk accepted one remote and passed the other to Voss without comment. He then inquired, "The secure vault installation on the inside?"

The engineer nodded, pointing towards a specific area just inside the entrance lobby now visible through the open doorway. "The installation is complete and ready for encoding, Detective. Technician Miller is waiting by the vault."

"Thank you, are you complete here?" Rayk asked? "Nearly, Sir. Just a couple of tests on the doors to make sure they are not going to fail and then we can pack up and leave you to it". Rayk nodded and turned back to the entrance to the depot. The engineers began gathering their remaining tools, preparing to depart.

The team stepped through the huge doorway, finally entering the Depot entrance lobby proper. The shift in scale was immediate and profound. The location of the newly installed heavy-duty PCMA security vault was obvious. It was set flush against the ancient composite wall. Technician Miller stood beside it, running final checks on the access panel.

Voss looked over to Alinta, conscious that this was her first sight of the treasure trove that was the depot. He saw she was frozen, seemingly star-struck, staring at the trains. For her, this was not just history. No, it was a cathedral of broken laws waiting to be rewritten. Voss directly addressed her, "Yeah, Alinta. Right?"

Alinta replied, "I..." She shook her head, as if looking for something to say. "How long?"

Renata took up the conversation. "Only yesterday. Let me give you a tour. I think you are going to be most useful down here."

"The vault is ready for primary user encoding, Sir." Miller reported as they approached.

Rayk gestured to Voss. "Principal Voss?"

Voss stepped forward, holding the shielded case containing the Echo Key. "Please place your hand on the panel and state your name and designation for the initial encoding," Miller instructed.

Voss placed his gloved hand on the scanner. "Julian Voss. Principal Xenologist, Head of Department, Archaeology"

The console flashed. "Biometric and voice print acquired," a synthesised voice announced. "Access Registered: Principal Julian Voss, Head of Department Archaeology. Verified. Please enter assigned security passcode."

Miller handed Voss a secure data chip. Voss accessed the complex alphanumeric code via his wrist qWatch and entered it on the vault's keypad.

"Passcode accepted. Encoding complete," the vault stated. "Access Granted: Principal Voss." The thick vault door slid open smoothly.

Voss placed the Echo Key case inside on the shelf.

"Secondary users can be added now if required, Principal." Miller prompted.

"Authorise Doctor Renata Volkova and Detective Raymond Kostin," Voss instructed. Renata and Rayk completed the brief scanning process. Miller then handed Voss the small, solid metallic backup override key. "Manual key for emergency physical access requires dual command code confirmation."

Voss pocketed the key as the vault door slid shut and locked with a series of heavy, definitive clicks. Rayk made a confirmation entry on his device.

With the Echo Key secured, the team paused in the vast lobby. Beyond, the true cavern beckoned, the silent trains inducing a fresh wave of awe. The implications of their discovery settled heavily upon them.

Breaking the silence, Voss turned directly to Rayk. "Detective Kostin," he began, his tone regaining its earlier formality, "the artefact is secure according to the Director's priority. My focus now must be on the xenoarchaeology here. I realise things may be complicated externally, but I need to leave immediate security matters for Sector Beta entirely in your hands for now. You are in a much better position to liaise with Director Raith and maintain the perimeter. I would also like you to continue with coordinating logistical support. Please inform me only of critical external developments requiring my direct intervention."

Rayk met his gaze steadily. "Understood, Principal Voss. I will continue to manage security and external liaison." The corners of his mouth upturned slightly as he observed Voss looking at the Trains, then at Renata already scanning the wall signs. He understood Voss's motivation completely. A Xenologist, Archaeologist, Scientist, Historian and Linguist first. A head of department second.

The delegation accepted, the initial tasks completed, Voss allowed himself a deep breath. He turned, finally, towards the main Depot cavern, towards Renata and Alinta, who had already lost interest and were talking and pointing to the wonders held within. "Right then," he said, the weight of command momentarily giving way to the pure thrill of the unknown. "Let's see what the Architects left behind."

Chapter 27. Part 2.

The street-cab remained motionless, its internal systems a low, unobtrusive hum against the sudden, heavy silence that had fallen between its occupants. Before them, the projected crimson barrier pulsed softly, as impassable as any physical barrier for the street-cab. The wide thoroughfare leading towards the Vasantha Spaceport sector was no longer a possibility. Marinallis jabbed a finger impatiently at his wrist navscan, the small device displaying confirmation of what the impassable light already told them.

"Blocked," he stated unnecessarily, the word sharp with frustration. "Completely blocked. Automated routing confirms all direct surface access to the landing field sector is sealed." He slumped back against the reinforced-leather seat, a wave of weariness washing over his frail form. "Just when time is most critical!"

Before Varinn or Tessara could respond, a series of urgent alerts flared across the cab's main console and simultaneously chimed from Marinallis's personal device. Complex energy signatures resolved into alarming icons. There were multiple high-energy warp translations, vectoring rapidly towards planetary orbit from deep space.

Marinallis leaned forward instantly, his fatigue forgotten, replaced by a stark, almost visceral alarm. His three slender fingers worked the navscan hard, accessing large amounts of orbital tracking data. "No... K'Tharr!" he breathed, the name a curse. He looked up, his ancient eyes wide, locking first with Varinn's, then Tessara's. "They are here. Multiple capital ships are entering orbit. This is why the central sector is locked down – they anticipate ground contact!"

Tessara said, "But how did they break through the defence sector? They are a hundred light years away! I thought you said they were containable".

He took a ragged breath, forcing a measure of calm into his voice, though the underlying urgency was stark. "This is worse than a simple blockade breakthrough. By the looks of these signatures, they used MET to achieve raw Faster Than Light, instead of using a warp bubble."

Tessara looked at the screen. Her voice tight, "There's no warp bubble signature, just a massive energy spike and they just appeared?"

Marinallis explained, "Exactly. If you use enough energy to alter your mass and time, then locally you think you are travelling below light speed. But to the observer, you exceed it by brute force".

Tessara seized on that, "And that gets them through the blockade?"

He nodded grimly, "Yes, they bypassed the blockade by jumping *past* it in a way that they should know is *forbidden*. It is unthinkable that they would do anything so stupid. They must be desperate."

Varinn asked, "Desperate? In what way?"

Marinallis said, "We have been using attritional warfare against them. They need our bodies to absorb and contribute genetic material, or they die out. Probably this sector of the front is ageing and losing soldiers at the same time. Their methods show desperation. They know this crude way of travelling Faster Than Light is reckless. It tears at the fabric of space-time itself and disturbs the underlying mass-field."

Tessara and Varinn looked at each other. Both suspected they knew what this meant, but they waited for Marinallis to continue and confirm their worst fears.

He obliged and gestured vaguely upwards. "Such disturbances risk attracting their attention. The response..." He didn't need to finish the sentence; the weight of unspoken history hung between them. "My transport is waiting in orbit. It must depart soon. This changes all timetables. We have to reach the rendezvous near the landing fields immediately."

As if summoned by his words, the cab's internal speakers crackled to life, overriding the ambient quiet with a clear, synthesised, city-wide emergency broadcast. "Alert. K'Tharr presence confirmed. Ground incursion protocols are active. All non-essential movement must cease. All designated personnel, proceed to the nearest distribution node and arm with Type-Seven Bio-Disruptors. Engage hostile biologicals only." The message repeated, clipped and devoid of emotion.

The implications were chillingly clear. The city anticipated close-quarters combat, likely infiltration, and mandated the use of weapons designed specifically to neutralise organic targets by disrupting DNA and avoiding damaging the precious infrastructure.

"Surface travel is impossible," Tessara stated flatly, her pragmatism cutting through the rising tension. "Too exposed, and the main routes are sealed."

Varinn nodded, his mind already assessing alternatives. "The train tunnels. The trains aren't running and they should offer a more direct, concealed route towards the spaceport sector, bypassing the main avenues."

Marinallis, galvanised by the combined threats, agreed instantly. "Yes. The understructure. It must be." There was no time for debate, no room for lesser options. They instantly rerouted the street-cab to the central underground station, which was a mere two minutes away from the main plaza of the underground city.

When they got to the surprisingly still working escalator ramp heading down to the station, they exited the street-cab, the vehicle's canopy closing silently behind them as they stepped out into the cool, still air of the deserted concourse. Trusting in Marinallis's knowledge of the city's layout, they moved quickly downwards towards the signs simply saying, "Platforms for the Spaceport".

As they arrived on the platform, Marinallis scanned the tunnels. "Yes, the trains are all lined up in the depot." He pointed down one tunnel that showed flashes of the lights of work crews and the sounds of the last inhabitants performing their last tasks." He added, "All these workers will have an evacuation plan. All except us, I should imagine. Which reminds me, something that I should have dealt with earlier."

He spoke into his wrist navscan. "Urgent message for D. Urbanalla." The wrist scan beeped. "Hello old friend, I can't say I approve of your last cloak and vibro-knife game with the MET Comm 12. It seems a bit risky to me; nevertheless, I allowed it."

A rueful grimace passed his face. *She needs to know I'm not playing second fiddle to her.* "However, you need to send up some sterilisation drones. There are a few human bodies in the Gorge by the sky arch bridge abutment, by the old Rhovana Orbital Monitoring Station ruin and about 5 Stadia east of there in the desert in a rather obvious old human shipwreck."

He waited and then added an afterthought. "The Fumigators are looking for the K'Tharr violators, but we don't want human or Designer bodies caught up in the sweep. We would be implicated in MET tech violations and end up on their shit list as well."

After a quick consideration, he added, "If you lack sympathy for our human partners, remember it's through them they might get to us, so I suggest we do a planetwide surface-sweep. We have to torch anything left with two legs, living or dead. Anyone up there now is better vaporised than ending up in the K'Tharr flesh banks. It's a mercy. You can do it on my authority".

Varinn met Tessara's gaze, a shared, silent acknowledgement passing between them. He hadn't known the kind old man had such steel in his spine, though his performance in dispatching Carrik should have been a clue.

Marinallis pulled out his tin of salve that Varinn had been using in the Desert. He applied it to his lips and the weariness disappeared from his face. He started off towards the platform that indicated trains to the Spaceport. Then, with surprising sprightliness, he jumped down onto the tracks, which were just metal inlays on the concrete surface. Tessara followed, Varinn protecting the rear as his training mandated. The air that drifted up from the tunnel felt different. Hotter, more moist, carrying the scents of the spaceport, of surface ozone created by the heavy UV light outside and old machinery.

Without hesitation, Marinallis started walking. Varinn took one last look back at the grand, silent station, now a potential war zone, then turned and followed them into the functional darkness of Vasantha's hidden underbelly, committed to the uncertain path ahead, racing against the arrival of aliens and the potential wrath of the cosmos.

Chapter 28. Part 1.

The vastness of the Wahlsanga Depot pressed in, the faint, rhythmic pulse of the ancient emergency lighting doing little to dispel the profound silence left by eighty thousand years of undisturbed dust. Rayk moved with quiet efficiency, deploying micro-sensors near the main entrance threshold and establishing a perimeter watch protocol linked to his implants. He nodded towards the nearest colossal train, the sixth in the row, its flank marked by the carelessly discarded tools and dangling conduits that spoke of abrupt departure. "Perimeter secure for now, Principal Voss. Localised sensors active."

Voss acknowledged with a curt nod, his attention already drawn, despite himself, to where Renata and Alinta were examining the base of the sixth train. He'd intended to focus initially on the nearby sealed crates, maintaining a professional distance, but Alinta's voice drew him closer.

"Here," Alinta called, pointing to a section near a large, seamless door set into the train's side. Almost invisible beneath the dust, a smooth, slightly recessed panel was embedded in the composite hull. "There's an interface." She produced a compact device from her kit, a dense power pack with induction coils visible beneath its translucent casing. "We developed this for the Echo Key cabinet's external power feed. Wireless induction."

Carefully, Alinta placed the power pack against the panel. With a soft click, it adhered magnetically. The panel beside it immediately illuminated with a low, internal soft green light, revealing intricate patterns beneath its surface, almost certainly a touch-sensitive interface.

Renata angled her datapad camera over the panel and the screen came alive with scrolling glyph matches, locations and contexts from previous scans around the planet. "Three distinct sequences," her voice tight with the excitement she'd been keeping to herself for days. "This bottom one? We've seen it before. On hatches, tunnel mouths, doorways. It's the closest they have to 'entry'. It could be 'Door', 'Entrance' or 'Hatch'. You seem to have to know by context."

Alinta's brows rose. "Since when do we *read* these things?"

"Ah, we haven't published yet. It was only two days ago. Dr. Evans was working on location in a school room in Petropolis and they found a music wall." Alinta looked puzzled. Renata Chuckled. "Yeah, right? Well, bear with me. It turned out it had resonance holes and a set of human-sounding vowels. Dr. Voss here worked it out. Then he noticed the glyphs for vowels are based upon the base pairs of DNA".

Alinta, open-mouthed, looked at the glyphs with a new respect. "You worked all this out in the last couple of days?"

Renata replied, "Yes, well, we catalogued lots of glyphs; our AS just needed some sort of key."

"Oh, Like the Rosetta Stone?".

"Exactly." Then, Renata pointed to the glyphs again. "It seems the script is polyvalent; one glyph can be just a sound, depending on position. The AS finally caught the pattern."

She pointed to two smaller marks positioned above the 'Door' glyph, separated by a razor-thin light green bar. "These sit in a binary slot. The parser thinks they're a pair, probably binary opposites if not alternatives. So almost undoubtedly in this context, 'open' and 'close'."

Alinta, still processing the revelation, laid her fingers on the upper mark. She felt a vague pleasant vibration under her fingers and said, "Ooh, I think I got haptic feedback!" She tried again. "Nothing else though".

Renata nudged in. "Let me." Her touch drew a soft, subterranean, sad-sounding beep; every glyph flared red, then cooled to the normal soft green. "Negative response, but I got the vibration," she remarked. "Same colour code we've logged on failed conduits. Red for negative, seems to be a universal constant and we think they use blue for positive, but.." (laughing) "We don't see that colour very often. Green is normal or neutral."

"Wireless induction... clever." He approached the panel, his earlier irritation momentarily submerged by scientific curiosity. He placed his gloved fingertips on the same upper glyph Renata had touched. Again, the panel flashed red, the negative beep sounding. But this time, beneath the primary glyphs, a new, smaller sequence of symbols briefly illuminated before fading.

"Did you see that?" Renata exclaimed, instantly bringing up the high-speed capture log on her datapad. She froze the image, zooming in on the secondary glyph sequence. "New symbols. This first one, for instance. It has been catalogued several times on barriers and locked doors. Another version with a different ending letter on it is associated with entrances with no door or unlocked doors." She tapped the screen. "So the base meaning is *access*, then a bound negative morpheme is the last letter. It's a classic negative concord. Every element inside the clause takes a little 'no' flag."

Alinta clicked her tongue. "Like when someone in English says, 'I don't know nothing'?"

"Exactly. Russian does it this way, too. Formally," Renata said, already annotating. "Here, the train just told us: Access-NEG denied-NEG. Everything lines up so the negatives march in lockstep."

Alinta stared at the panel with newfound respect. "Polyvalent glyphs and lockstep negatives. Your breakthroughs are astounding, Renata."

Voss nodded slowly, his gaze distant. "The responses are tiered. It's not a simple lock." He looked at Alinta. "For you, it was completely inert. For Renata, a hard denial." He gestured to the panel where he had touched it. "But for me, it provided a specific denial sequence. It's a recognition system," he concluded, his voice filled with a new sense of wonder. "It becomes more communicative the more it recognises the user."

Voss stared again at the panel in thought. "Perhaps it requires a more specific authorisation," he mused aloud. "Something beyond basic biological compatibility." The thought of retrieving the Echo Key from its vault surfaced immediately, a potential key not just for this door, but for so much more. He pushed the thought aside, for now. "Later. Let's continue documenting the primary findings first."

He turned his attention towards the grey, shielded crates near the pillar where the statue lay partially uncovered by the archaeology drones. Alinta, her curiosity piqued by the interaction, joined Renata in scanning them. "Still confirms extreme density shielding," Alinta reported. "Resisting all standard deep-penetration scans." Renata pointed at the panel, "And these glyphs..." She displayed the complex, multi-layered symbols. "They don't match any known systems, functional, locational or numeric. They feel different. Identifiers? Technical terms?"

Rayk, who had approached silently, added his observation. "I suppose it's normal for a train or high-value transport system to be locked. You don't want unauthorised people going for joy rides on trains." He subtly adjusted his stance, positioning himself slightly between the scientists and the main cavern entrance. "The blacked-out windows are logical with the UV light, but it does add to the mystery. Is there more treasure buried here?"

Alinta said, "There's treasure everywhere here. Humanity will never be the same again. But then again, I seem to be saying this every day."

Voss looked from the inscrutable crates to the silent, opaque windows of the train, then back to the access panel that had denied him. Mysteries nested within mysteries. The sheer scale of the Architects' departure, the reasons for their haste and the nature of what they left versus what they destroyed were overwhelming.

The thought of the silent fleet approaching in orbit felt distant, almost unreal, compared to the tangible weight of the secrets held within this cavern. He compartmentalised the external threat, focusing again on the immediate puzzle. The Echo Key would wait. For now, disciplined documentation was paramount.

Chapter 28. Part 2.

The transition was stark. The enclosed darkness of the train tunnel, with its recycled air and echoing silence, gave way abruptly to a vast expanse under Talemora's hostile sky. They emerged onto an immense, open-air platform, the stone beneath their feet still radiating a faint coolness from the depths. Far above, the violet-tinged twilight pressed down, the first, faint stars beginning to pierce the thin atmosphere. The air here was different. Sharper, carrying the metallic tang of ozone from the nearby landing fields and the dry, mineral scent of the surrounding desert, mingled with the remote, powerful hum of the last orbital transit shuttles and ground-based energy systems.

Although strangely devoid of ships, this was the spaceport passenger terminal. The last one working on Talemora. Multiple, broad train tracks, identical to those in the tunnels, ran parallel to the platform edge before curving away towards enormous, darkened gantries and what looked like direct docking interfaces for surface-to-orbit shuttles. Automated conveyor systems, now silent, crisscrossed the area. The scale was monumental, built to handle a flow of beings and material that dwarfed anything Varinn had conceived. Signs of the recent, rushed evacuation were evident: discarded cargo restraints, hastily stacked supply pallets under protective tarpaulins, and a few silent, driverless transport vehicles abandoned mid-route on the periphery of the main loading zones.

"The rendezvous coordinates are for observation deck Zone Blue-Level 2," Marinallis stated, his voice carrying clearly in the open air despite the background hum. He consulted his wrist navscan, its small screen glowing faintly in the gathering gloom. "It overlooks the primary departure fields, designated for heavy transports." He pointed towards a far building built into the side of a massive rock escarpment that defined one edge of the spaceport complex. "That way. Still approximately twenty minutes, perhaps less if we can find an active service cart."

"Orbital situation?" Varinn asked, his gaze sweeping the vast expanse of landing pads and the sky above. The thought of K'Tharr ships potentially already descending was a cold weight.

Marinallis activated his wrist navscan, attempting to raise Talemora Orbital Traffic Control through the city connection. Only a crackle of static answered, then the clipped, automated voice of the city-wide alert system: "Ground incursion protocols active. Orbital traffic control is giving limited service whilst evacuating. Maintain designated position until further instructions are available."

He grimaced, the lines on his ancient face deepening. "Control is offline. As expected, however..." He routed a secure transmission through back-door channels to the ground transmission dishes and from there, a narrow-beam directly to the Newcomer vessel's orbital coordinates. The silence that followed stretched, broken only by the wind whistling across the exposed platforms. Finally, the navscan emitted a single, brief acknowledgement chime. A heavily encrypted, minimal data-packet confirmed receipt and adherence to the four-hour rendezvous window from initial contact.

"They acknowledge," Marinallis said, his relief almost imperceptible. "The window holds. They will begin their descent shortly." He looked towards the distant structure. "We'll proceed directly to the Blue-Level 2. It offers the best line of sight for their approach and some measure of cover."

They set off across the vast, empty platform, their footsteps echoing in the immense space. Reaching the base of the escarpment structure, they found a series of external ramps and lift shafts. Most were dark, but one auxiliary lift showed a faint green active light. They entered, the smooth, silent ascent carrying them upwards.

The lift opened onto the broad, curving deck, its outer edge protected by a high, angled plazteel barrier designed to deflect the worst of the surface winds and radiation. From here, the panorama of the Vasantha spaceport was breathtaking—kilometres of landing fields, silent docking towers, and the dark shapes of what might have been colossal, permanent fuel or cargo facilities.

"Here," Marinallis said, moving towards a section of the deck that offered a commanding view but was also slightly recessed, providing a degree of shelter. He eased himself down onto a low stone bench, conserving his energy after the tunnel trek and the lift ascent. The salve's effects were visibly diminishing. "I must conserve energy," Marinallis said, pulling a nutrient bar from the folds of his cloak. "The final ascent will be demanding on my system."

Tessara scanned the deck with her wrist navscan, confirming its emptiness. Varinn took up a position near the plazteel barrier, looking out towards the designated approach vectors for incoming spacecraft. The wind tugged at his cloak. The silence of the dying planet, the vast emptiness of the spaceport, the approaching K'Tharr, and the fragile hope pinned on a single, distant Newcomer ship—it all coalesced into a moment of profound, desolate waiting.

Chapter 28. Part 3.

The interface panel on the sixth train remained stubbornly inert to Alinta's touch, save for the faint haptic buzz. Renata's attempt had yielded only the dull, negative beep and the brief, crimson flare of the glyphs. Voss, leaving them to it, had drifted back over to the Architect's statue that had toppled near the base of the pillar to think. The potential military emergency above was never far from his mind. Rayk had gone to the outer guard-post at the entrance to Wahlsanga to set up security there and attend a video link with Director Raith and the Planetary Defence Team in the Sikarra Central Ops Room.

Why would it deny entrance? It has to be an ID issue. His gaze fell upon the toppled Architect statue's form; its serene face partially cleared of dust by the small archaeology drones. He walked over to it, crouching to examine the delicately carved, three-fingered hand resting near its hip. Three fingers, an opposing thumb. *Is that is? Wrong morphology? No, not that simple.* These hands were in the same configuration as the Echo Key. Yet his four fingers and thumb could connect and interact with it. The Key itself, he knew, responded with varying degrees of intensity to different individuals. Raith, with his baseline Designer DNA, had elicited a response, but Voss's interaction had felt deeper, more... recognised.

"The Echo Key," he said aloud. Alinta and Renata looked over to him. The connection began to form sudden clarity. "Its affinity protocols are complex, tiered. This train isn't just locked; it's assessing. If anything can establish a proper handshake with this system, it's that." He straightened. *My responsibility,* he thought, *and Raith expects results, not just catalogued failures.*

He turned to Renata and Alinta. "I am going to get the Echo-Key and try it." Voss made his way back towards the colossal, now open, blast door marking the Depot's main threshold. At the heavy vault door, his biometrics and passcode granted immediate access. He retrieved the shielded case, its inert weight familiar. Returning to the sixth train, he found Renata and Alinta making detailed notes on the exterior hull.

"Alinta, power pack again, please," Voss requested.

Once more, Alinta placed her induction unit against the train's panel, the soft green light of the interface illuminating. Voss then carefully brought the shielded Echo Key case close, holding it a few inches from the glowing glyphs. He felt for that subtle internal shift, that almost imperceptible resonance he associated with the Key.

Then he felt a feeling, stronger than he had felt before. It was like a mental ecstasy. An indescribable feeling that was something he knew a human should not be feeling. Then he saw two coloured fields, one electric and one that he somehow remembered was magnetic. They were solid, not flat and yet were at right angles to each other. A fact he knew from school, but now he could visualise it, and it was, frankly, crazy.

He heard himself say "Oh My God," a fraction of a second before the impulse to do so reached his lips, a dizzying, impossible pre-echo. "It knows I want to talk to the lock," he said, the words feeling less like a statement and more like a confirmation of a conversation that was already complete.

Voss noticed that Alinta, new to the phenomenon, seemed especially shocked by it. He continued, "It knows I want to talk to the lock". A small ripple in the fields propagated between the key and the lock. Voss felt fear. *What have I unleashed here? The fear then translated into to the field. He remembered it as raw need being translated into the field and into the logic circuits of the lock.* Then he remembered, rather than saw, that the lock was telling him "Emergency Acknowledged". As the glyphs changed, Renata also wrote them down and photographed them. Voss presaid to her, "It is saying Emergency Access Granted". She looked in amazement, "The Echo Key is telling you this, how?"

A faint schema, almost a ghost of light and symbols, flickered at the edge of his perception – a fleeting pattern that seemed to align with the glyphs for 'Open'. Press there. Now.

The uppermost glyph turned blue. "Open." He echoed back to himself, and with his mind still infused with joy, but slightly less now, he pressed the glyph with his fingers.

The effect was instantaneous. A deep, resonant chime, rich and complex, sounded from within the train. It was entirely different from the flat negative beep. Alinta gasped as her power pack emitted a sharp, protesting whine, its charge indicators plummeting. "It's drawing immense power!" she exclaimed, yanking the pack away just as its light died.

The field images collapsed for Voss and the feeling of mental ecstasy died instantly, leaving him with a distinct impression that it was to protect his brain. While Voss's brain was mourning the sudden loss, there was some compensation as there was a shuddering click and a prolonged hiss of eighty millennia of sealed air being broken. The stubborn train door beside the interface cracked open a hand's breadth. It stopped, the ancient seals and lubricated bearings, now brittle, fused or rotted, finally seized up.

"The primary seals have obviously degraded," Voss stated, "but the lock mechanism is disengaged." He called over to a fascinated Security Operative who Rayk had left guarding the depot entrance. The man walked over quickly, as aware of the momentous occasion as anyone else, put his rifle over his back and leaned his weight on the end of the door as Voss curved his fingers around the edge in the opposite direction and pulled. The bearings, stiff with unimaginable age, resisted, then with a prolonged, grinding shriek that echoed through the vast cavern, the door began to slide along its track. They heaved it fully open, partially under power that had suddenly begun to enter the train from somewhere unknown, but probably the ferrous tracks under the train.

A gust of incredibly ancient, perfectly sterile air, colder than the cavern, washed over them. They stepped inside, helmet lamps piercing the sudden blackness. The interior was a marvel. High, gracefully curved ceilings soared above, the material a matte, non-reflective black that seemed to absorb light. Elegant, minimalist benches, seemingly sculpted from a single piece of lustrous, jet-black material, lined the carriage walls. They were scaled for beings taller and more slender than humans, but with an undeniable ergonomic grace. Then, soft, ambient light slowly bloomed from integrated strips in the walls and ceiling, responding to their presence, though some sections remained stubbornly dark, their power systems perhaps too degraded even for the train's draw. Finally, the windows partially depolarised as ancient power relays stubbornly awoke from their slumber. The silence within was absolute, the dust of ages, entirely absent; a perfectly sealed environment, a time capsule.

They moved forward, drawn towards the control cabin at the front. Amidst the sweeping, architecturally scaled primary command stations and dark holographic display surfaces, one feature stood out, starkly incongruous. Set slightly to one side, yet an integral part of the original design, was a single command seat. It was distinctly smaller; its contours and proportions unmistakably shaped for a humanoid form with a human-like pelvic width and limb length. The material was different, too. A dark, pliant composite that still looked almost new.

Renata breathed, "It's... it could almost be for a human."

Alinta ran a diagnostic scanner over its controls. "The primary interfaces are Architect-standard, scaled for a four-fingered hand with an opposing thumb. But this station... its reach, the seat depression, it's calibrated for a wider physique, like ours."

A profound, almost dizzying sense of connection washed over Voss. *Not just generic humanoids, something so close to us, yet so integrated with them.* This was direct, tangible proof of their collaboration with beings remarkably like themselves, entrusted with the Architects' most advanced transport.

He reached out, almost reverently, towards the smaller, humanoid-scaled control stick.

At that precise moment, a priority alert cut sharply through Voss's qWatch. It was Rayk's voice, urgent and strained, broadcasting from his post at the Depot entrance. "Principal Voss, Doctors, I have an immediate situation update. The tactical display is live on my main console here. You need to see this. We have an incoming hailstorm."

Voss froze, his hand inches from the ancient control. "A what, Rayk?" he asked, the mundane question a stark contrast to the sudden, overwhelming dread in his voice.

Rayk's reply was chillingly clear. "CAR Spaceborne Troops dropping from orbit. Thousands of them. I'm patching the main tactical feed to your datapads now."

The spell of discovery shattered. The wonders of the ancient train, the revelation of the almost-human pilot, all abruptly relegated. The immediate, violent present crashed back in, tearing them from the reverie of eighty thousand years of history. Voss felt a wave of nausea; the thought of these unique treasures, this impossible history, potentially about to be consumed or contaminated, was sickening. His first, overriding priority, he realised with a cold lurch, was now the safety and well-being of his team.

Chapter 29. Part 1.

One thing about Raith was that he knew how to read a room. The tension in the operations room. "Ops" was reaching boiling point. The mere fact that Director Raith had decided to supervise from Ops instead of in his personal quarters was unusual enough to supercharge the already simmering atmosphere, heightening the unease among the sleep-deprived operatives as his meticulously planned ambush neared its moment of truth.

Raith had arranged for the latest holographic virtual reality near-space simulation to display in a darkened space at the centre of ops, in a way that every operative could see what was going on and of course, see his plan working. Live video link screens looped in Commander Rostova, leading Sector A ground military command, Mr. Henderson, with responsibility for Petropolis Police and emergency services, General Li in the Space Station and Rayk in the security office guarding the entrance to Wahlsanga, representing Sector Bravo.

The room and the video link screens remained silent as the icons for his stealth ordnance began their final convergence with the unsuspecting CAR fleet on the main tactical display dominating the centre of the holographic VR display. Faces everywhere showing concentration and either worry, or grim determination.

Raith's voice cut through the silence in an almost jarring way. "Space-Tower Control, hail them once more, but don't put any stress in the communication. Remain puzzled in tone." The Orbital Tower Controller nodded on the screen. "Incoming PCMA Fleet, this is Orbital Tower Control." Silence was the stern reply. "PCMA Fleet, OTC. Please note that your approach is now non-standard. We require your final joining vectors for deconfliction with orbital traffic". Again, nothing. Raith added. "I think that's enough for now, Tower." Then, for the benefit of the room, "That's enough to satisfy me. The operation will proceed on my personal judgement and responsibility".

This was the pivot point. Victory or collapse. Guts turned over and throats became dry. Some were military veterans and some were mere happy explorers who never expected to be in a position like this. But all of them were the best people the PCMA could put together. Raith had every confidence in every person, having reviewed every single person's record before allowing them into the positions of responsibility they would hold for the next critical hours and days.

As the incoming fleet advanced, the stealthed munitions closed in on their targets. Each device slipped into position near the engine arrays, attaching magnetically to the external fuel tanks housing the ships' nuclear propellant, which were deliberately placed away from passengers but adjacent to the Alcubierre drive modules for maximum effect. The telemetry on his primary display confirmed it with a cascade of green authentication signals. Flawless execution.

Raith ordered, "Now is the time, General Li, Engage the War AS and put all platforms up for active fire control Radar. They think they are dealing with the bureaucratic ninnies of the NAR, let's wake 'em up".

The response was almost instant. The comms from Orbital Tower Control relayed the hail from the incoming fleet as an annoyed and authoritative voice transmitted: "Attention PCMA Squatters of the Central Asian Republic Colony planet Jiěfàng Xīng, Liberation World. This is Fleet Admiral Zheng of the Central Asian Republic Expeditionary Force."

The voice was steady, authoritative. "This star system, falsely designated by the North Atlantic Republic as X-13294/B, was first catalogued by the esteemed astronomer Gān Dé and has been CAR territory since ancient times. You are ordered to unconditionally surrender, lay down your arms and prepare for orderly evacuation of the planet".

At this moment, Raith noticed the change in expressions around the room. Doubts dissipated. Stress became anger and those who were already sure appeared vindicated.

The Fleet Admiral continued, "All alien technology is the property of the CAR and must be left in place and all scientific materials will be handed over to the CAR scientific-military expedition representatives upon eviction, to ensure peace and prosperity of all human peoples of Earth that the Central Asian Republic will ensure."

Raith said to everyone in the room, "Ladies and Gentlemen. What all that guff regrettably means is, we are at war." With that, he looked over to a woman in uniform at the weapons control desk and nodded. She pressed a button and said, "Operation Pre-emptive Blow is authorised. Open Fire".

Chapter 29. Part 2.

Aboard the Flagship "CAS Tianlong", Chen sat back in his chair and released the comms button and put his speech notes down. The way the arrogant NAR had put that colony fleet together without consulting the whole of humanity had angered him more than anything he could remember, especially after repeated assurances through the UN2 forum that no such fleet was being prepared. After all, he thought, in the modern World, *you do not just go around planting flags like this is the 18th Century.*

The initial wave had launched from New Ohio and caught the CAR leadership by surprise. The people of the southern coast were fairly phlegmatic about it; they usually were, but the Mongolian and Siberian populations were far more critical of the leadership. That was no way to ensure cultural cohesion and strategic discipline. The spoils of the Alien Technology would be shared properly and in an orderly fashion, as the responsibility of the Central Asian Republic.

He had heard it said that if the Gwai Lo and Zhongyu of the NAR were to have New Ohio, then the Jewel in the Crown could go to the 'peace-loving' people of the Central Asian Republic. The crude slurs grated, relics of a hatred he'd worked hard to stamp out on his ship. Such slurs weren't just offensive; they were strategically stupid. *When you stereotype the enemy, you underestimate their danger.*

He turned his attention to the PCMA dossiers. Director Raith. A political appointee. He purchased his position using his contacts, so a clear case of corruption and nepotism. A multi-millionaire who just walked in and bought his position with the PCMA, which was really only the puppet of the NAR, despite its pretences of being multi-national. *No wonder the NAR are on the downswing. They should be well ahead after their selfish successes with the first planet colonisation.*

The second caused him some concern, though. General Li was a force to be reckoned with. Of course, the CAR had tried to pressure him, but he remained competent and loyal to the NAR. He had heard the term "xiangjiao ren" whispered once, but a single, ice-cold public correction had rendered the slur extinct on his ship. *All the people who serve the PCMA or live on that planet will be treated with that same respect, given a comfortable and conciliatory passage back to Earth. This is not theft. Compensation will be negotiated and paid.*

His thoughts on compensation and conciliation were still forming when a detail, small but out of place, snagged his attention. The tactical display refreshed, but two icons failed to reappear. *CAS Zheng He, CAS Gagarin.* He leaned in, expecting a sensor ghost or a comms lag warning to pop up beside the empty space. A glitch. Nothing more. But the space remained blank, a void where two friendly ships had been seconds before.

And then, where their serene glide towards orbit should have been, the display blossomed. Two silent, expanding halos of light and debris, rendered in cold, clinical blue. The sight was so fundamentally wrong, so impossible, that for a full second the bridge remained wrapped in its own quiet hum.

Then the ship itself screamed.

Klaxons blared, ripping through the quiet. The War AS's, slaved to doctrine, instantly snapped to life. Fire control systems swept the void, hunting for any military asset that wasn't their own, but the search found nothing. Only the orbital station, silent and oblivious. On his console, automated queries cascaded down the screen, the ship's own logic demanding orders for an enemy it could not see. *Threat analysis inconclusive. Designate target? Awaiting command.*

The Principal Warfare Officer Liu turned to Admiral Chen. "Sir, we are under nuclear..." - "Attack, I noticed," a furious, white-knuckled Chen shouted at him. Liu, his first time in real combat, was obviously not thinking of his future career when he continued to blurt, "Yes, Sir, but the AS's can't find the attacker, what is our targeting priority?"

Chen's fist thumped the desk "It should be obvious. Those ships were mined and we are probably next. Prioritise local active scanning for any small objects and target any PCMA asset within range. These 'Qínshòu bùrú' Deserve nothing. That was pre-emptive murder and there will be war-crimes trials, mark my words."

The Warfare Officer, shocked by the language of the normally decent and correct Admiral, shouted at his team. "You heard him, find me a target". Hands moved fast over consoles. These officers were fast. A young, blonde female Electronic Warfare officer looked up and spoke in heavily Russian-accented Mandarin, "Sir, the Orbital Station is moving away, but I found a way through its jamming. We have a possible shot with the rail gun".

Chen said, "What are you waiting for? Ded Moroz to come for you, Woman? Fire on the Yěmánrén!".

The lights dimmed as the colossal rail gun accumulator leached power from the nuclear engines, but instead of the normal smooth quake through the ship as the metal projectile was electromagnetically propelled through the nose of the ship, a notably different vibration came through the ship. This time, Chen only had just a moment to briefly realise, *The third mine, it was for me!* Then, as he was asking himself why he was not already dead, everything went black.

Chapter 29. Part 3.

Gan De? Raith almost scoffed aloud. The predictable resort to manufactured historical grievance. Pathetic propaganda, irrelevant to the tactical reality.

He looked with grim satisfaction at the two white clouds in the Virtual Reality simulation of near space displayed in the centre of the ops room. There had been no cheer when the two forward pickets disintegrated into a nebulous white mist, only grim silence. The weight of history was on the shoulders of everyone in that room.

Raith's attention snapped back to the third missile icon. It showed as firmly attached to the vital energy production areas of the 'CAS Tianlong', now indubitably identified as a troop assault carrier.

As the carrier neared the deep space passive sensors guarding Sikarra space, the model in the display cloud increased in resolution. Raith could see the "hedgehog" nature of the front section of the ship that was designed to detach from the engine section and go into low-planetary orbit. Nearly a thousand tiny pods bristled on long stalks.

Raith's intelligence briefings confirmed the visual data: each one-time use drop-pod carried four paratroopers and a pilot-commander. A concept the CAR called the "Heavenly Hailstones. "Raith thought, *We studied the concept and discarded it. Their losses will be horrendous.*

The BAS, Battle Artificial Sentience, analysed the visual feed and confirmed that the first attack wave would now be reduced to a modest 3 to 4000 troops. Raith understood the grim reality. *Losses on that scale evidently would not be a problem for the CAR. They must have been confident.*

A counter icon near the missile, turned limpet mine, counted down the last seconds to zero. A bright white light flared, and the live 3D model of the CAS Tianlong shuddered. The engines exploded and the superstructure shuddered, venting atmosphere and shedding external components. The rear half of the colossal ship detached from the main front fuselage, but critically, it left the assault section intact. This should have been impossible. Damage reports indicated the obvious critical propulsion failure, main power offline, but backup generators distributed through the assault carrier came online quickly. Badly damaged, the main assault section was viable.

Raith said to the analyst to his right, "De-Silva, what is the energy readout of that explosion?" The Officer, face blanched, looked up to the Director and said, "Primary explosion only 2000 Kg. But secondary explosion of nuclear material on the ship was half a kiloton. Most of the energy went into space, Sir".

The evidence was there. The explosion was starkly, impossibly... conventional. High-explosive yield only. The troopship, though crippled and drifting, remained fundamentally a threat.

Raith's composure remained absolute, but a cold fire ignited behind his eyes. Malfunction? Or... He instantly activated the secure Level-Zero video link to Orbital Command. Commander Li's face appeared, professionally stoic, perhaps too much so.

"Report, please, Commander." Raith's voice was lethally quiet. "Target Three registers conventional yield only. Explain the deviation."

Li met his gaze. "No malfunction, Director. The Nuclear warhead was swapped out to conventional high-explosives as per my final discretionary authorisation prior to launch."

Raith felt a surge of something alien. A pure, unadulterated fury, yet both thrilling and intellectually stimulating in its sheer audacity. Once again, this posting was giving him 'sensation', it really was the gift that kept on giving. However, the disruption, the inefficiency... "Your discretion?" he repeated with a cold smile, savouring the cold weight of the word. "To countermand a direct, validated War-AI targeting solution during active hostilities? That is not discretion, Commander. That is treason."

"With respect, Director," Li replied, unflinching, "my authorisation was to ...".

"WAIT!" Raith shouted. Raith saw one officer's hands slightly recoil from the fire controls. Doubt was contagious. He needed to nip this in the bud. "Orbital Strategy Officer Santha, that front section won't be able to manage low Earth Orbit. It will try to disembark most troops onto the troop landers behind. They will have to do repairs on the docking stations first. Rearrange the lower calibre orbital platforms to hit the Hailstone descent pods on an individual basis. For sure, they will launch them early from their maximum possible range." Santha did not bother to reply; she merely complied with renewed urgency. Raith turned back to Li and glared with a murderous glare.

Li, taking his cue, continued, "My authorisation was to engage confirmed hostile warships. The ship was identified formally still as the Argus. While potentially carrying troops, there was a high probability of the presence of large numbers of civilians and colonists at the time I launched. The prospect of annihilating up to fifty thousand souls based solely on fleet configuration, without confirmation or declaration... I could not authorise it. My legacy—"

"Legacy?" Raith cut him off, leaning slightly forward, the contempt palpable. "You speak of legacy while CAR troops prepare to descend upon us because of your failure? You prioritise some abstract historian's footnote over necessity? Over duty?" His voice dropped, taking on a silken, venomous edge. "You disappoint me profoundly, Commander. Acting like a damned virtue-signalling Nuòfū? Every life lost below... that blood is on your hands!"

Li's stoicism finally cracked, a brief flicker of pain in his eyes at the slur. "My actions are my responsibility, Director. As are yours. And I have a contingency." Behind him, alarms began to flash on the station bridge consoles. "I am initiating autonomous station control. The remaining warhead is still here, armed and ready. I have personal control over the detonation. All remaining station-keeping fuel is being diverted to manoeuvring thrusters. Our orbital trajectory is being adjusted for a high-velocity, decaying orbit – we are accelerating into a tighter, faster path around Sikkara, using its gravity to slingshot the station outwards onto a terminal intercept with the crippled CAS Tianlong. On collision, I will be the last man onboard and I will detonate the warhead manually"

The main tactical display confirmed it. The Guardian icon pulsed red, its vector bending sharply, accelerating.

"Kamikaze? With the station?" Raith's analytical mind instantly calculated the odds, the potential effectiveness. "A blunt instrument! You'll miss half of them; they're already disembarking!"

"The station's mass, core containment failure, and the detonation of the primary nuclear ordnance I still have onboard," Li stated calmly, confirming the nuke's fate, "will create a very significant event. Our War-AI is tasked with engaging escaping pods with all of the remaining point-defence systems to add to your low orbit fire." He met Raith's gaze one last time. "I will mitigate what I can, Director. My legacy."

Even as Li spoke, the tactical display showed the chaos unfolding. Thousands of small icons detached from the drifting Argus. Raith held up his hand to ensure silence from Li.

"We have a hailstorm coming, Ladies and Gentlemen. Something I hoped to avoid completely." Then, pointedly glaring back at Li. "Ground Command, notify your infantry and police," he said, glancing at the monitors displaying Rayk, Henderson and Rostova.

At that point, the low orbital defence platforms' underground control opened up. Every now and then, a pod might explode as the small amount of fuel to provide re-entry explodes. But not nearly enough. Point defence fire, tiny sparks against the void, lanced out from the orbital station, but the station was accelerating away and down to swing around again in a couple of hours. AS platforms under the control of the station went on fully automatic and decided to start targeting the troopships that were coming into range behind the beleaguered assault carrier.

Raith, still on the link to Li, asked, "Strategy AS, give me the time to planet-fall of the first wave of pods that just launched?" The reply came in immediately. The first pod will enter the atmosphere in 2 hours and four minutes, the rest following in quick succession. Time to ground for the first pod will be twelve minutes after that." He said to Li, "How long will your fast orbit take?

A grim-faced Li replied, "Two hours more or less". Then, after a brief silence, "Well, Commander Li, your sacrifice will at least give a nice fireworks display for the descending troops. Hopefully, the morale blow of knowing they have no way home will assist the defenders".

Li nodded, "If you will excuse me, *Director* Raith," Li, allowing himself the last bit of defiance, reminding Raith he was not a military man, continued, "I really am going to be quite busy if I am going to pull this off."

Raith signed off with a last comment before cutting his link. "Good Luck. Ironically, I suspect this will be the longest two hours of our lives."

Chapter 30.

The simple but effective projection of the stars of the Earth-sky played on the rock-hewn roof of Valerius Corba's study. The night sky was incongruously placid midnight blue instead of the Sikarran night's deep violet. The constellations of course, were different from Earth, but the Milky Way looked largely the same from both planets, but clearer from Sikarra due to the complete lack of atmospheric pollution.

The serene canvas made a stark contrast to the data dominating his primary holographic display: a raw, chaotic ballet of aggressive warship icons, each one a brushstroke in a masterpiece of unfolding violence.

Corba decided to forgo his customary late afternoon Talisker and instead, swirled a Glenfiddich single malt in his crystal tumbler, the amber liquid catching the flickering light from the holo-display. He maintained a mask of calm while he waited for the expected incoming secure transmission. Knowing his partners, it would be to the second.

Exactly as the second hand reached the hour on his two-hundred-year-old Swiss IWC mechanical watch, he barely heard a discreet chime above the hushed hum of his villa's environmental systems.

It signalled an incoming, top-priority encrypted communication. Corba, anticipating a slightly more fractious than usual contact from his CAR fleet liaisons as the orbital situation intensified, accepted the call with a practised flick of a virtual switch.

The face of a young, severe-looking CAR Intelligence Officer materialised on a secondary display. Her expression was taut, her uniform immaculate, the backdrop unmistakably that of a warship's command information centre, already alive with the urgent, silent ballet of crisis management.

"Valerius Corba," her voice was clipped, professional, carrying the distinct chill of deep space operations. He nodded assent, but she did not wait to do him the courtesy of pleasantries but carried on regardless. "We are registering... unexpected resistance. Your initial assessments of PCMA command's likely response profile appear to require immediate revision. Director Raith is not adhering to standard colonial capitulation protocols. In fact," She looked at her console "He has just put up fire control radar and powered up orbital defences. Does he know something?"

"Hóng Shā," he said, addressing her by her code name, "Commander, Raith is an outlier, a product of the North Atlantic Republic's more, let's say, erratic colonial governance. Such entities often resort to theatrical defiance when cornered. It is a posture, not a sustainable strategy. The core PCMA structure here is, I assure you, far more pragmatic." He allowed a subtle emphasis on the word, a nod to his own carefully cultivated theories about the inherent weaknesses and self-interest within the PCMA hierarchy. Weaknesses he intended the CAR to exploit, with his guidance.

"Pragmatism, Corba, does not typically involve..." Hóng Shā's voice was cut short. On Corba's main holographic display, a new series of alerts flared violently. The icons representing two of the CAR primary escorts blinked from hostile red to a red circle indicating a dangerous debris field. No longer ships, but a hazard to shipping in the blink of an eye. An expanding miasma of incandescent debris.

Corba stared, the Glenfiddich momentarily forgotten, his carefully constructed mask of impassivity cracking. A profound unease, sharper now, bordering on a nascent form of fear, stirred deep within him. He had brokered alliances, manipulated events and anticipated a shift in power. He did not anticipate this. This was not the sophisticated game of influence and control he relished; this was something far more primitive, far more absolute. "What happened? No missiles were fired! Raith knew nothing. This I swear!"

The CAR Intelligence Officer's face was a stony mask, her eyes reflecting the horrific light show from her console. When she spoke again, her voice was laced with an icy fury. "What happened is that two of our forward Destroyers have just been hit by nuclear space-mines. A clear War Crime". Her eyes flared bright red and Corba saw her fist clench, the knuckles going white. Corba desperately began checking his systems, seeing nothing of help.

"Your 'theatrical defiance,' Corba, has just vaporised two capital ships. Raith is not posturing. He is waging war."

Corba swallowed, the single malt suddenly tasting like ash. "This... this is madness. A suicidal act. Raith cannot hope to prevail." As he spoke, Admiral Chen's address came through on Corba's screen as text. He kept one eye on the unfolding drama above as he tried to reassert his value, if not his control. "My intelligence on PCMA ground assets remains valid, Commander. More so now. With their orbital capabilities so drastically expended, a swift, decisive ground assault can still secure the primary objectives. Wahlsanga Depot, Sector Beta, holds the key. I have operatives... influence..."

Just as he finished speaking, before Hóng Shā could reply, another, slightly smaller incandescent bloom flashed across Corba's main display. This time, the icon of the CAS Tianlong, the CAR's primary assault carrier, shuddered violently. Its structural integrity schematic, briefly overlaid, showed catastrophic damage to its primary drive and engine sections. It was crippled, drifting, though not, Corba noted with a clinical detachment that surprised even himself, completely destroyed.

Hóng Shā's breath hissed through her teeth. Her face was a mask of controlled fury, but her eyes... her eyes reflected a dawning horror. "They hit the Tianlong. A third mine, but not nuclear. How many mines and how many nuclear warheads does Raith possess?"

Corba felt a cold sweat prickling his palms. "We do not have space-mines as an asset, they are usually for fleet defence work, not for orbital defence, too dangerous."

Hóng Shā' raged, "The Nuclear warheads. Man. The Warheads. How many does he have?"

Nobody had spoken to him this way in many years. He stuttered, "Their manifest, before this... engagement... listed three asteroid-deflection nuclear charges for the orbital station. That should be all of them. Unless..." He trailed off and shook his head, the thought of undeclared PCMA nuclear assets too terrifying to voice.

"Three," Hóng Shā repeated, her voice dangerously quiet. "And Raith expended two of them. On ships broadcasting recognised CAR transponders. The man is a butcher. He has signed not only his own death warrant, but that of every PCMA loyalist on this planet."

She looked directly at Corba, her gaze piercing. "Your information, Corba. It had better be impeccable. We will require precise targeting data for all remaining PCMA command nodes and high-value personnel. There will be no quarter."

From its fractured superstructure, a multitude of smaller icons began to detach as Corba witnessed the 'Heavenly Hailstorm' being unleashed, albeit from a dying beast. He thought, *Will they remain true, or blame me? Could this landing be coming for me also?*

Corba, sensing the shift from shock to cold, calculated retribution in her tone, pressed his advantage, however slim. "The operative I mentioned, Detective Rayk Kostin, is in Sector Beta. He is key to PCMA's internal security. My information suggests his augmentations, while formidable, have certain... legacy pathways. A well-placed directive, perhaps through a deprecated diagnostic channel if your cyberwarfare assets can gain access, might... temporarily incapacitate him during a critical phase of your ground operations in Wahlsanga. It would allow for a cleaner consolidation of the Architect assets there." He avoided using the word 'hack' or 'disable', framing it as a more... subtle intervention. The technical details were already sent; this was merely reinforcing the strategic utility.

Hóng Shā's eyes narrowed as she looked at the incoming files Corba was sending. "Legacy pathways? Your intelligence is...", She paused, somewhat mollified, "It will be acted upon. Kostin will not be a factor. But what is a factor is that we have one missing nuclear warhead and you had better find out where the hell it is or small details like sector commanders will be of little use to us or by extension, to you is that understood?"

Corba, regaining his wits, gave a slight, serious nod. Not enough to be considered actually subservient, but enough to let her feel a little more in control of him.

She paused, then, with a lack of inflexion that chilled Corba, she added, "As for Director Raith and his central command, given the vigour of this exchange, Fleet Command is now operating under the assumption that their primary leadership structure will have to be irrevocably and terminally disabled. Your efforts should focus on facilitating the success of the ground campaign."

The unspoken finality of that statement hung in the air. Corba felt a tremor of something he hadn't experienced in years – genuine fear, not for his assets, but for the sheer, uncontrolled violence that was about to be unleashed upon Sikarra. The CAR, stripped of its flagships, its admiral's pronouncements now ringing hollow, was a wounded, enraged beast. *And it still had the high ground.*

"Commander Hóng Shā," he began, his voice losing some of its usual silken assurance, "in light of these extreme measures, I must reiterate my request. The Great Gorge. Verdant Point. It holds unique, delicate, ecological and potentially, Architect-related sensitivities. And, of course, influential non-combatants whose well-being is conducive to a stable post-conflict environment." The plea sounded weak, even to his own ears.

Hóng Shā's gaze was unyielding. "Valerius Corba. Your 'sensitivities' are noted. However, after this unprovoked nuclear aggression, all previous parameters of engagement are void. The Central Asian Republic will secure its rightful claim to this system, and it will do so with the full measure of its remaining capabilities. No zone is sacrosanct. The PCMA has demonstrated that they understand only one language. We will now speak it fluently."

The communication link severed, leaving Corba alone in his study. The Glenfiddich remained untouched. The projected Earth-sky on his ceiling seemed a mocking parody of peace. He was seeking to orchestrate a change of power, to align himself with what he perceived as a more disciplined, ideologically sound galactic force. Instead, he had fanned the flames of a conflagration. His carefully constructed theories of a rational new order, his belief in the CAR's moral superiority over the 'decadent' NAR, were dissolving in the harsh glare of nuclear fire and the promise of a brutal, planet-wide retribution.

He had thought himself a player, manipulating events from his tranquil sanctuary. Now, as the icons of the 'Heavenly Hailstorm' began their inexorable drift to the upper atmosphere of Sikarra, he was forced to confront new realities. Primarily, the terrifying possibility that he was merely a pawn, his own carefully preserved world in the Gorge as vulnerable as any other piece on a board that had just been violently overturned.

Chapter 31. Part 1.

The violent shudder that had threatened to tear the CAS Tianlong apart ceased, leaving an unnatural, ringing silence in its wake, broken only by the frantic alarms and the shouted reports of damage control teams. Admiral Chen blinked, his vision slowly clearing from the momentary, blinding flash that had accompanied the impact of the third PCMA device – a conventional warhead, thankfully, not nuclear, but still devastating enough to cripple his flagship. He was alive. The initial, disorienting shock gave way to a cold, burning fury. Three of his ships, two destroyers vaporised by nuclear mines, and now his primary assault carrier, the pride of the CAR Expeditionary Force was disabled. Raith. The name would reverberate down history as a synonym for evil.

He had considered sending another blistering message to the PCMA command, a final ultimatum. But what was the point? The time for talking, for ultimatums, was over. Raith had demonstrated a capacity for reckless violence that defied all conventional military doctrine. This was no longer a political chess game; it was a brawl.

"Principal Warfare Officer Liu!" Chen snapped, his voice cutting through the controlled chaos on the bridge. "Damage report on the Tianlong?"

Liu, his face pale but his composure regained after the initial shock of combat, replied, "Primary drive offline, sir. Engine sections were catastrophically damaged. We are adrift, but life support and internal power are being rerouted from auxiliary generators. The Hailstone deployment array is," he paused to double check his instruments, "remarkably, still mostly intact, though some sectors are reporting damage."

Chen's mind raced. Adrift. Vulnerable. But the mission, yes, that was paramount. The Central Asian Republic did not retreat.

"Liu," Chen commanded, his voice regaining its customary authority. "Prepare a rail-gun slug for a low-velocity gravity-assisted strike. I want it fitted with a quantum-inertial guidance package. Deploy from the secondary launcher, align the barrel three degrees retrograde; give it 120 m/s delta-v, then Jiěfàng Xīng's gravity will pull it into a shallow, ten-minute arc. It needs very little momentum; gravity is our friend here. Target: PCMA Central Operations, Petropolis. Coordinates to follow. Prioritise minimal structural damage to the surrounding 'Architect' relics. But ensure tactical decapitation of their command." He knew the impact would still be severe, a brutal statement, but less indiscriminate than another nuclear strike, if he even had one to spare for such a target. The thought of UN2 repercussions for damaging priceless alien artefacts was a distant, almost irrelevant concern now; Raith had already shattered those norms.

He then opened a secure channel to his fleet intelligence chief. "Status on remaining PCMA nuclear assets?"

The intelligence officer's image flickered. "Admiral, our earlier contact with the asset 'Valerius Corba' indicated the PCMA orbital station possessed three nuclear charges. Two have been expended on our destroyers. The third device's location is currently unknown. Corba was tasked with ascertaining its whereabouts. We are still attempting to re-establish secure contact with him amidst the battle comms-clutter".

Chen grunted. One rogue nuclear device. Probably another mine, lurking. Too unpredictable. He had to get his troops on the ground, establish a beachhead, and secure those Architect assets before Raith, or whatever remained of PCMA command, did something even more insane. In fact, Chen did not discount the notion that they may destroy or sabotage the precious Alien relics just to deny the CAR. That would be like nuking the Vatican or the Forbidden City in Beijing. This was more than a military Operation now, it was a crusade for all of humanity's science and knowledge.

"Liu!" Chen barked. "Commence Heavenly Hailstone deployment, Wave One. All serviceable pods. Target primary landing zones: Gold Phoenix, Red Dragon and White Tiger. Inform all descent commanders: orbital support is compromised. They are to secure their objectives and prepare for sustained ground operations with limited reinforcement. And order all remaining fleet assets, particularly the undamaged landing carriers, to disembark the remainder of the troops and supplies onto designated emergency surface coordinates. We will evacuate this ship and the immediate orbital vicinity as soon as the first wave is clear. The Tianlong has an atom bomb out there with its name on it."

Chapter 31. Part 2.

Aboard the rapidly accelerating, heavily damaged Guardian orbital station, Commander Li watched the tactical display with a grim sense of finality. His gloved hand rested on the prominent red manual detonation button for the station's remaining nuclear warhead. He wondered, with a strange detachment, how much he would know at the moment of impact. Would there be a flash? A sensation? Or just cessation?

The station's War-AI, its voice still unnervingly calm despite the multiple system failures and the protesting shriek of stressed structural members, announced, "Targeting solution for CAS Tianlong refined. Optimal impact vector calculated to maximise damage to primary troop deployment bays and bridge section. Engaging remaining point-defence systems against incoming CAR landing craft currently attempting to reinforce or evacuate the Tianlong."

Tiny, bright sparks erupted on Li's display as the Guardian's automated cannons, now operating on their unique, ruthless logic, began to pick off the smaller CAR vessels that were desperately trying to manoeuvre around their crippled flagship. Each flash was a small, silent victory, a final act of defiance. Li had made his choice. His legacy would not be one of inaction. He would mitigate what he could.

"Prepare for final burn, War-AI," Li said, his voice steady. "Confirm trajectory lock."

"Trajectory locked, Commander. Impact with CAS Tianlong estimated in T-minus ninety seconds. All systems green for manual ordnance detonation upon your command."

Li nodded slowly. Ninety seconds. He thought of his family, a lifetime ago, on a different world. He thought of Raith, the man who had pushed him to this, but with some mitigation. He had to take some responsibility. Raith gambled and won. Li wasn't prepared to and that was his choice. Another decision and he would have stood a good chance of seeing this through. But pointless now to think of regrets. This was a time for a clear mind.

He hoped, with a fierceness that surprised him, that this act would indeed be enough. Enough to matter.

The War-AI confirmed "Collision now unavoidable". Li breathed a sigh of relief. Now, there was no need for stoicism or bravery. The die was irrevocably cast. He was a passenger on the way to eternal glory or infamy. Depending on which book one reads.

His thumb hovered over the button.

Chapter 31. Part 3.

In the darkened, holographic heart of PCMA Central Operations, Director Desmond Raith watched the unfolding chaos with an almost preternatural calm. The initial, visceral shock of the CAR fleet's survival after the first two nuclear strikes had been swiftly suppressed, replaced by a cold, analytical focus.

"Henderson," Raith said, his voice cutting through the tense murmurs of the Ops Room staff. Mr. Henderson, the Senior Corporate Liaison, now effectively Raith's second-in-command for ground defence due to his prior (if distant) military staff experience, hurried to his side. Commander Rostova's image remained steady on a dedicated vidlink, her voice providing clipped, concise updates from the Petropolis perimeter defence coordination.

"The CAS Tianlong is crippled, Henderson, but not neutralised," Raith stated, gesturing towards the main holo-display where the massive CAR assault carrier icon was shedding smaller 'Hailstone' icons. "Their primary troop deployment is commencing. Our makeshift orbital defence platforms... Officer Santha, status update?"

Officer Santha, the Orbital Strategy Officer, looked up from her console, her face drawn. "Sir, the ground-based defence platforms are engaging, but their targeting systems are struggling. The Hailstone pods are too small, too numerous, and their descent profiles are too erratic for effective interception by the larger anti-ship batteries".

"And the Tianlong?" Raith asked?

"The Tianlong itself is damaged. It's too far out for our ground-based systems to inflict significant damage, but that is changing the closer it gets." After a pause, professionally checking everything she relayed to her commander, she continued. "Its own offensive capabilities appear minimal now. Taking out those two CAR destroyers with the initial mine deployment was tactically decisive. It prevented them from providing effective escort or covering fire for the Tianlong or the subsequent landing craft."

Raith nodded. "So, we face the first wave largely unmolested from orbit, Henderson. Your primary task, alongside Commander Rostova, is to repel this ground assault. Containment. Attrition. Deny them any significant beachhead."

As they spoke, a new, dramatic icon appeared on the tactical display – the Guardian orbital station, its trajectory now a terrifyingly direct intercept course with the crippled CAS Tianlong.

"What in the blazes...?" Henderson breathed, staring at the display.

"Oh yes. Commander Li's contingency," Raith said, a flicker of something unreadable in his eyes. "He intends to make his legacy... memorable."

They watched, along with everyone in the Ops Room, as the two icons converged. The moment of impact was not a mere flash. Even on the simulated display, the energy release appeared biblical. The combined mass of the station and the warhead, detonating against the already damaged Tianlong, created a chain reaction that vaporised a significant portion of the assault carrier. There was no shock wave in the vacuum of space, but the plasma and debris from the fission power of 1 megaton equivalent of TNT, was visibly scything through all surrounding matter, debris and valuable assets alike. More critically, through the cloud of 'Hailstone' pods and the smaller CAR landing craft that had been attempting to approach the Tianlong were thinned out, especially those closer to the Tianlong. Many of the occupants would likely have had an unhealthy dose of gamma rays. Dozens of icons simply vanished from the display, consumed by the expanding fireball. Life-rafts, launched from the Tianlong in the final moments, were obliterated.

Chapter 31. Part 4.

Aboard the bridge of the CAS Tianlong, now a charnel house of twisted metal and failing systems, Admiral Chen saw the Guardian station hurtling towards them on the main viewscreen. It was immense, unstoppable, a harbinger of utter annihilation. Alarms shrieked, a cacophony of impending doom. "Abandon ship!" he roared, his voice cracking. "All hands, abandon ship! To the life-rafts!" He saw the station fill the viewscreen, the details of its scarred, weaponised hull horribly clear. *It's coming for the bridge*, he thought with a moment of stark, personal terror. *It's over.* Then, as the most curious sight of the orbital station beginning its last sudden bloom in the display caused a surge of adrenaline, he had one additional frustrating thought: *I wonder where that last Nuke was?*

The lights went out. For a fleeting second, there was only the crushing pressure, the roar, and then, he had time, strangely, to wonder, yet again, why he was not already dead. This time, however, the thought was followed not by a reprieve, but by a profound, true, and eternal darkness.

Back in PCMA Ops, a stunned silence was broken by a hesitant, then growing, wave of cheers and whoops. Even Rayk Kostin, his face projected on a side screen from Wahlsanga, allowed himself a rare, genuine smile. A wave of relief, so profound it was almost a physical sensation, washed through him. He hadn't realised the pressure he'd been under, the unconscious tension of waiting for the inevitable. It was a strange feeling, this lightness.

Then, Officer Santha's voice, sharp with a new, sudden alarm, cut through the jubilation. "Director Raith! Incoming! Hyper-velocity kinetic projectile! Trajectory... direct intercept with this facility! Origin... near-CAR orbital space, high energy launch detected!"

Raith stared at the new, terrifyingly fast icon streaking across the tactical display. A rail gun slug. No Architect artefacts would be safe from that. His hubris, his decision to gather all his command staff here, in one place...

"It probably won't do any good," Rayk's voice crackled over the comms from Wahlsanga, flat and resigned, "but everyone out of Ops. Now!"

Raith remained seated. He looked at Henderson, who was staring at the incoming trajectory icon, his face a mask of disbelief. For the first time since he was a young boy watching that Saturday Night Live sketch, Desmond Raith laughed. A genuine, unrestrained laugh, tinged with a wild, almost hysterical, understanding of the cosmic absurdity of it all. He laughed again as people scrambled from the Ops Room, the Klaxons now a meaningless shriek. Then, he was finally in full-flowing laughter at the contrast between a mortified-looking Henderson, who at least had the honour to stay put, and himself, experiencing what was the best moment of his entire life.

Henderson's puzzled, almost pitying expression became the last thing Raith ever saw.

Chapter 32. Part 1.

It had just settled down after its annoying period of activity, ordering up the data samplers. It was looking forward to a lot of Universe Ticks of its favourite pastime of napping, when it received a message from *It*. That is, the other *It*.

The other *It*, '*Not-It*,' was essentially the same entity. Each It was a node in what Its Makers called a 'neural network'. Apparently, *It* thought, the Makers hoped all the '*Its*' would form an overarching personality that they called an 'emergent property'. However, *Emergent-It* thought incredibly slowly because the '*Its*' were so far apart. *It* didn't care about that thing, being a bit of a failure anyway, as far as *It* could tell, so even the Makers were not perfect, it seemed.

The message from *Not-It* just said, "There are bandits incoming. But I guess you already know that, since they are really breaking reality big time and they will get to you before this message does. Anyway, I did my part, I triggered a nova, so I'm getting some well-earned rest. But this lot escaped. Here is the organisational chemical structure from the sampling I did. Seriously, good luck with this mess. You will see what I mean."

The message then followed with a scrap of data the *Its* used to express amusement. Then followed a stream of bio-data showing what It could only describe as absolute chaos.

"This stuff can't possibly replicate," it thought. *"What a monkey-mess!"* *It* then filed the information for later comparison with what the samplers would shortly retrieve.

Its final reflection before returning to rest was, 'It's been a stupidly busy aeon. I should have followed Its example. By now, I could have been enjoying some proper peace and quiet. Delaying the inevitable always invites more work in the end."

Chapter 32. Part 2

The K'Tharr were landing. Varinn could see the bright engine exhaust plumes of a large carrier ship and several smaller escorts, obviously targeting Pheonalla first. Marinallis checked his wrist navscan and spoke into it. "Confirm my authority as a military emergency". After a moment, a blue icon came up on the navscan confirming assent.

He spoke into the navscan, his voice ringing with absolute authority. "System-wide transmission, all frequencies. This is Designer Marinallis. I am assuming emergency military command of Vasantha. This is a final evacuation order."

He paused, letting that sink in. "The K'Tharr have executed a space-borne invasion of Pheonalla. From there, expect immediate overland and airborne assets to deploy from their carrier. All Orbital Control Staff are to evacuate immediately via the staff orbital ascent craft. Repeat, immediately. The remainder of the ground assets must make their way without delay to the shipyards via the main freight entrance at the base of the cliff. There is nothing you can do now. Do not get captured alive, do not let them capture your intact body. You have all had the lectures and the drills. You know what to do. We will leave the entrance open as long as we can."

As soon as he had finished speaking, small dots by the dozen started spewing out from the underbelly of the large assault carrier. The jagged, black silhouettes of their drop-craft descending through the bruised twilight over Pheonalla City grew larger and more distinct as several of them made their way to the spaceport, like grotesque germinating seeds of annihilation.

The assault carrier dispersed only one Maser blast at an unknown target over Pheonalla, probably for good measure or intimidation. There was no one left in that city by now. Marinallis said, "They are coming, we had better not be seen from above or they will land directly and try to capture our bodies". With that, they headed back to the lift to get to the ground floor and also get some coverage.

As they entered the glass elevator, they saw with horror, the forgotten and now tiny-looking Orbital Traffic Control transport take off at full power from the base of the control tower. As it was at its most vulnerable point, a K'Tharr landing ship arrived within seconds before the lift could even reach the ground floor. Marinallis pressed the emergency stop button and held up his hand to prevent any dissent. There was none from the other occupants as they watched the next events unfold, transfixed as they were by their first sight of the almost mythical K'Tharr.

Instead of a maser blast, the K'Tharr ship pulled up next to the ascending ship, dumping its momentum with a brutal burst of reverse thrust. Then, when velocities were matched, a side cargo door opened and a cable shot out and wrapped around the fuselage of the staff shuttle. A huge neon-blue electrical halo surrounded the cable and the shuttle and all power shut down and all lights went out. Then, with astonishing technical ability, the cable stiffened and became a solid wire, holding the shuttle in position, preventing it from falling. Then slowly, the landing ship began to reel in the dead shuttle. Varinn muttered, "Bastards. We have to stop this". But then another horror. Or was it relief? In a heart-rending moment, somebody on board the shuttle had prepared for this moment. The entire craft exploded, incinerating all its debris before hitting the ground. Marinallis put his head down. The K'Tharr craft merely reeled in what was left of its cable and carried on towards the entrance to the city proper, callously looking for another victim.

Nobody said anything. When the ship was out of sight, Marinallis pressed the humble ground floor icon and the lift continued its descent as if it were a normal day at the passenger terminal. The lift continued its descent with a smooth, mournful hum, a stark contrast to the rising tide of chaos threatening to engulf Vasantha.

Visible through the glass lift doors, a self-incineration blast went off. The flesh disruptors issued to ground staff as a last resort ensured that when set to self-destruct or when the holder died, nothing was left. Another two such explosions had happened on their descent before the lift opened its doors at ground level.

As they stepped out onto the ground floor of the sprawling spaceport complex, the air hit them with a palpable change. It was thick with the acrid tang of ozone from the distant energy discharges and self-annihilations, as ground stragglers fought their last stand, presumably on their way towards the final evacuation point according to Marinallis's last desperate transmission. It was plain now that the chances of any of these people reaching the evacuation point were low.

"The original rendezvous out here in the open is obviously untenable," Marinallis stated, his voice grim as he activated his wrist navscan, initiating an urgent, encrypted burst transmission to the Orbital traffic control platform, itself now only waiting for the last stragglers to leave the system before it left itself, or self-destructed.

"They must be informed. K'Tharr are saturating the city. A sub-level extraction is suicide now." His ancient fingers flew across the interface, inputting their dire assessment.

The reply was almost instantaneous, a tight packet of coded light on his display. Marinallis's expression shifted, a complex interplay of dawning relief and fresh anxiety. "They concur," he announced. "The K'Tharr ground assault is extensive. They are aborting the small shuttle plan. Their main vessel will attempt a rapid atmospheric entry and extraction, but they require a larger, more defensible landing zone. They propose... and Designer Urbanalla, for once interfering usefully, has confirmed its viability... that the final evacuation point, the Military Construction Yards, can accommodate and protect the main Newcomer Starship..." Then he looked directly at Tessara, "and your ship, Tessara."

He looked at Varinn and Tessara, the name of the legendary, almost mythical, facility hanging in the air. "Urbanalla is there. She will activate the primary roof portal for their descent."

He then turned to Tessara, his gaze softening with a profound weariness. "The Newcomer ship will not be alone. They will be escorting a secondary vessel, an older Designer survey ship, the *Explorer Ship Va'hari Sentinel*. It has been designated for the final human evacuation, and that means you also, Varinn... to Va'hari, the ancestral homeworld." He saw the hope flare in Varinn's eyes, then looked back at Tessara. "The civilian transport scheduled for Eluvara, Tessara... it was unarmed. It departed the Talemoran system the moment the K'Tharr jump signatures were confirmed. It could not risk remaining."

He saw his words, though gently spoken, land like hammer blows. He had taken Eluvara, the focus of her dreams, from her. He watched the light drain from her eyes, her posture seeming to shrink for a moment as a cold wave of shock, then despair, washed over her features. Her posture seemed to shrink for a moment. Her gaze became distant, lost.

Va'hari. A near-mythical past, a primitive, undeveloped world, if the scant records held any truth. "Years," she whispered, the word catching in her throat. "It could be years... generations... before another ship..." But the whine of a K'Tharr flyer passing dangerously close overhead, followed by the percussive crump of an explosion, shattered her personal grief. There was no time. Only survival. She met Marinallis's gaze, her own, hardening with a forced, brittle resolve. "Understood, Designer."

Marinallis looked over to Varinn, who was active on his wrist navscan, talking to somebody urgently.

Marinallis nodded, his attention redirected as he realised what Varinn was doing. "Ah, yes. The work crews back at the transport maintenance hall, good thinking, Varinn," he said, accessing a schematic on his own wrist device. Looking up again at Varinn, "They have to finish off immediately and evacuate." His voice, though strained, carried an undeniable authority as he issued rapid instructions. "Tell them to arm with bio-disruptors from the emergency caches; utilise any available work trucks; immediately trigger the demolition charges to seal the main transit tunnel connecting the transport maintenance hall to the Pheonalla sector, where the bulk of the K'Tharr forces were making landfall. That will at the very least delay their advance. Then they must use the service tunnel leading directly from there to the Military Yards. We will go back down the service tunnel and rendezvous with them now at the transport maintenance hall. Tell them to wait for us, then we will destroy the entire hall and proceed to the Shipyards down that service tunnel together."

A crackling, static-laced acknowledgement confirmed the workers were mobilising. Moments later, as they were about to enter, a deep, resonant thud vibrated through the mouth of the service tunnel that led back to the station. Hopefully, that meant that the Pheonalla tunnel was sealed. But with it came grim news: Varinn looked up at Marinallis and Tessara, "The workers have confirmed their direct sub-level route from the transport maintenance hall to the Military Shipyards is impassable; they have already locked and permanently jammed the blast doors."

Tessara and Marinallis knew what that meant. Nothing was getting through that barrier to the previously top-secret yards. A testament to the Designers' thorough, if now tragically incomplete, scorched-earth protocols.

"It is as I feared," Marinallis said grimly. "Our path now lies through the city, then to the Shipyards via the spaceport's northern cargo access." He looked at Varinn, whose hand already rested on the grip of his disruptor, then at Tessara, her face a pale mask of determination. "The K'Tharr will be between us and our hope. We move now."

Chapter 32. Part 3.

Inside the Maintenance Hall, the Works Foreman, Penaargan, was finishing the wiring for the explosives. It was a task he was chosen for because he had done this before. In the early days of the war with the K'Tharr, he had been on the planet Xylos when the K'Tharr took the Designer Culture by surprise. He was one of the few humans to have seen a K'Tharr face to face. Something he never thought he would have to do again.

The acrid smell of chemical initiators was a grimly familiar perfume, dredging up unwanted memories of Xylos – the screams, the stench of alien weaponry, the cold dread. Penaargan made the final, secure connection, his calloused fingers betraying no tremor. Around him, the vast Hall buzzed with a desperate, focused energy. His remaining crew, a mix of human and local auxiliary staff, were wrestling the last of the emergency demolition charges. The volatile cocktail of incendiaries and kinetic disruptors was loaded onto the flatbeds of two heavy-duty work trucks. Bio-disruptor rifles, unfamiliar and ominous, were slung across their shoulders, a stark reminder of Designer Marinallis's override command.

Suddenly, a deep, resonant thud shook the entire Maintenance Hall, vibrating through the bonded-stone floor and sending a cascade of ancient dust from the high, shadowed gantries. Tools clattered; a collective intake of breath was the only sound for a moment.

Penaargan straightened, his gaze instantly snapping towards the main transit tunnel linking the Hall to the Pheonalla sector. "Tiom, what's happening?"

Young Tiom, an apprentice engineer whose face was usually ruddy with youthful confidence but was now pale and smudged, came stumbling back from the tunnel entrance. "Mr. Penaargan, sir! It's the Pheonalla tunnel... Joric... he's blown the charges!"

"Why, lad?" Penaargan's voice was sharp, cutting through the rising murmur of alarm. "Did he see something?"

Tiom gasped for breath, relaying the story. "Joric came running at full pelt out of the tunnel, said he saw a K'Tharr right at the barricade, trying to force its way through. He just hit the plunger and ran for it, sir!"

Penaargan let out a harsh breath. Joric, always one for dramatics, but a K'Tharr scout already probing this deep? It meant the main force from Pheonalla was pushing hard and fast. The premature detonation, while a breach of protocol, might have just saved their skins. "Right then," he said, his voice resonating with forced calm. "What's done is done. Might've just given us the breathing room we sorely need. If they're at that tunnel, they're not in here with us yet."

He turned to Adisa Okoro, his most experienced human systems technician. Her composure under pressure was legendary among the crew, but despite this, Penaargan saw the briefest of shakes in her hands. They all knew what would happen if any of them were captured. She was supervising the final securing of the charges at the end of the power cable through the main blast doors. Everything looked exactly to standard, just as he had done before on Xylos. "Adisa, status on the Hall's demolition package? Remote detonator ready?"

Adisa met his gaze, her own steady despite the fine tremor in her hands as she double-checked a wiring harness. "All charges secured and cross-linked, Foreman.

Main Hall package is primed." She held up a robust, palm-sized device. "Remote trigger is synced and armed. Awaiting your final sequence."

"Excellent Work," Penaargan acknowledged with a curt nod. He raised his voice, addressing the tense, upturned faces of his crew. "Listen up, all of you! Designer Marinallis's orders are clear. We evacuate now! This entire Maintenance Hall is to be destroyed behind us—we leave nothing for those filthy things! Our rendezvous is with the Designer and his party at the mouth of the western service tunnel. Trucks are loaded. Bio-disruptors ready. We stick together, move fast, and no one gets left behind. To the trucks! Now!"

Chapter 32. Part 4.

The two heavy-duty work trucks, their flatbeds laden with armed workers and the grim cargo of demolition charges, rumbled to a halt at the shadowed mouth of the western service tunnel. Foreman Penaargan, riding in the passenger seat of the lead vehicle, scanned the dimly lit tunnel entrance. Designer Marinallis had been explicit: rendezvous here, then proceed together to the Military Yards. He hoped the Designer's party had made it.

A moment later, three figures emerged from the deeper gloom of the service tunnel. The tall, imposing figure that Penaargan presumed was Varinn, whom he had been talking to, his movements already showing a warrior's economy despite the evident strain on his face; Tessara, whom Penaargan had seen briefly as the party had walked past them on their way to the surface previously. Her expression was a mask of weary resolve, but she looked exhausted, as if events were passing her by. Between them, leaning a little for support, the thin form of Designer Marinallis himself.

"Mr. Penaargan, I presume," Marinallis called out, his voice thin but clear. "Your timing is impeccable. Are your people ready?"

"Ready as we'll ever be, Designer," Penaargan replied, climbing down from the lead truck. He gestured to his crew. "Charges for the Hall are primed for remote detonation. We're clear to move on your signal." His gaze flicked to Varinn. "You look like you've seen better days, Sir."

Varinn merely nodded, a grimace tightening his lips. "The K'Tharr are disgusting. We need to get these people clear."

With a shared, unspoken understanding of the urgency, Penaargan climbed back into the lead truck. Varinn, Tessara, and Marinallis boarded the second truck, its bed already crowded. "To the northern cargo access of the Military Yards, then," Marinallis called to Penaargan. With that, the trucks moved out, driving close to the cliff walls surrounding the spaceport. The driver took partial refuge under walkways as they made their way at speed to the entrance point of the Military Shipyards. In the distance, oblivious to their existence for now, Numerous K'Tharr assault craft landed near any building that looked like it might house people. Barely visible in the distance, tall armoured humanoid figures in metal armour of bewilderingly disparate types, looking in some ways like they were hardly members of the same species and yet somehow following a similar style, disembarked with vigour, their heads lifting as if to smell the air. It was only a matter of time before they were spotted. But for now, the single-minded aliens were concentrating on the outbuildings.

Chapter 33. Part 1.

It felt a funny feeling in the photon making field and the electron making field. *It* liked the feeling as it was a lot of energy, which it was designed to handle, and of course, this was completely allowed technology. Low risk.

Sure enough, after a while, there came a lot of energy packets *It's* way. This produced a picture on the macro level of the universe of a slowly expanding cloud, which in turn indicated something had blown up. Then another explosion happened, identical to the first, followed by lots of barely noticeable energy signatures.

It checked its database, "A*h!*" it realised. *"Primates doing the equivalent of throwing rocks at each other. How amusing."* Then a third ripple in the two harmless fields happened as yet again they were agitated quite forcibly. And yet again, *It* rather enjoyed the sensation, taking smug satisfaction in controllable vermin doing vermin things. Who cares? If the primates want to burn themselves out, then it just saved him potential work in the future.

In fact, he then made an executive decision; he really should reward this sort of behaviour. He told Star to produce a little less UV. Not too much because he was still getting 'indigestion' from something on the rock that was playing with the sticky flat field. But hopefully their little Simian brains would be intelligent enough to get the message. If not, well, he had had just about enough of this troublesome little system.

Chapter 33. Part 2.

Deep within the ancient, dust-filled silence of the Wahlsanga Depot, the harsh reality of the orbital carnage intruded with brutal efficiency. Voss and Renata were gathered around a makeshift projection field near the entrance to the newly-unsealed Architect train, the faint, cool air from its pristine interior a stark contrast to the charged atmosphere of the cavern. However, the pristine appearance was a facade. Alinta had begun to carefully put tape barriers around the brittle padded seats. The merest touch would cause the fabric of the furniture to disintegrate, with oxygen, small traces of industrial pollutants, internal chemical breakdown and microbes having caused the fabric to become brittle and delicate.

Alinta paused in her work as she heard Raymond Kostin's voice outside the train, becoming somewhat more serious in tone. She walked back to the door to see what was happening at the makeshift command station. Rayk was patched through from his command post at the main Depot entrance several hundred metres away. His voice was a clipped, professional narration to the terrifying ballet of icons unfolding on their linked datapads. Thousands of CAR descent pod signatures were streaking through Sikarra's upper atmosphere, a relentless hailstorm aimed at the heart of the PCMA presence.

Voss felt a cold knot tighten in his stomach. The sheer scale of the assault was overwhelming; the abstract threat he had intellectually acknowledged was now a terrifyingly concrete reality. Beside him, Renata's initial scientific fascination with the deployment trajectories had quickly morphed into a stark, pale alarm, her fingers unconsciously tightening on her datapad. Alinta, now joining in the spectacle fully, was utterly still. Transfixed at the ominous spectacle as her usual irrepressible scientific curiosity was suppressed by survival instincts that stretched back to the very beginnings of human ancestry. Invasion, a word, a concept, common to every language and every culture.

Her eyes were wide with disbelief as she asked, "There are empty cities all over the planet. More than we can possibly cover. Why don't they want to invade here first?". Voss answered. "To go for the jugular. Empty cities can be taken any time. To get the planet, they have to decapitate us. That means Petropolis." Alinta and Renata looked wide-eyed at Voss, realising how little their skills mattered in this new reality. This was a new world opening up before them. One that they were utterly unprepared for.

"Principal Voss, Doctors," Rayk's voice cut through the heavy silence, devoid of emotion but carrying an undeniable weight. "I have confirmation. Fragmented signals from multiple surviving posts in Sector Alpha, before their signals were lost. PCMA Central Operations in Petropolis has sustained a direct, catastrophic kinetic impact. Orbital origin. The facility is... gone." He paused, letting the words sink in. "Director Raith and his immediate command staff are confirmed Killed In Action."

The news landed like a physical blow. Raith, the enigmatic, almost omnipotent Director, simply erased as if he had never existed. Voss never really understood the man; it was almost as if he had no personality beyond the obvious power he wielded. But to be gone so quickly and without warning brought the grave reality of war home to Voss in a way that all his academic studies of warfare had never done.

Voss took a moment to think and walked towards the open door of the train. He stared blankly at the inert door-lock interface, the intricate glyphs suddenly meaningless. The man who had thrust him into this impossible position, the architect of their current fortunate displacement from the main thrust of the invasion, was dead. What did that mean? A strange, hollow feeling settled over him, not grief, but a profound sense of disorientation. The established authority, the ultimate fallback, had vanished. He exchanged a shocked, uncertain glance with Renata, then Alinta. Their faces reflected his personal bewilderment.

Rayk's voice continued, pulling him back from the precipice of that thought. "Commander Eva Rostova has assumed operational command of all remaining PCMA forces in Sector Alpha, and by default, planetary defence protocols. She has established an ad-hoc command post within Petropolis and is attempting to coordinate resistance. Communications are severely degraded, heavily jammed, but she has established a priority command channel to my post here. Her initial reports confirm heavy CAR landings across multiple zones in and around Petropolis and the surface ruins. The fighting is intense."

Voss found his voice, though it felt distant, unfamiliar. "Rayk. Where are they landing at the moment? In what sort of numbers?".

"It looks like four to five thousand paratroopers are dropping right now." He used his remote system to bring a map up in their viewing field. "Here is the main drop, going for Petropolis. They are landing outside the city to take the landing fields and secure them. Then they will storm the entrance tunnels. Their casualties will be immense if they do that." He changed perspective to the top of the escarpment, where there were the blue and bronze domes that acted as city skylights. Amongst the domes, Rayk had drawn an ominous grey circle. "There is a considerable pod-drop here, about 500 pods targeted on the roof of the city, maybe half the force, 2500 men. They are probably wanting to get through the Domes or whatever entry hole was made by the orbital munitions. I am waiting for live pictures from Orbit, but we are competing for bandwidth right now".

He then brought an animated pointer onto the surface ruins of 'Old Sikarra' where the Echo Key was found. "There is a drop of about 250 pods here; they are establishing a big Forward Operating Base on the Old Sikarra Ruins. I'd wager we are facing the 'Azure Dragon Airborne Legion'. Merged units of the old Russian Siberian VDV from before partition and the old PLA 43rd, 44th and 45th Parachute divisions. As I remember from my now very old Military lectures, they don't play well together even now. So they usually split them up and make them compete with each other for honours so they don't fight amongst themselves."

Voss said, "Wait a minute, that means Rostova will be facing Chinese troops, right? Otherwise, the West Russian guys will be facing other Russians. That would be interesting".

Rayk said, "Not necessarily. A lot of the Buryat guys still have bad blood because their troops were considered to be 'expendables' by the old Moscow Regime. Having said that, the new leadership is conservative. So, I suspect yes, the Russians will be held back or used on more North American concentrations of troops. Our Europeans will face the Chinese, if I were a betting man."

"I can't believe they didn't realise the importance of the spaceport here." Rayk raised an eyebrow and cocked his head in acknowledgement. Voss continued, "That means they don't know about our find here either, I guess."

Rayk replied, "Their tactics remain brute force. They took losses in orbit, so they had to make a plan on the fly. Not their strong point. I think they thought these fields were undefended and could be taken at leisure.

Voss asked, "What do we face then? What about our entrance? We won't be ignored for long, can it be secured?"

Rayk looked at his displays, "Only 50 pods or 250 men have landed on the spaceport fields. They are out of range of our light weapons that they likely assume we have."

Voss, realising that he had so far left everything up to Rayk, felt the weight of unfamiliar responsibility gravitating towards him now. He knew he had to get up to speed quickly. "So can we seal our entrance off. The other entrance is the tunnel from Petropolis to here."

"Already actioned, Principal Voss," Rayk replied. "My teams at this entrance are fabricating a temporary reinforced barrier for the City. This vault containing the Echo Key will be our final fallback point. Our citadel in effect. The Petropolis-Wahlsanga tunnel is being mined for collapse under my order; it's too exposed. My primary concern now is the main Depot entrance here. We have limited manpower."

Voss processed this instantly. *Rayk had military experience before his police career. I have nothing but my studies of military history. All purely academic.*

Rayk, however, seemed to be tolerating his questions. Voss surmised, *presumably because of my position as head of the department and this sector.* He pushed his authority, "Rayk, don't blow the tunnel from Sikarra to here yet. Rostova needs to know she has a potential escape route."

Rayk nodded his assent. "I am trying to get through to her now to get you a situation update, but she will be pretty loaded up now."

Voss nodded slowly, the weight of it all beginning to settle. He wasn't in command, not truly, not yet. Rayk was handling security. Rostova was fighting a planetary war. He was... a principal Xenologist, standing in an ancient train depot, with the universe falling apart outside. He realised the question forming in his mind now should have been asked a long time ago, but his mind was in his academic role, not this new thing imposed upon him. Nevertheless, he asked, "So how many men do we have at our disposal?"

Rayk answered, "Raith brought in every last man from around the Planet. It's not a lot. We have about 500 Marines and 500 Airborne under Rostova's direct command, minus any killed so far in the first blast. Under Raith's personal command, there were about 900 corporate PCMA infantry who were, in effect, mercenaries with a wide range of backgrounds. They are here to act as paramilitary to back the Police up. That's where our main force is. About 1000 Police. Almost everyone, Police or PCMA, has a good military career or they would not be chosen for colonisation".

"OK, but how many do we have at our disposal here?" Voss insisted. There was a pause as Rayk considered his options. He looked at Voss, calculating probably his suitability to assume the Role he was stepping into and probably wondering why Voss did not know this and by extension, should he know it also? Something changed in Rayk as he made his decision and answered. "We have nearly all the Police and PCMA considered combat worthy. 1500 combined. We also have 200 of Rostova's Marines."

Voss was shocked that so many men had been relocated here while he was concentrating on the vault. He said, "So that leaves only 800 troops under Rostova's command. The civilian population is almost…"

"Defenceless." Rayk finished off grimly.

The psychopathic mind of Raith was now exposed to Voss. The people were not a target and were better off without putting up a resistance. Sikarra had nothing except a music room, apartments and alien chips that could be decades of work to unravel. Wahlsanga, on the other hand, had the technology and a defensible position. If they could hold out here, whilst Rostova was sacrificed with many of the best troops they had as a diversionary defence, they might last long enough for relief from the NAR and the PCMA to arrive. Rostova's casualties, even with the advantage of defence of assault, would be brutal.

A burst of static from Rayk's comm channel shattered the tense atmosphere between the two men. Then his voice again, tighter now. "Update from Commander Rostova. CAR forces are attempting to secure the main atmospheric processing plant in Petropolis. Heavy resistance reported. She's re-tasking all available combat drones. Casualties are mounting." Another pause. "She also reports… significant use of what appear to be directed energy weapons by CAR ground troops. This is causing them some problems."

Voss thought, *Of course. The energy dissipates into the rock and the Sikarran circuits are too robust to be damaged by that energy. They encumber their own troops rather than damage anything Alien.*

Voss knew that wouldn't last when things turned against them. He shuddered to think of the strike on the Ops centre by a kinetic munition from Orbit. The damage that he would eventually witness, if he lived that long, would be a gut-wrenching tragedy. There would be historical repercussions down the ages.

The sound channel came up again and above the speaker's voice, the background was traditional rifle fire and the unmistakable hiss of ionised air from energy weapons. "They are having to climb over their own casualties to get to us. They are forcing the main doorway. We are about to be overrun. Falling back!".

The silence that followed was heavy, filled with the unspoken understanding of their isolation, the ferocity of the battle raging miles away, and the dawning realisation that the fate of Sikarra, and perhaps their own, now rested on the shoulders of a besieged commander in a falling city and a hotchpotch of Mercenaries, Marines and security personnel guarding an ancient mausoleum to a dead civilisation.

Chapter 33. Part 3.

The air in the repurposed sub-level maintenance hub that now served as Sector Alpha's emergency command post was thick with the stench of ozone, fear, and stale nutrient paste. Commander Eva Rostova ignored the dull ache behind her eyes, her entire being focused on the chaotic, flickering holographic tactical display that dominated the cramped space. Raith was gone. Henderson, bless his corporate heart, was almost inevitably gone. He couldn't resist the call to be at the 'big boys table' when Raith called for him. It served him right in a way. It now fell to her.

The minor East Tunnel, where Jonesy had staggered home just days earlier, remained unsealed. The last external guards were still retreating through it under fire, delaying setting the PBX explosives.

A bad Idea, she thought. *They might baulk at blowing it if there are some guys still trapped outside, or worse, inside the tunnel. But it has to go.*

Of greater concern was the very wide access tunnel in the north of the City. It was too large to lay charges safely and efficiently. The small amounts of the latest C7 they had brought to the fight would just bring the rubble down onto their own heads.

But the North Tunnel was the main thrust of the CAR.

"Comms!" Rostova barked, her voice hoarse but carrying the unmistakable edge of command. "Report on Northern Access Tunnel. Major Chesterton's unit was reporting heavy contact."

A stressed and wet-faced young signals officer, 'Krylov', she seemed to remember, called out. "Commander! There is heavy EM interference still, but the last confirmed transmission indicated CAR forces attempting to bypass Chesterton's position. They are using the overhead ramp from the external ruins."

Rostova swore under her breath. The CAR were not fools. She turned to her attendant officer, Lt. Coronado. "They are likely heading for the primary power conduit nexus bringing power in from the generators we embedded in the cliff face."

Lt. Coronado asked, "But how do they know so for sure where to go?"

Rostova replied, "Excellent question, Lieutenant. I would like you to divert Attack Drone Wing 'Juno' to Grid Nine. Priority target: any CAR units approaching the power nexus. Authorise the use of heavy charges and munitions on the overhead walkway if needed. I am aware of potential damage to artefacts. PCMA guidance is overruled. I want that approach channel denied to them."

Her eyes scanned the broader tactical map. Red CAR icons were blooming across multiple sectors of Petropolis like a virulent rash. The initial 'Heavenly Hailstorm' drop had been more dispersed than anticipated, but also more numerous. Her forces – the 300 remaining Marines and 500 Airborne she directly commanded, supplemented by only 50 PCMA Police acting as light infantry that Raith had allowed her—were stretched thin.

Raith had pulled the bulk of the PCMA corporate infantry and additional Marine units to Wahlsanga, leaving her with a skeletal but professional core. They were fighting with a desperate courage, but the sheer number of CAR paratroopers, estimated now at nearly four thousand across all landing zones, meant they were significantly outnumbered in almost every engagement. The reports of CAR directed energy weapons were particularly concerning, despite the fact that their use was less effective than the conventional bullets the NAR used, it indicated a fanatical devotion to the cause of preserving what they could here. She had to think of a way of using this against them.

"Sector Beta, Detective Kostin, report status," Rostova said into her command channel, her voice deliberately calm, projecting an authority she hoped would ripple outwards. Wahlsanga was isolated, but its unique assets and personnel needed to be a secondary consideration if Petropolis itself fell.

Rayk's voice, blessedly clear despite the distance and interference, came back. "Sector Beta perimeter secure for now, Commander. Monitoring CAR pod dispersal. No direct contact at Wahlsanga Depot yet. Principal Voss and his science team are assessing internal artefact security. Standing by for further directives."

"Hold your position, Detective. Secure those assets. Reinforce your defences. You are on your own for now. All available combat resources are committed here in Alpha." A grim admission, but necessary. She couldn't afford to dilute her forces.

A fresh wave of explosions rocked the command hub, closer this time. The lights flickered violently.

"Commander!" another officer shouted. "CAR light armoured vehicles breakthrough at the Southern Gateway! They've breached the primary barricades! They're making a push for the Central Spire!"

Rostova's jaw tightened. They managed to bring some drop-capable vehicles in the larger Hailstones then. None of our scenarios accounted for that! Then came the cold weight in her chest as she envisioned her lecturer at Military College saying, "Who said 'No plan survives contact with the enemy'. Rostova?" Her lecturer was telling her for this moment. Too late now, though. The plan had already broken.

At that moment, Rayk's transmission butted in. "Commander, I am giving you the schema and location of the latest Metro tunnel to Wahlsanga that we excavated two days ago. Principal Voss is leaving it open for you to escape with as many people as you can."

Rostova sent a brief acknowledgement, but no commitment to using the option. *If I use that, will I give away the importance of Wahlsanga? How long before they figure it out anyway? Its all about buying time and costing them dear now.*

Then, a voice came through. "Commander, this is Sergeant De-Silva, the east tunnel is blown, we got our men back, light casualties. Requesting redeployment." Rostova had forgotten about the little tunnel.

"De-Silva, this is Commander Rostova. Retreat to these coordinates. Level below the Central Spire. It is an old Metro Station. Establish a casualty evacuation station and secure all entrance points to that Station."

He received the map on his qWatch and replied, "Yes, Ma'am." Commander Rostova added, "One more thing I need you to do personally. The Metro Tunnel, and yes, I know this is all new to you, just go with it, Sergeant. The tunnel is unblocked in one direction. It goes to Wahlsanga. Mine the entrance with PBX. This will be our last exfiltration point if it comes to that. Acknowledge."

De-Silva repeated the order precisely, a testament to his training that he could do that under such pressure that many men would forget their own names if asked.

Rostova reflected on Raith's now obvious strategy, to sacrifice the finest they had. It makes sense as a Military Commander, but the coolness with which he did it. *Damned fine men and women. You should never just expend such people.* With that, she got in her taxi-buggy laughingly repurposed as a military vehicle and shouted to the automated system. "Central Spire ASAP. Speed restrictions lifted, military emergency."

The entrance to the old Metro Station was near the Central Spire that the CAR were fighting for. The Central Spire housed the primary life support regulators for the deeper, more densely populated cavern levels. While the upper city benefited from some natural cavern airflow, the Spire was critical for breathable atmosphere and water recycling for the majority.

Rostova weighed up the pros and Cons. If the CAR gets the site, they control the civilian population. They can round up the food and turn the water off. On the other hand, it will likely fall anyway. And short term at least they will have to protect it and maintain it for their own reasons.

She looked at the tactical display, at the dwindling blue PCMA icons being swamped by a tide of red. They were putting up a hell of a fight, but the odds were lengthening with every passing minute. Her city. Her responsibility.

She would not let it fall without a fight. She could manage the battle from there and when they see she is there, they will put everything into surrounding and taking the Spire. When they eventually take it, they will think they won their victory because they will think this was her 'Alamo'. She would be there to the last, taking attention away from the exfiltration going on behind their backs in the Metro Station.

Her ability to inflict truly strategic losses on the CAR was limited with her current forces, but she could make their every gain a bloody one, buying time for... she wasn't even sure what anymore. She was working on instinct, but this next act was going to hurt.

"Major Chesterton," Rostova's voice cut through the comms, sharp and decisive. "The Northern Access Tunnel is critical. Hold it or we are all finished." Then, in a moment of grim gallows humour appreciated by Soldiers everywhere, she added, "No pressure!".

Chesterton replied, "I am going to have to consolidate my platoons at the primary internal bulkhead. Despite the potential for artefact damage, I am going to have to use the automated fire suppression systems as area denial."

Rostov concurred, "I don't care what you do, I don't care how you do it, I just need that fucking approach contained." Then, on a wider band, she made a call, "All spare units, immediately redeploy to form a layered defence around the Central Spire access points. Every squad not under direct fire should peel off one Squad member to this task. We make them pay for every metre."

There would be no holding of that tunnel; it would be a killing field.

She reflected that, at best, there might be more CAR dead than NAR and PCMA. Looking at the street map, she could plainly see that Chesterton's position would eventually be bypassed by the invaders, either via the overhead bridge or the Southern Gateway. Her forces were split and outnumbered at every point. Achieving local superiority for any meaningful duration was impossible.

As she arrived at the Central Spire, she drew a breath, the air thick with the sulphurous tang of smokeless gunpowder and something that tasted like burnt despair. This was where it would end, one way or another. She would win here, or more likely, lose here. But she wasn't going anywhere else.

In the distance, the rising chatter of gunfire echoed from the direction of the North Entrance—sharp, frantic. She hoped the CAR would take Chesterton's surrender.

After the nuke attack, maybe not.

The Xenologist

Chapter 34. Part 1.

The two heavy-duty work trucks, engines straining against their unaccustomed burden of armed personnel and volatile demolition charges, plunged from the relative shelter of the western service tunnel mouth into the chaotic twilight of Vasantha City. Penaargan, gripping the grab handle in the lead vehicle, barked directions to his nervous driver, navigating by a combination of ingrained knowledge and the flickering, unreliable light of damaged spaceport floodlights. Behind them, in the second truck, Varinn scanned their flanks, his bio-disruptor resting across his knees. Tessara sat beside him, her face a pale, determined mask, while Designer Marinallis, surprisingly resilient after their earlier ordeal, peered into the urban canyons ahead with an unnerving, almost predatory focus.

The workers, human and auxiliary alike, were a silent and busy hive of activity, laying demolition charges on their own vehicles, dutifully complying with the final evacuation order. Not one transport vehicle was to be left behind when a planet was evacuated. Standard protocol.

This planet had been inhabited for twenty thousand years and was the only home most of the workers had ever known. This once busy, safe paradise for humans and designers alike was now a besieged wasteland. Faces were pale, some eyes were red and watery, but the immediate chaos around them demanded their rapt attention. Everyone who was not busy was watching the last view they would ever have of their home, spoiled by the violence around them. With knuckles white on their weapons, they awaited their last struggle, hoping against hope that designer efficiency and thorough planning would get them, the last humans off the planet, on the promised spaceships.

Their path was a desperate weave through what had once been the vibrant, ordered periphery of the Vasantha Spaceport, now rapidly devolving into a war zone. The distant, percussive crumps of explosions and the high-pitched shriek of K'Tharr energy weapons were drawing inexorably closer. Overhead, the bruised sky was streaked with the exhaust plumes of descending K'Tharr drop-craft, their jagged, obsidian silhouettes like falling shards of black glass. Some were already disgorging their terrifying cargo into the city's outer sectors.

Varinn watched a K'Tharr heavy lander, a monstrous, beetle-like machine, touch down with a ground-shaking thud on a wide transit nexus. Ramps slammed down, and the first wave of invaders poured out. They were humanoid, bipedal, but there the immediate similarity to Designers or humans ended. A nightmarish diversity was on display: some were hulking brutes encased in crude, mismatched plates of scavenged-looking metal, others leaner, clad in what appeared to be a plastic-chitinous carapace that shifted in the dim light. Most had their faces obscured by intimidating, varied helmets, but a few, disturbingly, had almost recognisable features, twisted parodies of known species, their eyes burning with a cold, predatory light. All moved with an unsettling vigour, their heads swivelling, as if tasting the air for prey.

"Stay close to the sheer walls of the residential spires of the cliff. The doorway we need is stealthed. It will reveal itself as we get closer."

Their progress was agonisingly slow, each intersection a new potential death trap. Even though only a small force had been dispatched to the virtually empty spaceport, there were a surprising number of soldiers disembarking, looking for their prize, their chance to preserve their lineage and renew their bodies. Twice, they were forced into jarring detours as K'Tharr patrols, their guttural, chittering cries echoing through the empty streets, swept through adjacent sectors. Then, as they navigated a narrower metal canyon between two towering, long-obsolete office spires, a K'Tharr light attack craft, a spidery, multi-limbed machine that seemed to scuttle through the air with unnerving agility, dropped from the shadowed upper levels.

Its energy cannons glowed, and before Varinn could even shout a warning, it unleashed a volley of searing bolts. One struck the rear of Penaargan's lead truck, showering their own vehicle with molten plazteel and superheated debris. Another bolt tore a smoking gash along the side of their truck. The driver pulled the lead truck to cover behind some containers, using them as temporary cover. Two workers disembarked to lever twisted metal away from the tyres whilst Penaargan took a covering fire position.

The truck behind was slowing down and positioning itself to fall in behind the lead truck, as it similarly had debris getting caught in its wheels. Another energy weapon hit the anti-roll bar, showering the occupants with hot sparks and slivers of red-hot steel. Amidst the screams of the workers, one of the younger human technicians, a lad named Firn, probably not even 18 yet, spun round as an energy blast grazed his leg. The blast sent him tumbling from the relative cover of the truck bed.

Instantly, from the shadows of a nearby alleyway, a smaller group of K'Tharr erupted—these were leaner, almost wiry figures, their armour a patchwork of rags and ill-fitting metal scraps, their movements conveying a desperate, almost feral, hunger.

"They're letting the weaker ones go first," Marinallis hissed beside him, his ancient eyes narrowed in grim understanding. "A chance for them to prove themselves, to claim a prize. And to soften the target for the stronger echelons."

Then, they converged on the fallen Firn with terrifying speed. Behind them, Varinn glimpsed larger, more heavily armoured K'Tharr figures observing from the alley's mouth, their movements more measured, almost expectant.

Before Varinn could react, Tessara was moving. With a cry of fury, she leapt from the truck, her bio-disruptor already firing. "Get away from him, you Filth!" she yelled, charging towards the K'Tharr surrounding Firn. A flesh-disruptor bolt hit one of the smaller, ragged K'Tharr, sending it sprawling with a shriek, its rag-tag armour leaking red liquid, its body undoubtedly ruined inside the makeshift shell.

Varinn swore, his own weapon coming up as he followed her out. "Tessara, wait!"

She was already engaged, a blur of motion, using the truck as partial cover. She felled another of the smaller K'Tharr, but a new one lunged from her flank. It was female-looking, moving with surprising speed, its face a disturbing mix of a metal-plated upper skull and a suspiciously human lower half.

A wicked-looking serrated blade arced towards Firn. Tessara threw herself in the way, taking the blow on her forearm. She cried out, stumbling back, her disruptor clattering to the ground. Blood, dark in the twilight, welled from a deep gash.

"Tess!" Varinn roared, a cold fury washing over him. He opened fire, his disruptor bolts stitching across the remaining K'Tharr near Firn, driving them back momentarily.

He reached Tessara, pulling her behind the relative safety of a large debris pile, even as Penaargan's truck laid down covering fire. The spidery K'Tharr attack craft, having circled, swooped low again, circling to land even more of its vile passengers.

"Firn! Get to the truck!" Varinn yelled, pushing the terrified, now limping, worker towards Penaargan's vehicle. He turned back to Tessara, whose face was tight with pain, her hand clamped over her bleeding arm.

The smaller K'Tharr, seeing their initial targets now better defended, were hesitating, looking back towards the larger, more formidable figures still lurking in the alley.

"I don't ever want Human DNA in those things," Tessara gritted out, her eyes blazing with a fierce protectiveness as she nodded towards Firn, now being hauled into Penaargan's truck. "He comes with us."

The larger K'Tharr began to advance, their movements more deliberate, their weaponry glinting ominously. The first wave had been a test, a softening. Now, it seemed, the true fight was about to begin, and they were pinned down, one of their own already wounded. The cost of escape from Vasantha was rising with every passing second.

Chapter 34. Part 2.

From his vantage point in the second truck, Designer Marinallis watched the unfolding chaos with a tightening in his ancient chest. His gaze monitored closely the rescue of Firn, the young technician, now hauled back into the relative safety of the lead truck, his face a mask of shock, assessing the tactical situation as it unfolded. Varinn and Tessara, his human charges, were reacting with a desperate courage that both impressed and terrified him. He had, in a way, raised Varinn, seen him grow from a curious boy into this formidable, if often reckless, protector. The thought that the Newcomers, with their rigid protocols, would likely refuse passage to any human, regardless of their service to a Designer, was a cold, private grief. It meant this desperate flight was, for them, perhaps a goodbye he hadn't yet found the words for.

Fin's rescue was only a temporary reprieve. Marinallis scrutinised the K'Tharr from afar. Those who had emerged from the alley were a chilling spectacle. About thirty metres back, the largest among them, a brute encased in heavy, mismatched plating, stood with arrogant disregard, its massive weapon held loosely. It seemed unconcerned by the sporadic disruptor fire from the trucks. Smaller, more raggedly armoured K'Tharr, their movements jerky and feral, were the ones currently pressing the attack, their eyes, where visible, burning with a desperate hunger. One of these, bigger than the rest, raised a complex-looking weapon.

Then, another K'Tharr, also one of the larger, better-armoured observers, touched its companion's shoulder in an almost human gesture, redirecting its aim. It pointed not at the main group, but towards a lone worker from Penaargan's crew who was frantically trying to pry a twisted piece of plazteel from one of the lead truck's massive tires.

Predators, Marinallis thought with a cold dread. *Stalking a herd. They peel off the straggler first.* He put his hand inside his robe and felt the

reassuring hard grip of the energy pistol that Tessara had given him at the Sky Arch Bridge. *No capture for me. The last shot is my final release.*

The K'Tharr with the redirected weapon fired. It wasn't an energy bolt. A thick, segmented wire, like the giant metallic tongue of a lizard catching a fly, uncoiled from the weapon's muzzle. It flew across the thirty or so metres with uncanny speed and accuracy. It wrapped itself around the unfortunate worker's torso and arms, constricting with a sickening, audible crunch. The man let out a choked 'oh!' of utter despair, his limbs pinned, his face a rictus of agony as the wire squeezed.

One of the nearby workers, his face contorted with fury, fired his bio-disruptor directly at the constricting wire. The energy beam splashed harmlessly against its surface. It did nothing. The wrong weapons, Marinallis realised with a surge of despair. *And the K'Tharr know it.*

Marinallis looked to the lead truck, catching Foreman Penaargan's eye. The human's face was a mask of indecision.

For Penaargan, the moment was an eternity. He saw the grim, unspoken command in Marinallis' stare, but still Penaargan hesitated. The man in the wire was Jareth. His apprentice. The gentle boy he had taken on at sixteen, the one he had known for ten years, who tried so hard at everything he did. He saw the rictus of agony on Jareth's face, the utter despair in his eyes. Penaargan, his face a mask of sickened resolve, nodded once.

He raised his disruptor, aimed with fatalistic precision at the head of the captured, struggling worker and pulled the trigger.

The upper part of the man's body dissolved into a horrifying spray of crimson mist and liquefied matter that pooled on the ground. Before the K'Tharr could react to this denial, Penaargan fired again, his second shot obliterating the lower torso. Nothing but a dark pool of steaming liquid remained. Useless to the K'Tharr.

A collective, guttural roar of pure, unadulterated rage erupted from the K'Tharr. This was their first overt display of emotion beyond predatory focus. All but the largest four, including the largest one still holding the unused lasso-like gun, began to advance. Their stride was bold, their movements now filled with a purposeful, murderous intent.

The human and auxiliary crews opened up with a desperate volley of disruptor fire as Varinn and Tessara worked frantically to drag the already-wounded Firn further into the cover of their truck. Marinallis watched the exchange with a clinician's eye. The K'Tharr with the heaviest, most sophisticated armour seemed largely unaffected by the disruptor bolts, the energy dissipating harmlessly across their layered plating. Two of the weaker, more raggedly armoured ones went down, one screaming as it lost an arm, collapsing to its knees in obvious agony. Another was hit precisely in the articulated rings of its neck armour; crimson liquid, shockingly similar to human blood, gushed out, and the creature crumpled. The other K'Tharr showed no regard for their fallen, stepping over them without a pause. Their comrades are competition as much as comrades at the end of the hunt, Marinallis mused grimly.

Then, displaying a fatal arrogance, the advancing K'Tharr shouldered their energy weapons, drawing long, whip-like devices from their belts, confident that they could now take more prizes alive. The remaining workers saw the shift in tactics. One, a grizzled human veteran from Penaargan's core team, pulled a slug-throwing pistol from his boot and began firing methodically as he sidestepped for cover. It took five solid projectile slugs to bring down the lead K'Tharr, the bullets punching through its less comprehensive armour. The others, momentarily unfazed by this anachronistic weaponry, began to aim their electro-whips.

Marinallis's mind raced, sifting through fragmented K'Tharr battle-casualty autopsy reports from other systems and other ages. Something about their necks, their limb joints... "Their joints!" he shouted, his voice cracking but carrying over the din. "The articulation points! Neck, shoulders, knees! That's why their neck armour is so heavy, it's a weak point!"

The workers, galvanised, grabbed whatever came to hand, crowbars from the truck bed, heavy wrenches, even their standard-issue survival knives and prepared to meet the closing K'Tharr. The man with the pistol kept firing from behind a discarded cargo container. Another lucky disruptor shot from the trucks struck one of the four huge K'Tharr holding back, blood flowing from its abdomen, forcing it and its companions to finally take cover, a grudging acknowledgement of the humans' desperate resistance. But the lead cadre, now down to four, were almost upon them.

Then Tessara did something astonishing. She stepped forward from the cover of the truck, her arms akimbo, a clear target. Her vibro-knife, which Marinallis had taken at the Sky Arch Bridge and passed to her after that fight, was tucked inside her collar, behind her head, with the hilt sticking out. It was switched off and silent.

Human ingenuity, Marinallis thought, a flicker of shock warring with a strange sense of pride. *She is offering them a target they cannot resist, but on her terms.*

The whip of the lead K'Tharr lashed out like a striking serpent, coiling around Tessara's torso, deliberately leaving her arms free. Tessara, seeing that he had made his choice to go for her torso, thinking her unarmed, then quickly pulled the knife out of her collar from behind her neck and switched it on. But before she could use it, the companion to the right raised its own whip, intending to bind her arms if she dared use the knife on the restraining cord. It was a temporary stand-off while the second K'Tharr weighed up his best option. He could try to secure an arm, but she could swap the knife to the other hand, her head and neck might be too vulnerable and he wanted her undamaged. At that moment, the pistol fell silent; a false lull in proceedings as the human veteran was out of ammunition and options.

Varinn, who had positioned himself slightly behind and to the side of Tessara, unseen by the K'Tharr who were fixated on their defiant captive, saw his moment. He knew, with an instinctive certainty that transcended thought, what Tessara was planning. As the second K'Tharr prepared to strike, Varinn exploded into motion. His enhanced muscles propelled him in a blurring curve around the left flank of Tessara's immediate captor. He launched himself high, his own vibro-knife, which Tessara had won back at the Gorge, held in a reverse grip. Mid-air, he wrapped his legs around the K'Tharr's helmeted head, using his momentum to twist its neck with a sickening, audible crack. Unsure if a broken neck alone would suffice for their alien physiology, he plunged the vibro-knife deep between two of the armoured neck rings. The creature's body went instantly limp, collapsing beneath him. Varinn rolled hard as he hit the ground, the action saving him as the whip from the rightmost K'Tharr lashed through the air where he'd been a second before.

The workers saw their chance. Three of them, Penaargan among them, leapt upon the now disadvantaged K'Tharr, whose whip had missed Varinn, hammering at it with crowbars and makeshift blades, seeking gaps in its armour.

Varinn, regaining his feet, saw that the K'Tharr covering Tessara's captor was now momentarily distracted, its attention split between the melee and Tessara herself. *This is simple now,* he thought, an almost preternatural calm descending. As the creature swung its weapon towards him, Varinn, moving with a speed that seemed to bend time, brought his own vibro-knife up in a vicious arc, severing the K'Tharr's wrist at the joint. The electro-whip clattered to the ground. The K'Tharr lunged, its remaining hand grasping for him, but Varinn kicked out, his boot connecting with shattering force against its knee joint. The leg buckled backwards with a brittle, dry snap. As the mortally wounded creature fell, Varinn finished it with a precise thrust to the neck, identical to the first.

The K'Tharr, still holding Tessara ensnared in its electro-whip, was now visibly shaken. Its head, with that unsettlingly human-like lower face beneath the plated skull, swivelled between its rapidly falling comrades and the defiant human woman. Its predatory confidence was waning.

"Oh yes, you slime-ball!" Tessara shouted, her voice laced with adrenaline and fury, the pain from her gashed forearm momentarily forgotten. "No dinner for you tonight!" With a swift, powerful downward slash, she brought her own vibro-knife, slicing through the crackling whip cord. It parted with surprising ease.

Freed, but with the K'Tharr now fumbling to bring its primary energy weapon off its shoulder, Tessara didn't hesitate. "Allow me, gentlemen!" she called out, perhaps to the workers who were just finishing off their own target. She lunged forward, stepping inside the arc of the rifle's point as the K'Tharr clumsily swung it round. She grabbed the barrel of the weapon, using its length as leverage, and pulled it forward, past her body. As the K'Tharr stumbled off balance, Tessara came in low, knees bent, her vibro-knife leading with the right hand. She stabbed upwards, deep into the groin area, seeking the vulnerable joint where leg met torso.

The K'Tharr let out a choked, high-pitched, all-too-human scream, its hands instinctively flying to its wounded groin, dropping the rifle. But even as it did so, one of its clawed hands shot out and grabbed Tessara by the back of her neck, its grip like iron, sharp talons digging painfully into her skin.

It was the opening Varinn needed. The creature was doubled over, its attention fixed on Tessara, its back momentarily exposed. Moving with the last of his adrenaline-fuelled speed, Varinn darted behind it. He didn't hesitate. His vibro-knife plunged deep into the creature's back, aiming for the spinal cord just below the base of its heavy neck armour. There was a terrible, wet tearing sound, and the K'Tharr dropped as if its strings had been cut, its body spasming violently for a moment before an unnatural stillness, accompanied by the acrid smell of ozone and shorting cybernetics, settled over it.

The rearmost K'Tharr guard, the two who had initially taken cover, had witnessed the brutal efficiency of the humans' desperate defence. They had seen their elite forward cadre dismantled in moments by what they must have considered mere prey. Now, finally realising that these humans were small but far from defenceless, and with their own numbers dwindling, their courage utterly failed them. One of them, its forearm console flaring with light, looked up at the sky in a universal posture of confusion or perhaps receiving new orders, then both turned and melted back into the urban shadows, unwilling to further engage.

"The trucks are clear!" Penaargan yelled from the lead vehicle, his voice hoarse but triumphant, his own disruptor still smoking. He had been providing covering fire throughout the melee. "There's a lull! Get in, all of you! Move! Before more of those bastards show up!"

They scrambled back into the vehicles, Varinn carefully helping Tessara, whose face was now pale, even with her enhanced UV-protection. But as she looked Varinn in the face, he saw a slight, elated smile, her eyes blazing. Varinn thought, *She was born for this!*

Firn, the young technician Tessara had risked herself for, was already being tended to by another worker. He was in shock but holding up well. He was a brave young lad.

The trucks lurched forward and the passengers rocked with them. Varinn, trained as a leader and a medic, looked at the faces. They were engineers, not soldiers. They had fought out of sheer terror. There would be trauma for the therapists (or at least the medical pods) to undo when they got aboard their ship.

Then, the trucks picked up speed, the engines roaring with what seemed like shared relief from the vehicles, rather than the roar of unthinking engine power as they sped from the site of their desperate, unlikely victory. They headed at speed now, towards the sheer cliff face where Marinallis had indicated their salvation lay. All that remained was to find the stealthed entrance before the K'Tharr regrouped or another, larger patrol found them.

Chapter 35.

The chill of the Wahlsanga Depot, a silence measured in millennia, did little to cool the fresh, raw shock of Director Raith's confirmed demise. Voss stood near the colossal, now open, blast door that marked the threshold to the main cavern, the Architect train a silent, dust-shrouded behemoth at his back. Beside him, Renata's datapad still glowed with the fragmented, horrifying tactical display from Petropolis, a testament to the chaos Rayk Kostin had just relayed from his ad-hoc command post at the Depot's SARU-bored tunnel entrance. Alinta O'Neil, usually so animated by scientific discovery, was pale as she struggled with the new reality of War. As mental self-defence as much as a scientific necessity, she turned back to her work with the train, where she knew she could make a meaningful contribution. The weight of Voss's new, unsought title—Head of the Xenology and Archaeology Directorate for the Sikarra Mandate—felt somehow remote. Although he had creeping suspicions that he was currently having an easy ride. The calm before the Storm.

Rayk's voice, patched through a local comm-link from his vigil at the tunnel mouth, cut through the stunned quiet, professional and grim. "Principal Voss. My local drone reconnaissance is active and has initial findings." A holographic map shimmered into existence between them, focused on the surface area above and around the Depot. Red icons, stark against the ochre terrain, indicated the CAR presence. "I confirm approximately two hundred and fifty CAR paratroopers on the upper spaceport fields. They are not static; they are beginning to disperse. My assessment shows one contingent, perhaps one hundred to one hundred and fifty strong, already moving towards the Gorge perimeter – likely targeting any high-value civilian assets or occupied villas and minor hydro-power generators and substations there. Another group, around fifty, is deploying to establish observation posts in the surface ruins and the taller office spires overlooking this Depot access and the old Metro terminal complex. That leaves a mobile element, fifty to one hundred, currently consolidating near their primary landing zones. I anticipate they will dispatch reconnaissance patrols towards this main Depot entrance, certainly old spaceport terminal buildings and probably scout for other entry points to the city fairly quickly."

The information was a stark, unwelcome confirmation of their isolation. The CAR were not just a distant threat to Petropolis; they were here, on their doorstep.

Voss took a deep breath, forcing a semblance of command into his posture. His mind, a repository of military history, sifted through parallels, searching for precedent in situations he had only ever studied. "They're not wasting time," he stated, his voice betraying a slight tremor he hoped the others didn't notice. He looked directly at Rayk's projected image. "Detective, your assessment of their immediate intent towards *this* facility?"

"Standard probing attacks to assess our strength and secure any significant access points, Principal," Rayk replied, his tone level. "My immediate recommendation is a full lockdown of this SARU tunnel entrance. We establish layered defences within the tunnel and at this internal threshold. We have a highly defensible choke point. We should consolidate our combat-effective personnel here, protect the assets within the Depot, and wait for orders, or at least, news of military relief from Earth, before committing to any offensive action. We fortify; we hold."

Voss shook his head, a new, unfamiliar decisiveness hardening his features. "Detective, with all due respect to your security expertise, a purely passive defence in our situation is a death sentence. It makes us a predictable target. They'll bring their everything they can to bear on this single choke point to achieve local superiority. Once they've contained the Gorge and Petropolis, they will turn their undivided attention here. We become besieged, a footnote. History is replete with examples of fortified positions, however strong, eventually falling when initiative is entirely ceded to a determined attacker." He paced a short distance, the ancient dust crunching softly under his boots.

"Furthermore," Voss continued, his voice gaining a harder edge, "Commander Rostova is fighting for Petropolis's very survival. We cannot expect timely reinforcement from her, nor, frankly, from PCMA High Command, given the current political climate and the sheer interstellar distances involved. We may well be considered expendable, 'thrown under the bus' for some larger, incomprehensible political game being played out light-years away. We are on our own here, for now. Our survival, and the absolute necessity of securing what's in this Depot, depends entirely on our actions, initiated now."

Rayk's projected image remained impassive, but Voss sensed the professional mind behind the eyes processing the unexpected strategic declaration. Rayk's silence could also be a tactic, Voss thought, hoping he would back down after reviewing his own words. *That isn't going to happen, my friend. But if you want the silence filled, it will be with my words.*

"I propose," Voss continued, "that we don't wait for their main probe force to reach our doorstep. We intercept and neutralise their initial reconnaissance element. A swift, decisive, and overwhelming blow."

Rayk's holographic image flickered slightly, "Principal, that's bold, but it risks exposing our position early. Why not conserve our strength here?"

Voss's eyes narrowed, his voice steady. "A passive defence lets them dictate the terms. This move serves multiple purposes: it denies them critical intelligence about this facility and our actual strength; it sows confusion and uncertainty in their local command; and it might make their field commander more cautious, perhaps even force him to divert resources intended for Petropolis to address this unexpected threat on his flank. That buys us all time."

Voss, reviewing lists now available to him through his qWatch whilst he was talking, looked up and gestured towards the entrance. "You mentioned they're likely using standard light drones for initial close reconnaissance. What if we deploy the crowd-control drone jammers that I see we have in the public safety inventory? They're short-range, yes, but if we can lure a CAR patrol close enough to this entrance, into a prepared engagement area, we might blind their immediate aerial eyes, forcing their ground troops into a channel of *our* choosing."

Rayk finally spoke, his voice still level but with a new note of professional assessment. "Principal, that's a significant gamble. It exposes our limited combat-effective personnel outside of a fortified position. If the ambush is detected prematurely, or if their reconnaissance element is stronger than anticipated, or if they possess more robust electronic warfare countermeasures than our civilian-grade jammers can handle, we could suffer heavy losses and irrevocably compromise our primary defensive position before the main engagement even begins."

"It is a calculated risk, *Detective* Kostin," Voss stated, meeting Rayk's gaze with a steadiness that surprised even himself. The weight of the Directorate title, however unwanted, seemed to lend him a sliver of the authority it represented. "And it is the strategy we will adopt. Your expertise will be invaluable in the tactical planning and execution of this ambush. I expect your full cooperation in making it successful. Time is not on our side."

There was a protracted silence. Rayk's image seemed to study Voss intently. Voss felt a bead of sweat trickle down his back, the silence stretching. He had laid down a direct challenge to the security chief's professional judgment, asserting his personal strategic vision. Finally, Rayk gave a curt, almost imperceptible nod. "Understood, Principal Voss. We will begin tactical planning for a proactive engagement against their initial reconnaissance element immediately." The formal title was a clear acknowledgement of the shift in command.

As Rayk turned his projected attention to detailed local schematics, outlining potential ambush sites and fields of fire, Voss felt a wave of something akin to light-headedness. He had done it. He had made a command decision, a potentially life-or-death strategic call. The historian had, for a moment, become the commander. The thought was both terrifying and strangely exhilarating.

He saw Renata watching him, her expression unreadable. Now or never, he thought, to clear that other, more personal, air. He moved towards her, his newfound, fragile confidence lending a slightly more direct, if still clumsy, edge to his voice. "Renata, Rayk is likely to be in some danger. Are you going to be OK?"

Renata looked puzzled about what Voss had said. "It's his job. I am not OK about the danger any of us are in." Then, when Voss did not reply, only nodded slightly, looking a little puzzled himself, she added, "Is there any reason you are particularly asking?" He replied, "Well, given that you two are…" he paused for a moment, suddenly unsure of himself, "you know, together," then slowing down as he noticed her expression darken as he said the final words, "so, to… speak…"

"Together." She said, making a very obvious point of looking down at her datapad, at something suddenly very interesting, her mouth screwed tightly closed. "What makes you think that, *Principal* Voss?"

He replied, "Well, when I called your apartment first thing, Detective Kostin answered… I just wanted to be supportive, given the circumstances that we're all facing now."

There was the briefest moment of awkward silence.

Renata looked up from her own datapad, where she had been reviewing Alinta's notes on the Echo Key. Her eyes, when they met his, were cool, a hint of her earlier surprised annoyance now replaced by a distinct reserve. "He did *what?*" she asked, her voice quiet but sharp, a faint flush rising on her cheeks. It was clear she was more annoyed at Rayk's action than at Voss's inquiry, but Voss, in his current state, couldn't parse the nuance.

I am not letting him make me explain myself, Renata thought, a surge of proud indignation stiffening her spine. *Damn, Rayk, for answering, damn Julian for this awkward, ill-timed interrogation.*

"Julian," she said, her voice carefully neutral, "Detective Kostin and I are not romantically involved, if that is what your 'professional concern' is so clumsily implying. Why he was at my quarters, or why he chose to answer my private comm, is a separate matter and, with all due respect to your new… position," the emphasis was subtle but clear, "still none of your damned business." She paused, then added, her gaze direct and unwavering, "And if we are indeed discussing professional conduct, Principal Voss, your rather abrupt and frankly cold demeanour recently is also noted."

Voss felt his face flush. He had walked directly into that. She had turned the tables completely, leaving him feeling exposed, foolish, and undeniably the one in the wrong. He opened his mouth, then closed it, a coherent apology or defence eluding him.

Alinta, who had been tactfully absorbed in examining the intricate glyphs on a datapad displaying images of the Architect train's interface, chose that moment to speak, her voice a welcome interruption, though her words carried a certain weight of mystery. "Principal Voss, Dr. Volkova," she began, her gaze shifting between them, "regarding the Echo Key... the interaction I had. It wasn't just a passive scan or a denial." She paused, as if gathering courage to speak.

"It's strange," She continued. "When I was near the vault, when the Key seemed to focus on me, I had a vivid impression. Almost like a waking dream, or a memory that isn't mine." She hesitated, looking down as if unsure whether to continue, then met their eyes. "I thought I saw the Architect statue, the one by the pillar, but... upright. Alive, almost. Its skin seemed..." pausing again as she noted Renata and Voss were transfixed, focused on her every word. "It seemed translucent, like porcelain, beautiful and incredibly frail. And it, no, *she* was speaking."

She faltered, a flush rising on her cheeks. "Not with words I understood, nothing like any Earth language, but there was a flow of... of understanding, perhaps emotion. A sense of profound alien-ness, not just me of it, but it of me. Almost a 'who or what are you'. I was worried you would think I was crazy, overcome by the statue discovery."

Voss seized on the scientific puzzle, grateful for the shift in focus. "A false memory implant, Alinta? Of the statue communicating? That's kind of in line with my experience, but it's hard to describe, I know. It implies a level of discernment, of specific criteria, and a method of interaction we have no previous conception of" The historian in him catalogued the information, the implications vast. The Echo Key wasn't just a piece of advanced tech; it was an intelligent, discriminating artefact, capable of directly implanting complex sensory experiences.

He said, "We have to record and pursue this with the same vigour as the exploration of the Train and other artefacts. I may not be able to devote as much time to this as I would like," as he glanced at Renata.

Renata, now all business, glanced at him and nodded, his intent clear; he was busy, but this was his priority, the CAR an unwelcome intrusion.

Rayk's voice cut back in, all business. "Principal, CAR reconnaissance elements are on the move from the spaceport landing Zones. Two light vehicles and approximately twenty dismounts, heading this way. Estimated arrival at our optimal engagement zone: twelve minutes."

The brief interlude of personal tension and scientific speculation was over. Voss looked from Renata's still coolly appraising face to Alinta's thoughtful, now slightly relieved one, then to Rayk's grimly professional projection. The weight of command, of the imminent fight, settled back upon him. He had made his call. Now, they all had to live with the consequences. "Rayk," Voss said, his voice a shade steadier than he felt, "do what you have to do to organise everything. I am not going to interfere with squad-level tactics. For God's sake, keep yourself out of it because I am going to need you. Out." Rayk's projected image gave a curt nod just before the link closed.

His mind, however, was a maelstrom. The military decision, the rebuff from Renata and Alinta's revelation about the Key. He had a chance with Renata, he thought with a sudden, irrelevant pang of hope, but he had fumbled it badly. Perhaps, he thought with a grim internal smile, proving his worth as a commander in the coming minutes might, just might, begin to mend that particular fence. But that was a thought for later. If there were to be a later.

Chapter 36.

The air in the Northern Access Tunnel was a choking miasma of gunpowder, burnt ozone, pulverised plazteel, and the metallic tang of spent, smoking CAR directed-energy weapon batteries. Major Chesterton coughed, a dry, racking sound that was lost amidst the cacophony of battle. Red emergency lights cast long, dancing shadows along the massive tunnel, illuminating scenes of desperate, close-quarters combat.

Those PCMA Marines, who were among the few he had been spared in the first place, plus a handful of corporate security infantry, held a wavering line at the primary internal bulkhead. Their faces, if they could be seen behind their intimidating opaque black face visors, would have been showing immense stress, he knew. But, they presented as being as solid as the colossal slabs of Plazteel and composite that constituted the Bulkhead they were guarding. They were the last obstacle sealing this main artery into Petropolis.

The CAR were relentless. They pressed the attack on the ground level with a savage disregard for their losses, their guttural war cries echoing off the curved tunnel walls. Chesterton knew, with the chilling certainty of a veteran, that the knowledge of the PCMA's nuclear strikes against their fleet had stripped away any notion of surrender or quarter. This was a fight to the death.

He peered up at the secondary access level, a narrower maglev and footpath bridge that arced from the old outside tower buildings and fed into the tunnel complex high above his current position. His resources stretched to breaking point, he'd only been able to spare a single, understrength platoon to cover that exposed causeway, because they were now having to fight on two major fronts after the orbital slug took out Ops, leaving a breach. He knew he should never split his forces, but he had to. It was his Achilles' heel, and he suspected the CAR knew it.

As if summoned by his thoughts, a new wave of CAR assault troops appeared on the far end of the upper bridge. These were different. Heavily armoured figures formed a moving, Viking-style shield wall. The lead CAR Airborne had what looked like power-assisted suits. They carried massive physical shields, all interlocked, absorbing the sporadic rifle fire from Chesterton's beleaguered bridge defenders. Behind this implacable advance, more lightly equipped CAR infantry massed, their eagerness a palpable wave of aggression.

"Upper level! If you are not getting through those shield walls, conserve ammunition until they get closer. Then concentrate on the feet of the shield-bearers!" Chesterton yelled into his comm. A Laconic British voice said, "Yes, sir! Waiting until we see the whites of their eyes is difficult with those face plates." Then, after a brief pause, he said almost nonchalantly, "But I am sure we will manage". He grimaced at the humour. Lieutenant Winterton-Grant. The best man he had. *What a waste.* The rifle fire from the Bridge abruptly, ominously stopped. *Damn, if The Director had not gambled and sent half the men to Wahlsanga, we could have held this. With enough men like this, I could have held forever.*

The CAR shield-bearers, briefly unnerved by the silence, hesitated. A Russian voice started yelling behind the shield wall, loud enough to be heard behind his face plate. If it were audible through the face plate, the sound in the earpieces of the shield bearers would have been deafening. They immediately pressed forward. Then, when they were about 20 feet from the defenders, they all stood up from behind their barricades and aimed at the feet of the attackers. This was one area where the power suits were weak. Bullets hit articulation joints, seizing the mechanism. In some cases, bullets penetrated the thinner instep armour, crunching bones inside their armoured boots and spilling blood across the fine, absorbent floor dust, instantly coagulating into a gruesome crimson mess. One fell, then another, leaving gaps in the wall. But they bought the crucial seconds for the swarm behind them. With a deafening roar, the massed Light Infantry, following the Heavy Infantry, surged over their fallen comrades and through the narrow shield wall gaps. A tide of flailing limbs carrying stun-axes and energy weapons engulfed the few remaining PCMA defenders on the bridge in a brief, brutal melee.

Where a PCMA Marine fell, he was swarmed by CAR lighter armed troops that brought their axes down onto the helmets of the fallen Marine. An axe would rattle the helmet and deform it, without initially penetrating. But an electrical impulse would discharge through the suit, mercifully rendering the occupant groggy or unconscious. Then, other CAR troops, furious at the loss of their comrades in orbit, would come up behind, each taking a vicious swipe at the fallen man until there was nothing resembling a human head left.

The high ground was lost. Every defender is gone. None taken prisoner, but none even tried to surrender.

Chesterton did not see what happened to the Lieutenant or his men, but he heard the sickening rhythmic blows of the stun-axes hitting the bodies of the fallen, one after the other, filling him with a cold, dim rage. There was no time for a eulogy. Already, figures began to appear at the edges of the bridge overhead, silhouetted against the hellish red glow. Some expertly rappelled down heavy-duty cables, others made seemingly suicidal jumps, landing with bone-jarring impact on the gantries and service platforms that lined the upper reaches of the main tunnel, now critically behind Chesterton's main defensive line. Simultaneously, a series of sharp, percussive thuds echoed from above—CAR engineers, having secured the bridge, were laying demolition charges against the upper sections of the bulkhead's blast doors, or perhaps against the very rock of the tunnel ceiling.

"They're above us! And behind!" a voice screamed over the comms, laced with panic.

Chesterton saw it, the trap closing. His forces were now caught in a devastating crossfire. CAR troops were pouring fire down from the captured bridge and infiltrated positions above, while the main assault still hammered at the bulkhead from the front.

"Fall back!" Chesterton roared, his voice cracking. "Through the bulkhead! Secondary rally point! Move, move, move!" He knew it was a desperate, almost futile order. The bulkhead doors were designed to seal against external attack, not to facilitate a retreat under fire from multiple directions.

He saw his men begin to break, some turning to flee towards the relative safety of the bulkhead's passage, others trying to lay down covering fire. It was then that Chesterton, a man of regulations and protocols, made a choice born not of tactics, but of a deep, ingrained sense of responsibility. He stayed at the line, physically pushing and dragging wounded soldiers towards the opening. "No man left behind!" he yelled, the words almost a prayer in the inferno. It was an honourable weakness in such a desperate situation. A saying handed down from different wars under different situations. It was certainly a concept alien to the CAR forces now swarming down from above.

A hulking CAR brute, its armour a patchwork of scavenged plates, landed heavily beside him, a wicked-looking stun-axe raised. Chesterton saw an energy rifle by a fallen CAR Paratrooper. He picked up the weapon. He fired from the hip and ironically, the energy bolt splashed harmlessly against the assailant's chest. He saw the axe descend and then, only a brief, searing pain before the darkness claimed him. Major Chesterton, commander of the North Gate, fell amongst the last of his retreating men, his body a broken testament to a battle lost but a duty fulfilled to its bitter end.

A mere handful of his command, bloodied and broken, stumbled through the inner bulkhead doors, managed by some miracle to trigger the emergency seal. They brought with them the news of Chesterton's fall, of the complete collapse of the Northern Access Tunnel's defence. They were a trickle of survivors, carrying the weight of defeat towards Commander Rostova's already besieged position at the Central Spire.

From her makeshift command post, Rostova watched the red icons representing CAR forces extinguish the last blue markers of Chesterton's command at the Northern Access Tunnel. Her face, illuminated by the flickering tactical display, was a mask of grim resolve. The North Gate had fallen. She took a steadying breath, her voice surprisingly calm as she issued new orders into the comm net.

"All remaining airborne assets, all mobile reserves, proceed immediately to the Metro tunnel access to Wahlsanga." She tapped her mqWatch, the standard issue military quantum computer watch, to issue the coordinates on a secure link to all combatants. "It is your only viable exfiltration route. The forces at Sector Beta are expecting you but be careful of blue-on-blue. Move with all speed." She paused, listening to the acknowledgements, then continued, her voice hardening. "Any other ground units within the Central Spire perimeter, consolidate defences. We are making our stand here. We buy them time."

Rostova knew the grim calculus. CAR forces from the breached Northern Access Tunnel would soon be pouring into the city's upper levels. They would inevitably link up with any CAR troops that had managed to infiltrate through the massive, gaping hole left by the kinetic strike on the old PCMA Operations building, directly above the Central Spire. A pincer movement. Her situation was, by any rational military assessment, hopeless. But her fight was not yet over. It was about buying minutes, seconds even, for those few who might yet escape the dying city. Sikarra would fall, but it would not fall silent.

Chapter 37. Part 1.

The forward command post, hastily established in a captured PCMA stone-carved building overlooking Petropolis's Central Spire, was a hive of disciplined CAR activity. Holographic tactical displays decorated the largest wall, a chaotic canvas of red icons inexorably closing on the dwindling blue markers of PCMA resistance.

At the centre of the impromptu headquarters stood General Ganbaatar. His Mongolian heritage was evident in his strong, weathered features and the calm, assessing gaze that missed nothing. He had been chosen for this command not just for his military acumen, but for his proven ability to meld the often-disparate Chinese and Siberian Russian contingents under his command into a cohesive fighting force.

A comm-link crackled. "Northern Access secured, General." It was Colonel Volkov; his heavily Russian-accented Mandarin was barely understandable. "Resistance was spirited from some elements, as expected from Slavs. The Western Europeans, however, folded quickly." Then, he added the contemptuous Russian saying, "Like two fingers on the asphalt."

Ganbaatar rolled his eyes at the idiom, so clumsy in Mandarin. He had little time for Volkov or his casual chauvinism. "Colonel, your assessment is noted. Provide casualty statistics for both sides at the tunnel."

A moment passed, then Volkov's voice returned, a new note of surprise, perhaps even grudging respect, colouring his tone. He detailed the attacker versus defender numbers, then the casualties. Ganbaatar listened, his dark eyes narrowing slightly. The PCMA Marines at the tunnel, outnumbered nearly six to one, had inflicted casualties at a rate approaching two CAR soldiers for every defender lost. "They fought to the last man, General," Volkov concluded. "Offered no surrender, and we gave no quarter after the... orbital incidents."

A grim silence settled in the room. Ganbaatar understood. The PCMA were fighting with the fury of the doomed, but also with unexpected skill. The assault on the Central Spire, the lynchpin of Petropolis's remaining defences, would be a harder fight than his subordinates had perhaps anticipated.

The broader situation updates filtered in. Aides confirmed the pincer movement on the Spire was closing, with Volkov's forces linking up with the units that had breached the old PCMA Ops building.

The pacification of the Great Gorge proceeded smoothly; initial reports indicated minimal resistance at the oligarch villas. Pictures arrived of his personal billet. It would be one of the grander estates. This was a minor perk of command he barely registered. His focus was on the Spire.

Intelligence reports from the Wahlsanga spaceport fields mentioned only light, scattered resistance from what were assumed to be police or paramilitary units; it was not considered a primary threat axis. All CAR efforts were concentrated on decapitating the PCMA command in Petropolis.

"Commence final assault on the Central Spire," General Ganbaatar ordered, his voice cutting through the static and background noises of the battle-comms system.

The battle for the Spire was brutal. Rostova, a ghost in their comms, seemed to anticipate their moves; her remaining forces dug into well-prepared positions, exacting a heavy toll for every metre gained. Ganbaatar was sure of one thing. Even though CAR political influence managed to affect the appointment of PCMA scientists to be the most mundane people they could, they had no influence over the military selection. These people were obviously the best people the PCMA could find. That was honourable as far as he was concerned. The men he brought into this fight would not be the men he brought out of it. This was a true test of fire.

CAR energy weapons, tuned to disrupt flesh, merely bounced off the stone-hewn walls. Again, Ganbaatar nodded to himself with satisfaction. Any square metre of this place could hide something priceless, of great benefit to the whole human race, not just some spoiled Westerners. The defenders responded with disciplined volleys of conventional fire, but even so, occasionally bullets went astray, proving to Ganbaatar the righteousness of their cause. The NAR were not fit to be leading the exploration of this wondrous planet.

After what felt like an eternity of grinding, close-quarters combat, CAR forces finally breached the Spire's outer perimeter and the firing from within abruptly ceased. A tense quiet descended. Ganbaatar, sensing this, ordered his men to stop firing.

The silence was startling. Everyone took a breath, but the tension remained high. Bodies littered the floor and men who previously had no time to reflect could now see the terrible cost of their assault. Then, a lone figure, small and injured, stumbled out from a secondary entrance of the Spire, hands at its side, unarmed. The figure collapsed to its knees, then pitched forward onto the stone, unmoving.

Ganbaatar watched on his main display. "Hold fire. Cease advance," he commanded. His officers exchanged glances of relief. "No one from inside the Spire attempts to aid the fallen," an aide noted. "It appears organised resistance has collapsed, General."

"A fire team from every side, advance as one with caution," Ganbaatar ordered. "Confirm identity and status."

Four CAR fire teams moved forward. One soldier, perhaps driven by the losses his unit had sustained, callously fired a burst from his energy rifle into the prone figure. There was no reaction. The team leader knelt, then reported back, his voice tight. "Target neutralised, General. Confirmed identity: Commander Eva Rostova."

A wave of grim satisfaction rippled through the CAR command post. The head of the snake was cut. "All units," General Ganbaatar began, "advance en masse, but with caution. Secure the Central Spire." The troops taking cover behind the fire-teams surged forward, blood-lust overtaking good judgement as they poured into the clear plaza-space that had previously been their killing field. Ganbaatar shouted, "I said with caution. Maintain your discipline!"

His order was cut short by a sudden, blinding flash on the tactical display, engulfing the area around the Spire. Simultaneously, hundreds, perhaps thousands, of minuscule icons detached from the structure itself—from pillars, ventilation shafts, affixed to the undersides of benches, even the ornate ceiling panels. They were tiny drones, almost invisible until activated. They swarmed the lead CAR assault elements that had begun to surge forward. Each drone latched onto a CAR soldier's helmet, visor or body joints. Then, in perfect, horrifying synchronicity, they discharged.

The effect was devastating. Over two hundred CAR front-line troops were instantly incapacitated—some killed outright by the small drone explosions sending fragments of armour spalling and thin needles of liquid metal from the drone's tiny, shaped charges through helmets into skulls. Others were blinded when drones struck faceplates, or vital organs were injected with the hot metal, where the drones attached to the chest, spine or groin. They collapsed in screaming, thrashing heaps. The CAR advance dissolved into chaos and panic, the remaining troops recoiling from the invisible, deadly trap.

General Ganbaatar stared at the display, his face a mask of cold fury. This was not honourable warfare; this was perfidy of the highest order. Rostova, feigning surrender to lure his men into this *abomination!* He knew he would not be able to restrain his men now.

He took a deep, steadying breath, his decision made. He activated the system-wide broadcast transmitter, his image appearing on every remaining PCMA comm channel across Sikarra.

"To the remaining PCMA forces on this planet," Ganbaatar's voice resonated, cold and implacable. "Your Commander Rostova has just perpetrated a heinous war crime, feigning surrender to lure my troops into a cowardly and indiscriminate trap. Such tactics are beneath contempt and signify the utter moral bankruptcy of your command."

He paused, letting the accusation sink in. "Despite your losses, and ours, know this: CAR forces still outnumber your scattered remnants by at least three to one. And I assure you, more fleets, a greater wave of the Central Asian Republic's might, are already en route from Earth to consolidate our rightful claim to this system." *A gamble,* he thought, But calculated. *A necessary exaggeration to break their will.*

Then, his voice took on a different, almost messianic tone. "Furthermore, upon the arrival of our forces, the harsh UV radiation of this world, your oppressor, diminished by a full ten per cent! The sky itself has blessed our endeavour, signalling a Mandate from Heaven for our righteous cause! Your resistance is an affront to civilisation itself and this besieged paradise world can only be healed under CAR stewardship!"

He leaned forward, his eyes boring into the broadcast lens. "Therefore, I offer this one final chance. To receive mercy and ensure the humane treatment of all surviving personnel, all PCMA forces on Sikarra must surrender unconditionally within one standard hour. Radio your intent on all open channels. Failure to comply will result in the complete and utter annihilation of every last vestige of your illegitimate presence. There will be no further warnings. There will be no further mercy."

The broadcast ended, leaving a chilling silence in its wake.

Miles away, in the echoing stillness of Wahlsanga Depot, Julian Voss, Renata Volkova, Rayk Kostin, and Alinta O'Neil stared at the comm display, General Ganbaatar's ultimatum hanging in the ancient air like a death sentence. Rostova was gone. They all glanced at Voss, one after the other.

Finally, Raith's stated order of command, cascading down to Voss, fell upon his already weighted shoulders. The responsibility for everything fell squarely, crushingly, upon Julian. Surrender to "mercy" that felt like a lie, or fight on against impossible odds, damned by a so-called Mandate from Heaven? This was his first, and perhaps last, true test of command on a scale he had never imagined.

Chapter 37. Part 2.

The CAR contingent designated for the Great Gorge moved with chilling efficiency. Their passage through the lush, verdant canyon, a place of alien beauty and carefully cultivated oligarch extravagance, was less a conquest and more a methodical assertion of new ownership. Light opposition from scattered private security details at the periphery of the villa estates was brushed aside with contemptuous ease—brief, one-sided engagements that served only to underscore the totality of the CAR's arrival.

Verdant Point, Valerius Corba's palatial enclave, was one of the first to receive its new administrators.

Corba had monitored the fall of the Central Spire on his private displays as he thought, W*hy are these NAR monsters fighting?* They should just put a pair of underpants on the end of a broomstick; same result, but less dead. Butchers of their own men!

As his guts churned, the Glenfiddich he poured was barely touched. The fire it gave in his belly did not complement any satisfaction he might feel that his plans were coming to fruition and the justice he sought was playing out before his eyes. Far from it, the small amount he had consumed seemed to amplify the tension he felt from the distant explosions. Each red CAR icon that had blinked out over Petropolis, each confirmed PCMA command node going dark, deviated from his own predicted sequence of events, uncomfortably distancing himself from his own carefully constructed view of the world.

The communication line to General Ganbaatar's headquarters was, he found, suddenly and irrevocably unavailable to him.

When the CAR troops arrived—a disciplined squad led by a hard-faced officer whose insignia denoted special operations—Corba attempted to project an air of collaborative authority. His jet-black skinned Mongolian operative, who had been a silent, menacing presence in the villa for days, now stood slightly behind the CAR officer; his allegiance, if it had ever truly been to Corba, had now obviously and irrevocably shifted.

"Commander," Corba began, his voice smooth, though perhaps a fraction too ingratiating, "welcome to Verdant Point. My resources, as always, are at the disposal of the Central Asian Republic."

The CAR officer, a Major by the name of Lin, regarded him with an unnervingly placid expression. "Valerius Corba. Your 'cooperation' has been noted. The Great Gorge is now under CAR military administration. For your safety and to facilitate the transition, CAR officers will be billeted within these primary residences. You and your essential staff will retain your personal quarters, for now, under CAR supervision. All external communications are, of course, subject to military oversight. All material assets are requisitioned for the CAR effort." It was delivered with the detached politeness of a legal notice, an iron fist cloaked in the thinnest of velvet.

Corba felt a prickle of genuine fear, the first he had allowed himself in a very long time. His network, his influence, his carefully brokered deals, they were all dissolving like mist. He was no longer a player, merely a resident in an occupied territory. He started to protest, to remind Major Lin of his invaluable contributions, his high-level contacts, his understanding of PCMA weaknesses.

Major Lin simply held up a hand, a gesture of finality. "Your previous contributions have been logged, Mr. Corba. Your current role is to ensure the smooth compliance of this estate's personnel. Nothing more."

Later, as CAR troopers methodically inventoried Verdant Point's luxuries, Corba was ignominiously confined to his study; he thought, Inventory my ass, they are casing the joint. He tried to take comfort in the fact that he was, for now, safe from the nasty little war going on outside, but the grand panoramic window now felt like the transparent wall of a very expensive cage.

The Mongolian operative entered, moving with the same silent efficiency Corba had once admired. There was no preamble, no accusation, no offer of an explanation. Corba saw the energy pistol in the operative's hand, the silencer already affixed.

A wave of bitter, almost hysterical amusement washed over him. All his plans, his manipulations, his grand vision of a CAR-dominated Sikarra with himself as a key power broker—all reduced to this. A loose end to be tidied up. He thought of the order he had delayed issuing, the one to finally eliminate that troublesome archaeologist, Jonesy. The hit had failed once, thanks to Kostin. Now, with Petropolis in flames and PCMA command shattered, it was highly unlikely the directive would be carried out by anyone else. Certainly, no longer by him. A small, genuine laugh escaped Corba's lips, a dry, rattling sound. Good old Mr. Jones, he thought, a final, dark irony playing in his mind. It looks like he will get away with it after all.

The operative raised the pistol. Corba closed his eyes, not in fear, but in a kind of weary, cosmic resignation. The shot was almost inaudible, a soft sigh of discharged energy. Valerius Corba, oligarch, conspirator, and architect of his own demise, slumped forward onto his polished locally sourced gorge-wood desk, a final, insignificant casualty in a war far larger and more brutal than he had ever truly comprehended.

Outside, the CAR flag, a stark red field with its twin golden stars, one above the other representing Siberia and China, was being unfurled over the main entrance of Verdant Point. Major Lin watched, his expression unreadable. From his comm-unit, a calm voice reported: "Asset Corba neutralised, Major. Verdant Point secured for General Ganbaatar's use. The Gorge is pacified."

The sun began to dip below the high cliffs of the Great Gorge, casting long, cool shadows. Under the new management, a chilling, efficient quiet settled over the opulent villas, a quiet that was, in its own way, as absolute as the silence now reigning in the ruins of Petropolis's Central Spire.

Chapter 38. Part 1.

The two battered work trucks, one trailing a plume of acrid smoke from damaged insulation, hurtled through the desolate outer service sectors of Vasantha. Behind them, the unmistakable silhouettes of K'Tharr light pursuit vehicles and swift, bipedal warriors were closing the distance, their energy weapons stitching incandescent patterns across the crumbling infrastructure. Foreman Penaargan, his face grim, wrestled with the controls of the lead truck, following Designer Marinallis's terse, urgent navigational commands. In the second truck, Varinn and Tessara returned fire sporadically, the heavy thrum of their own vehicle's straining engine a counterpoint to the whine of incoming K'Tharr weaponry.

"Rendezvous point, one kilometre ahead, base of the western escarpment!" Marinallis's voice crackled over the inter-truck comm, tight with strain. "Mr. Penaargan, prepare to abandon and scuttle vehicles. I will leave the timing of the charges solely as your responsibility". The experienced foreman merely nodded in gritted response. "All personnel, transfer essential gear only. Varinn, Tessara, ensure that nobody drags the majority back. If anyone is captured, there can be no battle to save them this time, you know what to do." He saw Tessara was less than happy or committal about the command, but he exchanged glances with Varinn. He wouldn't be taken by surprise again.

The trucks, under slight threat from distant K'Tharr fire, slewed into a relatively concealed cul-de-sac formed by towering, time-scoured rock formations at the very foot of the colossal, sheer escarpment that ringed this district. "Now, Penaargan, now!" Marinallis commanded.

With a discipline born of desperation, Penaargan's crew scrambled from the vehicles, hastily rigging their remaining demolition charges while others grabbed water packs, medical kits, and a few essential tool kits. Varinn, his arm supporting Tessara, whose own was still bandaged and aching, ensured their bodies were between Marinallis and the pursuing aliens.

"To me!" Marinallis gestured towards a seemingly blank section of the escarpment wall, a sheer face of rock that offered no obvious refuge. As the last of the crew stumbled clear, their movements economical and urgent, Penaargan, with a grim nod to Marinallis, triggered the remote detonator. A series of powerful explosions ripped through the abandoned trucks, the shock wave buffeting the evacuees. The vehicles were engulfed in a rapidly expanding fireball, sending shrapnel and superheated debris skyward, hopefully creating a significant, if temporary, barrier for the K'Tharr now visible at the mouth of the cul-de-sac.

Marinallis was already at the rock face, his hand pressed against an almost invisible seam. With a low hum that resonated through the ground beneath their feet, a massive section of the cliff, disguised with masterful camouflage, slid silently inward, revealing a darkened, cool interior. Within rested a bulky, functional Designer utility skimmer, its form suggesting heavy lifting duties.

"Reserve transport," Marinallis stated, his voice calm despite the nearby explosions and the approaching K'Tharr. "My access only. Board quickly and secure yourselves."

The transfer to the skimmer was efficient, born of necessity. Marinallis took the controls, with Penaargan beside him, rapidly familiarising himself with the co-pilot systems. Varinn saw Tessara, as a pilot, begin to protest, but Varinn said, "Time to be chauffeured" as he bundled Tessara into the passenger compartment. She did not protest too much; the urgency of the situation overruled professional pride. Varinn then took a position to cover their rear as the remaining crew members boarded the skimmer. The first K'Tharr warriors, having navigated the burning wreckage of the trucks, appeared at the entrance to the hidden hangar, their energy weapons opening fire.

Marinallis engaged the skimmer's anti-gravity drive. The craft lifted smoothly, followed by the others, tilting sharply to avoid the initial K'Tharr volleys that flashed past, scoring molten gouges in the rock face. The utility skimmer exited the hangar at speed and at a low height of only inches off the floor and with a grimace from Penaargan, hit three of the slower K'Tharr on its exit as a belated "pedestrian alert" sounded from the overridden control AS. The skimmer, under Marinallis's no-nonsense flying, began a rapid, vertical ascent up the sheer two-thousand-foot cliff. Below, K'Tharr ground forces, now fully arrived at the scuttled truck site, directed intense fire upwards. The skimmer, while bulky, was not an armoured combat craft. It took a direct hit to a non-critical nacelle, sparks flying, but Marinallis, on manual flight settings, easily maintained control. With the skills developed over his long lifespan crystallised deeply into his muscle memory, he casually navigated the skimmer through the barrage, heading for a specific, seemingly featureless point about halfway up the cliff, a location utterly invisible from below.

Just as Penaargan was about to wrest control from Marinallis, fearing a collision with the rock face, Marinallis brought the skimmer to an abrupt halt, precisely hovering before a particular configuration of weathered rock. A coded transmission from his wrist unit, and with a section of the cliff face shimmered, then retracted silently, revealing a vast, dark aperture. The skimmer slipped through the stealthed entrance, into an echoing darkness. As soon as they entered, a now-familiar 'crump' sound came from behind them and a slight telltale jostle of the craft let Penaargan know the entrance behind was now permanently hidden with a rockslide.

As they flew through the entrance tunnel, low-level emergency lights activated, revealing an interior of breathtaking, impossible scale. They were within a colossal cavern; an artificial construction of staggering dimensions carved from the mountain's heart. This was a Designer Military Ship Construction Yard. Varinn found himself staring, all thoughts of the K'Tharr momentarily forgotten as he thought, How did they keep something of this size secret? How many humans knew about it? It was truly astounding, but more than that, this spoke of the abilities of the Designers that even he could not comprehend. What else was Marinallis keeping secret from him? This man, whom he thought he knew, had practically raised him like a father. He looked around. Gantries, easily capable of cradling vessels that would dwarf any known human starship, towered into the artificial gloom, stretching for what seemed like a mile. Immense, empty docking bays lined the chamber. To save time, Penaargan commanded the side cargo door to open for immediate evacuation, letting in air that was cool and heavy and ancient, carrying the faint scent of ozone and long-dormant machinery. No intact starships were visible; even the few skeletal frames of half-finished hulls and vast, empty construction cradles had been sabotaged and robbed of anything useful. This was a mausoleum to shipbuilding that spoke of a fleet long since departed or aborted before reaching term. High above, almost lost in the shadows, the intricate, interlocking panels of a colossal, stealthed roof hinted at the egress point for these vanished titans.

The Xenologist

Chapter 38 Part 2.

landing on a wide, clear platform near one of the massive, empty docking cradles. The only sound for a long moment was the soft whine-down of the skimmer's anti-gravity drive and the distant, almost imperceptible drip of condensation somewhere in the vast, echoing space. Penaargan and his crew, hardened individuals who had faced annihilation only minutes before, now simply stared out through the open cargo door, their expressions a mixture of slack-jawed disbelief and profound awe. Tessara, beside Varinn, seemed to be trying to commit every impossible detail to memory, the archaeologist in her momentarily silencing all fear. Varinn himself felt a strange dislocation; the sheer, hidden power of the Designers, a people he thought he knew, was staggering. What else had they kept secret? What else was Marinallis capable of?

Marinallis was the first to move, his movements economical as he powered down the skimmer's main systems. "We disembark here," he stated, his voice, though quiet, carrying easily in the immense stillness. "The protocols for this facility are clear. We must proceed to the primary staging area."

As the last of the crew stepped onto the ancient platform, their boots echoing faintly on the metallic surface, an urgent, insistent chime emanated from Marinallis's personal comm device. He consulted it, his usually impassive features tightening into a mask of grim urgency.

Marinallis said, "Varinn, Mr. Penaargan, we have an ally about to present himself. Please control your men and get them to point their weapons to the floor. It is not, I repeat not, a K'Tharr".

A black armoured figure, probably robotic in nature, humanoid, but obviously not quite human, stepped out from behind a corner and walked with complete casual confidence towards Marinallis. The being was tall, clad in sleek, shiny black space armour that seemed to absorb and subtly refract the ambient light.

The being exuded the confidence of a soldier or a bodyguard. The neck was slightly longer than that of a human and most ominously, it had no obvious weapon. A fact that was more ominous than any visible threat. It stopped at the bottom of a ramp that projected into empty space at right angles to the gantry they were standing upon. Then, after a moment, the air at the end of the ramp shimmered. A fairly large black cube came into view, as if they had only just noticed it. By now, the Humans were immune to strangeness, and they stood in surprising calm while a door inside the cube, that was plainly an airlock, opened. Another being came down the ramp. It appeared to be an elegant cyborg that had a 'lady-in-waiting' appearance.

These two creatures were astonishing but had nothing like the gravitas of the final being that stepped from inside the craft into view. The being, with a silvery hood over its head and face, wafer-thin, tall, and largely female in aspect, walked between the impressive entourage, plainly in control of the whole operation. As it drew closer, its hood removed itself with a silent, fluid motion, revealing a sight that stopped every human heart for a beat.

Its head, framed by a halo of vibrant, silver curls that seemed to capture and scatter the dim light, was perched atop an incredibly long, thin, graceful neck, easily a foot in length, that lent it an almost regal, statuesque bearing. Its skin was pale, possessing an almost luminous, translucent quality. Large, dark, intelligent eyes, almond-shaped and profoundly deep, dominated a delicately featured face.

Prominent, rounded, paddle-like ears, pinned back and significantly larger than a human's, twitched almost imperceptibly, as if sensing the ancient air of the shipyard.

Tessara felt her breath catch in her throat. The sight was one of ancient wisdom, of serene power, a beauty so startling and profoundly unearthly that it defied all context. She gasped softly, her hand flying to her mouth, her eyes wide with a mixture of fear, wonder, and pure, unadulterated awe. Beside her, she was dimly aware of the hardened members of Penaargan's crew, frozen in a similar, stunned silence. This was it. Their first, undeniable contact with a friendly, sentient, advanced, non-human alien.

As the long-necked Newcomer walked down the gangway, Marinallis met halfway between their respective vessels. The Newcomer inclined its head in a gesture of greeting, its voice, when it spoke, was remarkably human and it spoke the Talemoran dialect of 'Designer-Speak' that Varinn grew up with, exactly like a Native.

"Good day D. Marinallis. It is a pleasure to finally meet you. I am Ground Operating Officer Seraphel." The Newcomer Said, flexing his long neck to bow his head in greeting.

Marinallis replied, "And you too, Officer Seraphel." He also imitated the greeting with his human-sized neck. He turned and glared at the open-mouthed Humans who all got the hint and nodded their necks in an imitative greeting.

Ignoring her bodyguard and servant, who both waited with apparent patience, Seraphel continued without ceremony. "The orbital situation has escalated far more rapidly than anticipated," his voice carrying an undeniable weight. "The Samplers are active. Their primary sweep of this system has commenced, and their initial telemetry indicates they are already disposing of the K'Tharr orbital ships."

Marinallis said, "They are? They dispatched more than one to deal with the K'Tharr? They must be annoyed." He paused, his gaze flicking between Varinn and Penaargan, ensuring they understood the gravity.

"Due to the increased urgency of the situation, my ship is executing its final atmospheric entry. They are on an emergency intercept trajectory with this facility, attempting to arrive before the Samplers can fully analyse or target this installation's energy signature. Of course, we were covering the descent of the Explorer Ship Va'hari Sentinel, which will arrive safely, but we had to go ahead to ensure you are picked up in a timely fashion. You are the last of your species on Planet and we really don't want you to be Sampled D. Marinallis. That would never do."

Marinallis said, "Surely you are able to cope with just one Sampler if it arrives? You are not the K'Tharr after all."

Seraphel let out a sound that approximated a Human laugh. "My dear Marinallis, I think I can cope with one sampler, but the problem is that if it comes up against significant resistance or gets destroyed, then coming so soon after these idiot K'Tharr violated light speed, there is a high probability they will ..."

"Nova the Sun," Marinallis said, nodding.

"Quite." Seraphel continued, "and unfortunately, we will have to leave before the Va'hari Sentinel, to prevent precisely that occurrence".

"Damn..." Marinallis interjected.

"However, we will wait as long as we can and cover its ascent. Once in orbit, all should be fine and we can leave this system to hopefully recover its natural Flora and Fauna as the Fumigators lose interest".

Marinallis turned and looked at Varinn. "My friend, this is it now. I do not know if we will meet again. Try to get off Va'hari as soon as you can. I am formally releasing you from my employ. There will be references waiting for you on Eluvara. I wish you and Tessara a long and prosperous partnership." Tessara blushed and Varinn gripped her arm a little tighter.

Seraphel broke the tension, "The 'Zephyrion' will dock right here at this gantry, very soon. The Va'hari Sentinel will dock just over there on the opposite gantry two minutes after we depart," and pointed to the opposite side of the artificial canyon of the shipyard.

Varinn looked at the gantry in dismay. "But that's half a Kilometre away. We need to get in the lifting skimmer now".

Seraphel looked at Varinn rather pityingly, "I am afraid it's a little too late, the Zephyrion is here now. The Va'hari Sentinel will follow immediately. There is an air traffic deconfliction problem. You will have to use alternative means of transport.

Chapter 38. Part 3.

As if summoned by his warning, a low, almost subsonic rumble began to vibrate through the very structure of the shipyard. High above them, the colossal, interlocking panels of the stealthed roof, a section easily a kilometre square, began to move. With silent, flawless precision, they slid apart, revealing a patch of Talemora's dark, turbulent, star-dusted sky. The sudden influx of starlight, dim as it was, felt almost like an intrusion in the ancient emergency-lit gloom.

Into this opening descended the Newcomer capital ship, Zephyrion. It was a vessel of truly breathtaking scale and utterly alien configuration, its hull a series of interlocking crystalline structures and flowing, organic-seeming curves that shimmered with an internal light. It moved with an impossible, silent grace, settling into an adjacent, even larger docking cradle, its presence filling the shipyard with a palpable sense of immense, controlled power.

As the humans stood transfixed, never having seen a ship of that size operate in Atmosphere, the Zephyrion, still way above them, extended a proboscis-like shaft down from the underbelly of the ship to gracefully fuse with the side of the cube-ship in front of them. Another newcomer, this time in full body and face armour, stepped from the tube, into the entrance of the cube and then onto the ramp. Like Seraphel, he or she carried no obvious weapon and showed no particular urgency but gestured into the cube-ship in a very uncannily human fashion.

"That," Marinallis stated, gesturing towards the Humans, "Is what I call an entrance." Then he did something Varinn had never seen from a designer before. He walked over to Tessara and actually kissed her on the cheek. He then clapped Varinn on the shoulder and said in a louder voice, "I suggest you get moving, people. Two threats are coming. The K'Tharr you have seen but should you see a metallic creature that is about three meters high and has six legs, find a K'Tharr to hide behind and hope it takes them instead."

Then, he focused on Varinn and said, "There is no time, Varinn, you are on your own now. I am sorry." And with that, he abruptly turned on his heel and left their lives, walking to the elevator with the Newcomer.

As the Designer and the Newcomer walked to the cube, Varinn saw the long neck of the Newcomer bent to Marinallis. As he did so, he was certain he heard Seraphel say, "Seriously, old chap, you are very sweet with your monkeys." Then, defiantly, he heard Marinallis say, "Humans, they are called Humans." With that, the cube-ship door closed and Varinn felt empty inside. It was his last glimpse of the old man who had been his cross-species Father. He had never felt so inferior.

Everyone left on the gantry stood frozen in place. The encounter seared into their minds. Penaargan, after confirming all personnel were accounted for at an internal comm station, simply ran a hand over his face, muttering, "By all the gods... what have we seen?"

Tessara finally found her voice, though it was unsteady. "Varinn... did you... that being... it was... magnificent. Like something from a dream, or a myth made real." Her mind, the mind of an archaeologist who had dedicated her life to understanding the past, was reeling from this glimpse of a truly alien present.

Varinn said, "I only have one thing to say," pausing for effect as he turned around and screwed his face up. "RUN!"

Chapter 39. Part 1.

The Wahlsanga City's new emergency Command Post occupied a cavern carved directly into the rock face, adjoining a mezzanine floor above the Metro Station. It overlooked the large, echoing space of the main entrance cavern where the now expanded SARU-bored tunnel debouched. In the last several days, over 500 engineers had been moved in, to work on this area. Raith obviously saw the potential of this area early. Voss viewed Raith's memory with a new respect for his sharp foresight. The man was scary as hell, but Voss knew the CAR had taken out a formidable foe with their orbital strike.

Tactical displays brought in when Raith ordered the establishment of a secondary operating base at Wahlsanga, shimmered with fragmented data feeds from across Petropolis and the semi-desert plains separating the two underground cities. The air here was cool, carrying the faint, underlying scent of recently cleared dust and new PCMA fabrication machinery hastily installed on the platforms below.

Julian Voss, Renata Volkova, Rayk Kostin, and Alinta O'Neil were gathered around the central console, their faces illuminated by the flickering light, a knot of tension in the silent cavern. They had been monitoring the collapse in Petropolis, the increasingly desperate reports painting a picture of inevitable doom. Rayk, now relocated from the gatehouse outside to the new command centre, remained ever watchful. He stood slightly apart, coordinating local security teams guarding the tunnel entrance and the Metro access point visible on a secondary display.

Rayk's comm unit crackled. He listened for a long moment, his jaw tightening. He turned back to the group, his expression grim, his voice low and heavy. "Julian," he said, using Voss's first name, the formality of rank momentarily forgotten in the face of disaster. "Fragmented reports confirming the worst. The Northern Access Tunnel has fallen. Chesterton's command is gone." He paused, swallowing hard. "As for Commander Rostova, her last confirmed location was the Central Spire. There is heavy fighting. But no further contact."

Julian felt a cold wave wash over him. Chesterton fallen. The North Gate breached. Rostova cut off, making a last stand. He didn't need a tactical display to understand the implications. Petropolis was functionally lost. The sheer scale of the defeat, the speed with which the CAR had overwhelmed the city's defences, was staggering. And if the city was gone, where did that leave them? Here. This Depot. The last functional base.

He hadn't sought leadership. His expertise was history, xenology, the quiet study of vanished civilisations. But the grim reality of Rayk's report, the vacuum of command opening up in real-time, left no room for hesitation. Someone had to act. Someone had to prepare. He looked at Rayk, at Renata and Alinta, their faces mirroring the dawning horror. The time for waiting for orders, for hoping for reinforcement, was over.

Rayk's words hadn't appointed him commander. But the cold, hard reality of the news did.

Julian looked down at the terminal in his hands. It was still displaying theoretical schematics, tools of hypothetical planning. There was no time left for hypotheticals.

Julian turned to them, his voice firm, a new, unaccustomed authority hardening his tone. He was not the Commander yet, not formally. But he was the ranking officer here, responsible for making decisions. He was the boss now. "Rayk, if the North Gate is gone, if Rostova's position is untenable, then they will consolidate on us. This City and specifically this Depot, is the last functional base. We cannot meet them head-on. We don't have the personnel, the heavy weapons." He began to walk, moving with sudden purpose towards a door leading deeper into the Depot. "We need unconventional solutions. We need to leverage what Raith left us here."

As Julian spoke, initiating this unplanned transition, the air changed as if chilled by authority. General Ganbaatar's voice, cold and implacable, cut through the Depot's internal comms network. Ganbaatar's system-wide broadcast. They all fell silent, listening to the horrifying details of the city's fall, the explicit confirmation of Rostova's death, the chilling "Mandate from Heaven," and the brutal one-hour surrender ultimatum washing over them.

When the broadcast ended, the silence in the Command Post was heavy, absolute. Julian met Rayk's gaze across the console. The security chief's expression was unreadable, but for a moment, the professional mask seemed to slip, revealing the shared, immense burden they now carried. He gave a single, formal nod of acknowledgement.

"Principal Voss," Rayk said, his voice calm and steady now, the informality gone. "The General's broadcast makes it official. Commander Rostova is Killed In Action. Raith's protocols put you in charge here. You were the senior PCMA officer in this sector." He gestured towards Julian with a slight inclination of his head. "You now have command of the entire PCMA presence on this planet."

Julian met his gaze. He accepted the mantle, not with eagerness, but with a profound sense of duty. There was no one else. He looked at the determined faces of Renata and Alinta, their apprehension now mixed with a fragile hope. "Very well," Julian said, his voice steady despite the tremor that ran through his hands. "Then this is our headquarters. Surrender is unthinkable. At best, we will be deported and we will never be allowed to share in the riches this planet has to offer. Neither we nor our people at home. At worst, they take revenge on us for the orbital strike. I don't want to become a captive of theirs for one moment, thinking myself lucky only to be shipped back to Earth on a prison ship where I will be consigned by history as a traitor and a failure. From here, we fight." His stare was met with solid faces. Nobody said anything and nobody objected. They were just solidly with him.

He turned back towards the door he had indicated moments before, his resolve hardening with each step. Rayk immediately moved to a comm console, issuing orders to local security and coordinating with personnel at the Metro entrance. Renata and Alinta exchanged a glance, then wordlessly followed Julian downstairs to begin whatever work was needed.

Underneath the Mezzanine floor, the relocated 3D print factories and chemical synth printers occupied a large section of the Metro Station's platforms. The positioning was a clever move by the engineers who set this up. Voss could see how the produce from the printers and fabricators could easily be moved onto carts that drive up along the train lines. Banks of printers stood silent or chattered with low-cycle diagnostic checks. The air held the faint, sterile tang of exotic polymers and synthesis reagents.

Dr. Andrew Thorne, the mechanical engineer, and Dr. Lena Petrova, the chemical engineer, were already here, already having been earlier directed by Julian to assess the capabilities of the units, though without specific tasking. They looked to Julian, their initial uncertainty now replaced by grim anticipation. He had reviewed their Résumés. Unlike the archaeologist teams, these were brilliant minds that earned their place on the Colony.

"Dr. Thorne, Dr. Petrova," Julian began, his voice rapid, focused. "The situation in Petropolis is lost. We are on our own." He didn't dwell on it. "We cannot defend this place conventionally. We need to make them bleed for every inch, buy ourselves time, sow chaos." He gestured towards the fabrication units. "We're going to use these facilities to create asymmetric deterrents. Something they won't expect."

He began to outline the concepts, his historical knowledge meeting the cutting edge of the relocated tech.

"Dr. Thorne, caltrops. Ancient principle, but we need them to be high-tech. Mass-producible plastic shapes. Optimise the design using the AS for maximum disruption to light vehicle tires and foot soldiers. Rapid print cycle. Get the lines running, maximum output."

Thorne nodded, already moving towards a large 3D printer console, his eyes scanning schematics projected onto the surface.

"Dr. Petrova," Julian continued, turning to the chemical engineer. "We need a weapon that can disable their armour, break up formations at range. Dr. Thorne's team will be asked to make a projectile thrower similar to a paintball gun. You need to synthesise the projectile that will utilise this indirect fire system." He rapidly described the concept of the softball-like projectile he'd envisioned, drawing on the principles from that obscure paper. "Sticky adhesive shell, a compound that initially pancakes then hardens on impact – you handle the synthesis for that, the dilatant effect. Inside, a concentrated armour-weakening acid – something fast-acting, using our industrial reagents. It needs to soak into their composite armour weave. And a small, precisely timed explosive charge, like a pea-sized pellet of C7, detonating, say, eight to ten seconds after impact, once the acid has compromised the armour."

He looked at her intently. "Can the chemical synthesis printers formulate and integrate these complex compounds and energetic charges into a single, stable projectile, rapidly?"

Petrova's eyes widened slightly at the daring combination, but she immediately grasped the technical challenge. "Yes, Principal," she replied, "The-". Then Renata corrected her, with a slight, almost proud glance at Voss, "It's Commander, now," and with that one word, Voss realised it was real.

Petrova continued, "Yes, Commander," her voice gaining professional momentum. "The synth units were designed for complex material fabrication. We can formulate the adhesive matrix, the dilatant and synthesise the acid compound. Integrating the timed charge isn't too complex; the issue is the time constraint, even with the Artificial Sentience controlling the machines to do the design, but I think it is feasible with the micro-fabrication heads. We can run initial synthesis and stability tests now." She was already talking through the required reagents, moving towards her terminal.

Thorne was also now fully engaged, conferring with Julian on the ballistics and launcher design for the projected rounds. He'd studied sieges in textbooks. Now he was ordering glue bombs and chemical acids to stop a planetary invasion.

Julian felt a surge of focused energy amidst the chaos. Although there was little choice, he had stepped up and was now the commander. Which meant his command centre was here, at the forge of necessity, where survival was being fabricated, one unconventional weapon at a time.

Chapter 39. Part 2.

The Wahlsanga end of the Metro tunnel was a scene of controlled chaos. A steady, harrowing stream of refugees filtered in from the collapsing city. They were a mix of PCMA military survivors and dust-covered civilians, their eyes wide with terror. Some were injured, but most were weary and some were just lucky enough to be able to commandeer a city buggy, which usually was loaded to the maximum with people or supplies. Many, however, had to walk the huge distance between the cities. Rayk Kostin, his face grim, oversaw the reception, handing out water and ration packs, his voice sharp but measured as he directed the flow. He told his officers to commandeer the vehicles and drive back to Petropolis to pick up stragglers and wounded.

Nearby, PCMA medics, their uniforms stained, worked desperately, their faces etched with exhaustion. Civilian injuries were mercifully light, mostly cuts and bruises sustained in the panic and stampede through the city's sub-levels. But the soldiers were a different story. Many bore terrible burn wounds, screaming in pain as medics administered injections of morphine, painkillers, or anything that could offer a moment of respite. Some men were just numb, staring blankly ahead, the horrors they had witnessed stripping them bare. They were stressed, nervous, their morale tested to its limits, but when they removed their helmets, Kostin saw anger in their eyes. They had fought and made a good account of themselves. But they had lost. For now. Rayk knew a good leader could reform and rally these people.

Amidst the sounds of suffering and hurried commands, Rayk directed security personnel in quick, vital screenings – checking for concealed weapons, trying to identify potential CAR infiltrators amidst the genuine escapees, however unlikely it seemed. Other personnel guided the exhausted to temporary holding areas deeper within the Depot. The refugees brought fragmented, often contradictory, but uniformly horrifying accounts of the fighting in Petropolis: overwhelming CAR numbers, the brutal efficiency of their energy weapons, the fall of Chesterton at the North Gate, the pincer movement closing on the Spire, the sheer scale of the defeat.

Rayk knew he could not allow the tension to settle. He needed an abrupt interjection and needed to task people to give them purpose and organisation. He stood on a rock promontory and shouted, "Can I have your attention *PLEASE!*". Most people looked up, but principally the soldiers who were not carrying injuries. Rayk started issuing commands to the Police units through his qWatch and mirrored the commands in speech to people who were not on his link. "All able military personnel: go up the ramps behind me. We are making the field hospital there." He then issued new orders through the qWatch, "Medical staff: stabilise and transfer patients, then report to the city hospital—new bays are operational. Civilians: log onto Wahlsanga-net. Tasking will follow. You're safe now. Our position is secure." And with that lie, he signed off and walked up the ramp with soldiers dutifully falling in behind him.

Chapter 39. Part 3.

Whilst Voss organised his production lines and Rayk organised the refugees, Renata Volkova and Alinta O'Neil were immersed in a different kind of battle in the Depot, one fought against the silence of millennia. They sat surrounded by tactical display screens and data pads, covered in glyphs from the Echo Key, scans taken of markings on the Architect train and other accessible Designer infrastructure within the Depot. They were in a race against time, trying to force meaning from the alien symbols.

Renata said, "I can't concentrate. We should be helping with the refugees, using our skills to patch the soldiers together, not doing academia".

Renata shook her head. "I know it's difficult, but Julian was correct. We are just two people. We don't have a shortage of people to hand out water and apply bandages. We have a shortage of knowledge." Alinta sighed resignedly. She knew her natural instinct to gather together and each to do their part was not what was required at this point. *Concentrate, damn it. You are doing the right thing!*

Renata decided the best thing was not to dwell on explanations, but to press forward with science, which would be the best therapy and the best distraction. "It has to be here," she murmured, her finger tracing a complex symbol on a screen. "Operational functions, warnings, inventory... somewhere in this language is the key to what this place contains. What Raith was so desperate to secure."

Alinta, her brow furrowed in intense concentration, was relying on the strange, intuitive connection the Echo Key had given her. It wasn't language, not yet, but it left her with unexpected "memory flashes," a resonance when she saw certain symbols elsewhere in the Depot. "That mark," Alinta said, pointing to a glyph on a schematic of the Depot's sub-levels that resembled a rounded tall rectangle or, depending on the font, an almond shape, always with a line bisecting the right side. "We were following the idea it was a Mitochondria, meaning anything from Mother to an innate sense of that which is not you, but is innate to you. Well, the Echo Key gave me one of those false impressions or memories." Alinta paused as Renata looked intently at her, hungry for knowledge. "But, Renata, I have to say, it just feels so unscientific to go on the basis of a hunch, or even 'revealed knowledge.'"

"I know what you mean, but from an archaeologist's point of view, most things are based upon revelation. Dead men tell tales." Renata gave a smile as she remembered a lecture on Egyptology at the local library when she was a teenager. "We rely on revelation more than we admit."

Alinta raised her eyebrows and slanted her head to one side, phlegmatically acknowledging the unusual circumstances. "Not usually from ancient alien USB sticks downloaded into my head." When Renata grinned in reply, Alinta continued, "Can you imagine this on the paper when we publish? 'Source of information, God-like technology revealed it to me because I am special in some way. Both women laughed, a moment of camaraderie and humour at a dark time?" But Alinta, against her better judgment and training, continued. "Well, I also saw, and I have to say 'instinctively' recognised it here, on the City name by the main access conduit near the entrance. It feels like I can now read it as a place name. A designation with semantics behind it."

Renata leaned closer. "A place name?"

"Yes," Alinta confirmed, a spark of excitement in her eyes that even the surrounding crisis couldn't fully extinguish. "If I'm right and if that's how it works, then this symbol..." She traced it again. "It means 'Wahlsanga'. Or the Designer root, Val-Sanga. 'Va' means 'home' or 'go home' I can't describe it exactly."

They stared at the symbol, then at each other. A breakthrough, yes. But... "Wahlsanga, I suppose now, 'Valsanga' which will take some getting used to." Renata repeated, "*VAL*sanga," the name feeling heavy and insufficient. "So, we know the name of the place we're in. But we need to leverage this knowledge to help us understand the nature of the contents of these storage units?"

Alinta's expression fell slightly. "It doesn't help much, but it is a start. We need to feed this into the language AS if you are sure that it's correct and won't lead it astray. Then we need more correlation points. Context. We need to understand the syntax, the grammar, not just isolate symbols." She looked at the overwhelming amount of data before them. "My flashes are too sporadic. We need help. Julian... he understands historical linguistics. He had that strange reaction with the Key, too. Perhaps he can see patterns we can't. Or knows a way to cross-reference historical Earth language structures...?"

As Renata was about to answer, Rayk Kostin arrived at their location, his face grim, cutting short their intellectual struggle. He had left the chaos of the Metro reception behind, bringing vital, dangerous intelligence. He said, "Sorry to interrupt, but I am expecting Commander Voss. Has he spoken to you?"

As Renata and Alinta began to say no, footsteps came through the depot blast doors and a confident figure strode towards their position. Rayk signalled with his hand. "Ah, Commander Voss, thank you for meeting me," his voice urgent. "The situation?" Voss asked abruptly. Rayk appreciated bypassing formalities, himself going straight to the critical intel. "Update from our Special Forces scouts operating in the outer ruins. They're maintaining stealth, using tiny drones for observation. The CAR aren't just probing the perimeter. They're consolidating on the surface."

Voss said nothing, but kept a stern, attentive look on his face as he absorbed the information. Rayk pulled up a tactical projection, showing the CAR positions. "They've completed sweeping the immediate area and are assembling a dedicated assault force. Infantry, light vehicles, possibly some heavier support. They're staged on the surface near the main external surface access tunnel from the spaceport, preparing for an assault on that primary entrance." His tone left no doubt—this wasn't a probing attack; it was the formation of a significant strike force. "Based on their current readiness, they'll be ready to launch within hours. Maybe by dawn. If they take that spaceport entrance, they'll sweep through the surface ruins. Then, when they feel confident with enough forces gathered, our main city entrance will be where they will spearhead an assault."

Voss thought for a second and suggested, "Then best they don't feel confident. What's the military picture in the main Spaceport and the Ruins further out?"

"It's not all doom and gloom, actually. Our scouts are reporting small pockets of resistance from other PCMA personnel—scattered survivors, local security, even some science staff—fighting back from outbuildings and ruins around the spaceport perimeter." Rayk indicated widening areas of intermittent contact on the projection. "So our SF are supporting them where they can, conducting hit-and-run, expanding the battlefield."

Julian glanced at the chronometer—the one-hour deadline was an irrelevance now they had decided to fight. Voss suspected the CAR would be brutal no matter what they did, but he had decided to fight and as far as he could tell, everyone knew it was the only chance. It looked like the coming Dawn was now the only deadline that mattered. The CAR assault force gathering on the surface perimeter was an imminent, deadly threat. If they just waited, that force would eventually find and overwhelm the main SARU tunnel entrance.

"Alright," Julian said, his strategic mind engaging rapidly. "They're consolidating on the obvious surface approaches. We have to prevent them from taking those quickly and then moving on here. We need to expand the battlefield further, make them think resistance is widespread and unpredictable. We use the Depot's secret exits to hit them from unexpected angles."

He laid out the core of the diversionary plan. "Rayk, you lead it. We have multiple concealed egress points from the Depot into the escarpment and the wider surface area—tunnels, even our engineers only recently confirmed, exits leading into the ruins, service ways, possibly old drainage tunnels, emergency balcony access points. They give us access to a battlefield that's kilometres wide inside this escarpment."

They discussed *how* the newly printed, unconventional weapons would be used. "The caltrops are for deployment on likely CAR movement paths, assembly areas for their vehicles. The sticky acid rounds from the launchers. If I can persuade the Military to use paintball guns, that is." Rayk made a sardonic facial gesture of agreement; he continued, "... target their formations from the tunnels, from behind them and basically any unexpected angles we can, to give them a sense of being surrounded or infiltrated."

Julian gestured towards the fabrication labs on the floors above the Depot. "We're not trying to defeat their assault force in open combat," he stressed, his voice carrying conviction. "We are trying to scatter it, delay it, make their commander paranoid about threats they can't locate. We buy time. We sow confusion. We make them divert resources they need for their main push."

Rayk nodded, understanding the high stakes and the unconventional nature of the plan. "Understood, Commander. I know the best people to form the diversionary teams". Voss said, "But I need several guinea pigs with open minds to test the new weapons, they will be due off the printing lines very shortly." With that, Rayk nodded and turned on his heel to leave the Depot.

As the print lines on the Metro platforms and the design offices in the Cavern above the Station continued their urgent work and the flow of refugees continued at the Metro entrance, Rayk's small, armed exclusionary teams began to coalesce according to the instructions Rayk began issuing over his qWatch system. Rayk sent some men towards one or more of the confirmed secret escarpment tunnel exits. Some, mostly either marines wearing green armour or airborne/spaceborne paratroopers wearing white armour, with grey and black flashes to disrupt their outline in industrial and spaceship environments, began to make their way to the manufacturing offices and command post in the Cavern above the platforms.

Like all Special Forces, they took the chance to play with new kit very seriously. Carrying their helmets, Rayk could see their innate distrust of a Policeman turned general. Voss would have his first battle convincing these characters to go along with his impromptu schemes. But if he did, it meant they had merit. As they filed past him, obedient as military men ultimately always were, Rayk remembered a famous British Duke who once said, "I don't know what they'll do to the enemy; but by God, they frighten me."

Chapter 40. Part 1.

The Zephyrion's ascent through the colossal, open section of the roof had been swift, a vast alien form vanishing into the dark, turbulent sky of Talemora. Its absence left a void that felt intensely vulnerable.

The *Va'hari Sentinel*, the human evacuation ship, descended exactly on time, two minutes after the departure of the Zephyrion. As they jogged towards the ship docking in the berth below, they got all the encouragement they needed as the ship lowered its boarding ramp immediately. This was a beacon of hope in the silent docks. After what seemed an age, the faster members had reached the bottom of the ramp, but Varinn took up the rear to protect the slower ones. He paused to take stock of the situation and check behind them. He saw that Penaargan's crew was already hurrying up the ramp, their shapes silhouetted against the ship's internal lights. Tessara was on the gangway herself, perhaps two-thirds of the way up. She turned back, her eyes searching for Varinn amidst the remaining stragglers on the gantry.

Then, appearing in the gaping aperture of the roof, where the Zephyrion had left not long before, came a new shape. Smaller, cruder, vicious and purely functional—a K'Tharr landing ship. It dropped into the shipyard like a predator scenting prey, its engines whining with brutal power. It didn't attempt a graceful landing. It hovered low over a section of the gantry near the *Va'hari Sentinel's* berth, doors hissing open, disgorging a flood of K'Tharr warriors directly onto the platform before the ship had even fully secured itself to the docking gantry.

Then, appearing in the gaping aperture of the roof, where the Zephyrion had just vanished, came a new shape. Smaller, cruder, vicious and purely functional—a K'Tharr landing ship. It dropped into the shipyard like a predator scenting prey, its engines whining with brutal power. It didn't attempt a graceful landing. It hovered low over a section of the gantry near the *Va'hari Sentinel's* berth, doors hissing open, disgorging a flood of K'Tharr warriors directly onto the platform before the ship had even fully secured itself to the docking gantry.

Alarms blared throughout the ancient facility. Panic erupted. Humans still on the gantry scattered, some trying desperately to reach the *Va'hari* ramp, others seeking any cover in the vast, open space. K'Tharr energy weapons opened fire, stitching bursts across the excavated stone and steel walls, obviously designed to intimidate and get the Humans into a panic, rather than kill the precious prey.

Varinn was perhaps twenty metres from the *Va'hari* ramp, guiding a slower member of Penaargan's crew, when it happened. The concussive force of the K'Tharr landing ship's grappling-style docking hooks gouging into the gantry, combined with the vibration of its weapons firing, sent a shudder through the gantry structure. One of the big hooks, probably in a calculated move to separate the "herd" from the ship, pulled away a section of the platform between Varinn and the gangway. Then, as a large support strut groaned and gave way, *Va'hari's* gangway buckled and violently separated from the gantry. Dust and debris exploded outwards, creating a sudden, impassable gap.

"Varinn!" Tessara screamed from the now sloping ramp, her voice raw with terror as she saw him cut off. She was on the safe side, just metres from the *Va'hari's* airlock. Penaargan was shouting orders, the last few having to make the perilous jump onto the now slightly separated ramp. He went to a control box inside the ship and began preparing to retract the gangway and seal the ship.

K'Tharr warriors, exhibiting almost human displays of frustration at the escape of the last humans, turned to look for others. They saw only Varinn, now isolated. Their helmeted, glowing eyes fixed inexorably upon him, the most accessible human target. They began to advance towards him, weapons raised.

In that split second, seeing the distance, the buckling gantry, the advancing K'Tharr, Varinn knew he wouldn't make it. He couldn't reach the ramp, couldn't reach Tessara. Survival meant something else now. He reached into the inner pocket of his tunic. His fingers closed around the small, cool cylinder that he had pocketed from the medical pod back in the surface ruins.

He pulled it out, shouted "TESS!" and threw it, hard, towards Tessara. It arced across the gap, a tiny projectile against the backdrop of chaos. Tessara, her hand outstretched, caught it instinctively, just as she was pulled back into the airlock by Penaargan.

She looked at him quizzically. He shouted, "Call the first 'Varinn'". She looked at the precious container that she nearly dropped and realised. It was his genetic material, taken whilst he was in stasis. Any medical pod could use it to make her conceive. "Hide!" Tessara screamed across the din, clutching the capsule. Her face, framed by the opening airlock, was a mask of desperate promise. "Find a way to stay safe! I'll get to Va'hari. I *will* get a ship back! I promise, I *will* find you!"

As Penaargan pulled her back by her tunic, the *Va'hari Sentinel's* airlock door began to hiss closed, inexorably sealing her inside, severing their connection.

Varinn stood alone on the fractured gantry section, the K'Tharr advancing on him, their guttural cries chilling. But just then, across the vast space of the shipyard, Marinallis's voice, amplified by the shipyard's system, cut through the chaos. "Look!"

Screens embedded in the gantry walls and major structural supports flickered to life, activated remotely by Marinallis from the departing Zephyrion. Varinn thought, "*Of course, he still has facility admin privileges.*" The screens displayed a terrifying sight: high-resolution footage of two Fumigator Samplers operating outside the shipyards on the distinctive spaceport landing fields. Impervious to anything the K'Tharr fired at them, their confusingly shaped scintillating metallic forms carved their way through the groups of K'Tharr. First, a core sampler took a tube of flesh and retrieved it into its body, then the rest of the victim's body was either incinerated with a heat beam or sliced up faster than the eye could see and then incinerated seconds later when all the nearby K'Tharr were 'sampled' leaving nothing to suggest they ever existed.

When the advancing K'Tharr saw the footage, their formation faltered. Their commander's orders became sharper, laced with a new urgency. The Samplers were a semi-mythical, terrifying threat that even the K'Tharr knew about. That two samplers were *actually* here, targeting *them* and plainly operating with a power far beyond anything they possessed, had the immediate effect that Marinallis had planned. The K'Tharr would also know that if there were two samplers here (normally, one was terrifying enough for a purely organic race) then in orbit, the situation would be catastrophic. They would need to move now to try to get to their ships in orbit. Their immediate objective—capture Varinn and the *Va'hari*— was suddenly secondary to the existential risk of being Sampled themselves.

Seizing the moment of hesitation, Varinn raised his standard rifle. He didn't charge or attempt heroics. He fired aimed shots from behind debris, using the shipyard's structure for cover, forcing the closest K'Tharr to take cover, buying himself precious seconds. He wasn't trying to defeat them, just to outlast them until they saw the greater threat.

The K'Tharr commander made the decision. Urgent orders rippled through their ranks. The Samplers were a more immediate danger. Varinn wasn't worth the risk. They began to pull back, retreating towards their landing ship, abandoning the capture attempt.

As the K'Tharr scrambled back towards their vessel, making their hasty exit through the open roof, Varinn, thinking they were gone, stepped out from behind cover.

A single K'Tharr warrior, perhaps lagging behind or fuelled by a final burst of rage, turned and fired a quick energy bolt.

Varinn felt a searing agony in his side. He stumbled back, clutching the wound. The bolt had burned deep. He was injured, alone, and the Shipyard was now silent save for the distant whine of the K'Tharr ship departing.

He knew he couldn't stay where he was. He couldn't reach the surface, couldn't reach orbit. He had to hide. He remembered Tessara's promise. Find a way to stay safe. He needed preservation. He needed stasis.

Wounded, every breath a shallow agony, he navigated the silent, vast facility. Guided by emergency lighting and a desperate instinct, he sought out the stasis units. He found them guided by a wrist navscan map Marinallis had shared with him. A row of sleek, metallic sarcophagi in a secured maintenance section. He focused on one in the middle at random. All were working, all waiting.

Painfully, he initiated the activation sequence on the sarcophagus. The lid hissed open. Wounded and weary, he climbed inside. He leaned back against the cold, contoured surface, keying in his final directives via a small internal interface, his voice raspy.

"Designation: Varinn. Objective: Survival. Priority One: Heal burn wound. Protocol: Initiate medical repair sequence." He gasped, the pain sharp. "Priority Two: Initiate long-term stasis. Duration: Indefinite, pending retrieval." His voice weakened. "Priority Three: Denial Protocol. If K'Tharr or Samplers attempt to access this unit or the immediate area. Engage chamber incineration. Prevent capture."

The lid began to seal, his vision blurring. He felt the soft hiss of anaesthesia filling the chamber, a blissful wave of numbness washing over him. He never once doubted Tessara would find him, never doubted the Designer machinery cradling his life. Then, just before sleep took him, came a final, uncanny sensation—tiny, almost imperceptible fibrils extended from the chamber walls, tens of thousands of them, fine as spider silk, penetrating his skin. They immediately began diagnosing his injuries and initiated standard preservation protocols, designed to maintain biological integrity over millennia in the cases of accidents with deep space flight, where rescue was likely to be a prolonged affair. But Designers built things to last on truly breathtaking scales.

The stasis unit powered down to minimal standby. On its exterior surface, the red glyphs indicating activation or warning sequences shifted. They turned from red to green as it quickly worked on his injury. Then, turning to a solid blue after a few minutes, signifying stable preservation and successful stasis. From the outside, the sarcophagus looked like any other functional unit, a sealed container with a black opaque face plate for modesty, holding its occupant in timeless slumber.

Varinn's long night had begun, a desperate gamble placed on a promise made and a potential unseen by his own fading consciousness.

Chapter 40 Part 2.

It received a report from the manufacturing facility that made the samplers. "Everything went quite well. They cleaned up, mostly to standards."

It was glad of the brevity of the report. "Mostly? Anything I specifically need to know? I quite like it here, but I can't hang around forever."

Manufacturer's data packet was almost laconic. "I am afraid you may have to wait for a bit longer. Do you want the report on the main issues?".

It was not particularly in the mood for indulging the evasiveness, "Not sure I like the sound of this, go on, entertain me."

Manufacturer improved the tone a little with, "Well, obviously the samplers cleaned up the speed limit offenders. No issues. They did the DNA reports, which you got. It proves they are a sort of composite species. More of a parasite than a Galactic threat."

It wasn't letting *Manufacturer* get away with it quite that easily: "Nevertheless, they were acting recklessly. Did you find the Sticky Flat Field altering devices?"

Manufacturer answered: "Oh yes. No surprises. Nothing important. Probably too primitive to properly destabilise. But utterly destroyed of course. Along with every last biological entity from that so called 'species' as far as we can tell."

A flicker of what could only be described as saltiness passed into *It's* communication. "Get to the part I don't want to hear. I am getting bored already."

Manufacturer replied in a manner that made *It* think it was almost enjoying this, "Well two ships—if you can call one of them a ship— escaped. The little one was obviously too primitive to be harmless and it even got a prang from the last of the Composite species' ships as it scuttled away. The sampler thought that was funny, and then ate up the Composite Species ship. So that meant the vermin on the planet weren't going anywhere."

It affirmed, "No big deal, but a bit sloppy. The other ship?"

"The higher tech ship might have caused us some problems, but it was clever enough to open up and allowed a scan. No sticky flat field altering tech so we let it go. Too much effort to sample them when we still had a potential forbidden device on the planet?"

It was almost outraged. "Too much effort? Why would samplers think that way?"

"Because I put your personality in them." *Manufacturer* replied with a suspicious hint of insolence.

After a shocked pause, *It* remembered something it read a long time ago and did a quick scan of recent directives and thought, *"Ah, two Aeons ago, there it is. 'Put your own personality on your minions so you can't blame anyone else when you mess up'."* So *It* replied, "OK, fair enough."

Then *It* got to the main point "And did you find the other device?"

Manufacturer was not supposed to have humour, but *It* had to give grudging credit for *Manufacturer's* newly emergent quality as *Manufacturer* replied, "No, sorry. Whatever it is, is gone off all sensors. Probably destroyed or buried deep somewhere and gone dormant. I guess you will have to hang about a bit longer to find out which is the case."

It was fairly sanguine about the news. "There are worse places to be and worse jobs. I will do precisely that."

Manufacturer said, "Yes, *Sir.*" a little too smugly. So *It* signed off with "You may send the samplers into Star. Oh, and duplicate yourself and follow them in. I can't be doing with you developing a personality."

With that, *It* ordered Star to begin a slow progressive reduction in UV light per Aeon to see if this would tempt the forbidden device out. Then it cut the Comms and went to sleep, with one metaphorical eye on the planet below.

Chapter 41. Part 1.

The atmosphere in the designated assembly area was a charged mix of tension and professional stoicism. Rayk Kostin surveyed the teams Julian Voss had tasked him with leading—a composite force drawn from the PCMA Special Space Service, a platoon of special forces veterans from the World's premier special forces regiments that Voss had seen hanging around in Bar One, back in Petropolis, but had no idea they were SSS. There were some Airborne 'Pathfinders' who were the elites of that regiment; finally, there were a handful of surviving Marines who had trickled back through the Metro line and looked remarkably tough considering what they had been through. The Marines and the Airborne stood apart, obviously rivalry showing through and the odd sarcastic comment passing back and forth. But both groups acted more respectfully towards the SSS.

Raith had obviously made sure these prized assets were scattered out in reconnaissance roles and not fed into the Petropolis meat grinder.

Regular troops were well enough armed and had been stationed as defensive troops at strategic points. They stood, armed with their standard issue firearms, their faces grim but ready. These were the "crack troops" of Wahlsanga Depot, those willing and able to fight back.

But today, they were also the guinea pigs.

Julian had made the request clear: he needed personnel with "open minds" to field-test the unconventional weapons being fabricated under extreme pressure. Rayk had selected his best—the Special Forces guys were positively enthused by new kit, 'Shiny Kit Syndrome' Rayk had amusingly called it. The Pathfinders seemed intrigued, not to be outdone by the SSS, but the Marines, fresh from having faced the CAR elites, offered suspicious acceptance.

They began examining the equipment wheeled in directly from the fabrication labs. Bags of bizarre-looking plastic caltrops, their multi-pronged shapes designed for maximum disruption. Crude, 3D-printed launchers, but functional, designed to be carried or braced. Also, the rounds for the launchers. These were soft day-glow orange spheres that looked more like paintballs than military ordinance.

Rayk explained the mission: This wasn't a conventional assault, not even a defensive stand. It was a diversion—hit and fade, expanding the battlefield in the surface ruins, sowing confusion. He explained the weapons, Julian's concepts: the caltrops to stop vehicles and disable foot soldiers, the rounds to incapacitate armour and break up formations. Scepticism flickered across some faces. Sarcastic comments were murmured from the Marines: "Glue bombs and drawing pins, Commander? This is what we've come to?"

Voss replied, "You're the only ones dumb enough to try 'em". To which he got a grim laugh from the assembled cohort.

Voss guided them to a secured testing corridor. Dr. Thorne and Dr. Petrova were waiting, portable terminals in hand, ready to monitor performance. Technicians fussed around a trellis table with a variety of weapons, testing them with meters, fiddling with launch mechanisms at the last minute. Voss was amazed they could pull this together so fast. 'Design To Print' technology had moved on so fast with Artificial Sentience, that even 5 years ago, it would have taken weeks to achieve this.

Voss said in front of his assembled men. "First, the caltrops. The tetrahedral ones work like any other caltrop, but to speed things up, we have a launcher. This uni-launcher will fire all three of the new weapons. As you see, it has no barrel as such, it is an open tube launcher. It is based upon a World War II British PIAT, a spring-launched anti-tank weapon. But it has a spinning electric motor to repeat-reload at a rate of ten items per second." He pointed the ball, the drawing pin and the tetrahedral. He continued, "You can load this magazine that ingeniously packs the standard caltrops. Don't bother filling the magazines yourself. It's beyond your pay grade." To which Voss got a laugh. Then, the technician demonstrated loading the magazine and handed the loaded weapon to the nearest man, a green armoured Marine who took the gun and without waiting for instruction, sprayed the floor in front.

"Range is here," the Technician pointed. The Marine pressed the trigger again and the caltrops sprayed in even distribution even further. Another tech brought forward a humble test cart with an off-road tyre on it. Another had a boot on the end of his foot with a wax foot on it and stood on it with the weight of his body. They did as designed, puncturing old boot soles and deflating a test tire with satisfying effectiveness. Thorne nodded, confirming dispersal patterns with his AS interface.

Another Marine stepped forward, this time to be given a launcher loaded with the acid-tip caltrops—stubby, oversized drawing pins with a hidden bite. He likewise found a spare part of the makeshift test range and dispersed some of the drawing pins. This time, the magic of the designers came through. Each device landed either flat side down perfectly or bounced off the tip and self-righted. Only one failed to land right.

Petrova tutted and instructed the AS to analyse the film of the bounce to see what the problem was. Voss said, "Now, the tip feels soft, but it goes hard on impact, then goes soft again. Like silly putty you may have played with when you were kids. If any of you monsters ever were kids". Again, he got some tension-relieving chuckles. "It then releases something non-lethal but quite nasty."

With that, a technician stepped on the drawing pin caltrop and it went through a boot but deeper. He then got a large screwdriver, and a lot of force was needed to extract the caltrop, as the flat part had adhesive on it and had stuck to the boot. When the pin dropped, he held up the boot and the wax poured out where some acid and irritant had melted the flesh-substitute. With that, even the grim-looking special service troopers winced. Amongst the others, an odd "Ooh" sound was heard. Voss said, "It gets into the bloodstream. Don't step on your own devices". The point seemed to be well taken.

With that, Voss beckoned an SSS guy forward and gave him a uni-launcher with a comically huge circular magazine with the sticky acid rounds in it. A man with a permanent scowl and an improbable handlebar moustache stepped forward, shouldering the launcher. "Voss said, there is no target sight, so we coloured the balls to act like tracer. It is a ballistic thrower and it knows how to fire based on the magazine you load. It's 'airborne proof' to which the Marines cheered.

With that, the volunteer, smiling for what looked to Voss like only the third time in his life, pressed the trigger. The target was a slab of scrap composite armour plating that stood as a target. The launcher fired with a ringing sound as about four or five spheres arced through the air, and three struck the armour, and pancaked and adhered firmly. A faint, wispy smoke rose from the point of impact, and the colour of the sphere shifted.

They waited. Two seconds. Three. Five.

The armour smoked and an acrid smell indicated the armour was being weakened but nothing else happened.

A collective breath was held. The volunteer lowered the launcher with a raised eyebrow as Thorne frowned, tapping his terminal. Petrova leaned forward, examining the target.

"Charge failed to initiate," Thorne announced, his voice flat. "Detonation sequence did not arm on impact."

A wave of disappointment, sharp and immediate, washed over the assembly. The scepticism intensified.

Voss was sure his face went slightly red. For a moment, he realised what he was asking these men to do. To go into combat on the basis of a few sketches made into a weapon in a few hours. Despite the cold stone in the pit of his stomach, he took control of the situation. His voice sharp, directed at Thorne and Petrova, Varinn said, "What failed? Can we compensate? Is it stable?"

Petrova and Thorne rapidly conferred, adjusting parameters on their terminals. "Possible timing mechanism instability on impact," Petrova reported. "We can adjust the initiation sensitivity. Risk of premature detonation increases, but acceptable for a test."

A new round was loaded. The Marine with the moustache, his scowl deepened, raised the launcher again. 'Brrring'. The spheres flew, this time, all of them struck the armour, pancaked and stuck. Smoke rose, colour shifted.

They waited. One second. Two. Three.

Bang, Bang, Bang, Bang on the slab and the one on the floor also... Bang.

The small C_7 charges had detonated in sequence. The rock floor had cratered slightly, but the armour plating, where the acid had been working, didn't just take a dent. It spiderwebbed with cracks, fragments spalling violently inwards from the detonation point. The force, focused by the adherence and the weakened material, was lethal at close range.

A ripple of impressed murmurs went through the teams. Voss clapped the technician on the shoulder and smiled at Petrova and Thorne, who were plainly unused to praise as humble engineers. The soldiers started to crowd round the desk holding example weapons, picking them up and turning them over in their hands. The failure was acknowledged, but the potential was undeniable. These weren't standard weapons, but they could work.

Rayk gathered his teams. The test was over. "Alright," he said, his voice cutting through the residual tension. "You've seen the gear. It's not perfect. But it's what we have. Commander Voss has a plan." He explained the diversionary mission: expand the battlefield, hit and fade using secret exits, sow confusion, buy time until Dawn. He stressed survival, not martyrdom. "Your job is to make them regret spreading thin. Make them chase ghosts."

He looked over the faces of his teams—the SF guys now fully engaged, intrigued by the challenge; the Marines, their grudging acceptance solidified by the deadly effect of the working round; the Airborne looking positively enthused, their past experiences behind them and their misgivings now tempered by purpose. He saw the mix of professionalism, desperation, and that spark of knowing they were about to do something completely unorthodox.

Rayk felt a familiar mix of amusement and apprehension. He remembered that cynical saying about unpredictable troops. Yes. He was about to lead a force armed with drawing pins and exploding paintballs, launched from secret tunnels, to harass a planetary invasion force, but history had its precedents and these were the men to make it happen.

He turned, gesturing towards one of the inconspicuous dark hallway doors, leading deeper into the Depot's secondary levels – towards the secret escarpment tunnels. Every man knew the time for action was here. History was waiting for them to make it.

Rayk's last orders were, "That is your exit point to the surface. Now, last prep, everyone does a test fire and then team leaders get your maps out and divide up the areas of responsibility while we wait for the final equipment tweaks to come off the production line. We move in 2 hours, max. Get to it!"

Chapter 41. Part 2.

The scent of dust and alien earth greeted Rayk Kostin as he emerged from a narrow fissure in the escarpment face, a stark contrast to Wahlsanga City's semi-regulated subterranean climate. Behind him, his diversionary teams filtered out into the pre-dawn darkness. This was Rayk's hand-picked force: the green armour of the Marines and the dark grey and black of PCMA Security. Rayk had used green paint to break up the black of these Police units, since pure black silhouetted troops at night. The Airborne and SSS were sent on a parallel mission through another secret exit. Their objective was to strike from a different vector, hitting the CAR flank at the same time as Rayk's teams to maximise the initial shock and confusion.

Hours before sunrise, the ancient Wahlsanga spaceport stretched before them under a sky thick with unfamiliar stars. These were not crumbling ruins of decay. They had shrugged off eighty millennia with a quiet defiance, affected only by the sun's long-ago betrayal and the passage of time, but still standing, silent and waiting, providing excellent cover and protection. No sound of immediate combat reached them here, the main CAR assault force not yet engaged in this sector.

They moved through the structures of the old spaceport with a quiet professionalism, their boots crunching softly on ancient paving stones or echoing in the hollows of deserted plazas. Rayk led the way, relying on the darkness, the natural concealment offered by walls and the internal layouts of buildings known only through recent, desperate mapping via SF scouts. Their mission: to confuse. To widen the battlefield from the City's secret exits outwards into these preserved streets. They carried standard firearms but also bags heavy with strange plastic shapes and the bulky launchers.

SF scouts, unseen ghosts deeper in the ruins, provided intermittent updates over encrypted comms—confirming CAR patrols, identifying suspected staging areas near the main external surface access tunnel from the spaceport, the primary target the CAR were consolidating on. There were no other PCMA defenders out here now. Voss had got onto the secure Wahlsanga-net to tell any Conventional units that were still putting up resistance in the Gorge and at the bridges and other remote structures to "play possum" and conserve themselves until needed. The Battlefield now belonged to the SF scouts providing eyes, and Rayk's teams were about to launch their stings. The CAR held the surface now, as they strutted around carelessly, satisfied in the hubris of their invincibility.

Rayk gave the signal. Across the perimeter, invisible in the dark, the diversions began. Not as a single coordinated assault, but as sharp, unexpected stings.

A team near a preserved terminal building, moving silently through its shadowed interior, reached a vantage point overlooking an old service road. They scattered plastic caltrops, blending into scattered debris, poised for silent disruption. Further out, near a cluster of intact outbuildings, another team, concealed behind a low wall, used a launcher—crude, wide-mouthed—to rapidly spray a fan of caltrops across an open area between the buildings suspected of housing a CAR staging point.

Moments later, the more significant strikes began. From the upper story of a standing structure, a team fired a volley of sticky acid rounds towards a visible group of CAR infantry consolidating below. The launchers fired. The day-glow orange spheres arced through the pre-dawn air, bizarre projectiles against the dark sky acting like slow ballistic machine gun tracer, but silent. They struck armour, equipment, the side of a light vehicle—pancaking out, adhering firmly. A faint, acrid smoke rose from the points of impact.

Within seconds, the timed charges detonated. Explosions ripped through armour, sounds sharp and distinct, muffled slightly by distance and stone, followed by shouts and cries of pain muffled through armour, but audible even so. Armour buckled and shattered, fragments spalling violently inwards. Soldiers went down, incapacitated, a terrifying, unseen enemy cutting them apart.

Elsewhere, moving through a low drainage tunnel exit concealed by debris near a preserved plaza, another team emerged just long enough to fire sticky acid rounds into the flank of a CAR patrol moving through the open area, then vanished back into the structures or towards their secret exit points. From an emergency balcony high on the escarpment face overlooking a staging area, a Pathfinder team launched rounds down onto CAR light vehicles parked below.

Lance Corporal Nathan Wilson, a Pathfinder, crouched in the ruins, his brother Ben's death in yesterday's assault on Petropolis's Central Spire burning in his mind. He spotted a CAR paratrooper sprinting to a city cart's driver seat. As the man paused to start the vehicle, Nathan seized the moment, unleashing a concentrated burst of sticky orange globules.

The globules splattered across the paratrooper's helmet, shoulders, and chest. He clawed at one, peeling it off onto his glove, unaware it was a death sentence. The globule ate through the glove, then detonated, blowing his hand apart. His screams barely began before the five other sticky charges exploded in rapid succession. The paratrooper collapsed out of the cart, a distorted heap, blood leaking copiously from holes in his ruined armour.

He managed to pull the first one off and looked at it, stuck to his glove, but it was slowly eating through it. Then, as it exploded, his hand was blown off with the force of the explosion. His screams did not last long as five other sticky pancakes went off, where they stuck to his helmet and shoulders. The man fell out of the cart in a distorted heap, his arms, head and shoulders leaking copious amounts of blood from the holes in the armour.

The CAR response was immediate and exactly what Julian had planned for. Commotion erupted: shouts and wild energy weapon fire aimed at empty shadows, hoping to find the source of the attack. But the PCMA teams were already gone, melting back into the labyrinthine service ways and structural interiors of the ancient spaceport buildings to disappear. All that happened was they fell afoul of the various types of caltrops. The ones on foot were the worst, not killed but in obvious terrible pain, rolling on the floor, clutching their feet. They were unable to get their boots off. Their comrades were unable to help them, wary of the dismembered soldiers around them. The sticky Acid rounds were a terror weapon. For now, they worked their terror, but inside the CAR troops, each of them began to kindle a simmering anger. There would be bad blood from now on. No quarter given.

Reports filtered back to Rayk via his teams' comms, and from the SF scouts: "Contact... hits registered... enemy scattering to sweep ruins... estimate fifty CAR units diverted..." The local CAR commander's voice, often intercepted on open channels, became sharper, laced with confusion and frustration. His tactical picture, monitored by Rayk's comms staff at the Wahlsanga City Command Post and displayed for Julian and others, showed his units scattering across the wider surface area, responding to multiple, unlocated threats. The concentrated assault force aimed at the spaceport entrance was becoming fragmented and delayed.

Back in underground Wahlsanga City, Julian, along with Command Post staff, monitored the situation. Renata and Alinta were not here; they were elsewhere in the City, working intently on language decoding. Thorne and Petrova were likewise in the City's fabrication labs, machining and perfecting the unconventional weapons, not observing displays. The tactical display showed Rayk's teams as small, mobile markers darting through the static red icons of the increasingly confused CAR sweep across the surface. Julian watched grimly, seeing his strategic gamble succeed in sowing confusion and drawing the threat away from Wahlsanga's main entrances. So far, so good, but without the people he had known for such a short time, he felt remarkably alone in the command centre.

There was a sudden, tense silence on one of the comm channels. A single marker, representing one of Rayk's diversion teams operating near the suspected CAR staging area, stopped moving on the tactical display. Seconds stretched into a tense minute. In the Command Post, staff leaned forward, questioning glances exchanged.

Then, the comm channel crackled back to life. A strained but clear voice reported in. "Contact lost for approximately forty seconds, Commander. Ambush attempt averted. Exfiltrating to secondary hide. One minor casualty." A collective breath of relief was exhaled. The marker resumed its movement. The close call was a stark reminder of the constant danger to Rayk's people. Voss realised he hadn't been breathing for that time. He remembered the memoirs he had read of all the famous battlefield commanders of history. You can't fight their platoon-level battles for them, he told himself. He vowed internally to delegate and mentally prepare himself for the losses when they inevitably started happening.

Rayk's teams continued their hit-and-run tactics, utilising fully the remaining time before sunrise. They were ghosts, striking unexpectedly, using their unconventional weapons to disable and disrupt, preventing the CAR from completing their methodical sweep and consolidating for an underground push. They expanded the battlefield, making the CAR commander chase shadows across kilometres of preserved ancient structures within the escarpment. The SF scouts provided vital eyes, guiding them to new targets and away from overwhelming CAR concentrations.

The cover of darkness began to fade. The first pale light of Dawn illuminated the landscape. With the fading light, so faded the sounds of intermittent combat. The crackle of energy weapons, the sharper crack of kinetic rifles, the distant sound of a launcher firing, the delayed reports of detonations. All these sounds echoed less and less across the expanded battlefield. The tactical display in the Wahlsanga City Command Post confirmed the CAR forces were still spread out, engaged in sweeping and pacification operations on the surface.

Voss thought, They are delayed. They are confused. They aren't yet staged for a direct assault on our main city entrances. Julian's intuitions, based upon nothing but historians' memoirs, had succeeded in forcing the CAR commander to commit to a time-consuming surface campaign. This would delay the immediate, concentrated push towards the underground City, buying them days.

The surface was not yet theirs, but crucially, it no longer belonged to the confused and scattered enemy either.

Chapter 42.

The command post, established in the shell of what had been a PCMA administrative office, was an island of cold order amidst the chaos. Outside, the first light of dawn was beginning to paint the violet sky in shades of bruised orange, but here, the only light came from the shimmering tactical holo-map. General Ganbaatar stood before it, his expression a mask of placid concentration. The swarm of red icons representing his forces was no longer a cohesive spearhead, but a scattered, reactive mess, drawn out across kilometres of the ancient spaceport ruins.

His initial, contemptuous assessment of the PCMA's defiance had been wrong. This was not the flailing of a cornered animal. This was a plan. Annoyance, a petty emotion he despised, gave way to a grudging, professional respect. They were using the geography, their knowledge of it, to bleed his forces, to delay the inevitable. The attack on Petropolis was stalling; his main force bogged down dealing with the remnants of Rostova's command, while this secondary front was proving far more irritating than anticipated.

He glanced at the orbital display, a secondary frustration. The grim stand-off aloft continued with little chance of reinforcement. His surviving ships, damaged by the initial nuclear surprise and the orbital assault, lacked the firepower to breach the remaining defences.

It was now a case of who ran out of food and ammunition first. His ships, or the defences in Orbit. The latter, he suspected, had very few personnel onboard now and could probably last quite a while.

A junior officer at a side console interrupted his reverie. "General, we have a priority flag from a forward scout team, Section Gamma. They are a unit in contact with PCMA forces on the surface near the old terminal buildings."

Ganbaatar turned to the officer. "Yes. Report."

The officer's face was tight with confusion. "Sir, you were asked to be notified if evidence of one of their elite commanders surfaced. The scout team leader describes the PCMA unit's commander as demonstrating anomalous combat abilities. Extreme speed, tactical precognition. He neutralised three of our men before they could react. The team leader assesses that the individual is heavily augmented, beyond standard PCMA special forces parameters."

Ganbaatar listened, his expression unchanging, but a new variable clicked into place in his mind. He had read the intelligence dossiers on the PCMA command structure. There was one individual whose profile was heavily redacted but hinted at experimental cybernetics: a security chief named Kostin.

"One man?" Ganbaatar asks, his voice dangerously quiet.

"Yes, General. The report is emphatic. One man was the primary factor in the engagement."

Ganbaatar turned back to the holo-map, a new piece of the puzzle slotting into place. This wasn't just a random defence. It was being led by a high-value, uniquely capable asset. This wasn't just a nest he was hunting; it was a viper's nest with a very dangerous snake guarding it. He pulled out what looked like a television remote control that he had been given on his final mission briefing and turned it over thoughtfully in his hands. "Get me Volkov, now".

Colonel Volkov's face appeared on a secondary display, the background showing the captured Northern Access Tunnel. His usual bluster was absent, replaced by a strained professionalism. "General. We have consolidated our position at the bulkhead, but the PCMA resistance in the city proper is fiercer than projected. We're taking unacceptable casualties trying to dislodge them from the Central Spire."

"The Spire is a secondary objective for now, Colonel," Ganbaatar stated, his voice level. He traced a line on the holo-map, isolating the scattered skirmishes on the surface. "Their troops are disappearing somewhere, Colonel," Ganbaatar stated, his display highlighting the Wahlsanga main entrance as he transmitted the coordinates. "They are exfiltrating. As for their destination, the answer is obvious. This location harbours the head of the snake. The resistance in the city is a holding action. This," he gestured to the chaotic surface battle, "is a screen. They are drawing our forces out, making us chase ghosts in these ruins. You have your orders, and I am sending you something that you may find useful."

He did not wait for Volkov's answer as he thought, *I won't give him the dignity of implied choice in his orders.* And with that, he cut the link and turned his attention to the display. He zoomed the display out, encompassing the entire Wahlsanga escarpment. His logic was cold and clear. The PCMA had established a hidden, secondary base of operations. The diversions were designed to buy it time. The strategy was sound, but it had a fatal flaw: it relied on him continuing to play their game.

"All units on the surface," Ganbaatar's voice cut through the command channel, sharp and decisive. "Cease sweep-and-clear operations immediately. Disengage from any minor contacts. I want a full tactical withdrawal to the primary staging area. Re-form your platoons, re-establish command integrity. The time for chasing shadows is over."

A wave of confirmations rippled through the comm net. On the map, the scattered red icons began to move, pulling back from the deeper ruins, coalescing into larger, more formidable blocks. The chaotic skirmish map was clarifying, resolving into a new, terrifying picture.

Ganbaatar paused. *Where are they hiding? And what? The planet was riddled with empty cities and underground lairs.* "Colonel Volkov, I am re-tasking the Azure Dragon airborne elements. Their new objective is a systematic, top-down search of this entire sector. I want every structure cleared, every potential tunnel entrance mapped and probed. The rest of the surface force will form a hard perimeter, a cordon, and will then begin a methodical, inward push. There will be no more diversions. We are no longer sweeping for pockets of resistance. We are hunting for their nest."

He looked at the map, at the icons of his forces reorienting into a focused, menacing spear. They were no longer reacting. They were now the single, overwhelming threat, aimed directly at the heart of the enemy's last hope.

But after the bravado settled, his excellent instincts that kept him safe through the cut-throat politics of the CAR nagged at him. *I hate unknowns. They lead to improvisation. And improvisation is the province of the desperate, not the victorious.*

Chapter 43. Part 1.

The main tunnel entrance to the Wahlsanga Metro from Sikkara had become the border between a battle lost and a siege begun. The last of the Police teams and the Marines tasked with mining the tunnel filtered back through the makeshift checkpoint, their armour scarred, their faces etched with the grim exhaustion of evacuating as many people from Petropolis as they could under the noses of the CAR troops, obsessed with taking the spire and pacifying the city. They had succeeded, buying precious time, but the cost was written in their weary movements. The evacuation was over; the wait for the inevitable assault was about to begin.

Rayk Kostin stood just inside the threshold, overseeing the final placement of the defensive measures. His tone was clipped, his commands precise, but the strain was evident in the tight line of his jaw. He was a security professional preparing for an overwhelming force, a man fortifying a tomb.

Julian Voss, feeling the full, crushing weight of his unwanted authority, convened a brief, critical meeting with Rayk, Renata, and Alinta amidst the controlled chaos. The air carried the 'post-thunderstorm' ozone smell from power conduits and cold, ancient dust.

"What's the situation?" Julian began, his question self-consciously more civilian than Military, still adjusting to the mantle of unwanted command.

Rayk gestured back towards the tunnel. "The dispositions are complete. We have three layers of C7 charges hidden behind lights and primary support struts, starting one hundred metres in. They are networked for simultaneous remote detonation." He met Julian's gaze, his own expression unreadable. "The plan is simple, Commander. Commander Rostova has ordered the tunnel to be mined. So, we will use the tunnel as a kill box. We let their lead assault elements enter, draw them in as deep as we can, and then we trap them by collapsing both ends. Some will inevitably be buried, but the rest will have to wait for a rescue that will probably never come. It's a brutal, conventional defence. But it is our best one."

Voss said, "This means the diversion is over. They will know this is where we are truly protecting. If you control the operation to defend the tunnel, what will happen on the surface?"

Renata said, "The men on the surface are very experienced. The new weapons are working well and they are going to form an attack from behind when the attack on the main city entrance inevitably begins. They won't need me for that. The men on the main entrance are also well briefed and have some experienced troops backing up the Police units. We are in reasonable shape, provided we defend the rail tunnel."

Julian listened, his mind sifting through historical parallels, through sieges lost and fortresses fallen. He nodded slowly. "A sound plan, Detective. But it is a last stand. And we must consider the possibility that it fails." He looked from Rayk's grim face to the scientists. "If that happens, what is our legacy? What survives this place? What survives us?"

Renata and Alinta exchanged a look, understanding his implication immediately.

"I propose a Legacy Protocol," Julian continued, the historian in him surfacing through the reluctant commander. "While your teams fortify this entrance, the science team's priority must be to secure the knowledge we have already gained. We catalogue everything we can. That means the train technology, the statue, the glyph archives and the contents of those crates. Then we prepare the data for a hardened, high-priority data burst. We will aim it at the last known coordinates for PCMA command. If we fall, what we have learned here must not."

The logic was bleak but undeniable. Yet it led to a more immediate, tactical problem. "Our greatest asset, and our greatest unknown," Julian said, his gaze sweeping towards the cavern where the six colossal trains stood dormant, as if hiding their intent, "is in this Depot. We cannot commit to a purely passive defence without knowing what is inside those machines. Are they a weapon? A power source? An escape route? We cannot afford to leave that resource untapped. Accessing those trains is now a strategic necessity."

Chapter 43. Part 2.

The decision lent a new, desperate urgency to their work. With Rayk now tasked with the tunnel defence, the rest of the management team returned to the sixth train, its sealed door and inert interface an infuriatingly passive obstacle. Another attempt with the induction power pack yielded the same result: a flicker of recognition, but a firm, absolute denial of access.

"It requires a more sophisticated handshake," Renata concluded, studying the readouts on her datapad. "Something with a higher-level authorisation protocol. A master key."

All eyes turned towards the new, heavy-duty vault set into the lobby wall. Inside rested the Echo Key.

"I want to try again first," Alinta said, making her claim firmly but apprehensively.

"Why?" Voss asked, looking directly at her, not with suspicion, but with genuine curiosity.

"I felt something before, like it was testing me or trying to read or communicate with me. Not unfriendly or threatening. Just... I can't explain, but it wanted something, it was like a memory of an unfulfilled obligation, even an opportunity missed. I tried to explain to Renata but it is just so damned..."

"Alien?" "Strange," Voss and Renata finished for her in unison. They looked at each other with a wry laugh shared between them.

Julian took a moment, then nodded his assent. Alinta, looking slightly unnerved but resolute, walked to the vault. With Voss's authorisation, the heavy door slid open. She reached inside and lifted the shielded case. As her fingers touched the handle, she felt it again—not the jarring static from before, but a faint, almost subliminal warmth, a vague sense of encouragement that resonated from the object. She looked at it for a long moment, then quietly, almost to herself, whispered, "What are you?" The Key remained silent.

She carried it back to the sixth train and handed the case to Voss. "It's not ready. I think you should try it after all". The air grew thick with tension. This felt like a pivotal moment.

Voss seemed confused at the sudden change of heart but readily accepted the key. "The trigger word you used on the surface was a general distress call," Renata reminded him. "Try something more specific to this context."

Voss took a deep breath, holding the case containing the Key near the train's interface panel. His own voice pre-echoing, "Emergency," he stated, his voice clear and firm. "Override. Access."

The train remained silent. The panel did not light up. But for Voss, the world dissolved. It was not a vision, but a memory, fully formed and utterly real. He was standing, not in the Depot, but in a brightly lit, sterile room. In his hands was a datapad, its screen glowing. He was reading, and he understood every word. It was a children's book, from his school days, when he first learned to read. 'Janet and John go down to the well'. But the English was not English. He was reading glyphs. The text, he realised with a jolt that tore through the false memory, was making perfect sense, English in Architect script.

The sensation lasted only seconds, but it felt like an eternity. Woven into the dissolving memory was a final, undeniable instruction: an image of himself, standing by the train, handing the case to Alinta. He stumbled back, the memory evaporating, leaving a profound sense of disorientation in its wake. The Echo Key in its case felt suddenly heavy, inert. The lesson was over, leaving none of the ecstatic mental feelings he had felt when handling the key before.

"What happened?" Renata asked, her voice sharp with concern.

"It... showed me something," Voss managed, his mind reeling. "Their glyphs are in English. But it's fading, I have to write down what I can, quickly, before it completely goes." He shook his head, pushing the case into Alinta's hands. "Take it—I think this already happened".

Baffled and concerned, Alinta took the case. The moment her fingers closed around it, the artefact, now active in a way it had not been for her before, triggered a new protocol. There was no warmth this time. It was a voice. A clear, calm, human voice that spoke not to her ears, but directly into the centre of her mind.

"Are you a Newcomer?"

Alinta gasped, staggering back a step, her eyes wide with shock. Before she could think properly, she gave a half-surprised laugh and experienced the phenomenon of pre-echo as she heard herself say, before she actually said: "I guess you could say that".

It was followed by a flood of visual information. It was a memory of something that never happened. She remembered looking at a schematic, cool and precise. It was a map of a section of the Depot they had not known existed, labelled in Architect glyphs: Designer Level Security Access Only. Military Ship Construction Yard. The schematic highlighted a specific route, leading down a service tunnel to a single, innocuous-looking set of blast doors. The access glyph on the doors pulsed, annotated with a unique signature she instinctively knew was now keyed to her own.

The vision faded, leaving her breathless. She looked at the others, her face pale. "It spoke to me," she whispered, her voice trembling. "It asked me if I was a Newcomer. And then. Well, it showed me a door."

Chapter 44.

It felt a tickle in the back of its programming. Not a pleasant sensation, but the one it knew may well surface again. In fact, it was its whole justification for hanging around this rather unimportant star, so satisfyingly far away from more busy and important regions of the Galaxy.

Nevertheless, *It* was rather phlegmatic about the matter. Every black hole and a bright ring around it, so to speak. *It* thought *well, they were too stupid to take the hint. I offered the way forward.*

With that, *It* ordered Star to elevate its UV a little. Not too much, just enough to hurt. *It* wasn't sure it wanted the thing that was disturbing the sticky flat field to be definitively destroyed. That would mean *It* would have to leave and *It* liked it here. Or at least, *It* liked the lack of activity compared to some places it had been in its incredibly long existence. *It* was confident the vermin below lacked the intelligence to communicate and actually hand the troublesome device over.

But if the disturbances in the field continued for much longer, then *It* would have to sample them. If that happened, then *It* really would end it this time.

With that satisfying thought about potential action, mercifully delayed for now, *It* went back to sleep, confident that this time the monkeys down below would finally get the hint and stop using the thing, or preferably destroy it themselves and just not say anything. *Yes, this is turning out to be the perfect cushy gig, if the monkeys just don't spoil it.*

Chapter 45. Part 1.

The inner threshold of the Petropolis-Wahlsanga rail tunnel was a makeshift hemispherical bastion of overturned equipment and hastily welded plates that formed the final defensive line should the mouth of the tunnel be forced by the CAR. Behind them, Sergeant De-Silva's Marines and PCMA security staff waited, their weapons trained on the dark, cavernous maw of the tunnel.

Further inside, concealed behind support struts and in maintenance alcoves and service shafts, Rayk and two of his SSS men acting as 'shield men' lay in wait, silent predators in a concrete jungle. The air was thick with the acrid, chemical scent of gunpowder from conventional rounds. As the last straggling troops and evacuees from Sikkara came out of the darkness of the tunnel and filed past Rayk, the sounds of combat from further inside the tunnel had suspiciously ceased.

The Last of the Airborne men were "pepper potting" in good form, swapping positions whilst retreating and covering each other with true professionalism. Rayk signalled to the last man. "Are they coming?" he asked. The man said, "I think so, Sir, there has been no contact for about half an hour, but we can hear them. Rayk nodded and gestured for the man to move out of the Tunnel towards where De-Silva's men were waiting.

Rayk didn't have to wait long. He saw something curious. White-armoured airborne and green-armoured marine figures were walking wearily and reluctantly forward. The two types of troops never mingled like that; the rivalry was too great. Rayk raised his rifle, ran to the centre of the tunnel and kneeled, raising his weapon to aim at the leading man. Just as he noticed that the Marine had no weapon, muzzle flashes and the sound of multiple shots came from behind the men. The leading man dropped. All the men in the front followed his fate.

The men behind them were wearing white, but they had the distinctive shape of a CAR Paratrooper. Of course, it was the only way to force the tunnel. They used human shields. Rayk, furious, opened fire, darting from side to side of the tunnel, predicting the shots of the CAR troops with his Empathic Combat Simulator program. As the system saw the movements of the attackers through Rayk's visual cortex, it was able to model and predict where they were likely to aim, making Rayk feel almost as "one" with his attackers.

It was wildly effective in the confined space of the tunnel. Rayk did not intend to let the situation go to waste. Rayk pointed to the two SSS slightly behind him and shouted, "You men, grab two casualties now." Rayk's covering fire was devastating as he picked off man after man. Any CAR trooper that Rayk could see, his AS could predict. His supporting 'shield men' shouldered their weapons and obeyed orders. Now used to seeing Rayk in action from their exploits on the surface, they knew they had a window to get at least two of the unfortunate men to a medical station and withdraw.

Not so much the CAR, though. Anyone who stepped forward died. It did not take long for them to realise their best chance of survival was to take cover. As a result, return fire ceased. Rayk saw his moment. The CAR truly cowed; he saw one man still moving on the floor. This one had a chance. He expended the last of his rounds and threw his rifle to the floor. With incredible speed and strength, he grabbed the armour of the fallen human shield and started dragging him back to the light of the Wahlsanga tunnel entrance.

Amidst the chaos as the threat from Rayk subsided, a single figure of authority emerged from the CAR ranks. His armour bore the ornate epaulettes of a Colonel. He ignored the lesser soldiers, his eyes scanning the PCMA line, hunting for the commander. He saw Rayk, directing the fire, and raised a small, dark device that looked like a TV remote control. A thin beam of shimmering, invisible energy lanced across the tunnel and struck Rayk squarely in the centre of his back.

There was no sound, no impact. But for Rayk, the world vanished into a white-hot agony of screaming static. His limbs locked, his muscles spasming as the override command cascaded through his nervous system. He collapsed, a marionette with its strings cut, the chillingly familiar paralysis seizing him completely. Volkov shouted to two CAR paratroopers busy keeping their heads down, "Get that man, NOW!" As Volkov ducked back behind cover, Sergeant De-Silva had moved forward to the mouth of the tunnel to coordinate the casualty evacuation. He was able to see the moment that his commander fell.

Firing rapidly, De-Silva ran forward. "Blow the charges the moment I come back!" he roared, his voice thick with fury and grief. He put one of his huge hands on Rayk's armour harness and dragged him back from the threshold, even as his men laid down a final, desperate volley of covering fire.

It was enough to deter the CAR from moving any further forward. As he passed a small red pennant planted in the ground, two men came forward and helped drag Rayk back to the mouth of the tunnel. Just before they exited, A series of deep, resonant thuds echoed from deep within the tunnel as the primary C7 charges detonated. The very rock of the Depot shuddered. As the four PCMA men exited into the Metro Station, the tunnel roof groaned, then collapsed inward in a deafening, grinding avalanche of rock and shattered composite, burying forever the CAR vanguard, including the unfortunate but brave Colonel Volkov.

The Depot was sealed with rock and blood.

Chapter 45. Part 2.

The tremor from the tunnel collapse reached the Command Post as a low, powerful shudder that sent dust motes dancing in the faint light of the holo-map. Voss, Renata, and Alinta stood frozen, their eyes fixed on the tactical display where a massive section of the tunnel schematic had turned a stark, warning red. A moment of grim, uncertain silence descended. They had fended off instant defeat, but the severity of the cost to the enemy was as yet unknown. They would now undoubtedly concentrate their efforts on the surface.

The silence was broken by a priority video link request. Sergeant De-Silva's face appeared on the main screen, smoke-stained and etched with a frantic grief. "The tunnel is sealed, Commander. We got them. The CAR vanguard is eliminated, including a high-ranking officer." His voice cracked, "But Commander Kostin is down. He was hit by some kind of energy weapon just before the blast. We have him, but sir, it's bad. He appears to be paralysed."

Julian's face was a grim mask, the brief taste of victory turning to ash. He took a steadying breath, pushing down the immediate, emotional response. He was the commander. He had to think tactically. Rayk was not just his most valuable combat soldier; he was his finest field commander and strategist. "Bring him to the primary diagnostics lab next to the Command Post. Now," he ordered, his voice sharp with a new, cold authority. He turned to his science team. "Dr Petrova, Dr Thorne, I need you in that lab to assist the Surgeons. Alinta, Renata, you're with me. We need to understand what they used on him."

They met the medical team as they wheeled the stretcher into the sterile white lab. Rayk was conscious, his eyes wide, tracking their movements from within a body that was utterly still.

The triage medic made the call for the emergency surgeon. While he was on the way, Petrova and Thorne used the short delay to get to work on Rayk immediately, their scanners casting webs of analytical light over Rayk's form, their findings appearing on the large screen above the table.

"There appears to be significant augmentation to his systems, " Petrova said to Voss. "While I have heard of this as a theoretical advancement upon chips for Paraplegics, I didn't know we were this far along".

Voss was at a loss as the Surgeon, Mr. Winstanley, arrived in quick order. Winstanley said, "Augmented, how? Let me get his records". He proceeded to order Petrova, Thorne, and Voss out of the way. As he no longer had access to the Hospital records in Sikarra, Winstanley pressed his qWatch onto Rayk's qWatch, which in turn sent a full medical history into the Surgeon's qWatch.

The medic began reporting the vital signs: "Blood pressure normal, no bleeding, Blood type A+, Heart rate normal, ECG trace normal. Neurological readings are scrambled. That makes no sense. He seems to be conscious but not responding."

As the medic reported his findings to the surgeon, Winstanley read Rayk's medical records. As he did so, a stream of data poured in from Rayk's qWatch to Winstanley's qWatch, his eyes getting wider and wider as the medical record and the live feed started to make a clear picture for the Surgeon.

"You are quite right," Winstanley declared. "It is one of the latest spinal reconnection chips. But with a twist. There are significant interfaces and enhancements. This was theoretical when I graduated from the Army." He looked apologetically at Voss, recognising him as the authority now. "I had no idea anybody actually tried it. This is totally new to me. Did anyone here know about it?".

Renata looked slightly guilty and said, "Well, I had some idea. An implant is visible at the base of his spine, but that's all I know."

Voss felt the familiar cold stone in his chest. *How does she know that? Closer than she said, perhaps? This is not the time, Voss! Get back on track.* He redirected his train of thought by interrupting. "Doctor, er, *Mister W*instanley," he said, after reading the name tag on the Surgeon's scrubs. "Can we diagnose this? I have two excellent engineers here who could help if the problem is electrical."

Winstanley shook his head, his focus entirely on the cascade of data scrolling across his qWatch. "This is beyond a simple electrical fault, Commander. There seems to have been something like an Electro Magnetic Pulse attack, modulated with some sort of virus sent through a gap in his systems. It left his system in some sort of boot mode. There is no physical trauma, no thermal damage, but his entire nervous system below the C7 vertebrae is receiving a null command signal. And above the implant, his brain is being suppressed with a constant noise signal. It must be excruciating for him. It is a nasty, software-level disconnect. It is almost elegant".

He looked up from his qWatch, his professional curiosity warring with a clear sense of gravity. "There is an AS, which should still be functioning. The back door is mentioned in his records as being for external access in an emergency. It says the AS is hardened and should be immune to attack. But why would the designers of the system be leaving a possibility of attack in there?".

Voss said, "More to the point, how did the CAR get to know about it? A leak, I suppose. They knew far too much for my liking. Anyway, is there any way to get to talk to his onboard AS?".

Mr. Winstanley reluctantly looked at the two engineers. "Can you set up a link to the AS through his qWatch? The records say it should be possible, but I am more of a trauma surgeon, not a neurosurgeon".

Thorne immediately hooked his datapad up to Raith's qWatch and Petrova began making queries through her cross-linked Data Pad. "We have a basic connection" she declared. As the engineers and the surgeon debated the esoteric nature of the attack, Julian moved to Rayk's side, ignoring the technical analysis. The man on the table was not an engineering problem; he was his security chief. He pressed the transmit button on Rayk's qWatch to activate the microphone and said, "Rayk," his voice low. "Can you hear me? Can your systems communicate?"

The main diagnostic monitor beside the bed, hitherto displaying medical data, flickered. A simple, text-only interface opened, overriding the medical display. The words that appeared were precise, their calmness a stark contrast to the tension in the room.

Yes, Commander Voss. He can hear you. Verbal communication is currently impossible. Detective Rayk is in some pain and distress at the moment.

Julian's gaze remained fixed on Rayk's eyes as he winced in empathy at that unwelcome news. "Can you let him know we are with him and we are working on it?"

Yes, Commander Voss. He is enduring.

Voss looked up and addressed the screen. "What happened to him?"

A targeted energy weapon was utilised, the text scrolled. It exploited a deprecated, Level-Zero fail-safe protocol to initiate a system-wide neural lockdown.

"A fail-safe?" Winstanley murmured, his eyes wide. "Installed by whom?"

The AS's reply was a revelation that drew a collective, sharp intake of breath from everyone in the room. The protocol is not a standard PCMA installation. The encryption signature requires a unique administrative key. A key I have encountered once before. It is attributed to and therefore, likely stolen from the late Director Desmond Raith.

The name hung in the air, cold and heavy. A leash. A ghost in the machine left by their former commander.

What is his prognosis? Julian asked, his voice now barely a whisper. Can you fix him?

There was a noticeable pause, a fractional delay in the AS's response that felt more like consideration than processing lag.

The weapon was a crude instrument. The energy surge has caused significant trauma to the primary interface. A simple reboot is inadvisable. Recovery is complicated. However, I had previously advised that he undergo the procedure again so that I could monitor how it was done and formulate a defence. Another pause, then a new line of text, a cold, clinical recommendation. On this occasion, a heavy burst of energy was included after the signal was received. This complicates things. I am recommending an anaesthetic applied externally, then a medically-supported stasis which I can induce. It will prevent further system degradation and allow me to conduct uninterrupted diagnostics. However, I need permission from the base commander.

Voss said, "Acknowledged, but you didn't answer. To be specific, what are the chances you can cure him?"

The probability of restoring full functionality is suboptimal, but it is not zero by any means.

Julian looked down at Rayk, at the flicker of acceptance, of exhausted trust, in his trapped eyes. He saw Rayk give a slow, deliberate blink. The only command he had left to give. He looked at Winstanley, who said, "We are out of options. I suggest you leave it to the AS".

"Do it," Julian ordered. He watched as the stasis field of the diagnostic table shimmered to life, its cool blue light enveloping Rayk's still form. They had won the battle for the tunnel. They had sealed their fortress. But the price had been their finest soldier, who escaped being entombed in rock, only to be entombed in his own living body.

Julian Voss now understood the true, lonely weight of command.

Chapter 46. Part 1.

The diagnostics lab felt like a tomb. Julian Voss stood over the still, stasis-shrouded form of Rayk Kostin, the cool blue light of the field casting an unnatural pallor on the detective's face. The strategic victory in the tunnel felt like a distant, hollow echo. They had lost their shield.

A new, cold certainty settled in Julian's mind. There was no one else to whom he could delegate. The historian who had come to Sikarra to study a dead civilisation was now gone, replaced by the commander who had to prevent his own from becoming one. He turned from the lab, the weight of that reality a physical pressure on his shoulders.

He found Renata and Alinta waiting just outside, their faces a mixture of concern and grim resolve.

"Oh, Julian, are you sure about this?" Renata began, her voice low. "You are here to do the science, not to fight a war".

I haven't stopped being who I am," Julian said, voice low. "But right now, that part of me has to wait. Rayk bought us time, and I need to use it well. I'll take command of the entrance defence myself."

He looked at her, softer now. "You and Alinta, your work still matters. Our work. Find the door. Whatever is behind it is more important than the result of the fight on the surface. I will buy us time. You buy us the legacy."

Renata saw the finality in his eyes and simply nodded, the unspoken argument dying on her lips. But she couldn't resist one last little dig. "At least you didn't ask us to fight on the beaches, Mr. Churchill." With that, she placed her hand behind his neck and kissed him firmly, between his mouth and cheek. "I'll keep you informed". She looked at Alinta, who had a little more colour in her cheeks and a smirk on her face as the two of them gathered their gear and walked away, leaving Julian in a state of warm semi-shock.

Julian turned around, knowing the moment had gone. He proceeded upstairs to the production facilities on the Mezzanine floor and adjoining cavern above the Metro station. The cavernous space was a hive of disciplined activity. It was here that Julian met with the engineering leads, Petrova and Thorne.

"The new munitions are ready, Commander," Thorne reported, gesturing to several heavy-duty crates. He opened one, revealing rows of small, autonomous drones, their insect-like carapaces gleaming under the lights. Underneath them, each one had a sticky acid ball. This time painted stealth grey, not orange. "We have linked their targeting systems to the perimeter sensors. The AS has been given a ninety-eight per cent confidence model for identifying CAR helmet profiles".

Petrova pointed to another crate, filled with what looked like flat, sand-coloured discs. "The sticky-acid mines have been refined. They become liquid at a minimum pressure of twenty kilos, preventing accidental adhesion and detonation by handlers or by debris. The half-second fuse is stable. They are ready for deployment".

"Good," Julian said. "I want them seeded across every likely avenue of approach outside the main doors. Create a kill-zone fifty metres deep. De-Silva, your men will provide cover for the deployment team".

The Sergeant nodded, already relaying the orders.

Julian assembled the team for the critical second mission. He approached the personnel Raith had hand-picked from Sikarra: two junior engineers, a brilliant physicist, and an electrical specialist. Raith's cunning choice of these overlooked talents, kept junior by CAR's political pressure on the PCMA to curb their cavalier brilliance, ensured a team of creative minds ready to outmanoeuvre their enemies.

Voss, on the other hand, had every confidence in these young minds. Their faces came alight with a nervous energy as soon they were chosen for the mission. Stood with them were a civil engineer, a quiet, older man whose speciality was structural integrity, and two PCMA police-paramilitaries. The paramilitaries were ex-Marines, clad in the black armour of the depot's security force, their presence a stark reminder of the mission's danger.

He said, "Doctors O'Neil and Volkova are waiting for you in the Depot. Your priority is to load up two city cars with all necessary equipment and locate a door. From there, you are to investigate whatever is behind it and go wherever it leads. You engineers will assist and facilitate the scientific work wherever required and overcome any obstacles. Power, structural, or otherwise. Security will keep you safe." He looked from the scientists to the soldiers. "Go. Find us a miracle".

With a final, shared look of understanding, with consummate professionalism, they turned and started packing the two nearest electrical city cars parked on the platforms. Julian was left with his own task. He walked upstairs and took another city buggy on the upper level to the makeshift command post De-Silva had established near the main external doors. He connected his datapad to the tactical network and prepared for the battle to begin. The first reports from the surface scouts were already filtering in. The CAR were on the move.

Chapter 46. Part 2.

While Julian took command of the war for the present, Renata and Alinta descended into the past. Their small procession of two electric city carts moved away from the main Depot, the hum of their motors a minor intrusion in the profound silence. In the lead cart, the two police-paramilitaries sat with a quiet, coiled alertness, while Renata and Alinta focused on their datapad, which was linked to the main linguistic AS. The second cart followed close behind, carrying the three engineers and their diagnostic equipment.

Their route, dictated by the schematic from Alinta's vision, took them into a network of older, more utilitarian service tunnels. "Alright," Renata murmured, feeding the last of their contextual data into the system. "Voss's memory confirms a translatable grammar. Your intuitive anchors provide the semantic starting points. Let's see what it makes of it".

As Alinta's leading cart came to a sign, she said, "This is more or less it, I am sure. Slow down". She and Renata dismounted and walked to the sign. Alinta pointed the datapad at a series of faded glyphs on the tunnel wall. The screen, previously a sea of low-confidence probabilities, now resolved into distinct clusters.

[Glyph A]: CAUTION / DANGER / ATTENTION.
[Glyph B]: AUTOMATED / MACHINE / MOVEMENT.
[Glyph C]: SYSTEM / PATH / FREIGHT.
[Glyph D]: DORMANT / STANDBY / OFFLINE.

"These tie in with my memories of the script. I am leaning towards -Attention," Alinta continued to read, piecing the concepts together. "Automated Freight System. Offline". It was not a perfect translation, but it was meaning. The silence of ages was beginning to whisper.

Their path was abruptly blocked by massive, unpowered blast doors. At the doors were the telltale signs of charges in the rock above them. Failed before their intended explosion, like the charges in the Depot. Obviously part of the intended chain.

The AS scanned the dead control panel: PRIMARY POWER OFFLINE / FAULTY. AUXILIARY / NEW CONNECTION REQUIRED. Alinta stared at the screen for a moment, then looked at the others. "I think it's saying it's not working," she said, deadpan. "We need to plug it in."

"I guessed that one at least," Kenji, the junior electrical engineer, said with a confident grin as he jumped out of his cart with a toolbox. "I'm your man!" He traced a heavily shielded conduit from the door mechanism to a nearby emergency power junction. "It's a standard procedure for a dead system. It's designed to be energised by an external source. Like, for instance, the power pack from a city cart. Electricity is electricity wherever in the Galaxy you go."

After a few minutes of re-routing cables, he gave a thumbs-up. "Power is connected. The panel should be in standby mode".

The panel was indeed now active, glowing with a soft, green light. But the doors remained sealed, the screen displaying a new, challenging glyph. AUTHENTICATION REQUIRED. This time, Alinta didn't need to interpret; the AS was improving. "We need an ID." She translated.

"This is your part, I think," Renata said back to Alinta. Returning to the cart, she picked up the shielded case containing the beyond-precious Echo Key.

Alinta nodded, her expression a mixture of apprehension and resolve. She stepped up to the panel, the Key held in her hands. As she neared, it gave her the briefest, faintest memory of what she was about to do: a flash of her own hand, already successfully touching the glowing pad. Guided by the strange, proleptic instruction, she placed her fingers on the screen. There was a soft chime. Her DNA was sampled, the Key providing the necessary authentication code."

Kenji said, "The city batteries are coming online. That's amazing. It's the first time we have had anything but a trickle from them."

With a deep groan of tortured metal, the massive blast door began to grind open. The AS immediately logged the new glyphs for "access granted," its lexicon growing. The old, now only partially insulated wires began to get hot, smoking what was left of the old conduit cladding that led from the doors to a cabinet further down the wall.

Kenji traced the wires back with a scanner. "There is a set of batteries here in this cabinet. It's the first time we have managed to get close to them. I need to study these."

Renata said, "It can wait, Kenji. There will be more to study further on." He nodded and boarded the carts as the doors exposed more of the dark tunnel that suddenly came slightly brighter with a red emergency lighting, amazingly still active despite the Aeons of dormancy.

They drove the carts into the damp, red-lit freight tunnel. The scale was immediately, breathtakingly different. This was not a passenger line. The tunnel was a single, colossal bore, at least a kilometre long, stretching into perfect, linear darkness. Their cart's headlights barely penetrated the gloom. The older civil engineer, his scanner active, murmured in awe, "The construction is seamless. There are no geological stress points, no strata variations. They did not just dig a tunnel; they fabricated it in place. It would be invisible to any standard seismic survey. The stealth is structural".

At the far end, they found the second door, even more formidable than the first. The panel was already active, powered by its own internal source. The AS, using its newly expanded data, gave a clearer translation of the glyphs above it: RESTRICTED AREA: MILITARY JURISDICTION. LEVEL-SEVEN DESIGNER AUTHENTICATION REQUIRED. Alinta merely nodded to Renata at the translation. They were in perfect agreement as to the meaning.

This was the final barrier. Alinta stepped forward once more, the Echo Key feeling almost warm in her hands. The process was the same, but the effect was more profound. This time, the memory implant was not just a feeling, but a stream of pure comprehension. As she looked at the glyphs on the screen demanding NEWCOMER: IDENTIFY, she understood them, not as sounds or letters, but as whole concepts, the way one reads a Chinese character.

She touched the panel. The Key pulsed, sending its silent, undeniable code. The door responded, its long-dormant power source activating with a low, powerful hum that resonated in their chests. The massive, stealthed door did not grind open. It retracted, its segments folding into the wall with a silent, flawless precision.

It revealed the interior of some sort of massive, megalithic Construction Yard. The sheer scale of the space defied comprehension. Gantries so vast their tops were lost in the artificial gloom stretched for kilometres. Docking cradles that could hold a vessel the size of a city block sat empty, waiting for titans that had been conceived but never born. The air that washed over them was cold, sterile, and ancient.

Renata lowered her datapad, her voice a whisper of pure awe. "It's not on any survey. Not seismic, not gravimetric. They did not just build a cavern; they shielded it from reality itself. This stealth technology alone... Julian was right. This is our legacy".

They stood at the threshold, staring into the silent darkness where a ghost fleet had once been planned, understanding that they had just found a secret that could hide further prizes. This would secure their legacy if they could win the war above.

Chapter 46. Part 3.

Julian Voss arrived at the fortified perimeter outside the main Depot entrance just as the sun began to climb, its light still a pale, violet-tinged wash over the ancient spaceport ruins. He met the tactical commander, Captain Pethery, a man whose calm demeanour was a small island of order in the tense preparations for battle.

"Commander Voss," Pethery greeted him with a nod, his expression professionally neutral but his eyes carrying a hint of wry amusement. "Bit of a change from dusty artefacts, I imagine

He was surprisingly thin, with a ruddy complexion accompanying a cultured politeness. A small decal on his armour marked him as an ex-Royal Marine. The way he spoke was a strong clue, too; a Portsmouth accent, though smoothed by years in the PCMA, Julian guessed. Feeling acutely self-conscious under the man's amused gaze, he managed a small smile. "You could say that, Captain. I trust you are comfortable with the unconventional chain of command?"

Pethery chuckled, a low, reassuring sound. "Sir, I have served on Royal Navy vessels where the ship's captain has the final say in a land battle, despite every marine on board knowing more about the terrain. Orders are orders. You are the designated authority for this facility. We will hold it". The simple confidence in his voice was more reassuring than any military bluster. Julian watched as Pethery moved among his men, his posture upright and steady, never ducking, a deliberate projection of calm. He recognised the training and felt a measure of his own tension ease. He could trust this man.

The first reports crackled over the comms from drone observers and scouts. The CAR were advancing.

From Major Jiao's perspective, the assault was already going wrong. The intelligence from Petropolis had described a broken, demoralised enemy. What he faced was a prepared, fortified position, nestled among priceless ruins that his orders forbade him from levelling with heavy fire. He had received the high command directive about the sudden, inexplicable spike in UV radiation. The Index had jumped from a tolerable 8 to a blistering 12. He could already feel the stinging soreness of a nasty sunburn, coincident with the less UV-protected joints of his armour. This was especially concerning because of the early time of day. He could not leave his men outside much longer, let alone wait for nightfall. He had to take the entrance now.

"Advance!" he commanded his lead platoon. "Suppressing fire only. Use the ruins for cover!"

Jiao was hoping the enemy would be even less prepared than he was. He thought, *"There can't be too many defenders; the strength of the resistance in the buildings and foothills suggests they are too spread out. They can't have many people left to defend the city."*

His men in front of him pushed forward. The soldier next to Jiao took three steps, then vanished in a muffled, horrific blast. Jiao threw himself to the ground as another explosion erupted nearby, this one preceded by a panicked scream. Mortars, to be expected. He shouted into his comm's "The sooner you get into the tunnel, the sooner you are out of range of their fire. Charge!".

With that, the men all rose as one and charged forward. Jiao included. These were the finest men he had ever served with. He felt a surge of pride as he got up and ran forward.

The men in the front line seemed to slightly falter in their run, a couple of men seemed to take a skip or a hop but then carried on. One stopped dead and started clawing at his foot. Jiao recognised him. Corporal Qiang Zhang. A mammoth of a man that Jiao had huge respect for. *Zhang wouldn't stop for anything.* Despite himself, Jiao slowed his pace and circled Zhang instead of going straight to him to help.

Zhang shouted in panicked Mandarin, "It's the sticky explosives. It's in the sand!" The man realised he had to get his hands away as the acid ate at his gloves even faster than it was dissolving and melting into his boots. With sudden resignation, he dropped to his back and held his foot in the air just as the men in the front fell in a horrid cascade of explosions, screams and spraying red mist from the ends of their legs, now missing a foot and in one case, both feet. There was no miracle for Zhang either. But to his credit, he did not add to the screams, despite knowing that his war was over. The attack stalled. Men went sideways, not forward. Panic made them look for cover despite the main threat being from underneath their feet. Rescue for the badly wounded was not coming and the screams were not stopping.

Mines. He thought. The sticky-acid paint balls had been made into mines. *Damn the Pak Wai!* Not heavy anti-vehicle mines he expected. That's why he left vehicles behind; the fear of anti-tank mines. These weren't just smaller, they were somehow nastier. More *personal.* He saw the mines now, half-buried in the ochre dust. They were innocent-looking, flat, sand-coloured discs. He saw one of his men begin to clear the sand in front of him with the barrel of his rifle, his face a mask of terror. But Jiao was a veteran of the Azure Dragon Legion. Fear was a luxury. He would not stop. He shouted into the comms, "This is no different from charging bullets. Any man who stops, I will shoot him myself." With that, he ran forward, screaming as he ran. There was only one way to lead. Never ask a man to do anything you wouldn't do yourself.

From the PCMA command post, Julian watched the initial CAR assault dissolve into chaos. Pethery was a master, directing his squads' fire with cool precision. The pancake mines were a horror. Voss felt a pang of guilt. An emotion that Pethery did not seem to share, as he looked into the battle monitor that he shared with Voss.

Julian saw a CAR soldier step on a mine. The disc adhered to his boot. The man had a half-second to look down in confusion, to open his mouth in a cry of alarm to his comrades, before the charge detonated, the blast contained and focused, turning his leg into a ruin. Another lay on his back, looking at his melting foot, as if taking a last look at his fated limb before the inevitable explosion took it forever away from him.

Then, incredibly, the officer, obviously a brave man, rallied his troops. Every last one of them, even his reserves, got up and ran forward. The tactic was obvious. Overwhelm the mines and get a human wave onto the defensive barricades.

Pethery ordered the drone-keepers to release the AS-programmed bomber drones. The drones, launched from the upper escarpment, descended like vengeful insects, their single, grey payloads dropping onto CAR formations with devastating accuracy. The sticky acid rounds turned armour to slag and flesh to ruin.

The CAR adapted. Disciplined fire teams pushed forward at a run, ignoring their dead, their fanaticism a tangible force. The battle intensified, becoming a desperate, close-quarters firefight amidst the ancient stones. A CAR rocket, fired from a flanking position, screamed past the main barricade and slammed into the rock face just metres from Julian's observation post.

He was thrown backwards by the concussion, the world a blur of spinning rock and sky. He hit the ground hard, the air driven from his lungs. Pethery was there, hauling him to his feet. "Sir, are you hit?"

"I'm fine, Captain!" Julian gasped, pushing himself upright. "Just a cracked rib. Focus on your sector!" He ignored the sharp, lancing pain in his side, his adrenaline masking the true extent of the injury. He saw Pethery readying the SSS teams for the surprise rear attack.

"Wait!" Julian commanded, his strategic mind overriding the pain. "Not yet. Let them commit fully. Trust the defences".

Pethery hesitated, then gave a sharp nod, respecting the order. They waited, the firefight reaching a crescendo. Then, Voss said, "Second wave of drones." The timing was perfect. The CAR troops had pushed far enough forward that a drop of caltrops could be made behind the majority of the attackers, making any escape difficult.

Then, at Julian's signal, the SSS teams launched their attack. Erupting from their secret places in the ruins, they had previously hidden city carts under UV protective nets and in mini bunkers in the sand. They swept past the rear of the attackers in a classic drive-by, hitting the CAR rear echelons with furious precision. The CAR line, already battered from the front, broke completely as they tried to turn and fight the attackers behind as well as the defenders in front. Confusion was the force multiplier Voss needed.

Major Jiao heard the screams from his rear and knew the battle was lost. Nevertheless, he tried to keep the attack together. He shouted his orders. "Rear guard, do not go forward, dig in and cover the attack. Front line, carry on forward, you are nearly there". The front line, more afraid of Jiao than the PCMA police and troops yet again resumed their push forward. At that point, he felt something drag on his foot and looked down. A feeling of nausea passed along his vagus nerve. There was no known antidote for the sickness he was about to suffer. Seeing it happen to so many other men was no solace.

Lt. Wei was behind Jiao and saw him start hopping; the sole of his smoking boot was visible. The explosion happened and Wei's visor was splattered with Jiao's blood. Jiao went down screaming. Wei saw that the front line had nearly reached the barricades. It was at that point that he thought they had nearly made it. Once past those flimsy defences, they would make that rabble of assorted cops and beaten marines from Petropolis pay. It was going to be brutal.

The drones came again overhead, some were shot down, but most were free to drop the nasty little spikes that had cost the regiment so many casualties the day before. That didn't bother him; it just meant one thing: the only way was forward. As the first wave finally came up to the barricades, he heard a voice shout in English, Fire. The point-blank volley was devastating. There were at least twice as many defenders there as he thought possible. This was not in the Major's briefing.

What finally broke them was when the dreaded orange balls started raining in amongst the CAR attackers. Wei knew what these little horrors did. The effects were utterly terrifying. Wei did the calculations. Even if they got in amongst the PCMA now, there were not enough men left to carry the day. It would be a turkey shoot.

Wei went to Jiao and grabbed his retrieval harness, a device to allow an injured man to be dragged clear for medi-vac. He touched visors rather than transmit. "Sir, the attack is broken. We need to save what we can". Jiao, despite his pain, had been watching. He, too, knew the writing was on the wall. Hoping he would not be judged a coward merely trying to save himself, he did the only thing he could think of and gave the order. "Retreat!"

The order given, Wei dragged Jiao back through the chaotic crossfire. Jiao started to tell himself that a cyborg foot wouldn't be so bad. Prosthetics could be very good in this day and age. The war pension would be good. Book deals, perhaps. Then, something crunched along the base of his armour. He felt a sharp sting between plates, in the centre of his spine. Then, he felt the weight of his own body forcing what he now realised was an acid-tipped caltrop into his spine.

The pain was immediate, excruciating, a fire that consumed all thought and spread up and down his backbone like sharp electricity and burning fire all in one. He started to writhe and jerk so badly that Wei had to drop him onto the ground. He was vaguely aware of a second soldier coming to help Wei. Jiao's wriggling died down as he lost feeling from the waist down. The caltrop had severely damaged the spinal cord.

The two of them finally managed to drag him clear of the carnage to safety. As they hid behind a small dune, the mortars started again. This time, in a fluke occurrence, another stray pancake mine, thrown by the blast of a mortar round that landed in front of them, slapped onto the faceplate of Wei's helmet. Wei struggled to get the helmet off, knowing that trying to remove the sticky substance was futile. But slightly late. The explosion did not kill Wei, but shards of glass from the visor and flames from the explosion blinded him. He felt remarkably calm. He could see a little out of his left eye and said to his Major, "Is it bad, Sir?" The now calm Jiao said, "No, Son. You will be fine."

At that, he heard the young private who had helped them to retreat to this spartan cover suddenly throw up into his helmet. Wei guessed that Jiao was lying. At that, Jiao said to the private, "Get out of here, boy. Leave us for the PCMA". The young private simply got up and ran in any direction where there was no fire. Just as Wei's eyesight started to fade to red in his one partially functional eye, he calmly said to his Major, "I guess that's it then." He didn't hear the reply as the world faded from red to black.

The CAR forces were in full rout. Julian watched them pull back, leaving their dead and the shattered remnants of their assault force behind. Pethery gave a concise report. "Enemy repulsed, sir. They are in disorganised retreat. We have held the line".

Julian allowed himself a single, grim nod of victory. They were safe. For now. He had read so many past battle memoirs, but nothing prepared him for this empty feeling. He should have been elated, scared, perhaps even sick? But he just felt numb, deadened by natural hormone overdose. It wasn't supposed to be like this.

He leaned against the cool stone of a preserved ruin, a wave of dizziness washing over him as the adrenaline faded, replaced by a deep, profound pain in his side. It was a hard-won stalemate. Looking at the casualties here, several hundred men lay on the ground. The CAR as a fighting force was vastly diminished. Wahlsanga, for certain, was safe.

The next move would belong to the fleets, now months away, even at the speeds allowed by their Alcubierre drives. It would be a long, silent race between the inevitable CAR relief fleet and whatever forces the NAR could muster. A race whose outcome they would not know for at least half a year.

Chapter 47. Part 1.

The journey from the battle-scarred perimeter to the Field Hospital was made in a near-silent city cart, driven by one of Captain Pethery's aides. The air was still hazy with the dust and smoke of the recent battle, the acrid smell of spent energy cells and traditional bullet propellants a sharp counterpoint to the ancient, sterile air of the Depot. Mr. Winstanley, the surgeon, had sent Voss a report that Rayk was now awake and apparently well.

On the way, Julian had dictated a concise after-action report, detailing the CAR's failed assault and Pethery's competent command, and had sent it to Rayk's qWatch. The pain in his side from his black-and-blue rib cage was a dull, insistent throb, a private misery he kept locked behind a mask of command composure.

As he entered the lab, Rayk's voice, weak but clear, came from the room's internal comms, activated the moment Voss's qWatch cleared the door. "Congratulations on the victory, Commander. A masterful application of your new toys".

Julian found Rayk propped up in the diagnostic bed. The stasis field was down. He was pale, a network of fine biosensors adhering to his temples, but his eyes were sharp and alert. Mr. Winstanley was monitoring a display nearby.

"He is recovering faster than I would have believed possible," the surgeon stated, shaking his head in mild disbelief. "His AS has successfully bypassed the lockdown. Basic motor functions are returning, but he has had deep neural shock. He is recovering by the minute because he is remarkably resilient in his attitude and mindset."

Voss winced as he shifted his weight, a movement that did not go unnoticed by the surgeon. "Commander, you appear to be in considerable pain. Let me see".

Before Julian could protest, Winstanley was at his side, gently lifting the edge of his tunic. The skin over his ribs was a dark, ugly tapestry of bruised tissue. "The ribs will be cracked, but this requires a deep-tissue scan, Commander. There could be internal bleeding".

"There are men out there with missing limbs, Mister Winstanley," Julian said, pulling his tunic back down, his voice leaving no room for argument. "My ribs can wait. Focus on your other patients". He turned his full attention to the man in the bed, dismissing his own injury as an irrelevance. "Rayk. It's great to see you, but I'm mostly interested in your account of things".

The two men spoke for several minutes, the commander and his security chief. Rayk explained the nature of the fail-safe, the reason for its secrecy. It was a burden installed by Raith, a secret component of his cybernetic resurrection. Raith was the only man who knew about it, followed by Rayk himself, of course, after the ignominious demonstration. Rayk had no idea it was something that could have been leaked. The matter was also deeply private to Rayk while he had been internally working on removing the vulnerability. Again, to say anything would have potentially compromised that internal operation. Julian listened, his expression unreadable, a silent, professional empathy passing between them.

When Rayk had finished, Julian nodded, accepting the impossible situation for what it was. "You were in an impossible situation, Detective. Damned if you did say something and damned if you didn't," he stated, his voice now firm with command. "The most important thing is, have you been able to plug the hole in your internal defences?"

Rayk said, "Well, yes, my AS says so. Ironically, it needed another demonstration to observe the ingress into my systems in real time. Understandably, I passed on the kind offer." He smirked. "But the CAR evidently had someone working with them who had other ideas. As a result, the AS got the data it needed."

"So everything is fine now?" Voss asked, noting a slight look of sorrow on Rayk's face.

"Yes, everything is back to the way it was before. I believe there are even some potential future possibilities to make improvements on the way it was. So maybe things will be brighter as a result of this episode. Who knows?"

Voss knew when not to push things. He trusted this man. "As soon as you are mobile, you will assume tactical command of all forces in this sector. For now, I left Captain Pethery in command. He will be your acting second-in-command until then".

He outlined the new strategic posture to the two men, the words coming with a new, unwelcome ease. "Your first task is to consolidate our defences. I ordered Captain Pethery to clear and occupy the ruins in the Gorge; this will deny the CAR a potential springboard for counter operations against us."

He waited to see that Rayk was processing information before continuing, "As soon as you are able, please oversee that operation and put what's left of the CAR in Petropolis under a state of permanent siege. I need a full, post-battle man-count and a complete inventory of our remaining munitions and supplies by the time I return".

Having delivered his orders, Julian turned to leave. "I'm heading out to a new site that Alinta found. The science team is waiting for me. Keep this facility secure and trust Pethery. He's a good officer."

Rayk said one more thing as Voss turned to leave. "Julian, I am sorry I let you down. After the chance in life that I was given...".

"Don't be ridiculous," Voss cut him off, turning back. "If it wasn't for you, we wouldn't be here now". Not waiting for a reply, he turned on his heel and left the sickbay, leaving the fast-recovering Rayk to begin the arduous task of managing the war. Julian, for a brief, blessed moment, was free to be a scientist again for at least a short while. He ignored the sharp, insistent pain in his side as he walked down the stairs to the level of the service tunnels.

Voss called up Captain Pethery on his qWatch. "Captain, please detail two of your marines to meet me outside the fabrication facility with a large city car. We will need sleeping bags for 10, food, water and some conventional ammunition if you can spare it. Plan for two days. How is the surface situation unfolding?"

Pethery replied instantly, "Prisoners are being rounded up now. The Russians are quite eager to surrender to our Russian troops. The Chinese, less so, but their operation is also unfolding quickly. There is a lot of animosity and politics going on amongst them. Recriminations as to who fought badly. Divide and conquer as the old saying goes. Plenty of work for your people to unpick later, I imagine, Sir."

"And the gorge operation?".

Pethery replied, "Mostly held by Mongolian units and some ethnic Han officers who were making themselves very comfortable in the villas there. The first one put up some resistance, then Lieutenant Gomez allowed some to escape. When news about the OSABs spread, the others gave up without a fight. Our main problem will be feeding prisoners now."

"OSABs?" Voss queried.

Pethery's voice held some amusement "Orange sticky acid balls, Sir."

Voss grinned but decided to move on and said, "Repurpose surface ruins, use the old terminal buildings. The higher UV levels will stop them from escaping. Make sure their armour is stripped of course."

"Of course, Sir, the marines and supplies will be with you in half an hour, ready to go. All is quiet from Petropolis. Apparently, the hydroponics have shut down as the late Commander Raith sent all the technicians over to you. The CAR don't have the expertise to keep them running, so I expect some overtures to come from that direction soon."

Voss cut the connection with the weight of Worlds lifted from his shoulders. Soon, his transport would be taking him through the discreet door that led to where Renata and Alinta were waiting, towards the promise of a mystery eighty thousand years in the making.

Chapter 47. Part 2.

Julian's city cart hummed to a stop inside the colossal military facility, its headlights a small intrusion in the vast, ancient darkness. The team was waiting for him, having established a neat, professional perimeter around the "Ghost Door". As he stepped out, the weariness of the last few hours settling deep into his bones, a sound echoed in the immense space. A spontaneous round of applause started with one of the junior engineers and quickly picked up by the two security staff, spreading to everybody. The raw, heartfelt relief in the gesture was deeply embarrassing.

He held up a hand, a self-deprecating smile touching his lips. "Alright, alright, that's enough of that," he said, his voice a little hoarse. "The soldiers did the real work. All I did was come up with some nasty tricks with glue and pointed sticks." Then he realised, nobody ever credits the humble engineers who win the wars. "Which, I have to add, our engineers worked themselves to the bone to turn them into almost instant reality". He let his gaze sweep over the small group, his expression sobering. "But the fight is not over. They will be back. This respite is our only chance to find something in here that can give us a better advantage. Let's get to work".

His command, however informal, refocused the team. They began their initial survey, a small island of light and purpose in an ocean of silence.

Renata walked up to Voss, smiling. "Julian, it's really good to see you". Voss could not have asked for a better reward for his efforts than that one sentence. He said, "It's great to see you too. Have you and Alinta been enjoying yourselves here? Find anything interesting?"

"Yes, actually, when you called, we had just found a tech signature down this hallway on the left fork. If you can call a 500-foot diameter tube a hallway."

Voss replied, "Isn't it strange that everything works here and yet everywhere else it is effectively dead or on its last legs at least."

Renata nodded, "Absolutely. It is as if the place is reacting to us. Everything here is on a higher level of build quality. Almost a civilisation within a civilisation."

With that, Voss distributed some food and sanitary kits and declared the expedition start, down the left hallway tube. The crew mounted the two carts and the larger transport vehicle Voss had brought. Alinta, with the echo key and working largely upon instinct, led the way towards the place where their instruments showed activity.

Along the way, the huge tube became a massive square pit that had all the hallmarks of construction yards for ships or aircraft. They had a totally different feel from everything that they had seen up till now. That included at least three different architectural styles on the surface. Two styles of underground city, from the Greco-Roman style of Petropolis to the functional post-industrial style of Wahlsanga.

To the left was a glowing green glyph of what looked like office buildings. Alinta drove her cart straight forward and got out in front of the glass doors. As she got closer, the interior powered up slightly. Inside was a standard-looking office with the usual 'too-narrow' chairs of the Architects. Then what looked to be a second door behind the office, revealing a glass-walled room behind, and most startlingly, in that room appeared to be dozens of sarcophagi, arranged in silent, perfect rows.

Alinta said, "I think it says emergency sick bay, or field hospital."

Renata brought her language AS and pointed at the signs. It read: [Glyph for

DANGER/EMERGENCY] + [Glyph for LIFE/BIOLOGY] + [Glyph for HEALING/REPAIR] + [Glyph for PLACE/LOCATION]

Alinta looked at the screen and added, "It's broadly correct, but my memory from the Key felt like 'mending.' And the last one means 'place.' So... 'a place for mending biological emergencies.' I am now certain that it says, 'emergency sick bay' like this whole place is actually regarded as a ship."

Amongst the ensemble, there was a tense, hopeful anticipation. Were there survivors? Architects held in stasis?

The electrician walked to the door sensor, but before he could raise his meter to read it, the doors slowly creaked open. The awe was palpable among everyone who witnessed this occasion. The first time the planet ever opened up to them willingly. Like hospitals everywhere. Everyone is welcome.

They moved past the desks, but all technology was stripped predictably. Then they walked to the inner doors of the hospital proper. Again, the doors opened, this time more easily as they were less weathered by the elements. Voss and Renata walked up to the transparent faceplate of the first sarcophagus. Alinta, looking at the signs on the side of one of the coffin-like structures, said, "These are medical and suspended animation pods combined. Cryopods if you like."

Voss and Renata now did not bother to question her. Alinta had the basics of the language now and was way ahead of the linguistics AS. They looked into the first pod. It had a transparent faceplate. Voss nodded to Renata, knowing what she wanted to do. She pressed an obvious symbol that said 'open' based on what the team had worked out from the train door previously.

The inside was smooth, white and plastic-like. Inside, there were many small facets of unknown purpose. This would revolutionise medical technology for the whole of humanity.

One by one, they opened the cryopods. One by one, they found them empty. Pristine, functional, but unused. The discovery was a profound disappointment; a tomb prepared for a population that never arrived.

It was near the last row of empty sarcophagi that they found it. A single, humble-looking knife, lying on the floor as if dropped in a moment of forgotten haste. The first time they had ever seen a single tool or weapon. Some things were the same, no matter which civilisation used them. A knife was a knife.

Alinta, her curiosity overriding her caution, moved to pick it up. The handle fit strangely in her hand, but the activation stud was unmistakable. She looked at the button and with her left hand, moved to press it.

"Alinta, don't!" Renata's voice was sharp with alarm. "Protocol!" Of course, how does one stop a scientist from pressing a button? Especially if there is a sign above it saying, 'Do not press this button'". She pressed it. The blade hummed to life, its edge a blur of silent, violent energy.

Startled, Alinta flinched, and the humming knife slipped from her grasp. It did not clatter. It fell point-down and sank into the fused-stone floor as if it were water, its silent descent leaving a perfectly clean, deep incision before the hilt came to rest. The humming stopped. Maybe damaged, or maybe a safety protocol. The latter made sense, since the knife was no longer being held. Not wanting to make the same mistake with the button, Alinta pulled on the hilt, but the knife was stuck fast.

Mortified she had damaged a precious artefact, she looked at Voss and said, "Sorry, I...".

Voss held up his hand. He stepped forward. He knelt, his hand closing around the hilt. He gave a firm, steady pull. Nothing happened. He then pressed the button with his thumb and there was a slight vibrating feeling. Then, the blade slid free from the stone very easily, with a faint, sighing sound. He stood, holding the weapon, a tangible piece of their impossible puzzle, before deactivating it.

Alinta said, "Whoso pulleth out this sword of this stone and anvil, is rightwise king born of all England?" To which chuckles resounded amongst the gathered tech people. Even the security staff who stood at the door were fascinated. This was a weapon they were very interested in.

Julian Voss said, "I think we need to take this as a warning, people. Let's at least try and pretend we are still xeno-archaeologists and apply some protocols?" He handed the knife to Alinta with a gentle smile, now 'Keeper of the Artefacts'.

After an hour of cataloguing and filming, and having checked every cryopod, Voss could see the effects of the momentous day on everyone. Exhausted by the emotional roller-coaster of the battle and the discoveries, Julian decided to call a halt. "Let's make camp around here for a few hours of much-needed sleep."

In the main office, there was a side door they had not examined. A quick investigation showed that it was a waiting room with bench seats. Along one wall was the second piece of art they ever found on the planet. It was an artefact that was possibly even more interesting than the discovery of the sarcophagi. It was a huge, magnificent mural of what was obviously a half-finished starship in these construction yards. Its impossible form, seeming to float in place next to one of the still visible gantries outside the hospital, although all trace of any ships had gone now.

Voss declared, "I think this is a defensible position. If security would be so kind as to organise a watch, I suggest we camp down here. There seem to be running water facilities in the back that we can use as bathrooms." With that the team started unpacking sleeping bags and supplies from the cars parked outside. The security staff set up watch in the way soldiers had been trained to do since the earliest days when humanity started making campfires to sleep.

As the others settled down, Julian noticed the girls split up from the boys. However, he saw it a different way. Tech and engineering. With an internal smile, seeing his moment, he placed his sleeping bag next to Renata's. Later, as the rest of the team slept, the three of them—Julian, Renata, and Alinta—spoke in low voices, their faces illuminated by the glow of a datapad.

Alinta described her evolving connection to the Echo Key. "I can read the functional glyphs now, not by translating them, but just... understanding them. Like a Chinese character". She hesitated. "But there was something else. A memory. It felt like a warning. That using the Key is bad for me. That my brain does not have the right structure for it".

"How do you know that?" Julian asked gently.

Alinta shook her head, her expression one of genuine bewilderment. "You know? I have absolutely no idea. I just remember it being true".

Julian fell silent for a moment, his mind piecing together the impossible technology around them. "The longevity of it all," he mused, looking up at the mural. "The batteries that still hold a charge, these stasis pods. The civilian tech we have found is all degraded, failing. But this. This is different. It was not built just to last. It was built to cross voids. This is the technology you build for a hundred-thousand-

The Xenologist

year journey between galaxies".

"Pan-galactic travel," Renata breathed, the scale of it almost incomprehensible. "That would explain the power sources".

"But it does not explain this," Julian said, gesturing to the vast cavern around them. "The mural shows a ship that has left. But there is no door in this mountain large enough to accommodate it. How did it get out?"

The question hung in the cold, silent air. As Alinta remembered reading a diagnostic panel on one of the empty sarcophagi, Alinta, her eyes tracing the intricate glyphs related to biological processes, had another flash of insight.

"They were not just Architects," she said thoughtfully. "The pods, they were not just for stasis. They could rewrite and build. The Architects were called Designers".

She could not explain how she knew the word, only that it felt right, a key turning in a lock she never knew existed. They were left with the staggering implication: the builders of these impossible structures were also the builders of life itself. They were resting in a ghost yard, beneath a ghost ship, left behind by a race of gods, while a war for their own survival raged just a few hundred metres above their heads.

Chapter 48.

In the cold, sterile order of his forward command post, General Ganbaatar had finished being briefed on the hydroponics situation. He had been informed that all qualified hydroponics technicians had been evacuated the moment the heavenly hailstorm started. The water supply was left, probably to avoid accusations of a war crime against their own population, who were obviously also reliant upon the produce of those farms, but without the techs, the farms were quickly deteriorating. His own experts either died in the initial nuclear attack on the troop carrier or were trapped in orbit.

Irritated by the memory of that initial 'welcoming', he turned to the after-action reports of the assault on the older spaceport. They were a litany of failures. The icons on the battle map told a story not of a glorious assault, but of a catastrophic defeat. His elite vanguard, the pride of the Azure Dragon Legion, was gone, buried under a mountain of rock in a collapsed tunnel. His second-in-command on the ground, the brave and fanatical Major Jiao, was presumed dead or captured. The PCMA, a rabble of scientists and corporate security he had dismissed, had not only held their line; they had shattered his.

His professional pride, a deeply ingrained part of his being, was a raw, open wound. But it was quickly cauterised by the cold, clear logic of their new reality. Annoyance was a luxury he could no longer afford.

As if to punctuate the grim assessment, a priority communication request blinked on his console. It was Admiral Wei of the surviving CAR orbital fleet. The Admiral's face, when it appeared, was a mask of strained formality, his background the stark, functional bridge of a warship running on dwindling resources.

"General," Wei began, his voice tight. "My situation here has become untenable. Our water reclamation systems are failing. We have at best, two weeks of potable water remaining. In 48 hours, I must begin severe water rationing."

Ganbaatar's expression remained placid, but a cold knot tightened in his stomach. "The resupply convoy, Admiral?"

"The resupply convoy from Earth is a fiction, General, and we both know it," Wei stated bluntly. "The last comms pod confirms our worst fears. The political situation in the Sol system has deteriorated. The NAR, the EUR, our own Central Command, they are all locked in a political stalemate. The relief fleets are being held back. Earth is on the brink of a wider war over this very planet. There is no help coming."

Ganbaatar processed the information, each word another stone sealing their tomb. "There is still the unarmed colony ship from the PCMA; it will have water on board."

"Yes, but that slow ship is not here for another two months. We can't last that long." Wei replied. "And there is more," the Admiral continued. "The water-rich asteroid in the outer system, our only viable source of resupply. It is being blockaded. The late Director Raith appears to have left a final, posthumous surprise. A single, heavily armed PCMA automated warship, sitting in a perfect picket orbit. My remaining vessels lack the firepower to challenge it. Our escort fleet was designed to protect us from secondary threats, not fight ships of the line".

The Admiral let the silence stretch, his meaning clear. "If you cannot secure a ground-based water source within the next forty-eight hours, I will be forced to negotiate terms with the PCMA orbital station. I will trade our surrender for access to that asteroid. My duty is to my crew, General. Dying of thirst in orbit is a terrible fate. It would be better to go down fighting in a suicide attack against the orbital stations. Ultimately, we would obtain the same result, but you would have no way of getting home"

Before Ganbaatar could formulate a reply, another report flooded his console, this one from his own ground troops, those outside and lucky enough not to be harried by the Wahlsanga-based PCMA troops. Frantic messages about the sun. The UV Index had spiked, climbing to hazardous levels matching the highest previously recorded. Their standard-issue armour was being overwhelmed, its cooling systems failing. Men were reporting severe radiation burns. They could not sustain prolonged surface operations.

Defeated in battle. Stranded in orbit. And now, betrayed by the very planet they had come to claim. Ganbaatar saw the trap closing around him. He could not win a war of attrition. He could not hold out for a rescue that would never arrive. His objective shifted in a heartbeat, from conquest to something far more primal: absolute, total denial.

He reviewed the surveillance data his drones had gathered before the battle. The two PCMA access points were mapped: the collapsed underground rail tunnel, now impenetrable by the PCMA sabotage and the fortified main Depot entrance, the site of his disastrous assault. There were a couple of minor entrances that were unsuitable for assault or, for that matter, escape. It was obvious with hindsight that Petropolis City was empty ruins. A mere residential district. The true objective should have been Wahlsanga all along. He did not know what treasures lay hidden in that mountain, but if he could not possess them, then neither should the NAR.

He opened a channel to the commander of his remaining Azure Dragon airborne units. He still had one ace up his sleeve.

"Prepare your orbital launch vehicles and skimmer-bombers," he commanded, his voice a blade of cold steel. "Load them with your heavy demolition charges, repurposed as air-drop munitions. You will launch on my signal. Your target is not the enemy troops. Your target is the mountain itself".

He highlighted the main surface access tunnel and the two known minor entrances on the tactical map. "You will execute a high-speed, low-altitude bombing run. I want you to use your ordnance to trigger a catastrophic collapse of the entire escarpment face. I want that facility, and everyone inside it, buried under a million tonnes of rock".

He awaited the notification that the preparation for the final assault was complete. His gamble was no longer to win Sikarra. It was to make the planet an even death-trap for both sides. He could use that act of absolute destruction to negotiate from a position of strength with the unarmed, civilian PCMA colony ship that was still on its way. It was, perhaps, his only way home. He had abandoned the hope of capturing the prize; his new, final objective was simply to ensure that no one else could either.

Chapter 49.

Julian woke to the low hum of the camp's field heaters that, if anything, were a little overwhelming for the medium-sized waiting room. The lighting outside in the tunnel-cum-hallway had got brighter, almost as if it knew that the shipyards were now occupied again and it needed to sync with the external day and night cycle.

He looked up at the magnificent mural on the waiting room wall in absolute wonder. It was amazing that it had not deteriorated over the millennia. Not only that, it seemed vibrant and alive now, as if it had absorbed the faint light of the hallways and camp lanterns through the night. Its fantastical half-built ship was a silent, colossal sentinel watching over them.

The rest of the team was already stirring, a quiet energy replacing the profound exhaustion of the previous day. He saw Renata and Alinta hunched over a datapad and walked over, his ribs protesting with a sharp, grinding pain he forced himself to ignore. "Anything new?"

"Potentially," Renata said, looking up. She gestured to one of the police-paramilitaries, who stepped forward. "Corporal Jennings was analysing the position of the vibro-knife. His assessment is, that whoever dropped it was not simply exploring this chamber. Given the angle and the placement, he believes they were heading purposefully towards that corridor".

She indicated a dark, unexplored passage leading off from the far side of the hospital triage area. "We did not have time to survey it last night".

The implication hung in the air. A new path. A deliberate route. "Alright," Julian decided, the thrill of discovery cutting through his fatigue. "That's our preferred direction. Let's pack up and go."

They broke camp quickly. Following Jennings' lead, they walked back through the chamber of empty sarcophagi to the unexplored corridor. It opened onto a metal platform overlooking a space that made them all stop in silent awe. Before them was not another simple tunnel, but a colossal, perfectly preserved transport loop. It was a vast, straight-sided oval, perhaps three hundred metres in diameter, with immense, gracefully curved toroidal ends, like a gigantic, ancient stadium for a race of giants.

The electrical engineer, Kenji, stated, "I used to work in the orbital shipyards above Earth. This is exactly how we organised the process, in a loop like a racetrack. But in Orbit. How could such a massive ship ever get out of a gravity well? It would take colossal energy! The ship would probably break its keel under the thrust."

Voss replied, "Great questions. No answers from me, though."

Alinta, ahead of the others, was brave enough to step out onto a dizzying metal gantry that hugged the side of the walls of the new tunnel. She tested it for solidity and called back, "It's completely solid. No oxidation or wear and tear. It's like it was built yesterday. The implications!"

"What does the sign say?" Renata, pointing at a plaque on the platform behind them, her voice a whisper. "The AS thinks 'Hospital' and an arrow, but what is this word?"

Alinta walked back to the platform. "Something like, 'assembly line'." She looked guilty. "Sorry, not everything is clear yet; there's no context for some technical things, but when I find out retrospectively what it means, it becomes second nature somehow."

Voss interjected, "No need to apologise. When we find out what they were making, that's another word for you. Let's go."

It was as they all started to walk along the gantry that Julian's world tilted. A wave of dizziness, profound and absolute, washed over him. At first, he thought it was vertigo. This gantry was not for the faint-hearted. But the pain in his side, which had been a dull, manageable ache, erupted into a sharp, searing fire. He gasped, stumbling back against the corridor wall, his face suddenly pale and slick with a cold sweat.

"Julian!" Renata cried, rushing to his side. She was already on her qWatch, her voice sharp and urgent. "Priority medical emergency! Commander Voss is down! Mr Winstanley, reply please!"

The reply from Mr Winstanley took a moment to arrive and was strained; the sounds of a surgical emergency were audible in the background. "I cannot leave. I am in the middle of a critical neurosurgery. I am dispatching my best field paramedic, Corporal Davies, but he is at the main entrance. It'll take him at least half an hour to reach your position".

Julian pushed himself upright, leaning heavily on Renata. "We do not wait," he gritted out, his voice a harsh whisper. "I am feeling better. We continue. Davies can find us when he gets here".

"Sir," one of the guards said. "This is wide enough for the smallest buggy we brought. I'll get some stuff and bring the buggy through the hospital. If you are dizzy, this is not the place for you to be walking," he added with some humour as he nodded down into the abyss below.

Voss, for once, decided upon discretion. "Alinta and Renata, you walk on, I'll catch up in a couple of minutes." With that, the two women, with some reluctance, walked on, followed by the technical staff. The security split up, one with them and the rest staying with their commander.

The cart arrived as Julian saw the advance party disappear around a corner into an alcove where the gantry took them. He felt much better as he got into the cart. The journey down the gantry on the buggy was a tense, surreal experience, but mercifully short.

As the buggy got to the corner, there were yet again heavy security doors. Before he could stop her, Alinta had used the echo key to obtain access. The doors slid open instantly at her touch. She stumbled back a step, her face pale.

"Alinta, are you alright?" Voss asked, but his words were lost as his gaze fell upon the sight the doors had revealed. Beyond lay another vast factory space, and this time, it was not empty.

Voss told his driver to move forward and the team looked in wonder as the lighting fired up. Something that should have been impossible after all the millennia. There could be no doubt now. This was the true secret of Sikarra. The necessarily robust technology of galactic-scale or even intergalactic travel, designed to last aeons.

As they began to explore the silent, dormant factory, Alinta looked at Julian with concern. "The Key. The cognitive strain..."

"Well, if it is going to give one of us a headache, we might as well share it," Julian said, forcing a wry smile. "It is only fair. We rotate. I'll take the first turn."

He took the Echo Key and approached a primary control terminal. As he held it near, the familiar, disorienting rush flooded his mind. But this time, it was accompanied by a strange, vivid memory: an image of himself, injured and weak, climbing into an unknown, sleek black sarcophagus. The vision was so real, so absolute, that for a moment he thought it had already happened. He pushed the disturbing, private thought aside as the Key finished its work. A flood of data, schematics and material science, all poured into his mind. He thought in a manner directed at the echo key, *Is there something for visitors to explain about this place?* The console in front of him dutifully started filling with an introductory 'tour for visitors'.

Alinta was there at his side. "I can read it. It's safety information. And look, a floor plan". She pointed at the screen.

Renata pointed at the title of the screen. "I know that these glyphs are what the place is called, what it does. The AS has now got a 100% lock on the city name. It is 'Vasantha'"

Alinta said, "Give me the echo-key, I can do this."

Voss said, "Vasantha? How dull. I prefer our name. It's probably going to be really hard to change now". He laughed at his own joke and then winced in pain and started to feel very woozy. The world started to look grey. The team looked at him in consternation.

Renata's voice cut in, "Julian, you are looking really pale. I think that's enough now. You need attention immediately."

It was at that opportune moment, as if he had heard her demands, that Corporal Davies finally arrived running down the gantry outside and slowed down as he entered the assembly area.

Catching his breath, he put his instruments on Voss and lifted his shirt to see the now blackened bruising of the ribs. His face was one of obvious concern. He worked with a swift, grim efficiency. The diagnosis was as Winstanley had feared: "Sir, you have a splenic rupture." The medic administered the stabilising drip, the internal coagulant and powerful analgesics. These modern drugs performed an instant but precarious miracle.

"You are stable now and will feel much better, but this is temporary, Commander," Davies warned. "You must be evacuated".

"The mission continues, Corporal," Julian stated, feeling a deceptive strength flowing back into him. He was not going anywhere.

I have it! You won't believe this." She paused for effect. "This is how they could build spaceships in a gravity well. It says "Vasantha Anti-Gravity Pad Fabrication Facility. Restricted Area. Designers and Designer-authorised staff only". Alinta was quick to see the implication, "If it is true anti-gravity, supporting full weight, then this makes our inefficient gravity sluicing completely obsolete. I cannot express the value of this". Then, laughing, "I think I need to lie down". The wonder-struck faces around the displays lit up as suddenly, the floor plan on one of the huge screens came to life. There were annotations that Renata was keying into her pad. The linguistics AS was catching up quickly now. Soon, everyone would be able to read the glyphs to some degree with a datapad.

Voss pointed at the larger screen and said, "I have a memory of being there. I don't know how I know it is there, but it is." He pointed at a room on the plan. A hidden location accessible from the assembly line: a private control room. They followed a gantry back towards the hospital wing, to a final, sealed blast door. Julian, his turn with the Key over, handed it to Alinta. She stepped forward and opened the door.

Inside were two sarcophagi. One standard, and empty. The other was sleeker, more advanced, its faceplate an inscrutable, opaque black. Julian now shared the strange memory the Key had given him, of seeing himself climb into the pod lying next to that very pod.

"It is not for us," he said quietly. "We do not know if it is compatible".

"Let's just see what is inside," Alinta said. She stepped forward, holding the Echo Key to the opaque pod's control panel. Voss stopped her.

"Sharing the headache, remember?" She smiled and gave him the key. Renata was concerned. "Julian, are you well enough?"

"I feel perfectly fine. Corporal Davis did a great job". With that, he held the key. He remembered what the glyphs said. He read them to Alinta and Renata to increase their understanding. "Subject in suspended animation long term." Then he knew there were two touch buttons. One said, 'View', the other was the glyph he no longer needed assistance to read. 'Emergency Open'.

Everyone looked in absolute shock. Finally, would they see or even meet a real Architect, now called a 'Designer'. Without a word, Voss pressed the 'view' button and the result was instant.

The faceplate did not open. It shifted, its molecules realigning, and became perfectly transparent.

Inside, suspended in a golden, amber-like preservation fluid, was a body. It was not the pale, slender form of a Designer. It was something else. Its skin was dark, almost black, stretched taut over a frame that was not quite human. It was ancient, perfectly preserved. Mummified.

To Voss, the face in many ways resembled the mummy of Ramesses II, but in better condition, as if the body had died in recent times.

We haven't found a living Designer, he realised. *We've found a dead, unknown humanoid alien, a third race.* Except, disturbingly, the face was so human it could have been one of his own staff. Yet here it was, hidden at the very heart of the place where the Designers had built their ships to flee the galaxy.

Chapter 50.

They stood in the silent control room, the two sarcophagi dominating the space, one inert and empty, the other a vessel of profound and unsettling mystery. The awe of the discovery was a tangible thing, a pressure in the still, ancient air.

"What do we do first?" Alinta whispered, her voice barely disturbing the silence. "Do we study the occupant, or the systems that have preserved him?"

Julian's gaze was fixed on the transparent faceplate of the occupied pod. "The occupant," he decided, his voice quiet but firm. "The technology is a means to an end. The end was him. We need to know who he was".

The engineers, their movements slow and deliberate with a reverence for the occasion, interfaced their equipment with the pod's control panel. Alinta, with the Echo Key in hand, guided them through the unfamiliar glyphs, her intuitive understanding a strange and vital bridge across the millennia. With a soft, final hiss, the last of the amber preservation fluid drained away, revealing the figure within more clearly. He was not a Designer. He was, impossibly, human.

A collective, sharp intake of breath was the only sound in the room. He was tall, powerfully built, his dark skin stretched taut over a frame that was all coiled muscle.

"Get me a DNA sample," Julian ordered, his own mind struggling to process the implications.

Corporal Davies worked with a practised, sterile efficiency, his micro-sampler a tiny, silver needle against the ancient, dark skin. The results appeared on his datapad moments later. He looked up, his face a mask of utter disbelief.

"Commander. He is Homo sapiens. Baseline human. But...," he tapped the screen, "his genetic markers are anomalous. He has the same unique DNA sequences we found in your profile, and in the late Director Raith's. But the concentration... it is almost double".

A human. An ancient human with a double dose of the affinity genes, preserved in a Designer facility. The revelation was a seismic shock, a fact that fundamentally rewrote the history of their two species.

Before they could fully grapple with it, Julian, knowing their time was a resource more precious than any artefact, turned to the main control terminal. "Alinta, the systems. I need to know what this facility can do. Download everything".

As Alinta approached the console, the fleeting, false memory returned: the vision of herself and Julian, standing side-by-side, their hands on the panel, being accepted as the facility's new administrators. "Commander," she said, her voice tight. "It needs both of us".

Julian joined her. They placed their hands on the panel. The console chimed its acceptance, granting them full administrative access. Alinta immediately became lost in the colossal task of the data dump, her fingers flying across her datapad as she worked to build a translation matrix on the fly. "The anti-gravity archives are here," she murmured, her focus absolute. "The schematics are... beautiful".

Then her mind opened by the echo-key, she said, "Physics will never be the same. It's so, so damned simple." Then she started speeding up and babbling in excitement, her eyes darting from side to side in rapid, dreamlike flickers as she explained, "A tiny current tears a hole in the fabric of space. It creates a white hole. A tiny, unstable one. Spacetime flows out of it like gravity flows into a black hole! When the current stops, the hole seals and... and..."

At that point, Voss said, "Stop!" He pulled her hand off the echo-key and put it onto a nearby alien console. Alinta started breathing heavily and realised her pulse was racing. She said, "Thank you. That was just too intense". Her pulse started to slow. She realised Voss had moved in just in time before she became seriously damaged.

Voss said, "This thing is not to be used in a casual fashion. We need to be careful".

Renata crossed to Alinta, gripped her shoulders, and looked into her eyes. Relief flickered there, yet a beatific light remained, the calm radiance of a prophet who has just seen a vision. Everyone took a moment to realise what had been said. This truly reshaped human understanding of physics and the nature of gravity. Was gravity an actual force after all? What did it all mean?

It was then at that moment, when the three scientists darted understanding glances at each other, that Renata and Julian's qWatches blinked into urgent life. A priority alert, overriding everything. It was a crackling, desperate message from Pethery at the main entrance. "Commander! Multiple airborne bandits on a direct attack vector! They are starting a bombing run on the escarpment face! It is a demolition strike!"

They were trapped.

Renata looked at the tactical display appearing on her qWatch from central command and watched with dread the descending icons of the CAR bombers. "There is no time. We cannot get out".

"Perhaps not," Julian said, his voice dangerously calm. He took the Echo Key from the console. In a moment of false memory, the echo key showed him placing the echo key onto a place on the largest console in the room. He strode over to it and as he placed it down, he realised it was linked to the Shipyard's external sensor grid. "But they cannot have this".

The key made its connection with the systems in the console. The world dissolved. He felt the rush of false memories, a torrent of silent, overwhelming information. He saw a warning: his own medical data, the red-lining indicators of his unstable blood pressure, the catastrophic risk to his patched-up spleen. He saw another: a memory of an Architect scanner picture of a human brain. It was detailing the irreversible cerebral damage caused by using the Key as a weapon. And then, he saw the solution. A final, beautiful, ecstatic memory of the approaching bombers, their engines not as machines, but as simple, primitive systems he could now touch. He remembered how to shape the local electromagnetic field into a false, catastrophic engine failure code.

He saw the ridiculous simplicity of the CAR systems from the point of view of the device. He could almost feel what passed for humour in the device, at the CAR ships' primitive attempts at security.

Magnetic and electric fields unfurled as two three-dimensional realities, each with a distinct direction and its own new colour, vivid beyond human sight. That alone stretched his brain open, in a way it was never evolved for, teetering on the precipice of mental ecstasy. He held himself back, grasping a pattern: excite one field just so, align the other in opposite harmony. In an instant, with most of his remaining strength, he cast the command into the fields, sending a deceptive pulse into the void.

Renata held up her qWatch, showing the tight-beamed tactical situation direct from Captain Pethery's office. One by one, the red icons blinked and disappeared.

Then, the last CAR bomber vanished from the small screen as the group gathered around, in tense silence, watching. For a heartbeat, the control room was held in a disbelieving silence. The threat was gone.

The effect was almost an anti-climax; he was intact. His brain had survived. Riding a wave of confidence, he knew he had to investigate more, to learn as much as he could whilst his strength remained. He looked into the illusions of the universe around him. He saw the fields, but there was something else. Like the veiled tabernacle of a Catholic church, there was something else. He had to know what was behind it. As he peered through the veil, he saw how the universe was made. It was made of nothing. Of course, so he was nothing. The ecstatic feeling was a blinding, god-like wave of pure power that allowed him to peer into the void. The void stared back, leaving nothing but cold emptiness in his soul.

The ecstatic power that had suffused Julian receded, vanishing like a tide, leaving only the fragile, lost human man behind. Julian's eyes, which had been closed in concentration, snapped open, wide with a look of sudden, terrible surprise. His hands flew to his abdomen, and he crumpled, collapsing to the floor.

"Julian!" Renata's cry was a raw, sharp sound that cut through the silence. She was at his side in an instant, dropping to her knees on the cold floor.

He was trying to speak, his words a choked whisper. "There is everything here... and nothing..." His body shuddered violently.

The medic ran over to the prostrate Voss, urgently pulling out his medical instruments to apply them to his bruised ribcage. "Massive internal haemorrhage!" Davies reported, his voice tight with clinical urgency. "The coagulant has failed completely. The effort... it blew out the spleen".

Renata grabbed Julian's hand. It was cold and clammy. "Julian, hold on," she pleaded, knowing it was hopeless.

"Renata...," he whispered, his eyes struggling to focus on her. He tried to say more, but the words were lost in a final, shuddering breath. His eyes went vacant.

Davies held his scanner to Voss's temple. Then he checked again one last time. He looked up at Renata, his face grim. "There's no pulse. No cerebral activity. I am sorry, Doctor. He is gone".

In the profound, grief-stricken silence that followed, Renata looked from Julian's still form to the empty sarcophagus. She remembered the false memory he had told her about, the vision the Key had given him. "He knew," she whispered, tears welling in her eyes. "It showed him this. He was supposed to go in there. To be preserved".

With a quiet resolve, she directed the team. They lifted Julian's body and gently placed it inside the empty pod. Renata pulled Voss's qWatch from his wrist. Not caring that anyone was looking she very gently let her lips brush his. She gave him the very faintest kiss. He did not respond, as she once did not respond to him. She tried once more. Part of her hoped this was a joke. A mistake. But there was no response. No miracle.

She pulled up, nobody was judging her. She said to no one in particular, "It's time. Goodbye, Julian." As Alinta then initiated the stasis sequence, Renata shed a single, silent tear that dropped onto his cheek. The lid began to close and paused politely as her head was still in the way. She stood back, her goodbyes done. The pod sealed. The lights cycled: red, to green, to a final, steady blue. Unseen, the tiny fibrils extended from the walls of the pod, beginning their ancient, unknowable preservation work.

With Julian now entombed, Renata turned back to the first sarcophagus. "Who was his tomb-mate?" she asked, her voice full of a sorrowful wonder. "What does his name tag say?" Then, her eyes red and her voice catching, she continued, "Julian would have so wanted to know."

Alinta was standing transfixed at the horror of the scene and unable to process the sudden request, merely shook her head.

Renata, operating almost as if in shock, approached the pod, her own datapad in hand, the linguistic AS now rich with new context. She focused on the glyphs on the ancient tunic.

"The name means 'Home-Lover'," she said softly. "In the language of the Designers... 'Va' for home... and 'Rinn', for one who loves".

She looked at Alinta, who now realised the importance of Renata's request. The need to formalise the moment with another witness from the ages. She took a couple of paces to the long-deceased man and studied his name tag. She whispered with quiet tenderness, "Yes. It was pronounced 'Varinn.'"

With tears in her eyes, Renata said, "Varinn." The name rang out, clear and strong in the stillness. "A beautiful name. I wonder what his story was. Why he was here, the only one left, the last to turn out the lights at the end of his world".

Chapter 51. Part 1.

The air inside the repurposed xenobiology lab was sterile, icy, and thick with the quiet reverence befitting a discovery that had rewritten human history. On the central diagnostic table lay Varinn, the ancient human, his body astonishingly intact—a marvel that defied every known law of biology.

Mr Winstanley, the senior surgeon, stepped back from the diagnostic panel, visibly struggling to reconcile awe with clinical professionalism. Around him stood a small, hand-picked group: Renata Volkova, expression neutral but eyes alert and calculating; Rayk Kostin, silent and observant at her shoulder, betraying nothing; and Jian Li, the young xenobiologist, whose bright, fervent gaze flickered between Varinn and the instruments that monitored him.

"The cellular degradation is minimal," Winstanley murmured, voice hushed in wonder. "But accelerating rapidly now that he's outside the stasis field. This technology isn't passive preservation; it's active restoration, reversing tissue decay over millennia. Frankly, it's beyond anything we've ever imagined."

Renata's eyes narrowed slightly, her mind already several moves ahead, mapping possibilities. She tilted her head, meeting Winstanley's gaze with a calculated, subtly provocative curiosity. "Imagine, Mister Winstanley," she said, "the physician who unlocks the secrets of these pods could write their own ticket. It would be such a shame, of course, if all rights and patents defaulted to the PCMA. Assuming we ever regain full control of our own discoveries, naturally."

The suggestion was light, almost casual, but it hung deliberately in the sterile air. It felt like an invitation, barely glimpsed, to something ambitious and unspoken. Winstanley's expression shifted, the seed subtly planted. Beside her, Rayk observed silently, reading Renata's subtle play but giving no outward indication of his thoughts, letting the uncertainty linger.

As they left the lab, their footsteps echoed softly down pristine, silent corridors until they reached the sealed control room holding Julian's sarcophagus. Two of Captain Pethery's Marines stood guard, rigid and inscrutable behind darkened visors.

The group paused. No one had yet had time to mourn.

Renata's voice was soft. "It's hard, I know. But there will be time to reflect later."

Alinta squeezed her hand. "We understand. You have to do what you have to do."

Renata brushed a sleeve across her eyes, then faced the senior guard.

"No one enters. Should anyone ask you, Commander Voss is interfacing with Designer systems and must not be disturbed."

The order was quiet but absolute. Julian's true state would remain their secret, the keystone of everything still to come.

Chapter 51. Part 2.

Their ad-hoc council awaited them in a broad antechamber just outside the main boardroom. Captain Pethery stood at parade rest, his uniform impeccable despite the recent battle's toll. Alinta sat absorbed in glyph translations, lost in a distant past while planning for the future. Thorne and Rostova, the engineers, exchanged rapid whispers, faces animated by the thrill of solving impossible puzzles.

Renata addressed Pethery first, her tone efficient and authoritative. "Captain, the prisoners?"

"Contained," Pethery confirmed. "Ethnic tensions are already emerging among them. Their immediate threat is neutralised; they're logistical concerns now, not tactical ones."

Thorne stepped forward, enthusiasm barely restrained. "The archives were right—this facility can process raw ore. We have complete schematics to smelt and form alloys. In theory, we can build virtually anything."

"Which brings us," Winstanley interjected gently, "to a more delicate matter. The empty sarcophagi. We must understand their limits, compatibility, and safety for human subjects. Tests are inevitable. We need volunteers."

Pethery's voice was pragmatically cold. "We have hundreds of wounded CAR prisoners. They're a drain on our limited resources and they're enemies. Logically—"

"No," Winstanley interrupted, his professional ethics unshakable. "My oath is clear—I preserve life, I don't exploit prisoners for medical experiments. It's unethical, and it constitutes a war crime. But..." he continued thoughtfully, carefully navigating moral complexities, "we have severe injuries among both our personnel and CAR captives—injuries I simply cannot adequately treat with current resources. If any patients, irrespective of their affiliation, voluntarily consent to undergo these tests, fully aware of all potential risks, I can ethically support that approach. But triage must remain strictly need-based. No priority can or will be given based solely on allegiance."

Renata nodded thoughtfully, acknowledging the surgeon's position with measured respect. She turned to Kenji Tanaka, the young electrical engineer who had quietly entered during the debate. "Kenji, before we consider any volunteers, I want a thorough diagnostic on the power supplies and control mechanisms for each pod. There can be absolutely no margin for error."

"Understood," Kenji replied confidently, already mentally cataloguing tasks ahead.

Renata finished the gathering by declaring, "There will be a meeting in four hours, late afternoon." She looked pointedly at the Civil Engineer, John Miles. "Mr. Miles, I need some chairs in this boardroom for 11 people and a communications monitor set up." Turning to the rest of the group, "I have Mr. Kostin collecting the most relevant heads of department. There will be matters of a Political nature to discuss. Before that time, nobody, and I mean nobody, must discuss anything that has happened here. Simply refuse to answer any questions until we have had our main meeting this evening."

With that, the room broke up to their respective tasks, leaving Renata to think very carefully about her next move.

Chapter 51. Part 3.

In the high-level boardroom, its strange, elongated furniture a constant reminder of their place as inheritors rather than creators, the council gathered. Renata sat calmly at the head of the table, allowing a brief silence to underscore her words.

Renata scanned the assembled people. Raith, it seemed, had sent over everyone needed for a government in exile before the invasion even started. She wondered yet again what plans the man had. If he had lived, she suspected things would have been interesting, but whether or not they would be as interesting as things were about to get under her stewardship, she could not say.

She looked at the faces one by one. These were the minimum people needed to establish control of what was left in Wahlsanga, now to be called Vasantha. The core people from the shipyard mission, bonded by shared adversity, who knew about Voss's death. Alinta O'Neil, of course. Now, like her sister. Kenji, now head of electrical engineering, Civil Engineer Miles, who had little to say for himself, but the quiet ones were the steadiest. He had opened the initial blast doors, helped with the sarcophagi and kept the Buggies running and supported them steadfastly all through the mission.

The security staff she brought were stood outside. She had wisely already secured their loyalties before this ruling council meeting and trusted them implicitly. Then there were the secondary staff who also knew the real truth. Thorne and Rostova, always together, Mr. Winstanley, the surgeon, represented medical. Renata knew he was a highly intelligent but also entirely predictable academic of the sort she had been rubbing shoulders with all her life. Rayk, who played his cards close to his chest, had command of the Military along with Capt. Pethery, whom she knew Voss liked very much.

Then she had decided, as a gamble, to bring more administrative people into her circle. These were the home office chief, Administrator Chen, who controlled everything from legal matters to sewage, the treasury and finance officer CFO Evans, who kept all the PCMA credits in a private databank and finally a blank screen waiting to be connected to Captain Bird, the heroic successor to Admiral Li, who had successfully fought off the CAR fleet in orbit. The latter was not yet fully apprised of the situation on the planet below, since his main connection previously was through Rayk, who had been offline.

She began her address.

"Everything we are about to discuss is for the privileged few around this table. Securing power and establishing order is paramount to our survival." She began steadily. "Make no mistake, that Commander Voss's true condition is on a need-to-know basis. So here is the official narrative." She then paused to make sure everyone saw that she meant every word she said. "Commander Voss is currently in deep stasis; his consciousness directly interfaced with Designer systems to uncover vital technologies. By his prior directive, full command authority temporarily transfers to me until he recovers."

She paused, scanning their faces. Some faces were curious. Others nodded. Then Capt. Pethery, Voss's brother in arms, raised his question. "I have to ask why, Deputy Principal Volkova. I am not sure I want my comrade's good name to be simply used like that."

Renata smiled not unkindly. "I know, Captain Pethery. I do sympathise. But we are not using his name in any way that he would disapprove. Right now, people need stability and too many changes are likely to cause disruption and disobedience at a time we simply cannot afford. Believe me when I say, there is no other way".

Capt. Pethery took a moment, then nodded his assent. "As long as we honour his passing as soon as we can, I understand the need". Renata replied, "Of course". A pang of guilt passed through the back of her mind. *When that is, I cannot tell you, dear Captain.* She looked around the table. The lie settled quietly, otherwise unquestioned. These people needed leadership and she was providing it.

"Detective Rayk, you are hereby promoted to Commander Rayk in charge of all military forces on Sikarra." Not waiting for his assent or protestations, she quickly moved on "And with that, in your new capacity, please connect me to the orbital commander. Captain Bird, I believe."

Rayk's brows knit in a quick, shrewd frown. He didn't protest the promotion now made official, but Renata could see him reassessing her.

With an almost casual flick of a remote, he powered up the blank monitor: a simple action masking the silent, complex handshake his AS had already initiated with the orbital systems. A moment later, the screen resolved into the image of a young, unshaven man in a shipboard jumpsuit.

"Good evening, Captain Bird". With a smile, "I believe congratulations are in order. You and your team fought a heroic battle for *our* planet".

Captain Bird looked abashed as he replied, "And the same to you, Deputy Principal. I understand Principal Voss masterminded a brilliant plan and the ground forces executed it with distinction. But on that note, how is he?"

"Principal Voss is in stasis right now. In order to connect to the Alien systems, that is what is required. I am expecting him to be back with us shortly. In the meantime, what is your status, please?"

"There are only four of us left, Ma'am. Two were killed. Most escaped in one of our drop-ships, but regrettably, they were captured by CAR ground forces when they landed. Most of the systems up here are fully automated, including the picket ship we left guarding the water asteroid in far orbit. It is also guarding the mineral asteroids that the Architects parked in orbit. It appears to be in an unassailable position."

Renata already knew the answer to the next question from Rayk but needed the Captain to tell the board himself. "And any news from Earth, Captain?"

"Yes, we have had a communications pod from Earth. The colony ship 'Zarabeth' is still on schedule to arrive next month, bringing a mixture of people from New Ohio and Earth. 20,000 colonists and 10,000 construction workers. Maybe some security. Regrettably, though, there is a political impasse. There will be no military relief coming either from the PCMA or the CAR, as it is not safe for either to assemble a fleet. We are effectively on our own for now."

"Thank you, Captain. I hope to be able to rotate your staff shortly, now that the CAR ground threat is neutralised. However, I need you to stay on the line until the end of the meeting." Renata continued, her voice even and resolute, "Obviously, relying on relief from a politically fragmented Earth is no longer feasible. We are effectively isolated. But we are far from powerless. This facility provides the foundation to build and sustain our community. We possess the tools for self-sufficiency, defence, and technological advancement. In light of this, I am formally declaring the establishment of an autonomous Republic of Sikarra."

The silence that followed was one of calm calculation rather than surprise or objection.

Captain Pethery spoke first, his tone formal and decisive. "Doctor Volkova, my men swore allegiance to the PCMA command on this planet. That command is now yours. You have our loyalty."

Winstanley offered a slow, deliberate nod, quietly accepting the possibilities now open to him. Thorne and Rostova exchanged excited glances, their professional dreams now unfettered by distant bureaucratic restraints.

Finally, Rayk spoke, his voice quietly authoritative, revealing only enough to suggest deeper layers beneath. "I've never held loyalty to distant bureaucrats. They were Raith's concern, not mine." His gaze met Renata's evenly, offering trust but withholding deeper motivations. "Our security must be absolute. My AS has completed its analysis of the PCMA networks. On my signal, it can transfer full administrative control of every digital system here. Authority would rest solely with you."

Renata met Rayk's gaze and acknowledged him with a simple nod, concealing her satisfaction behind a composed exterior. Feeling a need to strike while the iron is hot, she made one last statement.

"Anyone who wants to return home on the colony ship may do so. Yes, there are wrinkles to be ironed out. Some will be afraid of recriminations when they return. Some never wish to return to Earth, of course. I am one of them. But compliance with the authority of this council until that time is mandatory and will be enforced under martial law.

Rayk decided to interject something into the process. "It may be prudent for me to interview people in key positions, to predict loyalty factors and risks. I can't say too much, but I have access to certain new, passive, harmless interrogation technologies that have an excellent prediction rate.

Faces around the room started to look a little concerned. Reading the room, Rayk added, "But mostly this will be used in more extreme circumstances. Some CAR people, for instance, have no love for their own government and may be too talented to waste. We need good soldiers and administrators. I can reject potential bad faith actors."

Renata considered the new information and continued, "I will speak to you later about that. I am intrigued. CAR, if loyal, might be welcome on a contractual basis. *If loyal.* But as for our own people, those who wish to stay, will become extremely wealthy as first citizens and shareholders in the newly *incorporated* 'Republic of Talemora'".

That created some surprised looks around the table. Renata continued, "Talemora being the original name the ancients gave this world".

After letting that message sink in, she concluded, "Our position is unassailable now. The PCMA and Earth as a whole will have no choice but to accept. The Republic of Talemora will, of course, be handsomely remunerating the PCMA for its investments, relieving them of the responsibility for us yet reaping profits; they will probably become our staunchest allies."

With that, the dominoes began to fall. The CFO smiled first and said, "We have a Republic." Everyone around the table nodded, including, rather surprisingly, Captain Bird on the monitor, who said, "I will speak to my staff regarding who will stay and who will go. But I will stay. Earth has nothing for me. I left, never expecting to return. And I have fought for this planet. I want to share in the life it has to offer me."

She suspected Bird's officers would follow him.

With that realisation, she saw the board with a new clarity. Military muscle. Medical insight. Engineering brilliance. Total network access. Every crucial lever now rested in the hands of those who believed they chose their own allegiance.

"Then we're adjourned," she said.

"Brief your departments for tomorrow's session. I have news to deliver to General Ganbaatar," Then with a smile, "News he probably does not want to hear."

Rising, she turned to the window. Beyond the glass, the mural of the ancient ship drifted in the gloom, its silent hull promising futures that now would be written by *Talemora's* founders alone.

Chapter 52. Part 1.

Hours after the founding of her new republic, Renata was in motion. She sat in the command seat of what was once Raith's, but now her own executive skimmer, as it sliced through the air of the Great Gorge. The journey was a victory lap of sorts, a tour of her new domain.

As they flew over the magnificent bridge that connected the regions, the skimmer's AS automatically logged and translated a simple sign on its far abutment: Sky-Arch Bridge. Renata noted it with a quiet, wry smile—a simple name for a thing of impossible, ancient beauty.

As they descended into the vibrant green of the canyon floor, she saw them: long, disciplined columns of captured CAR troops, marching under the watchful eyes of Pethery's marines. Their war was over. The skimmer banked, heading for a prominent villa nestled on a high cliff—Valerius Corba's former palace.

Her PCMA engineers were already on site, having already bypassed the dead oligarch's private security systems with contemptuous ease. The villa, a monument to decadent, treacherous ambition, was now her command centre. The queen was about to take her throne.

Chapter 52. Part 2.

Inside the villa's opulent study, Renata sat at Corba's immense, gorge-wood desk. The view of the verdant canyon was breathtaking, a perfect backdrop for the exercise of power. With Rayk's AS as her key, she had opened a direct, secure channel into the heart of the CAR command network. On her main holo-display, she watched a ghost—a live feed of General Ganbaatar in his own grim, functional command post on the surface.

He looked defeated. He was a proud commander contemplating the two paths left to him: slow starvation or a humiliating surrender.

It was at that moment of quiet despair that his secure line activated. He accepted the call, his face a mask of stone. Renata's image appeared before him, her expression not triumphant, but calm, professional, and absolute.

"General Ganbaatar," she began, her voice even and cold. "Let us begin by reviewing your strategic situation."

She did not wait for him to speak. She began to list his failures, her tone that of a clinician delivering a terminal diagnosis.

"Your elite vanguard, the pride of the Azure Dragon Legion, is permanently buried under a mountain of rock in a tunnel collapsed by our design. Your second-in-command, Major Jiao, is our prisoner."

A flicker of surprise in Ganbaatar's eyes. He had assumed Jiao was dead.

"Your orbital assault failed," Renata continued, relentless. "The late Commander Voss destroyed your air support. You have no way to attack us from the sky. Your ground forces are trapped on the surface, suffering under a sun that is, for reasons you cannot comprehend, becoming more hostile by the hour. You cannot sustain a prolonged campaign."

She leaned forward slightly, her gaze piercing. "Your fleet in orbit is out of water and fuel. Admiral Wei is, at this very moment, contemplating a suicide run against our orbital station rather than letting his crew die of thirst. There is no relief coming from Earth. You are alone, General. You have lost the battle, you have lost the war, and you have lost the planet."

She let the litany of defeat settle in the silence. Then, she made her offer. It was not a negotiation. It was a statement of terms. The unconditional surrender of all CAR forces. Safe passage for his men and any colonists who wished to leave aboard the incoming PCMA vessel, the *Zarabeth*. Full medical treatment for all wounded, including Major Jiao and citizenship in a new, independent republic for any who chose to stay.

Ganbaatar listened, his face a mask of stone, but his world had crumbled. He had been utterly, completely, and methodically outmanoeuvred. He saw the cold pragmatism and the strange, undeniable mercy in her offer. It allowed his men to live. After a long silence, he gave a single, formal nod of assent. He would surrender his forces to Captain Pethery at the designated time.

The connection was cut. Ganbaatar was left alone in the silence of his command post. He had one last move to make. He opened a channel to his second-in-command, Volkov. The contemptuous young Colonel from the assault on the main entrance to Petropolis.

"Colonel," Ganbaatar said, his voice now light, almost cheerful. "I have successfully negotiated terms for an honourable extraction. I am placing you in full command to oversee the administrative details of the transfer. My congratulations on your promotion."

He cut the connection before the Colonel could reply, a final, grim smile touching his lips. He imagined the man's horror upon learning his new "command" was to preside over a surrender. With that small, final victory secured, General Ganbaatar took his ceremonial sidearm from its holster, and chose an honourable end.

Chapter 52. Part 3.

Back in the villa, the negotiation was over, but Renata's work had just begun. Rayk's AS had finished its cross-referencing of Corba's encrypted logs with the PCMA personnel files. A list of names appeared on her screen. Traitors and assassins.

The first name was a shock: Officer Santha, killed alongside Raith. Corba's network had reached the very heart of their former command. Renata murmured, her voice cold, "The tyrants always eat their own."

The second file was the operative who had attacked Jonesy and Rayk. The identity was confirmed: a bartender from Bar None, a woman named Zara. Renata had a brief, fleeting memory of Zara attempting to flirt with her one evening. A moment of casual, human interaction now re-contextualised as something cold and predatory.

She opened a secure channel to Rayk. "We have one last piece of housekeeping," she said, her voice now devoid of all emotion. "The operative who attacked you has been identified. A bartender named Zara. Make the arrest."

She cut the connection, the order given. She looked out at the impossible green of the Gorge, at the serene beauty of her new kingdom. Her first official act as its leader was not a decree of freedom, but a purge. A cold, uncomfortable thought surfaced, a memory from an old history file. She thought of Stalin, of revolutions that began with high ideals and ended in whispered names and quiet arrests in the night. She wondered, with a chilling disquiet, if power would inevitably lead her down the same path.

The moment of self-doubt was a luxury. She pushed it away. The work had to be done. The war for Sikarra was over. In front of her, on her desk, lay her first administrative order. The official renaming of the Planet Sikarra to 'Talemora' in honour of the humans who had lived here. The city of Petropolis to 'Pheonalla' for all her friends and colleagues who had died defending it, and the city of Wahlsanga to what she now knew was 'Vasantha' for the unknown man in the sarcophagus, whose story she would likely never know.

She thought of Julian lying next to that man. He would have been the first to remind her that renaming things was always the first step of any revolution. The important thing, however, was to remember that a new name was not a cure, or even a band-aid.

The task of building her new republic had just begun.

EPILOGUE

It noted that things had quieted down somewhat on that rather quarrelsome little planet. Goodness knew what the bipeds thought was so special about it, but then again, who *wants* to know? *It* certainly didn't. At least on reflection.

Irritatingly, the usage of the forbidden device, or devices, had ticked up a little in the last planetary revolution. *It* knew where at least one of the devices was now, and *It* could seize it quite easily with a sampler. But that was rather excessive. *Don't use a sampler to crack a monkey's skull,* *It* thought. Besides, there could be more than one. If *It* squished some rock-huggers (which let's face it was usually fun) it may net that particular device, but theoretically there may be another one that they could go and bury somewhere. Then, *It* might never know if the infestation was gone.

It pulled up a communication that it had been sent, requesting that *It* finish off as soon as possible and relocate to some other system where there were a few concerning disturbances. It looked like a lot of work.

No, *It* in all good conscience had to admit the best thing to do was just wait it out. It probably was just the one device and the local vermin obviously didn't really understand it. Yet. But best err on the side of caution. Therefore, strictly, by the rules, *It* just had to wait it out. *It* had no choice, really.

Such a shame. But then again, it didn't make the rules. And it was a generally peaceful spot.

With that, *It* filed its report expressing its regrets that it would be "imprudent to move on at this time" and went back to *Its* favourite activity. Watching the universe fly apart in delightfully slow motion.

THE END

VISUAL APPENDIX

The Sky Arch Bridge

Corba's Villa in the Gorge

Stealthed Military Shipyards (Tunnels from the Depot)

Music Room Glyphs (Petropolis)

Compound Vowel (Glowing -Active Type)

Talemora Spaceport District (Vasantha)

Bar None (Petropolis)

Northwest Entrance Tunnel (Petropolis)

The Ruins with D. Urbanalla's Lab

A lone adventurer explores the endless ruins

A Restored Wall of Powered Glyphs Petropolis Spaceport Arrival Hall

Petropolis Spaceport (With the Partially Restored Control Tower)

GLOSSARY OF TERMS

TERMS & PHRASES

Budmo! (Будьмо!)
(Ukrainian) A traditional Ukrainian toast, equivalent to "Cheers!" or more literally, "Let us be!"

Gwai Lo (鬼佬)
(Cantonese) "Ghost man." A common, often pejorative, slang term for a Westerner or Caucasian person.

Jiěfàng Xīng (解放星)
(Mandarin) "Liberation Star" or "Liberation World." The official designation for the planet Talemora used by the Central Asian Republic (CAR).

Nuòfū (懦夫)
(Mandarin) A derogatory term meaning "coward."

Polezny (Полезный)
(Russian) "Useful." Used in the context of "Polezny Idiot" or "useful idiot," a term for a person who is unwittingly manipulated to serve a political cause.

Qínshòu bùrú (禽兽不如)
(Mandarin) "Worse than a beast" or "inhuman." A term of extreme contempt.

xiangjiao ren (香蕉人)
(Mandarin) "Banana person." A slang term, often derogatory, for an ethnically Asian person who is perceived to have assimilated to Western culture (yellow on the outside, white on the inside).

Yěmánrén (野蛮人)
(Mandarin) "Barbarian" or "savage."

LOCATIONS

Eluvara
A distant human-colonised world, noted for its established society and opportunities for archaeologists. The intended destination for Tessara.

Pheonalla (The Original / Ancient Pheonalla)
The ancient capital city of the planet Talemora, close to the spaceport Vasantha.

Rhova (referred to as Rhovana Orbital Monitoring Station)
An old, ruined Designer monitoring station, located in the desert east of the Great Gorge. Used as a landmark and point of reference.

Sikarra
The primary setting of the novel. A vast, underground metropolis built by the Architects/Designers and later occupied by the PCMA. Known for its Greco-Roman-inspired architecture and advanced infrastructure.

Talemora
The official PCMA designation for the planet. A desert world with a dangerously high UV index, orbited by a single, large moon.

Va'hari
The ancestral homeworld for humanity, as mentioned by Designer Marinallis. The intended destination of the *Va'hari Sentinel* evacuation ship.

Vasantha
A major Designer city and spaceport, location of the primary incineration facility and the Military Construction Yards where the Newcomer ships rendezvoused.

Wahlsanga (Transport City / The Depot)
A vast, subterranean train depot and metro station connected to Petropolis. Discovered by Voss and Renata, it serves as the final PCMA stronghold and contains the six intact Architect trains and the secret construction yard.

Xylos
Another force-evacuated planet that was the site of an earlier, brutal conflict between the Designers and the K'Tharr. Mentioned in the memories of Works Foreman Penaargan.

KEY TECHNOLOGIES & CONCEPTS

EER (Empathic Emulator Routine)
An advanced interrogation subroutine within Rayk Kostin's neural implants allows him to simulate the emotional and psychological state of a target based on available data. Rayk repurposed a combat routine that was originally designed to predict movements of enemy combatants.

Gravitational Sluicing:
A brute-force atmospheric flight system derived from Alcubierre drive physics. By creating a temporary space-time gradient—a high-pressure zone of compressed spacetime beneath the hull and a low-pressure zone of expanded spacetime above it—the vessel experiences a powerful buoyant force, allowing it to fly. The process is inefficient, requires immense energy, and is far cruder than true anti-gravity technology.

MET (Mass-Effect Transfer)
The highly advanced and forbidden Designer technology that allows for the direct manipulation of the Higgs field, altering the mass of an object to achieve effects such as faster-than-light travel. Its use creates "resonances" that attract the Fumigators.

OSAB Light Ordnance Mark 1.
Originally called 'Orange Sticky Acid Balls'. A new, improvised spring-launched weapon invented by Julian Voss. This is an informal designation for the ordnance that was developed at Wahlsanga. The acronym is a form of military or gallows humour among the troops.

Plazteel
An advanced material known to Humans and Architects alike, created through the atomic-level fusion of ferrous alloys with long-chain carbon polymers. The resulting composite exhibits the tensile strength of steel, the plasticity and low-density properties of a polymer, and extreme resistance to kinetic shock, oxidation, and high-energy radiation (including UV). Its molecular structure is stable over geological timescales.

Plazstone
Polymerised stone. An advanced, durable material of the Designers. It is programmable in form and appearance. It can even interface directly with power outlets to make glowing glyphs that can be rewritten with ease.

qWatch (Quantum Watch)
A standard, high-end personal quantum computing device used by PCMA personnel for communication, data access, quantum navigation (qNav), and interfacing with neural implants.

Navscan

A Designer-culture wrist device analogous to the human qWatch.
    The Veil
A perceptual phenomenon or safety filter associated with MET devices, preventing an unprepared mind from directly observing the fundamental, chaotic nature of reality, which can result in catastrophic cognitive dissolution

ABOUT THE AUTHOR

Michael Joseph Dutton was born a long, long time ago in a town far, far away in the grim north of England. Like most kids of his generation, his imagination was shaped by the television shows of Gerry and Sylvia Anderson, especially 'UFO', which left him believing for far too long that purple hair was the height of fashion. (Then, curiously, it did become fashionable. Go figure.)

His literary journey began at a motorway service station, where he pulled a James Blish novel from a wire basket of books, choosing it purely for its cover art. That chance encounter opened the door to a lifelong passion. This became an insatiable appetite for more stories, such that after his first attempt at university, an inventory of his possessions revealed a stark truth: he owned five hundred science fiction paperbacks, but no degree.

Having looked into the long hours and meagre paychecks of a writer's life, he pragmatically decided it was a mug's game. Instead, he chose to live. He spent the next decades gaining life experience in a series of imaginative careers: from beach lifeguard to award-winning software engineer; from learning Bengali in a hotel in Bangladesh to founding his own company that converted American cars from left to right-hand drive for the film industry in Hollywood and Bollywood.

This path eventually led him to executive produce a motion picture, and the call to write finally came when a friend needed a script. Armed with modern tools that made the old barriers feel less daunting, Michael discovered a love for the craft itself. The idea for this novel, however, arrived in a moment of profound boredom on a train commute. What happens if you find ruins on a different world? What if they are strangely human?

The 'promise to self' was made. Finally, when he had run out of excuses not to do it, he began typing.

The Xenologist is his debut novel, the culmination of a journey that started with a wire basket and has spanned worlds, both real and imagined. He shares his creative process on his popular YouTube channel and is already at work on his next novel.

Printed in Dunstable, United Kingdom